Praise for AC Benus and *Mojo*
from the members of gayauthors.org

"These chapters are more fun and entertaining than real life, but not necessarily more ridiculous."
— knotme

"You cannot help but be drawn into this wonderfully written story. The characters are vivid and come alive within AC's beautifully described locations. You can see it all in the words he chooses to paint with. Tag along with this zany crew as they travel . . . find out if things will ever be as they should be again. First class writing and entertainment!"
— MichaelS36

"Kohl's come-about was exquisitely written."
— Defiance19

"Be still, my heart!" What a chase scene! What a confrontation . . . just how many scenes can be sent up? This was like watching a firework show, one spectacular burst after another . . . I was breathless by the end. But I still wanted more."
— Parker Owens

"Witty, fast-moving, filled with a collection of colourful, eccentric, and somewhat questionable characters. Superbly written and thoroughly entertaining."
— Dodger

"Mojo will probably generate a cult following."
— knotme

"This story surpasses itself in each chapter!"
— Parker Owens

"I loved *hankering* down to read this . . . I love these guys. The place descriptions had me there on the street; it was so well done but not dull like so many of these can be . . . Truly wonderful!"
— Mikiesboy

"Can I just say that this story is akin to *Much Ado About Nothing* or some such Shakespeare play where everyone is double-crossing everyone, and there's so much sex and intrigue and comedy throughout that you don't know whether to gasp or groan or laugh as you read it? It's like an overzealous literary carnival ride. And I mean that in the best way! I am humbled by your writing craft, AC. Each sentence is purposeful and moves the story forward. Your characters sizzle with personalities. I think this would make a brilliant play."
— MacGreg

"Cliff hangers, mad donkeys, Assauer, Kohl, Gordon . . . wild rides, vivid characters and beautifully written scenes put us right there and make this book what it is. A crazy madcap adventure that made me laugh out loud sometimes. You can't go wrong here . . . don't miss it."
— Mikiesboy

"I became quite attached to Kohl in the end. The lovable rogue that he is . . . . The dialogue was wonderful throughout."
— Dodger

"I do not know how to say this – every line AC writes sizzles with innuendo and hidden meaning. Each chapter is golden. I envy his skill with both characterization and plot."
— Will Hawkins

"I had to suppress laughter, as I read this chapter in a public area."
— Parker Owens

"This is a wonderful book . . . irreverent, naughty, brilliant, hysterical, and just downright entertaining. Thanks a million times for writing it."
— Mikiesboy

"Iced-tea glass raised, I want to toast AC for his untiring efforts – or maybe persistent efforts despite fatigue – to entertain and engage us in every scene of every chapter."
— knotme

"This story is great! I couldn't stop reading. The main characters are very vivid and lovable for all their faults."
— Lyssa

"Delightfully disorienting. Between the sarcasm and the satire, I don't know up from down, better from worse."
— knotme

"Two Bananas, a hard-boiled egg, Eleanor Roosevelt, two Gay sailors, a Second World War Luger and some hot spanking. How's that for a prompt? This is turning into a masterpiece. No one can ever accuse AC of being predictable."
— Dodger

"AC creates detailed pictures through all the high speed of the story that fit together perfectly. The scene where Kohl and Assauer shared memories and started to laugh about it was fascinating. I love it."
— Lyssa

"This has been an absolutely marvelous tale from beginning to end. You did it perfectly . . . *Bravissimo, maestro.*"
— Parker Owens

"Oh, my . . . this writing is incredible . . . it sweeps me away and I am in that place and with those characters. Each chapter is no different: 1,000 words or 10,000, it's never enough."
— Mikiesboy

"What an interesting bunch AC has introduced us to. They are, by turns, over-sexed, under-sexed, scared, and funny. It's like that old movie *It's A Mad, Mad, Mad, Mad World* trying to keep up with who's doing what to whom!"
— Mollyhousemouse

"It's so fun to read an actually witty story with brains behind it; it perks up my evenings, and it's interesting to get to know these people more and more. Glad to see Gordon giving as good as he's getting."
— Puppilull

"The writing is very good and brings the emotions forward strongly for the reader."
— Lyssa

Also Available from AC Benus

Love is Love
Poetry Anthology: In aid of Orlando's Pulse victims and survivors, Lily G. Blunt, Editor, 2016 (Contributor)
ebook: ISBN 153514369X; paperback: ISBN 153514369X

The Thousandth Regiment
A Translation of and Commentary on Hans Ehrenbaum-Degele's War Poems "Das tausendste Regiment", 2020
ebook: ISBN 1657220583; paperback: ISBN 9781657220584

Rima Fragmenta
Or Fragments of a Rift: Fifty Sonnets for Kevin, 2020
ebook: ISBN 9781734561005; paperback: ISBN 9781734561012

The Easiest Thing in the World
And other poems: marking the third anniversary of the Pulse Nightclub attack, 2020
ebook: ISBN 9781734561029; paperback: ISBN 9781734561036

Same Love
Short Story Anthology: a compendium offered during this time of pandemic, D.K. Daniels, Editor, 2020 (Contributor)

Mojo

A Post-Modern Satire and Sex Comedy

AC Benus

an AC Benus Impression
San Francisco

Grateful acknowledgement is here offered

for the support and encouragement
I've received on the literary site
www.gayauthors.org.

Inclusive of those appearing on the endorsement pages,
I'd like to further mention the following site-members for their validation of this project:
aditus; Timothy M.; Lisa; Brayon; droughtquake; Lux Apollo; Stephen; Blind Ambition;
dughlas; Carlos Hazday; deville; MJC; anthyrium51; Canuk; Cajbor

THANK YOU!

Cover photos: Dainis Graveris
https://unsplash.com/@dainisgraveris

Original Artwork: Anika Benz-Jaeschke

Chapter Vignettes: modern reproductions
of ancient lamps in the author's collection

Library of Congress Control Number: 2020908151

for

Timothy James Landon

who was with me every step of the way,
dealing nobly with my daily doubts
and always doing so
with a smile

Table of Contents

Part Eight – Seaborne ~~Venus~~ Priapus

Part Nine – Temptation in the Desert

Part Ten – Spanish Fly

Appendix – All the Priapean Extras!

Mojo

"Talent borrows;
Genius steals."

Oscar Wilde

— Part One —
Divorce, L.A. Style

#carmina-club, #linda-blair,

#Petronius, #Satyricon,

#Flying Dutchman,

#donkey-dick-folk,

#alone-together,

#on-the-sheep,

#racial-kink,

#eggplants,

#seedy

Chapter 1: An Asinine Situation

"So, in other words, you're saying belief trumps truth?" I couldn't help grinning at my own witticism.

Napoleon withdrew a cigarette from his pack and offered it to me. Once I'd taken it, he tapped out another for himself and said, "Ugly reality will rear her lovely head eventually, my boy, but for now, the last time Truth was seen, she was duct-taped and kidnapped from a taxpayer-funded golf outing on one of the president's properties."

That was kind of funny, so I laughed. "As you probably already know, Americans have a strong reputation for being gullible. You are famous around the world for believing the first thing you hear, say about a Nigerian prince who has a fortune waiting for him."

"Slight correction, Kohl. Not the first thing, but the last thing they hear before shutting out the rest." He lit up, puffing a little chortle. "However, speaking of princes and kings and foreign potentates, you just said something wise there." He passed me his cigarette so I could light up too. "I think one of the best analogies to what's happening these days comes from that old fairytale *The Emperor has no Clothes*. Think about it. Of course, the king's duped by the conman selling him an outfit he said only the pure of heart could see, but this description transfers to everyone. The moral of this tale lives in the pompous belief in one's own goodness. The confrontation of the naked ruler, i.e. exposed as a highly flawed individual, means the person seeing his nakedness is not as morally innocent as he thought. Thus, the easy way out is belief, with a capital 'B.' The people in the story tell themselves 'I *believe* I see a suit of clothes, because I have *Belief* in what a good person I am at heart."

The first tweak of nicotine hit my bloodstream, and I involuntarily relaxed a bit. Handing back his smoke, I said wryly, "Is that related to the dreaded 'Fake News' portion of the deception?"

Napoleon Trueblood's thin, middle-aged lips cracked a smoky grimace of pleasure. It appeared from behind the cherry-red microphone attached to his face via a headset from the ear. "Exactly, Kohl. Exactly. Sadly, in this country, the poor hostage known as Truth has been bumped off already, mob style, or she's at least hooked up to wires and beep-machines in a ICU somewhere overseas. Because now in this country, people think and speak in terms of 'My truth,' 'His truth,' and the like, which is damn stupid. Obviously, there is only The Truth, and it's not subject to anyone liking it or not; it can't be shut out big-baby fashion by covering the ears and shouting 'I won't listen, because I don't believe it!' However, as a self-help guru"—he crossed himself sacrilegiously with his glowing cancer stick—"I have to admit this gullibility is my bread and butter. I exploit it all the time."

I scowled a bit.

"Think about it. My rich clients, with more funds than brains, pay me big bucks because they are insecure about their own sense of worth. I find *their truth* for them, or so they believe, and they show gratitude with bank drafts and pricy presents. They treat me like a god for uncovering what should have been all too self-evident in the first place."

"You ever expose your fat-cat customers to the real facts?"

"Which ones are those?"

"That they are mediocre pieces of shit who won't help improve this world one—"

"Fuck no! I like my Beemer, thank you very much."

I slowly shook my head, chuckling softly.

"What?" he asked.

"Oh, nothing. I was just thinking this whole thing – the lecture series, this convo, your 'job' – it's all so perfectly...California."

"Damn right it is. And you're here, aren't you? Instead of some bum-fucked *Hänsel-und-Gretel* village out in the sticks, right?"

"Yeah." I cracked up. "We're here all right." The fact that life in L.A. was so cult-of-personality-driven made it painfully ironic the organizers of this afternoon's high-dollar self-help seminar decided to hold it in the region's oldest church.

Now, with a lecturer droning on and on in the holy sanctuary to our side about 'Maximizing People Activation,' whatever the hell that was supposed to mean, me and Napoleon stood in the courtyard of Our Lady Queen of Angels and smoked. We'd slipped out once Trueblood delivered his self-improvement 'sermon' in front of the gold altarpiece, and made the crowd salivate with thoughts of how much better they could be – be someone like Napoleon in fact. And why not? Audience members had shelled out a grand each to be told what ineffectual space-wasters they were, and it made them hellbent on getting their money's worth of belittlement.

Me and Assauer got freebie tickets from Neil Campbell, the self-help guru's boyfriend, and a guy I occasionally hustle. In truth, Neil's too thirsty for my tastes, but when he coughs up something good, I grudgingly top him. He's into the 'grudging' part of it, lol.

I looked around as I took a drag on my cigarette. This court was enclosed by tan stucco walls, capped with red roof tiles. The front end of it had an archway with wooden gates out to the street. The arch was pretty, covered with papery bougainvillea in full bloom, and Assauer moved below it with bored listlessness. My ex's into camo gear, so now had hands thrust into his blue Navy surplus trousers – the ones that made his ass look like a sailor's – and who knows, he might attract a real gob to service for cash before the day was through. Above that blue-on-blue flash, he wore his French Marines tank top, with the horizontal stripes of black and white. He seemed underdressed for this crowd, or maybe I was overdone with my chinos, hoodie and blazer. What does one wear to a pricy self-pity fest anyway...?

In contrast to our best casualwear, the motivational guru had attired himself in a shiny suit of gunmetal fabric, a black shirt and tie, and he'd torturously done up his thinning hair in that most unfortunate of modern trends: the man-bun. It rode the front portion of his skull like the extra ball of dough stuck atop a brioche.

'They say clothes make the man,' I thought, suppressing a chuckle and smoking. 'But I suppose *fake it till you make it* is what I'm seeing before me.'

"As I was saying," Napoleon continued, after a quick glance at his phone, "yes, it's true. So, like the emperor's no-clothes story, even the So-Called's most rabid supporters hate him, laugh at him, know he's the worst ever to be appointed by a foreign power over them, but can't admit it openly. And why? Because that means they'd have to confess they are as deeply flawed as him. I heard Howard Dean say it best: 'President of the United States; leader of the free world? I don't think so. The man can't even govern himself.' But mainly it's those few asses at the top of his party – and their endless corporate special-interest money – keeping that constipated, carrot-top piñata in pretend-charge anyway."

I puffed out a cloud of smoke. "I don't think you'll get much disagreement from around the world."

"Sadly, I know. This tyranny of opinion over fact makes America and Americans seem untrustworthy right now. And the rest of the international community wonders if we've lost our damn minds."

He took a long, whimsical drag on his cigarette again, no doubt expecting me – a foreigner – to have some piquant affirmations for him.

I didn't disappoint. "Don't worry about it too much. We're used to your politics being a Wild West show of some sort or another."

"Ah," he exhaled. "As I suspected, you are more than usually bright. Intellectual and engaging in a way far above the average. I suspect it's because you're German."

'*Gott im Himmel...*' I mused. 'It's always because we're Germans. These Americans—'

Trueblood went on. "Kohl, your culture is a thousand years older than ours, so you naturally bring a broad perspective when viewing everything."

"*Several* thousand years," I corrected him, and then joked, "or it could be me and Assauer are smart simply because we have our substitute teaching certificates."

Napoleon ogled my sun-dappled companion for a moment and then said, "That could be, but you're the hottest substitute teachers *I've* ever seen."

I smoked and teased him with my eyes for a moment; he may be fond of me because I'm 'cultured,' but I 'like' him because he's an easy mark.

The life coach stamped out his smoke in the gravel. "Yes, I suppose ultimately you are right. Nowadays, belief trumps truth, and what's real becomes about who can create and maintain the most entertaining screed to shout out electronically. To him goes the spoils of what the public thinks is true or not."

"Just fearmongering topics, and blowhard prattle," I said. "I think I've heard someone say that before." [2]

"Yeah, or we could call it 'spaghetti on the wall' ism."

"What?"

"Just create fact-free-isms and throw them at the wall to see how many stick. Flat-Earth-ism, Creationism, Alt-Rightism, Denialism – hell, these days, Republicanism too for that matter – all just ways for people to stick fingers in their ears and shout down The Truth by screaming: 'Na, nanna boo-boo – I can't hear you!'" He laughed. "It's asinine behavior."

I considered him closely as he shoved hands in his smugly shiny pants, and thought, 'You *would* know asinine....'

What I actually said was: "Yes. I guess I can't argue against that."

"And where is that hunky twink boyfriend of yours today?" Napoleon inquired casually.

"He's back at the motel."

Trueblood shot me a dirty look.

"What?!"

"Oh, nothing. Just a coincidence I guess your barely-legal twunk, and my feisty, roving-eyed boyfriend *both* couldn't make it to the seminar."

My heartrate accelerated.

Napoleon turned up the heat. "You don't think they could be alone, *together*, do you?"

Although I realized the guru was tugging my chain – and I knew my boy wouldn't have anything to do with Neil Campbell, even for cash – none of that could stop the red heat from rising through me.

He slapped my back, hard. "Gottcha! Neil had to see his parents today. He'd never miss one of my public speaking engagements. It's because he can't is why he gave you the tickets, and I ragged on you just to see some of your famous jealousy for myself."

Truth was, Gordon had refused to attend today, saying he hates Trueblood's fake-ass nature. Come to think of it, Assauer can't stand him either... but he agreed to come....

Just as I was turning my head towards the bougainvillea again, Napoleon grabbed my shoulder and laughed.

"Heed my warning, Kohl. You are still young, so maybe you don't know it yet, but overprotectiveness might drive that boy of yours into the arms of another."

'Well,' I realized, 'maybe he thinks me and Assauer are still 'young' at twenty-four, but I feel every one of the six years separating me and Gordon.'

The man chortled again, dipping his bun towards me. "That pithy observation's a freebie, by the way, but don't tell my Hollywood *ceelebs*. They're the ones who pay big bucks for these nuggets of wisdom. But, as it seems I'm so full of life-lessons, I can't help giving them away for nothing,"

'*Gott im Himmel*. He's so full of something—'

Suddenly he pushed me away. The So-Cal guru took a couple steps back, crouched, and bent his creaky middle-aged elbows into a rapper pose. "Lemme lay down the kind of rhyme my bigwigs flip for.

> "Yey-ya, yey-ya
> It's true, I'm True –
> My peeps know me
> As *Trueblood*,
> But Napoleon to you!
>
> Vice-Prez said it best
> 'Fool me once,' Ace,
> 'And shame on you' – yey-ah,
> 'Fool me twice, I'll shoot you in the face.'
>
> Politics today is all a test,
> Fall in line like all the rest,
> You a fool or one that got schooled?
> Let 'em see the cards at your chest.
> Improve yourself and quit the nest,
> Take flight and find your own quest,
> But let no schlubs be the boss of you,
> Cuz they'll lie to you with zest.
>
> Cheney said it best
> 'Fool me once,' Ace,
> 'And shame on you' – yey-ah,
> 'Fool me twice, I'll shoot you in the face.'" [3]

Just as I was wondering if he should change his rap name to Wondra Bread, a loud cheer went up from within the church. The conference was ending, and almost instantly, people streamed out to schmooze with Napoleon.

While he was crushed with requests for autographs and praise of his 'lifestyle,' I knew it was a chance to make my getaway.

I walked to the gate, and then stopped.

Assauer was gone.

I moved to the sidewalk in front of the church and looked around. Across the quiet road was a plaza of tall eucalyptus trees. A cast iron bandstand, surrounded by low brick walls for flower planters, resided in the center of the public space.

I thought I caught a streak of blue-black move left from the edge of the plaza into the next street.

"Assauer?" I muttered, crossing over and pulling out my phone. I sent him a text: "*Wo bist du, du Arsch!*"

By the time I pressed 'Send,' I was in the middle of the plaza, right where I had seen the shadow dart. In front of me was not what I expected to see at all. It was a wide pedestrian way: a brick-paved street with color, vitality, noise from music and people, and the good smells of food.

It was nearing twilight, but the blue of the sky framed the fancy street sign perfectly. "Olvera."

'Hmm,' I thought, 'I've never been to this part of Los Angeles.'

I started walking it. Shops on both sides nestled beneath arching shade trees, while down the middle stood open market booths with glass lanterns hanging from the eaves on graceful metal hoops. These kiosks brimmed with merchandise, so much so, colorful knickknacks spilled onto the walkway in baskets.

Families were strolling, some eating Mexican ice cream sold to them from men pushing carts with bells strung between the handles.

Troupes of Mariachi glided along while they played. One, who was always the youngest and cutest, trailed behind with his sombrero held upside down for cash and coins; his smile richly rewarding all contributors.

Shops in the main buildings – which were a combination of brick and adobe – lured shoppers inside with rows of *lucha libre* wrestling masks for the boys, and frilly sweet-sixteen dresses for the girls.

As for the restaurants, one in particular had appropriated space on the sidewalk for diners to sit *al fresco*. This eatery also featured a pair of curved staircases going up half a level to where happy bar sounds emanated. Potted flowers graced the handrail-end of every step.

I kept scanning the crowd as I went along, looking for more flashes of blue camo. At one point I thought I caught a glimpse of it duck into a gift shop selling glassware.

I followed, and the lady behind the counter smiled, asking me something in Spanish with warmth.

"I don't speak—"

"Can I help you with anything?" she asked again.

"Um…" I was looking around the aisles of the shop. "Did you see a guy come in here? About my age and height, but hair a little darker than mine?"

"A *gringo?*"

"Yes."

"No, *señor*. No one."

I thanked her and left, pausing by the steps of the monumental stone cross in the middle of the pedestrian intersection.

I pulled out my phone. There were no texts from Assauer.

I got up on tiptoes and glanced over the heads of the crowd once more. Seeing nothing, I shrugged and decided to move back towards the plaza.

The same color and life occupied the street as when I traveled up it, but this time I noticed more details, like the ceramic jugs for sale in brilliant colors, the various piñatas hanging like massive marionettes from the branches of trees, and I especially took note of all the semi-tropical flowers in bloom. Such sights never failed to impress, and remind me I'm not in Kansas anymore – or, in my case, not in Landschaftsschutzgebiet Harz und südliches Harzvorland anymore, lol. I didn't grow up with this amount of color and California sun, so I'm sometimes reminded to slow down and appreciate it.

Back in the public square, I climbed the steps of the bandstand to get a better view. Unfortunately, because of the amount of tree leaves and branches, I couldn't see very far.

I sent a second text, one simply saying *Assauer...?* and waited.

Ten minutes went by while I watched the light in the sky fade a notch.

A bit tired and frustrated, I descended the steps again and discovered an old lady had set up shop at the bottom.

"*¿Tamale, señor?*" she asked, hefting a sort of space-blanket-covered box on a shoulder strap.

"No," I said, starting to walk past her. But then a funny notion born of fatigue popped into my head. I went back and asked her, "Do you know where I'm supposed to be?"

She didn't snicker. In fact, I wondered if she had any idea what I'd just said, but she smiled and took my hand. "*Sí.*"

Going along with the conceit, and half-wanting to laugh about it, I held onto her pudgy-but-hard fingers as she led me out of the plaza and across the street. In an indescribable way, I felt like she was a dollar-store Divine, but one who had *behexen* me.

Ahead of us was a different kind of building, a Victorian one I suppose – three stories tall with white-painted arches and fancy iron work. "Pico House," the monument said on a giant sign above the cornice.

As she began taking me around to the back side of an alley, I suddenly thought better of allowing some old crone to lead me astray.

I tugged on her hand. "Here?"

"*Sí, aquí.*"

She let go of me, but moved farther into the alley and gestured for me to follow. At a little stairwell into the cellar of the old building, she held out her palm and I greased it with a dollar.

She gave me a gentle push, and I started down the steps, catching one last glimpse of her wrinkled face, which appeared anything but benign.

Getting to the bottom, I saw a door; a sign on the wall to the right of it said Carmina Club. I raised my hood and slipped in.

Quietly, I entered an empty lobby. The lights were on, but there was no one in sight, so I closed the door and nosed around a bit. The walls were mostly exposed brick, which contrasted sharply with the chrome and glass reception desk. Above black leather sofas and armchairs to my right, a plastered wall held little shelves – about a hundred of them.

Walking up to them, I saw each little wooden platform supported a handheld appliance from days gone by. I leaned in and got close to one painted yellow. Suddenly, the fact that a 'wand' lay neatly tucked under the machine, and that the words "Acme Sure-Fire Autostimulator" were embossed on the chrome number plate, made me realize it was a vibrator. I stepped back in something like awe. These were antique sex toys; each and every one a separate model. All of them!

I went back to the desk and picked up a card.

Carmina
*L.A.'s Most Selective
and Secretive Sex Club*
phone number: *"private"*

'What was that...?' I pocketed the card after hearing an oddly muffled noise. It came from somewhere beyond the interior archway.

I passed beneath it, wondering where everybody was, and what would happen if I was discovered snooping. But I admitted how undeniably curious I was too.

Walking slowly along the darkened corridor, I heard the same sound again. This time it seemed oddly animalistic.

I crept up to an open doorway at the end of the hall. Facing it, I leaned my shoulder against the frame to partially hide myself, and just as I was about to peek into a light court, I felt my phone vibrate.

My heartrate instantly shot through the roof. I lifted the screen to my face. Assauer's message simply read: "I'm here."

"But where, you ass?" I mumbled.

"Right behind you, numb-nuts," I heard out loud.

I started and jumped around. My ex was equally startled by my action. "How did you—"

He shushed me, so I started again in a hoarse whisper, "How did you get here?"

"You'll never believe it."

"Try me," I said without amusement.

"I couldn't stand being in earshot of that egomaniac anymore, so I started exploring, you know, checkin' the area out. I got lost after a while, and my phone said I had no service. I couldn't tell one street from the next, one Mexican souvenir stall from another, so I wandered around asking if anyone knew where the church was. Eventually this elderly guy took my hand and talked Spanish at me, but I felt he was all right somehow. Anyway, he brought me here, led me to a room and said he wanted a BJ. I told him $50 and he could blow me, but when I unzipped, he said 'I'm not a pencil sharpener' – the deadbeat prick. He strolled out and left me with my pants down. When I came out, I got lost again in the maze of corridors until I saw you standing by this door. Now, what are *you* doing here?"

"It's kind of similar, but I asked an old woman if she knew where I was supposed to be, and she brought me to this club."

As Assauer was about to pipe up again, that weird noise sounded once more from across the court, this time more muffled.

"Hear that?" he asked.

"Yeah. What do you think it could be?"

"Who knows, but in this place, I wanna find out."

He slipped past me into the central courtyard of the building. I reluctantly followed.

This open-air space was definitely creepy. Slender black columns held up two stories of walkways above us on every side. No lights were on, so everything was cast into deep shadow by the setting sun.

More noise followed, and we slinked our way under a brooding archway. Over it was a red panel bearing a rearing animal of some sort.

We crept along a dark corridor and realized we were in amongst the ropes and pulleys of a backstage area. Muffled chanting could be heard from somewhere deep in front of us now; it sounded like Latin.

Splitting up our single file line, we both ducked behind black curtains and stood like rigid poles. We knew on the other side of these panels of fabric was the stage, with people in the auditorium in front of it doing the chanting.

We held fingers up to our lips and inched back our respective pieces of material.

A beautiful woman with dark, waist-length hair, stood on the stage and led the assembled in their droning on and on. She had a silver cup in her hand, and garlands of flowers encircled her head and shoulders.

"What the...*ficken*...?" I murmured.

Assauer violently hush-fingered me.

The woman wrapped up the reciting, and I dared to peek out at the audience. Men and women stood there wearing the same loose-fitting robes and toting the same flower swags. In truth, they looked provocatively high as kites on meth and ED medicine. They suddenly cried out together, "Parthia, our great leader, the God's blessing be upon you."

"As it may be with you," the woman on stage replied placidly. "Now is the time, as He is pleased, and all preparations have been properly made to host him. Thus, let us begin."

Four men from the 'congregation' came up and put together something like a cot, or maybe, more like a swing set...? It was odd.

Her helpers left, and as Parthia sat on the contraption, my gut told me whatever was about to go down was not supposed to be seen by me and Assauer.

I tried to get his attention with exaggerated facial gestures, but he only seemed more and more engrossed by the unfolding scene.

I sneaked a peek out front again, and gulped. Clip-pity-clop sounds preceded the appearance of a naked young man leading a donkey on stage.

The animal had a two-toned face, and likewise wore a crown and sash of blossoms.

"Assauer!" I hissed, getting frightened.

He waved to silence me with lackluster energy, his eyes never leaving the spectacle.

"We better go…" I mumbled, not fighting the urge to watch myself. It was then I noticed how unusual the animal seemed – self-aware, or intelligent, if you will. Some keen spark of acknowledgement resided in the doughy, appreciative gazes he spread about the room and audience. Or at least I thought so for a moment or two. But of course, that was impossible, right…?

As the creature was led towards the waiting lady, that's when panic struck.

I accidentally let the curtain go to raise my hood, and was exposed.

Standing there like a deer in headlamps, it was the donkey who spotted me first.

Brays of bloody murder rent the air as the quadruped's possessed eyes locked onto mine.

Women screamed.

A second later, Assauer's hand encircled my wrist – thereby breaking my enchantment – and we ran for our lives.

Chapter 2: In a *Brunst*

The Red Line subway station had been bright, crowded and noisy, but now as me and Assauer walked on the side streets to our West Hollywood motel, the distractions fell away and left us to our own contemplations. The street-lamps were on and pooling light at our feet.

"What about dinner?" I asked at last. "Gordon must be hungry."

He shrugged, barely glancing up. When we came into a puddle of light again, I noticed something. "You all right? You look pekèd – I don't know, flushed."

Assauer nervously twisted the ring on his finger, hesitating a moment before feeding me a line. "That old man at the sex club gave me half a pill of something, and I've been feelin' weird since seeing.... Don't know what we saw."

I was not sure I believed that. Maybe he was feverish....

"Yeah, I don't know either," I told him. "We saw some freaky cult shit, I guess. They looked possessed, and so did the beast for that matter."

Now Assauer's naked shoulders brushed against mine in a friendly way; he walked swaying a bit and showing more of his usual animation. "And did you get a look at that emblem over the door?"

"That thing was messed up."

"Some kind of lion—"

"It had wings, so more like a griffin."

"Well, whatever – lion or griffin – it had an erection for a head."

I chuckled. "Yeah, a real 'dick for brains,' as these Americans would say."

"Anyway, it was weird."

I glanced down to his dark camo trousers. They seemed tighter than ever, especially right in front, if you know what I mean. "It was very strange, but are you sure you're feeling all right? You look a bit—"

"I'm fine. Just don't want to talk about it anymore."

At that moment, we came to a brightly lit intersection. My tummy rumbled and I got inspired. "There's that Bangladeshi take-out place up the block. Let's go get food and bring it back."

Assauer stopped walking. All of a sudden, a glassy look slid over his blue eyes. "Can you go? I'm beat and just wanna head back to the room. I'll see you in a bit."

Saying that, he thrust hands in his pockets, and with hunched shoulders, briskly strode in the direction of our motel.

'Talk about *weird*,' I thought. 'But whatever. I'm starving.'

The Bangladeshi place was nice. It was one of our regular spots, and the people were always smiling. Even though I'm six-foot and shaggy-haired, they welcomed me like a brother.

I scanned the items in the warming trays and selected the stews and curries I knew Gordon liked the best. Plus, at the end, I got the special little custards baked in earthenware dishes the size of *sake* cups. I wanted to see my boy smile – despite how much fuss they made over returning the shallow plates afterwards. "From Bangladesh! Cannot replace...."

I reassured them I would bring their custard saucers back, like we always did, and they let me pay with broad smiles on their faces. As I watched them wrap everything up, and freshly bake our *naan*, my mind drifted to my boy's face. Napoleon had referred to him as barely legal. Today the life coach only half suspected the truth of it. The feeling of 'guilt' is supposed to pass after the eighteenth birthday, right, which happened to Gordon Sanchez two months ago...but I don't know. Actually, I'm not sure I feel any remorse at all, because if I had to do it all over again, nothing would change. Well, maybe nothing except the two of us going it alone, without my ex in tow.

In any event, it's been a wild time since, well, since we went 'on the sheep,' or is it *on the lamb* – I get confused. But anyway, that phrase still makes me chuckle, even though our situation has been anything but laughable since skipping out of small-town Aptos, California, eighteen months ago.

As I walked along, feeling the weight and heat of our good-smelling food, anticipation of seeing my boy's smiling face quickened my step. I may know where we've been on this journey, but what will become of us is still up in the air.

I dashed across the street. The shabby aura of the Alta Cienega Motel, with its 1970s style blue lettering on an orange background, came into view. Assauer wanted to stay here, because they keep Jim Morrison's room as a graffiti-laden memorial to the musician who once lived here – or died here, I forget which.

Passing under the dead rock icon's room, along the driveway to where you check in, I saw someone slumped on the bench outside the front office.

I walked up to Gordon in a bit of a panic. "Hon, what's going on?"

The sexy teen immediately flew up and hugged me. I stroked the top of his wavy, chestnut hair. "Are you trembling...?"

He pushed me back, and I could see he'd been crying. My heartrate accelerated, but in an instant, he smirked, making a sour face.

"You've been doing it again," he stated with disappointment. "I can smell cigarette smoke on you."

I held his big brown eyes and tried to explain as if a complex thing to a simple child. "Don't be upset with me. I sometimes have to do it, socially, for work. You'll understand, and I'm sorry; I'll shower and gargle right away."

"Assauer is in the shower right now...."

Why did tears threaten to well as my boy said these seemingly harmless words?

I set the food on the bench and took Gordon by both shoulders. "What's wrong?"

"That ex of yours, he came back to the room looking like Linda Blair from *The Exorcist*."

Adrenaline began to pump through my veins. "What did he do?"

"Stay calm, please. Your temper—"

"What. Did. He do?"

"He tried to force himself on me, Kohl."

I let go of his arms and took a deep, clarifying breath. "Where is he now?"

"Like I told you, in the shower. He said if I was gonna act like an ungrateful little bitch and leave him blue-balled, he'd have to rub one out and relieve himself."

"Come on," I said.

I didn't look back until I had dragged the naked and dripping Assauer from the shower to the center of our room. I briefly noted Gordon standing in the open motel room door, holding our food and looking worried. For half a moment, I thought he seemed frightened of me, but that could not have been the case.

He was scared of this monster, the one under my grip.

"How could you?!"

Assauer wrenched himself free. "What the hell's your problem?"

"You, *Arschloch*. You tried to hurt Gordon?"

"No. I—"

"How dare you try to hustle me, you cut-rate fluteplayer. You, whose very breath belies your seedy profession."

He attempted a shocked routine for a second, but then his slumped posture straightened and he yelled even louder than I had. "Oh, just shut up! You're so goddamned self-important all the time, a star in your own movie. Just. Shut. Up."

"So you admit it."

"Admit what?! Admit that twink of yours fantails his sexy little ass under my nose night and day? Yes! I *admit* it, but we're supposed to share and share alike, aren't we, brother? So what? I tried to get some; learn to let others have a go once in a while."

"The *so what* is you're way out of line. The boy doesn't like you like that."

"Oh, yeah. *That's* outta line?! How's this for out of line: I think you're a tampon, douchebag and nightpad all rolled into one."

I raised my fist. "What the hell has come over you, Assauer? You're the one who left me high and dry at that seminar today."

"Yeah, that's cuz I'd rather hear glass shattering or watch stupid YouTube dream interpreters prattling on than listen to that self-motivational crap." He caught his breath, raising its pitch. "And call *me* a two-bit tart?! You're the more shameless slut between us, batting your cow-eyes at that idiot *scheister*, just hoping he'd take us to dinner afterwards."

"Well, at least I was trying to get us something. *Gott!*"

"Kohl, wake up. That asshole is broke! Who knows what his day job is, cuz it's certainly not 'celebrity life-coaching.'"

"But regardless of what it is, you're the one who left me there on my own. He was fucking rapping at me, while you gave your partner the slip."

"What'd ya think I shoulda done – oh, wise jackass – tell me. Let hunger overtake me, waiting for you to grow a brain?! It's not my fault you let yourself be caught in the clutches of master rapper Milk Tea, bustin' mighty-white rhymes on yo' ass."

"You still didn't have to abandon me—"

"What'd you want me to do about it?!"

"I wanted you to act like a friend. What the fuck else."

"Oh, you make me sick sometimes. A friend? Like the friend who saved you from prison in Germany. That friend not good enough for you? Oh, memory short? Then, how about the time you seduced that rich mobster's wife in Palm Springs and then begged me to step in because you couldn't actually do the nasty."

"You're bi, aren't you?! So what's the big fucking deal? She was blindfolded, wasn't she?"

"God, you're so ungrateful!" His eyes briefly fell on Gordon.

"I want you gone," I said. "Me and you, we've been through a lot together, but it's over."

"A lot of shit, you mean. In fact, what are you gonna do without me around to constantly save your pathetic ass?"

"We'll manage somehow."

"*Manage!* Manage like that mess you got into as the mascot of a *49er's* game?!"

"I came out on top, didn't I?"

"Because of me! That punk *cholo* tackled you from the third row – leaped over the heads of families to slam you on the field and make his buddies bust up watching the debacle on the big-screen jumbotron."

"Yeah…" I said smiling; I couldn't help it. "And then you chased the guy down for me, halfway to the middle of the field."

Assauer coughed up a brief laugh. "I held him down as 50,000 people cheered you on. You gave that guy two black eyes—"

"…As I pistol whipped him with the costume's foam rubber guns."

We stood still for a moment, daring each other.

Then me and Assauer burst into uncontrollable laughter. The memory of the event, and indeed all of the situations we'd gotten ourselves in to and out of over the years, proved too much for our anger.

I popped in the bathroom and hooked a finger onto a towel, which I tossed into Assauer's waiting arms.

As he dried off smiling, I told him calmly, "It was a good run, but let's divorce amicably."

He agreed, flinging the wet towel on the back of the desk chair and slipping on a pair of boxers.

Gordon finally entered the room and closed the door behind him.

I got down my ex's bag and pulled out the roller suitcase we used for storing all our common-stock property, pilfered or borrowed from here or there.

I flung everything out on Assauer's bed as he dressed. By the time he was done, I'd split our worldly goods, and he nodded assent before stuffing his clothes and pawnable merchandise in his carryall.

It was over; we'd had a good long run, but the cleaner the split the better.

Just as Assauer slipped on his jacket and shouldered his heavy satchel, he glanced significantly at Gordon. His clear blue eyes were glassy again.

I scooped up his car keys, placed them in his palm, and escorted him to the door.

Open and out of it, he gave one last look into the room, and I told him matter-of-factly – before closing and locking the portal – *"Tschüss, Exfreund.* Break a leg out there."

Satisfied, I went and hugged Gordon possessively. I could feel my heartrate slowly lessening.

I sat us on the bed, my arm draped around his shoulder. "Are you hungry?"

"No, Kohl."

"Me neither."

It appeared as if my boy wished to say something serious to me. "What is it?" I asked.

His doe-eyes played about my face earnestly. "Are you sure about this divorce?"

"Sure, as in—"

"Sure it's going to last? Sure as in you are sincere about a goodbye with him this time."

My brows wrinkled in concentration. "That's a funny thing to ask."

"Maybe. But you and your ex have a funny relationship."

While it was true, and Assauer had come to my rescue on many occasions, including the one that had us coming to the United States in the first place, I was sure of my resolve. "It's over."

I bristled with love for this boy, and guided his lips to mine. But when we parted, and I had opened my eyes, I saw a dark cloud settle over him.

"What is it, Gordon?"

"I just wonder about him having your heavy gold band, the one that you gave him, while all I have is this." He held up his left hand. On the ring finger was the nickel-plated Pride souvenir I'd bought for him at a San Francisco gift shop. The bezel was set down the center with square-cut, glass rainbow 'stones.'

He went on, "I know I'm the reason you're broke, but why should your ex have it and not me…?"

I didn't have an answer. All I could do was pull him into my lap, rest his ear against my chest and stroke the top of his hair.

It was soft, and as lovely as every other aspect of him. I reassured my boy, "He can't threaten you without consequences. Assauer crossed a line, and you don't have to worry about me taking him back again."

He raised his tender chocolate eyes to mine. "It's him taking *you* back that worries me."

I chuckled, gently rubbing his chest over his tee-shirt. "Gordon Sanchez, my love, that's the last thing you need to fear."

He responded by slowly slipping his fingers between my sweatshirt and skin.

The excited breath caught in my throat as I told him, "I'm glad he's gone at last. Good riddance! He's been an unwanted chaperone on our full privacy since the beginning."

"Oh, I'm glad too, Kohl," he said, brushing his ruby lips against mine. "So much so – Kohl...."

I caught his pleading and filled it with my tongue. My hand went to the back of his head and drove his moaning sighs fully into my mouth.

His hands began to tenderly push and pull at the flesh of my chest, teasing my hardening nipples as he went.

I lifted his shirt off, and struggled out of my jacket. He helped me slough it off my shoulders, and instantly drew my sweatshirt over my head.

His tongue was at my chest – flicking my left tit – while his hands worked my zipper.

I closed my eyes, kicked my hands back on the bed, and let him take me out.

Carefully, because he was a good and very experienced boy, he worked my stiff cock free of the fabric and brought my nuts with it.

His nimble fingers felt incredible as he pressed them down into the metal bite of the zipper, and then cupped them up and out.

In half a second, his mouth was toying at the tip of my dick, making it flare to full attention.

He excited it, like only he knew how to do, and caused me to kneel upright on the bed.

I dug my fingers in his hair and gripped with force into the furrows of his scalp.

He let me throat-fuck him – sinking my shaft all the way to the balls within his moist and silken mouth.

A bit of a gag later, I lessened pressure on his skull, and he sent waves of incredible pleasure through me. They went up and down my spine, and out to toes, fingertips and even hair follicles standing upright from individual mounds of goose bumps – tremors of sensation rippled through me as he applied the first pressure and sucked my dick.

He was so good at it, it was almost unreal, and through the hazy fog of my indistinct contentment, a keen notion of why I was sometimes so jealous of this boy's affections came into focus. Who wouldn't fall in love with him

"Kohl," he pleaded.

"Do you—"

"Yes. With all my heart," he reassured me.

"Me too. Can I cum, baby?"

"Fuck yeah."

"You sure," I teased him, both of us knowing he was about to get seeded anyway.

He kissed me, drawing my head forcefully, and making me pause full-bore in his ass.

I grunted into his mouth, toying with him the millisecond before I shot a mass of cum into his likewise throbbing passage.

He felt it and wriggled his ass even deeper on my cock, making me black out for a timeless instant of eternity.

He did it again, and I again – still in the throes of my orgasm – lost control of my body entirely for one, gloriously transcendental second. God, I loved this boy. God help me, I did.

Lost in the moment, only a very faraway piece of me acknowledged Assauer's voice mumbling something about "Forgot my phone charger...."

Gordon started to scramble under me, and I partially wondered why, when suddenly my ex rent the air with applause and laughter.

As I was groggily trying to turn around, another sound ricocheted from the corners of the room like a bullwhip.

My ass stung from where Assauer's wet towel struck me, forcing a rude and rough withdrawal from my boy.

The towel rang out again and slapped my other cheek. "Hey!" I said, rolling onto the floor and shielding my tush from another possible on-slaught.

Gordon scrambled for his shorts, and Assauer howled like a banshee. "All I wanted was a little 'share and share alike.' Was that too much to ask?!" More wild laughter erupted.

In my head, the only thing I knew was me and Gordon would have to move out of this motel room.... I wondered where we'd go, but then I thought of Napoleon Trueblood and his thirsty throt of a boyfriend.

Chapter 3: Wayfarers

"Okay, Kohl," the figure drawing instructor said. "Grab that pole."

I surveyed the small collection of props on the platform where I stood. Sure enough, there was something like a cut off broomstick with a pinecone screwed in for a finial.

As the teacher made his way up to me, through all the students and their drawing pads, I bent over, flashing my naked ass towards the hottest young bearded guy in the loft space. The late-afternoon/early-evening light coming in the large industrial-sized windows framed my body definition perfectly, and I knew it.

I liked being naked, and I'm anything but shy, so why not make a few extra bucks and titillate my fellow Flying Dutchman inhabitants in the process? [4]

"Now," cried Dryden, who was likewise bearded and sexy, "let's pretend this beach ball is a giant globe."

He had said this more for his students than me, but fetched it from the collection and placed the striped plastic sphere near the front of the dais.

"Stand holding the staff in your right hand, and prop your foot on the globe...." After he mused silently in my direction for a moment, he added, "Yes...almost.... Don't move!"

In a flash, the art drawing teacher was up on the stage, rummaging in the pile of set pieces behind me. I winked at the hottie with his charcoal all set to go. Just then, my eyes cast themselves upwards in time to see a dusty wreath of plastic ivy descend upon my head.

Dryden clapped his hands together once in triumph, and announced to the class of students: "Perfect! Now, this will be a twenty-minute pose, and think of Kohl here as 'Dionysus conquering the world.'"

I held my chin a little more erect; I'd been promoted to demigod status.

Being a figure drawing model exerts strains on the muscles, but this pose was relatively easy, and holding it for twenty minutes would not be so difficult.

If I slid my eyes to the right a bit, I could see the sexy guy holding his charcoal twig to 'measure' my thigh, or arm, or maybe even my cock – nah, he'd need a bigger stick for that, lol. But while watching, my mind wandered from him and on to the trappings of the room around us.

Neil Campbell had put us up with him in Long Beach. Me and Gordon were happy to be away from West Hollywood, but this building was just as weird, albeit in a different way.

Our week, submerged in the raggedy earth-tones of the Flying Dutchman's interiors, had been interesting to say the least. Getting lost had been a regular happening, because back alleys and dead-ends abounded through-out this 50,000 square-foot, three-story warehouse of the olden days. It had been converted into an artists' live-work commune, where everywhere you went smelled pleasantly of patchouli and *oregano* – wink, wink. The pressure on the city fathers downtown must have been great to 'get rid of the hippies,' for the views west from the acres of windows onto the scenic bay were incredible. A developer now would snap up this property in a heart-beat, thereby taking it out of public use, and auction it off piece by piece for private, blue-blood condos at several million dollars a pop.

We had packed our stuff the same night my ex broke in on our privacy and laughed like an ass at our intimate moment. After taking the room key from him, and shoving Assauer out the door, we jammed our clothes in bags and got ourselves over here, away from wherever he was back in L.A.

Living in the Flying Dutchman had taken the stain off our minds, except for the unpleasant task of me having to sleep with Neil from time to time as 'rent.'

Napoleon's boyfriend was annoying – a forty-year-old Australian who hated America and Americans because he secretly loved all things red, white and blue. I've found a few Germans behaving in such a messed-up way, but this intense love-hate psychosis seems endemic among Aussies. Whatever's at the root of it, this mentality is certainly a handicap for the one carrying it around in their heart at all times. Worse yet, Neil was a sham hippie – a middle-class surfer with blond dreads down to his shoulders and spray tan to orange-cover his wrinkled, UV-furrowed face. He must have gotten incredibly prune-like from sun damage caused two decades ago on Down Under beaches. I don't know, maybe all the lobster-broiling of his skin fried his brain too, lol.

Oh well, better I top him than he turns his jaded sights on my beauti-ful Gordon.

Snapping back to present, I saw Dryden move about the room, en-couraging the artists and suggesting subtle approaches to best capture my amazing physique. This space was one of many common rooms in the Fly-ing Dutchman, this particular one being known as the Mannequin Store, because plaster dummies lined the walls and collected themselves in the corners.

The owner had done nothing by way of painting the exposed wooden beams, pillars or floors, and hadn't used any drywall to partition off areas for folk's private spaces. Instead, architectural salvage items – like entire antique wood and glass storefronts, some even retaining the striped metal awnings from out in front – sectioned off some live-work apartments from the common areas. Places of other functions were demarcated by mis-matched wooden doors, bolted together in a colorful line.

In front of these varied backdrops, the owner had assembled an impressive collection of shabby-chic everything. Cool rugs of minimalist de-signs delineated sitting areas of Louis XV hotel-settees and Walter Gropius backless armchairs; hanging lamps, apparently from the love niches of every defunct motel in the region, shed light over end tables in motley styles as diverse as pirate chests to milk crates.

Where there was no seating, upright pianos and organ consoles proliferated. Piled on top of them were veritable walls of stereo speakers, the kind 1970s audiophiles thought were cool. For them back then, size did matter and bigger meant an automatic better – I've known some guys with the same attitude about eggplants....

But anyway, on top of these defunct sound amplifiers lived artwork: both frameless paintings and ceramic sculptures.

Tibetan, African and Asian religious articles were everywhere as well, some grouped into little shrine settings, where, say a Vishnu statue presided over votive offerings of crucifixes and Dharma wheels. Most times, the little shrine-ettes like these stood in front of backdrops. A popular decoration were sacred parasols from Nepal and Ethiopia canting overhead this way and that while their bases rested in umbrella stands.

More Far-East flavor was provided by Bali beds tucked at the ends of hallways; the only way you'd know you were entering a private space was by glancing at one of the hundreds of darkened and unplugged television sets on the property. With these, people used the screens like chalkboards, scrawling such messages of hospitality as "Welcome to Pat's Bohemian Palace," or "Now entering King Arthur's dungeon."

The figure-drawing instructor went on the move again, shifting my attention briefly to the entryway. A gaggle of tittering guys and girls passed by outside the room, spotting my dick and balls with grins.

I stood a little more erect with pride. All the better for my admirers to see, lol.

Some people I've met here at the Flying Dutchman are really cool, and I've discovered the building's intricacies provide a great venue to indulge in brief-but-intense encounters! Surveying my prospects for such another one, besides Mr. Hottie with the beard, there was one super tall African American guy with a nose ring I'd seen around. He wasn't in the room now, but my imagination saw him all too clearly: an appealing, six-foot-six tall-drink of a man, and I wondered if he were into bottoming at all.

The types of people living at this artists' commune were quite familiar to me and Gordon, even though most of them were strangers to us. When you're without family and on the run, either from your past, present or future, then you are part of a community like this, and it's one I can relate to.

"Five-minute mark, people!" Dryden called out. "Let's get the concept down and you can finish on your own later."

I shifted my eyes to the left, in the instructor's direction, and stiffened a bit – by which I mean it's possible my dick actually pulled back a tiny degree – because Neil Campbell leaned with folded arms in the doorway, licking his chops.

'Nope. Not in the mood,' I thought. But not only did he have his leery sights set on me again, he had me cornered.

I righted my view and pretended not to see him, all the while considering my options.

I hit on a plan, and it was none too sophisticated.

As soon as the instructor called time, every student stood to stretch, as I knew they would. They blocked the aisles, so I instantly dropped the staff, snatched my silky robe and took off.

Behind me was a private passage, leading I knew not where.

Odysseus-like, spurred on by a wrathful fate, I hurriedly shouldered my sleeves, pulled the belt loosely around my middle and took the first turning to the left. Another corridor, this one made of recycled shutters of green, white and gray, stretched on for fifty feet. I picked up my heels, thinking I heard Neil's footsteps appearing from where I had veered off the main course.

The end of the louvered corridor opened into a living area of car seats on the floor, and accordions on the walls.

"Kohl...?" I heard someone Australian faintly call from behind me.

I booked it across the open space, not knowing where the hell I was, but hung a hard right at a piling of demon figures from Indonesia.

If there was a television milepost here, I missed it, for the new passage was strung like a circus tent with dozens of Himalayan prayer flags and twinkling white Christmas lights.

Glancing over my shoulder, I thought I saw a shadow move within the exit from the car-seat lounge area, and wound up bumping into a person coming out of a bathroom.

"Sorry," I whispered, not even seeing who it was before I continued on my way. But I didn't have far to go, for after another twenty feet, the hallway dead-ended at the fancy carving and thick drapes of a huge Chinese bed.

I immediately ducked in, standing barefoot on the silk bedspread and pillows to draw the curtains shut.

I held my breath, listening as footsteps approached. The guy I had passed in the hall stuck his head in. It was that tall guy with the nose ring and handsome smile I'd seen around and liked.

Now his expression said: *WTF.*

"Dude, this is my room."

I dragged him in by the collar and slapped the drapes closed again, pleading for silence with a finger to my lips.

We both listened, and soon more footsteps sounded. A pause followed.

"Bertram, mate! You seen a scruffy fella wearin' a dressing gown come this way?"

Neil's brassy brogue from the other side of the curtain made the sexy Black guy eye me up and down.

"No," he said. "I've been asleep, man."

"Kay," Neil said dejectedly and walked away.

I hushed my savior one more time and peeked through the curtains to make sure the tormentor was gone.

Relieved, I turned around and gave the guy a huge smile.

"What's up, man?" he asked, sitting comfortably on a pile of cushions at one end. "You can sit down."

I did, crossing my legs under me.

"You always go around like this?"

I chucked the lapels of my robe. "Like this? No."

"I mean like that?" His grin blossomed, raising a hand to make a halo motion over my head.

"Ah." I felt up my hairline and took down the dusty demigod diadem. "Thanks for telling me. Might have gone the whole day like that.

My host reached over to his side, pulled out a lighter, ashtray and joint. "No problem. Smoke?"

"Yeah, that'd be great."

As he lit up and took the first draw, I explained the 'what's up' part of his initial question. "I'm avoiding that guy because he's thirsty; been crashing on a cot in his room for the last seven days, and I'm getting tired of his company, if you know what I mean."

He exhaled, passing me the blunt. "I do."

I took a drag and held it in my lungs. Almost instantaneously, I began to loosen up.

"Like it?" he asked.

I nodded and took a second hit.

"You know, I've seen you around. Didn't know you were assigned to Neil though."

I coughed "I'm not," and handed him his joint.

He chuckled. "Like the strain?"

I did; I was feeling really mellow. "It's good shit."

"Ought to be. I worked hard for it. Hand-trimmed *Bubba Kush*."

"I don't know much about pot, but this stuff is awesome. How do you know it's handpicked, anyway?"

He laughed again, the erotic silver ring of his septum piercing bouncing gleefully in the light. "Because I trimmed it!"

I admitted confusion. "You mean like *Knott's Berry Farm*, pick your own ganja?"

"No, no. During the autumn and early winter months, me and my friends harvest weed at an organic grow operation in Humboldt County. We have a good time, but it's ten- to twelve-hour days, and we have to sleep in tents."

"Oh, wow."

He took a hit and passed the *porro* back my way.

"Yeah," he said. "But I can make a lot of money in a short amount of time, and part of the pay – if I want it – is in product. I've got some *Blue Dream* around here too if you'd like to sample it."

I shed a smoky grin on him. "No, this is perfect." And then, after I took another deep draw, felt like laughing for no reason.

"Bertram," he said, taking the joint back.

"I'm Kohl. Nice to meet you."

"Likewise. You have an accent."

"Yeah. I'm German."

"Cool."

The open smile he gave me was really warm; I liked him. You can tell a good guy right away, and Bertram was one of them for sure. "What led you to the Flying Dutchman?" I asked.

"Cock."

I choked on a stream of laughter. "That's as good a reason as any!"

"Yeah, no doubt. But I mean one particular dick. See, a guy I liked was a painter and he hung out here before he broke my heart with a hooker-slut from Brooklyn and moved across country to live in sin with her."

"Ah. I'm sorry, man."

"No worries. It's his loss, right?"

"Defo. From what I can see, he was an idiot to leave you."

He chuckled once through his nose, and then inhaled from his blunt while his eyes squinted at mine.

"This place is pretty cool," I admitted. "But I can't quite figure it out."

"The whole concept?"

"Yeah."

"The owner is an artist and musician, and he felt the corporate squeeze on decent space due to gentrification, etc., especially for our LGBT kind. So he set up this nice, queer space that's acts like a safe haven too."

I started to laugh, the pot melting the marrow of my funny bone. "That's cool, but is it just me, or does this place look like the biggest antique mall in America?"

We both busted up. And I have to say, my joke was pretty funny.

Bertram calmed down and explained a bit more, after he kicked his tall legs out and reclined. "The owner is the organist at the old movie palaces around the L.A. area. When he's not out playing for a silent film, giving a concert or something, he's back here, playing for us Flying Dutchies, as we like to call ourselves."

"Ah. That explains it." I had heard a couple nights' worth of organ music, but the space was so massive and confusing, I'd never been able to track down where it was coming from. "And that's why there are organ consoles everywhere! I get it."

"Yeah, he can't let any of them be scrapped, so they all come here."

I was feeling nice and cozy now. I adjusted my robe and really stretched out, a hand supporting my head so I could look at the handsome guy from close to the bedspread. "What do you do?" I asked. "If you do anything at all."

"I'm a racial-kink cult leader."

"What's that?!" I sat up.

"I'm like a sex therapist, only helping guys deal with one particular hang-up."

"And which one is that?"

"Guilt. White-guy guilt: the sins of slavery, and for still feeling today like they are better than African Americans."

"Fucking hell—"

"Yeah. My followers all have the same desire to atone with their bodies to superior black dick. They beg to be belittled, shackled, spit on, told how worthless their tiny little pee-pees are, but most of all they love to hear how pleasurable their holes feel while I fuck 'em."

I started to get hard, really hard, and I think he noticed. "Um—"

"My last name's Hammerick, so I go by *The Black Hammer* on social media. I've got a pretty big following, and post daily non-affirmations about what pieces of shit my devotees are."

"Cool. Is that how one goes about being a modern sex cult leader?"

"It is for me. My internet followers sign up on waiting lists, and I travel all over the country for well-paid one-on-one 'Atonement Sessions.' I've got some big-wig clients, let me tell you!"

"Oh, yeah. What's the busiest region of the country for you?"

He paused a moment, before we both shouted the obvious: "Washington, D.C.!"

We howled with laughter, but then a serious thought crept into my mind. Maybe he would know....

"Um, as you're in the sex cult biz and all, I wonder if you've even run into another group operating around here with a weird kind of logo."

"Describe. There are a lot of cults out there; you'd be surprised how many and how diversified they all are."

"This one's logo is like a winged lion, except where the neck and face of the animal should be, there's an erect human phallus. A dick. Although, I think they might have a fetish for animals too."

Even before completing my question, I could read Bertram Hammerick's answer was going to be 'complex,' no matter what words he used in reply.

"I don't recognize that, man." An aloof sharpening of his eyes hinted the subject was too hot to handle. "But I don't think it's something you should be messing around with anyway."

"Okay." I let it drop.

"Are you single," he asked all of a sudden.

"No. You?"

"Yeah, I am. It's kinda hard to keep a boyfriend with my busy work schedule."

"I can imagine. You only into...?"

"Oh, not exclusively, but I *do* like to fuck white guys on and off duty."

There was more free and easy pot-fueled laughter.

"So, what's your boyfriend like, Kohl?"

I tried not to blush with pride. "He's a very cute Latino guy, curly hair and fair skin – kind of like a masculine Eros without wings. A little shorter than me, but he's very bright, friendly and outgoing."

"Oh, yeah. I've seen him around too in the last week. Where's he at now?"

"Gordon's out doing his part-time waiter gig. He'll bring back food in a bit. I'm starving. Want to join us?"

"Thanks, man, but I've gotta go and be wined and dined by a local GOP officeholder. Part of his penance is to be seen in public with his racial kink advisor. Later I'll need my ropes and whips, cuz he's a tough *nut* to crack. Work, work, work."

We laughed.

"You guys ever been to Burning Man?" He was asking about the artists' festival held yearly in the Nevada desert.

"Nope."

"You both should come with us this year. It's like a sexual Disneyland, without the overpriced souvenirs. A great time is guaranteed for all."

Just as I was about to answer, my phone vibrated with a text. "Sorry," I said. "It must be from my boyfriend."

I took it out and blinked disbelievingly at the screen.

It was not from my boy, and the message read cryptically: "I'm coming by your place tonight. It's serious, and I have to see you. I think we're...in some kind of danger."

The view from the roof of the Flying Dutchman was spectacular. Darkness had fallen, and the green and violet lights of the Queen's Way road shimmered along the waters of the harbor's shore. Lollipops of lights over the pavement easily led the eye to the strip of land on the other side, and the spectacularly moored ocean liner, the *Queen Mary*. Her vermillion funnels glowed with their black tops, and a continuous string of bare light bulbs – longer than the entire Empire State Building was tall – rose up from the bowsprit at the front, to the top of the forward mast, then arced gracefully over the funnels, all the way to her stern mast, and then down to the aft deck. It was enchanting on this calm, warm evening, and there was only one view like ours in the world.

A short time after getting baked with Bertram 'The Hammer,' Gordon showed up and I told him about the text. He grudgingly accepted there was nothing we could do about it, so the two of us ate dinner hurriedly – after a quickie, lol.

Now, me, my boy and Assauer sat on folding chairs up here while organ music wafted in surreal artiness from somewhere below.

Gordon didn't have time to change, so although his pencil-thin necktie was loosened – where, ahem, I tugged on it from behind – he was still wearing his black waiter pants and white shirt. Glancing at him like this made me hard and hungry for a dessert course.

My boy caught my inspection and shot me an 'ask him already' look.

Despite the anger I harbored for my ex, I had to admit Assauer washed up in Long Beach looking really haggard. I couldn't help but reach out and hug him at first sight, even though Gordon was right next to me and watching coldly.

Now, we were sitting here in silence, and I'm not sure why.

"So," my boyfriend blurted out.

"So...?" I tried to soften the question.

Assauer leaned forward on his chair, propping elbows on his knees. "Ever since those donkey dick people, I've been feelin' weird."

"Yeah?" Truth was, I had been a bit paranoid and 'off' as well, like some shadow was just out of sight, watching over my shoulder.

"Yes. Word on the street in L.A. has it these crazy cult members are on the hunt for the two guys who *defiled* their sacred ceremony. Honestly, I'm startin' to get scared."

I glanced at Gordon. He was concerned, I could tell.

My ex continued in more urgent tones. "I think I'm being followed."

I panicked. "*Idiot!* You led them here, to us?"

"*Nee, Dummkopf.* I got off in downtown Long Beach, at the 1st Street subway station, and stepped right into a ride-sharing car to come here."

Gordon asked, "How did you know anyway?"

"Where to come? I went down to Olvera Street to find Napoleon. He told me you guys were here."

"So what do we do?" I wondered out loud.

Assauer cupped hands behind his head and leaned back comfortably. "I say we skip town until this whole thing blows over."

Since my glances at Gordon, looking for signs of fear of Assauer returned none, I asked my ex, "But where would we go?"

"I have a former client – remember him about a year ago? He's rich and at his summer house in Laguna Beach now. I already texted him, and he said to 'cum on by.'"

I tenderly turned to my boy. "What do you think?"

He replied, unfazed, "I say we go. Something's not right around here."

I had to agree. "I know what you mean, and you're okay with an end to the divorce?"

Gordon laughed. "Dude, I didn't think it'd last long anyway. So, whatever."

We all smiled and nodded at that.

"Okay," Assauer asserted, "let's crash one last night here and head to Captain Hojax first thing in the morning."

After we had sealed our pact, we settled back and wordlessly watched the twinkling harbor scene.

Along with the chilly, minor-key notes of Bach's "Phantom of the Opera" music coming from below, a poem built on the strains of the current circumstances formed in my brain.

> Do any lights really lead the stray
> To a place a wayfarer might lay,
> If he but feels like a runaway…?

"…fascina fugiens…"

— Part Two —
The Laguna Beach (Mis...)Adventures

#think-of-Prussia, #pointy-ears,

#mean-streets-of-Braunschweig,

#cosmetic-justice, #McDump!

#cougar-crossing, #corndog,

#quiet-as-a-rat, #Lotto!

#ve're-werse, #beard,

#quality-stitching,

#coppin-feels,

#Slut!

Chapter 4: Slocked Affections

"So, what does this big-mac-daddy client of yours do again…?" I was casting eyes upwards.

We stood in front of a large but spartan-looking house, or more accurately, before its black iron gate. A six-foot wall of undressed cinder blocks abutted the sidewalk, and from the top of it rose vertical siding, stained sage green. Altogether the structure informed stranger, passerby, Jehovah Witness, door-to-door salesman, burglar or common punk like me: I may be rich behind these walls, but stay away. In other words, it projected the drunken 1960s idea of sobriety.

We'd already had a long day, even though it was only about four in the afternoon. Assauer's exertions had been great, for not only did he do all the driving – my reward for which was giving him the pleasure of my beloved Gordon's company in the front seat while I stayed isolated in the back – but last night, after we had agreed on our plan of escape, my ex returned to West Hollywood in the wee hours to fetch his car. He told us he drove through empty streets returning to Long Beach. No headlights followed him, he said, and I suppose late at night, with traffic at a minimal, he'd be able to tell.

Despite our intentions to hit the road at first light, we crashed most of the morning. After we woke up, we ate a bit, packed and left. Ninety percent of the drive down here had sadly been all too typical for SoCal forays; we traveled long stretches of featureless freeway, tediously playing stop-n-go taillight tag, all the while ducking in and out of the chasms created by towering trucks in the lanes on either side of us.

That changed spectacularly once we turned west on 133, or onto Laguna Canyon Road, for that's exactly what it was – a scenic and not very busy pass through a winding valley. Out my backseat window to the right were verdant hills apparently untouched by man, while strawberry fields rolled by for wide-open country miles on the left.

Eventually the highway swept us along a final gentle curve, and the entire vast blueness of the Pacific opened before us.

Once in the ritzy community of Laguna Beach proper, we pulled off the main drag and started climbing switchback lanes, which only narrowed and became more tree-shaded the higher and richer we rose into the posh neighborhoods.

At last we parked at the top of a hill and trudged with our bags to this gate, glimpsing vistas between the plantings and walled properties.

"He's the headmaster of a private military academy, one for small boys," Assauer said.

I immediately quipped, "Didn't Trump go to one of those?"

"He did," replied my ex. "One that went bankrupt recently because of all the abuse lawsuits."

"Oh, geeze," muttered Gordon.

I smiled. "Need I say more?"

"I'm texting the guy we're here."

"Now this house makes sense," I told my boyfriend, directing my sights up again. "It looks like army barracks."

The gate buzzed, so I grabbed it.

"He says to come in and head up to the pool."

My ex led the way and gave me a moment to raise a crooked eyebrow in Gordon's direction. "The *pool...?*" The uninviting abode appeared too severe to have any such amenities.

I followed my boy up a plain set of steps, not resisting the feel of his teenage buns working underneath his denim. His reaction was to shift the weight of his ratty old gym bag and swipe my hand from his ass.

"You should get rid of that...that piece of tat," I said peevishly.

"Why?" He grinned back at me, hefting the strap so the slate-blue Aptos High School logo – an 'A' over an anchor outline – was right in my face. "Don't like thinking about our past...?"

We laughed, but he was right. I didn't.

Upstairs, the main level opened up the house a little, but it still resembled a compound of buildings rather than a typical residence, for breezeways had overhangs and doorways to what I imagined were many guest rooms.

We heard Assauer return greetings to a manly voice up ahead, and in another minute, I followed Gordon's back into the sunshine.

I paused and had my breath taken away. Jutting over a cliff face, a huge terrace was dominated by a spacious and impeccably maintained swimming pool.

An iron handrail on the other side framed a killer view. A living fringe created by the top of mature palm trees rooted to the earth some eighty feet below punctuated a symphony of clouds and waves; the shimmering blue tones rippling underwater from the pool were matched by the views of sky and sea beyond.

A burly man, with an old-fashioned, silver gray buzz cut and wearing a terry cloth robe, was hugging Assauer. After shoving him back an arm's length and latching on by Assauer's shoulders, the man administered a painful backslap before releasing his grip on my ex.

He then turned his attention to us, smiling and calling out, "Welcome! The more the merrier."

"Captain Hojax," said Assauer, "it's great to see you again."

"I always knew you'd be back, son." He actually winked at my German companion, and caused a slight riffle of jealousy within me.

His appearance spoke of a hard life of faking it. In his particular case, the role was *Commandant*, a tough one at that, but only geared to frighten little boys. His features were round and somewhat flabby, but his scowls more than tensed up his facial muscles into a hypercritical whole. Fifty-ish, the peek of manly chest hair through the terry cloth opening of the robe, and powerful calves sticking out from below it, said he was not faking his youthfully fit physique.

Our host led the way, his gruff voice commanding, "Come. Let's meet the others."

Once the captain wasn't watching, my ex rubbed his sore shoulder, giving me a look like he regretted the decision of coming back into Hojax's clutches already.

To the right side of the pool was a shady cabana. In the cool underneath its linen roof were two people. They were sitting around in swimsuits and drinking like tourists to this private swimming hole.

The captain did the honors. "May I introduce my old friend Lloyd and his enchanting partner. This is a sexy German I know, Assauer, and his friends."

The three of us dumped our gear and sat down.

"This is Kohl, my ex," Assauer said, "and his boyfriend, Gordon."

One of Hojax's guests was a thirty-ish Asian. He whipped off his designer sunglasses and thrust a ladylike hand towards my boyfriend. "The name's *Sang Trọng*. But everybody calls me Trọng. And yes, I *am* Vietnamese," he said with immense pride, and quite a large accent to boot.

Gordon took the moist fingers gallantly, but I could tell he wanted to wipe his own right away.

In contrast to his younger partner, Lloyd was a darkly brooding man, the strong silent type, and no doubt considered a bad-to-the-bone stud in many circles. Over six-foot, and perhaps forty-five, he was endowed with raven hair slicked back and wet from the pool, and emotional eyes used to not showing a thing.

"Drinks!" the captain called out. In a moment or two, a boy in a white polo shirt appeared. A blond teen of the rich-kid variety, he was the type you'd usually expect to see part-timing it as a caddy on country club greens.

"Armand, mix up a pitcher of Mai Tais, lad."

"Yes, sir," the boy said with a slight bow, hands laid one over the other near his crotch. There was also a slight sparkle in his glance at me. He turned and went, with me noticing how well those black trousers gripped his tight little ass.

"So, Kohl," our host asked with another wink, "are you German too?"

"Yes. Me and Assauer are from the same little back-country region in Germany."

"Bavaria?!" Trọng inquired with raw enthusiasm. He had laid his shades on the table.

"No…" I smiled. "No leather shorts, or hunter-green socks I'm afraid."

While everyone laughed, Trọng's leer at me scanned down to my lap.

"Well, whatever," Lloyd's boyfriend said. "I think your accent's adorable."

As he drained the last of his drink in anticipation of a fresh round, I wished I could say the same about his umlauts.

"Speaking of Germany, I suppose my little Ass-Hour told you," said Hojax, "that I have quite a collection of Nazi memorabilia."

"You do?" I swallowed. Of course the *Arsch* had said nothing about it.

"Oh, yes! A fascinating time in military history. Fascinating. I have one of Hitler's *ex libris* stickers. It's one of my most prized possessions."

"What's that, anyway?" questioned Trọng.

"*Ex libris,*" the collector explained, "is – because a book can far outlive its people – the piece of paper glued to the inside of a book to show who once owned it."

"Yeah, right," chuckled Trọng. "As if Hitler's nightstand reading list is why we still remember him today."

"You know," Assauer suddenly chimed in with a scowl, "why is it you Americans are so interested in the Nazis in the first place, and with all things World War II in general?"

I shot my ex a warning look. This was not the place or time to antagonize our host.

"I can tell you that one," Lloyd said. It was the first time he'd spoken, and his tone was deep, mellow and sultry. "We're intrigued by how one of the world's great cultures – Germany before the war – could be seduced and destroyed by crudeness, bigotry and anti-intellectual boogieman-baiting."

"Lloyd is right," Hojax affirmed. "How the country of art and science and tolerance – of Schiller, Goethe, Einstein! – could turn its back on greatness and instead embrace xenophobia and fear."

Assauer flushed and rather aggressively pegged elbows on the table. "Then it sounds like people in the near future will be collecting Mar-a-Lago cocktail napkins and wondering the same thing about the nation of Emmerson, Thoreau and…and, Bill Nye."

The table was jolted as if by an electrical current. The truth is always right, but rarely comes the right time to say it.

After a tense moment, the captain laughed brightly and administered another punishing blow of affection on my ex's shoulder. "Bill Nye!" he called out. "That's a mismatched comparison to Albert Einstein! I would have said Edwin Hubble, Robert Oppenheimer, or even Carl Sagan."

Assauer relaxed back in his seat with a twinkle. "I stand corrected."

"Well, anyway," Hojax continued, "you won't find any of those Gop-endorsed 'Make America White-Bread Again' people around here. We're all aligned politically on the side of progress and calm."

I said, "That's a relief to hear, but do you mean Republican-endorsed?"

"Yes!" chirped Trọng. "You know, *holier-than-thou Gops*. Rhymes with *fake morality Cops*."

We all laughed until the sight of Armand returning made us turn and watch him instead. The sexy blond was rolling over a drinks cart, one that rattled with ice in a tall pitcher. The boy set out three new glasses for us, and as he poured mine, I made sure this kid knew I was interested. When he smiled briefly and moved on to fill Gordon's glass, I caught my boy's eyes on me. Let's just say he was not a happy motorhome, but I'd make it up to him later.

Almost as bitchy payback, Gordon picked up his glass and sipped it with lewd intent towards Trọng.

The Vietnamese guy fingered his sunglasses and plied glances between me, my boy and the teen waiter. Finally, he settled on Gordon, saying, "You are way overdressed for a pool party. Get changed and we'll go for a dip."

I hurriedly coughed up a lie. "Gordon has no swim trunks."

"Oh, tsk, tsk," said Trọng, rising elegantly and reaching for my boy's hand. "You need to find someone to take better care of you. Come on." His words turned to me. "I have just the perfect thing for him to *slip into*, back in my room."

My blood boiled as I watched this seductress lead my boyfriend straight into the lion's lair.

I tugged at my necktie. Dinner at the Hojax house turned out to be an oddly formal affair, or regimental, I guess you'd call it. Nevertheless, I had freewheeling plans for later, as Gordon looked extremely hot in his suit coat, tie and gelled hair, which accented his curls in just the right way.

I might have been the only one at the table to notice though, because some catering firm had supplied both boy servers and the fare. In terms of food, it was basic-bitch offerings. *'Gott im Himmel!'* I thought as I speared another tasteless one. 'How many grilled zucchini can one country eat?' As for the waiters, sexy guys in gray blazers appeared to be moonlighting surfer dudes and kept the boy-hungry stares of Hojax and Lloyd off of us, for the most part.

Armand had his role too, and he polished up attractively with a bow-tie and arm towel to pour dinner drinks.

However, the more California Merlot went into him, the more Trọng's eyebrows flickered at me in open flirtation. I guess he'd forgotten about my boy, or already had his fun with Gordon while putting those designer trunks on him.

"The *Mary Jane* all safe and secure for the evening?" Hojax mildly inquired of Lloyd.

I glanced at Assauer to see if he knew what they were talking about. He only shrugged.

"Yes, Captain. She's in good hands, with the full crew onboard and on duty for the night."

"Lloyd's a captain too," interjected Trọng.

"Well, my three-hundred-foot yacht is anchored offshore. Maybe we can all go out on her tomorrow."

"That'd be awesome!"

I found Gordon's enthusiasm to be a little bare-naked. It aggravated my green-eyed monster to see Lloyd sparkle so suggestively at my boy.

"If the weather is fine," I added, trying to dampen the fun.

Sang Trọng languorously drained his glass and got Armand's attention. "He's more than a yacht captain."

"Is that right?" Assauer began doing his own flirtations with Lloyd.

"Yes," said Hojax. "The way I'm captain over troops of little boys, Lloyd shepherds lots of little bundles by sea, from one 'destination' to another."

Me and the members of our gang looked at one another; what did that mean?

Armand poured more wine.

"Shipping," continued Hojax with a knowing glint to his expression, "is a cutthroat business."

Trọng's hand went over to stroke his partner's arm. "And my Big Strong Man is big and strong in both his love life and business dealings. Let's just say, he's respected by all."

"The sea has been good to me. I've always felt drawn to it, and I respect Neptune's bounty as much as his threats." Lloyd, who by candlelight only had his shadowy, 'dangerous' edge whetted, leaned forward to conclude with gravity. "I feel blessed, but it's more than that. It's about strength too. Put a weak man in a compromised position and he'll act recklessly. In contrast, put a strong man in a tough position and he'll show leadership."

Captain Hojax bristled with laughter. "I thought we were done talking politics for the day."

"Well, maybe just a little more," Lloyd said as he tapped his glass for Armand to top off.

Our host continued in a bright tone. "You know what I think, I think it's a story as old as history: a shyster, let's call him Mister McDump, blows into No-Wheres-Ville, USA, and tells the rubes 'I can fix all your woes. Just trust me!' Then he proposes schemes for brass bands, monorails and other useless things – like border patrols against the peaceful neighboring county – all of which the people have no earthy need for, while at the same time closing down the schools and hospitals as 'a total waste.' Then he sells off the public park to a developer for a ritzy, private golf course. So soon the man's supporters are the ones left paying more and more taxes to get these crazy extras they don't need. Meantime he's fucking their wives and daughters, stashing the cash for himself, and will eventually blow out of town, leaving the suckers robbed and knocked up." Hojax lifted his glass, a big grin appearing behind it. "...Sound familiar...?"

"Oh, yes. A Mister McDUMP indeed," Sang Trọng said.

We all laughed.

"Serves his few supporters right, I guess," affirmed Lloyd. "As they say, the devil eats his own first, and now they're the ones sending their money up to the rich." He drank.

I considered the captain's axiom for a moment. "You know, in Germany we say the same thing, only in a slightly different way. We say: *'Die Revolution frisst ihre eigenen Kinder,'* or, to loosely paraphrase, 'The revolution eventually devours the revolutionaries.'"

"Very good, Kohl," schmoozed our Vietnamese dinner companion.

I smiled at him before turning a goading expression on Assauer. Nothing wrong with scoring a few extra cub-scout points against my ex.

"That's the difference between a Lit major"—Assauer gestured to me with his head—"and a Math major like me. That translation's a little too artsy for my tastes."

"Oh? And how would you have it," asked Hojax.

"I'd make it say: 'Revolutions eventually consume their own offspring.' There. That's more precise; more scientific."

Okay. So, he scored a few points for himself....

Just then, the surfer waiters came around with steak and potatoes. Once placed before us, Hojax called out "Dig in!", and we did.

Just as I was about to take my first bite, Lloyd said, "Kohl, have you ever done any modeling? You have 'the look,' you know."

If the look was to be flattered and charmed, I sported it on the spot.

"Him!" exclaimed my *Exfreund*. "No!" And then he pealed off sheets of laughter like rain. Oddly, this caused Hojax to openly place his hand on Assauer's in a gesture of either turned-on tenderness or lust; I couldn't tell which.

"I haven't," I explained to Lloyd very calmly, "except for a brief stint as a figure-drawing model, but thank you for saying so."

I 'accidentally' kicked Assauer's shin under the table. His laughter died into a hostile glare, one that made Gordon giggle. My boy was used to seeing us at odds.

"I mention it," said the cryptic sea captain, "because there's a charismatic modeling agency I could put you in touch with, if you like. They're in San Diego, which is one of the ports I operate out of."

"Thanks, Lloyd. I'll keep it in mind." I could finally take a bite of my steak.

"And oh, by the way," Lloyd continued in tones of mild warning, "if you do meet up with them, you should know they're not too welcoming to out folks."

"Gay guys?" Trọng asked.

"No..." Lloyd shook his head. "For them, men sleeping with men is fine, especially their members with each other, just as long as they don't talk about it, or do public stuff to—"

"Promote *it?*" Trọng asked dismissively.

"Yeah."

"Geeze," muttered Gordon.

The shipping magnate lifted half of his mouth in a sultry smile, one aimed squarely towards my boy.

"Tsk, Tsk." Trọng wagged his finger before taking Lloyd by the hand. "No being lovey-dovey in the open and spreading the germ via our sinister *fairy* dust."

After a sip of wine, I said, "Thanks for the heads up, Lloyd. Since I'm so pretty, they may not mind either way." Premonition-like, I jerked my leg out of the way just as Assauer tried to kick me. His knee banged the underside of the table, rattling dishes, causing him pain, and making Gordon laugh outright.

After I glared at my ex for a second with a 'serves you right' sneer, I suddenly noticed the degree to which sexual tension was pinging around the room: Trọng to yours truly, Hojax nearly salivating as he asked Assauer if he was all right—causing my ex to roll his eyes at me—and now Lloyd had turned his considerable magnetism to attracting the attentions of my sweet little Gordon Sanchez.

I was instantly hot under the collarbone, and knew I needed to step away.

Excusing myself for a visit to the restroom, I instead ducked into the butler's pantry. The door to the kitchen was closed and I used the hand sink to splash water on my face.

What's that expression about being blind with jealousy…?

Yet, not being able to see as I was, I could still hear the door from the hallway click shut, and then sense fingers hand me a towel.

I wiped, opened my lids, and smiled. Sexy-ass Armand was already un-zipping my fly, and heading down to his knees….

Hours later, me and Gordon knew Assauer had been called to duty, and was currently 'at attention' in Captain Hojax's room. So we slipped out in nothing but our trunks and had a private moonlight swim. And is there anything more blissful than a midnight dip, other than doing it with the one you love?

I was still in nothing but my swimsuit, back alone in our room again, rubbing my head and listening to the stiff hotel-grade towel sound in my ears like sandpaper, when my stomach rumbled. In mid-thought about how grateful I was my boyfriend had ventured off to the kitchen to fetch us a snack, I heard a noise. Pausing, with the fabric still covering my sight, I called out softly, "Gordon?"

Nothing.

I lowered the towel. Not a thing seemed changed. 'Weird,' I thought, but shrugged and went to the bathroom.

While brushing my teeth, I smiled a sudden grin remembering how that sexy teen drinks-boy had gotten on his sexy knees in the butler's pantry, and all without uttering a—

Was that another sound?

Using the terry cloth now draped over my shoulders, I dabbed my chin and left my toothbrush hanging out of my mouth as I crept back into the bedroom.

Some vague urge led me to the closet.

Flinging open the door, I saw nothing. Well, nothing other than Gordon's clothes on the hangers and his gym bag on the floor.

Back in front of the bathroom mirror, I glanced at my own sandy hair and devilishly good-looking green eyes and thought how lucky my boy was, lol.

A fleeting memory of Armand's skillful lips on my cock shadowed the mirth of my gaze in reflection, and after I rinsed off my toothbrush and set it aside, I wondered if my boyfriend would be hurt to learn about the pantry tryst.

The water went on. I bent down to scoop some in my mouth and spit.

When I straightened up, Sang Trọng was smiling in the mirror behind me. "Evening, Kohl."

I whipped around, grabbing the counter in back of me for support. "What are you doing here?"

"What else, looking for a quickie." His gracile fingers landed expertly on my Speedos, front and center.

"Um—" I glanced towards the room door, fighting the natural reaction of getting hard.

"I saw Gordon go in the other direction."

I retreated to the other room and found Gordon's tee-shirt. As I tried to lift it over my head, Trọng halted my progress. His grip lingered on my forearm and wound up caressing me.

"Better to wear nothing," he said, "than *that.*"

"What's wrong with it?"

"Nothing except everything. It's not good enough for you, sexy. I'll take you shopping sometime with Lloyd's credit card. You into Gucci?"

I shrugged.

He took my hand and led me to a position in front of the bed.

"You like me so much?"

He guffawed. *"Like?* Like you in the way our host's Mai Tai boy liked you in the pantry?"

"No secrets in this house, huh?" I smiled.

"Nothing faster than the Gay Grapevine, hunty."

I moistened my mouth. "Wouldn't want Gordon to find out—"

"My lips are sealed. Well, to him at least."

Now I was hopelessly hard, but still unsure.

His hands reached out again and slid across the erotically sensitive area just in front of my hips. He kissed me, aggressively, all tongue and mouthwash, and my hands rose instinctively, not wanting to further in-flame him.

Just then the door burst open and Captain Hojax entered in a heart-broken rage. He seemed blind to Trọng's presence and came straight up to me.

"It's all your fault!"

"I didn't— He—" I gesticulated vaguely towards my original intruder, who was now easing himself down on the bed to enjoy the show.

"Assauer told me what's going on!"

"...He did...?" I was totally confused.

"He won't have sex with me, and said *you're* the one turned him against me. He told me you two are back together, and in love."

The final pair of words apparently made him sick, and while I was wondering if my callboy ex ever had more than a paid-by-the-hour thing with the captain, I glanced down at Trọng languorously spread with one elbow propped on a pillow, his hand supporting his head.

To Hojax, I shrugged and smiled. "What can I say. It's just one of those...things...?"

The officer's irate cast was eclipsed by something else. He moistened his mouth, and all at once I noticed what he was wearing: a pair of patent black leather shorts equipped with some sort of cock ring on the inside, a ribbed tank top in white with a harness over the top. A small military cap rode his head at an angle, and a punishing-looking crop twitched in his right hand.

Hojax didn't answer my question, at least not with words; things slowed down and unfolded in molasses-grade slow motion.

"Um—" stuck in my throat.

His fingertips ghosted the divot of my naked chest as carefully as an inchworm measuring a marigold. "Know what I think?" he asked, huskiness appearing in his voice.

"Umm..." I slowly shook my head.

"I think since you made him douse my affections with cold water, and now my Ass-Hour won't put up his ass anymore, it's your duty to pay the tab." The man's crop reached back and stroked my exposed thigh. "I think it's time for you to pony up, son."

"Um, but, sir, I'm a top, only—"

Without making a sound, Trọng had risen and was standing next to us. Hojax and I glanced into his crafty face and watched the seductive Asian take control of the situation.

Using one hand, he lifted the crop to a fully erect position and drew it slowly to his lips. Licking it, once, his head tilted, and Trọng's cinnamon-brown peepers locked fiercely onto the pseudo military man's.

"But, Captain," he teased. "I'm a guest too. When's my chance to show some 'preciation?'"

The pout worked its magic on the older guy, causing his mouth to tremble, and yours truly to be utterly forgotten.

In another moment, Trọng had full possession of the whip and was leading a bewitched Hojax out of the room, one finger looped through a harness ring.

"'Night, Kohl," he said with a wink while closing the door behind him.

All was silent for a second, and I let out a breath of relief. That Sang Trọng is a braver man than me, that's all I can say, lol.

Just as I was searching for something to put on, and thinking about locking the door, Gordon burst in flushed and grinning.

"Where have you been?"

Below his blushing torso, he wore his bath towel like a kilt, the leg slit revealing he was still in his swim trunks.

"With Lloyd. He was mooching in the kitchen too."

I suddenly realized he'd brought nothing back to eat. "With Lloyd...?"

"Yeah. He's a fun guy, if by fun you mean sexy as shit."

I was about to lose my own doo-doo and go all jealous lover on my boy's ass, when the door opened again!

Assauer skulked in and locked it immediately behind him.

Me and Gordon stood amazed. Our buddy was in some kind of costume – a giant schoolboy uniform: black shoes and knee socks; army-green shorts, jacket and cap; and a white shirt that was ripped, exposing half his chest and abdomen to view.

After a moment of restraint, me and my boyfriend busted up in laughter, laughing so hard we collapsed on the bed together.

"That's it!" shouted Assauer, whipping the cap off his head and throwing it at us.

"Awww," I said like his mommy. "Captain Hojax too hot to handle, little boy?"

"Shut up, *mein* ex," he said before starting to chuckle too. "Time for a group meeting." He shoved me out of the way and sat on the bed next to Gordon.

I noticed he winced and re-adjusted his ass cheeks on the mattress. I went over and sat on the floor in front of them.

"Group meeting about what?" Gordon asked.

"Coming here was a mistake." Assauer's tone begged for agreement. "I didn't have to do this, you know. I should have called up that rich mobster's wife in Palm Springs – she'd be safer for my health."

Me and Gordon chuckled.

"What do you propose?" I asked. "We just got here, and Trọng is keeping Hojax busy for the night. And by the way, thanks for making the captain hate me. He thinks I turned you against—"

"Yeah, yeah, I know. I had to tell him something."

I rolled my eyes. *"Arsch."*

"Spitzbub."

"Well, it's funny you mention it," Gordon said.

"Mentioned what?" Assauer puzzled. "That I called him a…a…scally-wag?"

"Yes, he's a scally for sure, but I meant escaping."

Me and my ex exchanged looks. "What do you mean?"

"I mean Lloyd. While we were eating leftover bean sprouts in the kitchen, he invited us to stay with him at *his* country house. He complained about Hojax being too stingy a host, and he wants him and Trọng to bolt, tomorrow in fact. Do you see? We can go with them."

"That's a great idea!" Assauer exclaimed, rising excitedly and getting pinging by his sore ass cheeks.

"No, no, brother," I said. "You're staying right here. This whole mess of Hojax hating me – and Gordon – is your doing. Plus, your 'client' is hot to entertain you for a while."

"Kohl—"

"He's right," Gordon chimed in.

"Look," I said. "Here's what we'll do. You stay put and scout out this place for valuables. You know the captain has some someplace. In the meantime, me and Gordon will do the same at Lloyd's. We'll meet you back here after we've collected some choice pieces to pawn."

"I don't know…" he said, but I could tell Assauer was already warming to the idea of robbing our host blind, or at least near-sighted.

"And, as for that whip of his, Hojax wants you to take charge. I saw Trọng do it, and Captain Crew-Cut positively drooled at the idea of a decent thrashing."

He relented a bit more but still didn't say yes.

"Come on, Assauer," Gordon entreated sweetly. "Enrich our common stock. Share and share alike."

That got him.

"Okay," he sighed. "But just so you know, I'd rather be slammin' some chick right about now."

I laughed. "Whatever, Mary."

Chapter 5: I Left My (Dignity) in Avalon

That boozy, bebop, swing-it-to-the-rafters Nat King Cole hit kept coursing through my head. My foot tapped infectiously to the beat as I gazed across the open waters, allowing the melody in my mind to meld with the gentle swells of the Pacific Ocean.

We were on Lloyd's palatial yacht, sailing over crystal blue waves off the coast of Santa Catalina Island, not far from its iconic marina town, Avalon. Our captain steered us with a steady hand several decks above, behind the dark glass of the bridge, with its radar and GPS thingies slowly rotating on top.

The distance to shore was only a mile or so, allowing us a perfect view from the right side of the boat – or starbuck, I think it's called. We could see that massive white rotunda built nearly a hundred years ago to host all the topnotch entertaining for this retreat of the rich, a mere twenty-two miles off the coast of Southern California. The Casino stood at the end of its own peninsula, while gradually curving away from it to the left, countless masts of sailboats swayed gently like a living pine forest. Beneath them, as if grazing sheep, the lumbering white masses of pleasure craft fanned out in all directions in the safe shelter of the bay. Cradling arms of green hills, sloping down to a wide ribbon of public beach, had Spanish Revival houses climbing up them. It was all indescribably enchanting in the summer sun.

"Why aren't we heading into port?" Gordon suddenly asked Trọng.

"Silly!" he exclaimed. "Lloyd's yacht is much too large to fit in Avalon's harbor – it's as big as what the poor people have to use. The Catalina Ferry, I think they call it. But no, our captain has his own private cove, just the other side of Church Rock, on the southwest corner of the island."

"And I bet it offers exciting views of the sunset."

Trọng liked my statement: showed so in a sultry leer.

"Yes, Kohl. Very good. Plus, his protected pier leads straight up to the grounds of his mansion. It's lovely. Gordon, you'll love to be pampered there as I do."

"Well, lunch was delicious, if that's any indication of the spoiling we have in store."

And my boyfriend was right. About an hour ago, while we were still on open waters between here and Laguna Beach, we sat down to a sumptuous spread on the rear deck. We had Maine lobster, little neck clams, and steamed corn on the cob with seaweed. It was all good, except the seaweed, which we were not intended to munch on anyway, lol.

"It is!" enthused Trọng all over again. "Lloyd is a man of fine tastes. He knows what he wants"—those cinnamon-brown peepers locked fearlessly with mine—"and goes after it, just as I do."

The Vietnamese guy leaned back on the railing after lowering his shades from the crown of his Velcro haircut. With elbows propped like that, he licked his lips wantonly in my direction. "Give you any ideas, sailor?"

My boyfriend laughed.

Shouldering both a backpack and Gordon's gym bag, I felt my feet transition from the smooth boards of Lloyd's private dock to the lush lawn before his 'house.'

It was enough to make Tiberius – peeking down from his hilltop fortress on the Isle of Capri – contract a bad case of villa-envy, for a glimmering mansion in white stone had every window shaded in striped awnings, rustling indolently in the breeze. It fronted the water for a thousand feet or more, surrounded by terraces stepping up to it with Mediterranean ornaments and plantings. Blossoms were everywhere.

Behind the red roof tiles, rolling hills shone verdant with native shrubs, wildflowers and stands of wafting trees.

Lloyd and Trọng caught up and led us towards a beautiful woman with long dark hair. She stood in a vibrant summer dress, near a bougainvillea-encrusted obelisk, and maintained a bland smile with hands folded dutifully over her modesty zone. From this distance she almost seemed like an ornament of the place, say a modern knockoff of a Venus statue found in the Vatican museum gift shop.

But arriving next to her side, I revised my opinion and took her to be some manner of servant – but then Lloyd kissed her.

The strong man's voice crackled with a bit of uncertainty as he announced, "I must have the pleasure of introducing – Doris – my…."

Trọng filled in the information gap with a wry grin. "His wife."

"…Wife…?" slipped from between my lips. Gordon elbowed me back to decent manners, and I held out my hand. "Oh, yes. It's nice to meet you."

The woman's grip was firm and dry. Even first impressions conveyed Doris was no dye-bottle brunette with ditz for brains. Possessing soulful eyes, perfect posture and poise, and beauty of both face and composure, she brought an almost glove-like fit to Lloyd's physical appearance, only in an undeniably feminine form.

"This is Kohl," informed her husband, "and his boyfriend Gordon."

She shook hands with Gordon as well. "A pleasure, gentlemen. Welcome."

Trọng quipped under his breath, "Yes, a pleasure to see me too, I'm sure."

Doris righted her head; a halfway convincing grin spread like an algae bloom. "Trọng – darling – *mi casa es su casa.*" Lloyd's wife leaned over and loudly Hollywood-kissed the man's boyfriend on both cheeks.

Just before I exchanged amazed looks with my Gordon, I noticed the expression on our host's face. If I had to characterize it, I'd say it was one of settled pride: perhaps even self-congratulatory on the concord of good will being displayed, sham thought it might have been.

Trọng pulled away gracefully, ungallantly murmuring, "*Mi casa* – you got that right."

Venom shot from the woman's eyes, but Lloyd stepped in. Before I could regroup my thoughts about there actually being 'a wife' tossed into our holiday mix, I felt our host lift the weight of the luggage from my shoulder.

"Why don't you," said Lloyd to Doris, "show Kohl the nature preserve behind the property, dear? In the meantime, I'll be helping Gordon unpack and settle in."

This ludicrous proposal had not been presented in the form of a question, so even though my jealousy flared mightily seeing Lloyd's hand resting on my boy's back, neither me nor 'the wife' had any say in the matter.

Contemplating letting this woman take me away, knowing Lloyd had intentions of leading Gordon astray, gave birth to a stratagem. If I played my cards just right, I could make my boyfriend jealous of Doris.

"Well," I sang out. "I'd be delighted to have a tour conducted by such a beautiful woman." I picked up and kissed the back of her hand; she flushed.

"He's *continental*," Trọng informed her with a sturdy dash of sarcasm.

"Yeah, he is," muttered Gordon as Lloyd began guiding him towards the house. Had there been a wisp of wistfulness in his tone…?

I laced arms with Doris so that my boy could see, and chuckled intimately. "Lead the way, lovely lady."

The trail was narrow, dusty and hot. The thick foliage – all of the dark, dark-green variety accustomed to semi-arid conditions – penned us in and kept the cool sea breeze at bay.

An opening appeared, and me and Doris stopped to admire the house, yacht and Pacific Ocean hundreds of feet below, and maybe a half-mile in front of us.

"Funny," Lloyd's wife said suddenly.

"What is?"

"Listen."

I did; there was nothing to hear.

She smiled, revealing great intrigue. "See? Back East, a wooded thicket like this would be alive with birdsong, but out here, at the margin of the continent, everything is still."

I couldn't help but like this woman. She had poetic thoughts, and I admire that in all people.

"How long have you—" I halted myself, thinking better of what I wanted to ask.

"Lived here?"

"Yes," I lied.

"Lloyd picked up this place three years ago. It was built by one of L.A.'s water barons about a century previous, long before Catalina became a state park."

"A water baron…?"

"Yes. Back in the day, money was pouring into Los Angeles – mainly from offshore oil drilling – but the town could only grow as fast as drinkable water was discovered, which was slow because of all the benzene polluting the wells. A consortium got together, built hundreds of miles of pipeline and tunnels to divert the Colorado River straight to a thirsty tinsel town. There were millions in old money to be made – trillions today."

"Fascinating," I said, suddenly realizing something else. "Poisoned drinking water from oil wells? Isn't that what those Frickin-Frackers are allowed to do now, all over the country?"

"I'm afraid, Kohl, it is—"

"Then what will we do for drinking water?"

"I imagine it's going to boil down to two choices. Either we'll have to ween our kids on the flavor of oil waste as 'natural,' the way we've already accommodated the taste of chlorine bleach in our kids' water – like the way grown-ups pretend not to taste the sulfur we've allowed corporations to contaminate every bottle of wine—"

"Or…?"

"Yes, I'm sorry. *Or,* we let the 19th century concept of a 'Water Baron' crawl back as a 21st century reality."

I felt a bit lost. "But what about renewable and clean energy sourc—"

She laughed so hard, a hand needed to fly over and grip my forearm for support. Through her gasps for air and lingering champagne giggles, she sputtered, "No. Come on, noooo." Then she caught a good deep inhale and stood upright. "Look around! We're still pretending we can send people to Mars using dinosaur juice. It's the equivalent of building the Titanic to run on whale oil. Modern times, modern fuels, but, sadly, such progress has not happened since Reagan monkeyed his way into office." Doris appraised me frankly, smiling like I'd made her day. "Oh, Kohl, the powers that be— Well, never mind, but I do have to say, it is so refreshing to spend time with someone so perfectly…shall I say, innocent…?"

Before I had time to protest, and attest to my personal wickedness, she'd laced her arm through mine and said, "Shall we see more?"

Doris gestured with elegant flare, and we continued to walk.

"Anyway, concerning the house, Lloyd had to spend many millions too to get this place – had to pull in some political favors as well – but it's a sound method to process some of his cash."

'Process,' I thought. 'Yeah, like the patented French-Connection laundry process.'

She picked up on my silence with a smile and shrug. "Well for now, the nation's thirst for water is quenched, but Lloyd and his business partners south of the border are the lords of slaking a different thirst – one that seems as insatiable as dehydration in shriveled men."

"And more profitable, apparently."

She smiled at my attempted witticism, but quite frankly, the woman's obvious scorn for her man was palpable. It seemed like an infinitely dense black hole she carried around in the core of her being, and it reached out to draw me in.

The leaves overhead unexpectedly stirred into motion, acted upon by an errant sea breeze, and I found my hostess' moroseness blent with the inhospitable environment to form an unbidden snippet of verse. I recited it out loud, glancing up at the brooding leaves and spots of blinding sunshine; it appeared we were moving farther away from any signs of civilization.

> "Cruel stepmother,
> As heartless as the sea,
> Nature seeks no embrace
> From her children – man –
> But only a jealous wish
> That we not rise up and
> Challenge her authority to seed."

"That is beautiful. Beautiful and desolate, Kohl."

"Yeah." I had to agree with so obviously wise an opinion, but then she startled the hell out of me by slipping her fingers into mine and kissing me.

After she removed her tongue from my mouth, I mentioned with a little too much volume, "But I'm Gay!"

Her expression dappled as she cocked her head with a smirk. "So? So is my husband."

"Yeah, I've been meaning to ask—"

"No words, Kohl. Let's not spoil the moment with words, okay…?"

Another 'not a question,' her grip on my hand tightened and she took me off-trail.

In another minute or two, she'd found a sturdy Aleppo pine to prop me against and began to unbutton my jeans. In response, I leaned my head against the bark and concentrated on getting hard. The leaves twittered overhead like they were enjoying an inside joke; the breeze licked my member a moment after Doris took it out. My hands landed within her hair as the doubtlessly beautiful woman sank to her knees.

I tried following Queen Victoria's old sex advice, closed my eyes and thought of Prussia. But as images of Königsberg Castle, the Brandenburg Gate and *KaDeWe* department store did nothing for me, I tried to think more erotic thoughts. And then, an odd set of impressions – visions really – filtered down on my brain like mottled starlight.

The pleasure built down below and I saw Gordon's smile. It made me stiffen all the harder and grin in my darkness too. There's no doubt how much I loved my beautiful boy.

This lovely meditation was interrupted by a frightful sound. At first indistinct, I clenched my eyes tighter and pivoted my head against the tree as if trying to bring the phantom tone into better clarity. All at once it burst onto my consciousness – the horrendous screech of that donkey in the L.A. sex club. It caused a painful queasiness in the pit of my stomach and I forced it away by will.

In another moment, Doris' skill had re-asserted itself and I saw her sexy face before my mind's eye. It sent a thrill along my spine to know those were the lips servicing my flaring cock right now.

As I inched closer to climax, I imagined I was pleasuring my boy in the most intimate way possible. Stroke for stroke, watching him writhe under me in pleasure, and then being vaguely aware of Assauer's laugh and the biting sting of his wet towel on my exposed ass cheeks.

Just as I was on the verge of giving Doris what she wanted – gripping the woman's head deep down on my dick – I got a weird, sickening whiff of something fetid and natural in the extreme. This was followed by the image of a maniacal looking man with curly locks and pointy ears. The expression on his face was full of loathing, and it appeared like he were the one about to hate-cum on me.

I opened my eyes, sunlight searing my pupils, and the goaty smell lingered as I ejaculated over and over again into Doris' receptive wetness. I did so, but helplessly let go of the woman's hair while trying to drive the nature spirit's intense visage out of my head.

'Same old bullshit,' I thought as I surveyed the scene. 'Drinks and dinner with someone going over my boyfriend as if he's an empty house to move into and plant a SOLD sign in front of. Makes me sick.'

And so it did. I felt bleak and alone, despite the crowded and grand setting, sitting across a spacious round table from them and watching Lloyd's partner ply Gordon with ogling attention.

I gazed around the room to distract myself. The Casino – the massive round landmark defining Avalon's harbor – resembled some oddly large concrete water tank at its base, but several stories up, a loggia looking like it was lifted from the Doge's Palace in Venice, wrapped itself around a domed ballroom of mesmerizingly perfect proportions.

That's where we were now, having a lavish candlelight supper, per Doris' suggestion, in the storied restaurant at the top of the structure. A band cranked out some old standards, and more noise coming from the soft-soled shuffling of feet on the circular dancefloor joined the music. Our table was just one of many near the open doors and fresh sea breeze coming in from the wrap-around terrace.

My eyes followed the shallow ribs of the dome up to the rather Classical-looking oculus. Here an Art Deco grille supported five lighting fixtures of Lalique-esque crystals.

Lloyd leaned against my right side and asked in a deep tone, "Like it here?"

My gaze momentarily alighted on his wife's retiring stare – as she was sitting opposite me – before turning to the handsome sea captain.

"It's unique. I'm not sure I've seen any place quite like this before."

My response made Lloyd smile warmly, and I might add, it appeared he would have taken my hand if we weren't under such close scrutiny at the moment – from his wife *and* partner.

'It's all bullshit.' I thought. 'Guess he's done with Gordon already and sent him back to Trọng's clutches to slock my green-eyed gremlin with water.'

While I fumed, the band music reasserted itself; Gordon laughed at one of Trọng's stupid jokes; Doris' eyes were on mine again, and I wondered if I looked as miserable as she felt.

Trọng burst out, "Lloyd's wife has *such* good taste. She suggested your first night on Catalina be spent here, and who can argue with a woman of *quality?*"

Doris leaned over and endowed a husky-but-fake smile on her Vietnamese rival. "Some foolish few, I suppose."

Lloyd laughed, and we all wound up gawking at him; he explained nothing.

Trọng continued, his accent growing more pronounced as a vindictive edge crept into it. "Being a good hostess is all right, as far as it goes. I suppose compensation can come in many forms—"

I took a sip of wine.

"So, Kohl," interrupted the man of the sea, "what did you think of the nature trail behind the house?"

I nearly spit it out.

"We had a very nice time," Doris said plainly.

"Oh, I bet." Trọng planted fascinated elbows on the table, chin in palms, and batted cow-lashes at me. "See much of the view?"

'*Gott im Himmel,*' I thought. But I actually said, "Unbeatable, and our hostess falls into the same category."

Gordon seemed to swallow those words wrong.

"Oh!" exclaimed Lloyd's partner. "Reminds me of another woodland adventure. Involves one wolf"—his glare landed on Doris—"and three little naïve piggies." Trọng's glance rounded the table with calculating ease from me, to Gordon, and then settled on Lloyd. "'I'll huff, and I'll puff, and I'll blow your house down,' she said."

Lloyd was the only one to laugh. "I think, dear Trọng, you have your old

Disney cartoons mixed up."

He sat back, triumphant. "Maybe I do; maybe I don't."

"But if I remember correctly," I offered as peacemaker, "the wolf was okay in that one."

Cold stares greeted me from around the table.

"I mean, he knocked down a couple of shacks with his bad breath, but did not meet any awful fate – no cosmetic justice, if you will."

"Cosmetic...?" Doris asked.

Gordon instantly chuckled. "He means *cosmic justice*. Kohl is always mixing up his sayings, at least in English."

While the rest of them laughed, I flashed a little bit hot inside. Who among us is perfect, after all?

The band's current song finished. A smattering of applause rewarded their efforts, mainly from the dancing couples. Almost immediately, another one started. *Avalon*, the song stuck in my head as the *Mary Jane* glided us past Catalina's main harbor town.

Doris visibly changed. "Do you know, Kohl and Gordon, this place is very special to me?"

"No," said my boyfriend.

Lloyd appeared shaken.

"It is," continued the lovely dark-haired lady. "It's where my husband and I held our wedding reception. Remember this song, darling?"

"Yes." The sea captain, a decisive man of action, stood up. He went around to his wife's side – undeterred by Trọng's amazement – and held out his hand. "It's *our* song, so shall we dance?"

She rose with total command of herself, took hold of his fingers and let herself be led off to the dancefloor.

When I glanced back, Trọng had already taken Gordon's hand and was chatting with him quietly, as if his heart had not just been broken.

"Excuse me," I said, standing up. "I need some fresh air." As I walked to one of the terrace doors, I barely let myself register the hurt look in my boyfriend's eyes.

The loggia curved away gradually in both directions from the railing where I had planted myself to brood. Lights bobbed from the harbor vessels and climbed the otherwise dark hills behind town.

I recognized I was feeling very uneasy, but the queasy discomfort in my gut...or, maybe not my gut. Where exactly was it coming from?

"Kohl?"

I turned.

Gordon slid in next to me. "What's up with you?"

"Don't sound so smug—"

"Kohl!"

I instantly relented. "I don't feel right, Gordon. I'm not myself."

"Yeah, I sensed that. But don't worry."

"Don't worry about what?!"

"Watch your temper," he warned.

I nodded and repeated myself very calmly, "Worry about what, honey?"

"Lloyd."

"Lloyd…?"

My boy rolled his eyes, like it was all *so* obvious. "Yeah. He never had any interest in me. He's shoving me and Trọng together to get a rise out of you."

"You think?" This possibility had not even been on my sonar.

"Hell, yeah. I see his ploy to make you jealous – not a difficult task. He's pushing your buttons to make you 'hurt' me so I go flying into Trọng's arms. And then he'll sweep in, Zeus-like, to scoop you up and out of your pants. It's all as plain as Ganymede's little red cap."

"But still…" I stammered.

"Still, what?"

"You—"

"Kohl…" his tone cautioned again.

"But still you seem to like that Vietnamese guy." Turned out I couldn't help myself.

Gordon stood up straight, mad. "Fuck you. Is that all you think of me?"

"Wait!" I grabbed his arm. "I—"

"What is it?"

"I don't know. I had…." How could I tell him about a weird vision occurring while Doris blew me in the woods?

"We'll talk later," Gordon said, pulling away. "That is If you can see past your jealousy long enough to form a coherent sentence."

Helplessly, I watched him go back to our table all smiles and jovial gestures. Gordon slid back down next to Trọng once more.

Disgusted with the whole display – and with myself too – I looked out over Avalon again. The music filled my head, allowing my thoughts to climb up into the silent, brooding wilds of Santa Catalina Island.

Chapter 6: Alligator Tears and Dollar Signs

I was a bit lost in the vastness of the upstairs bedroom corridors. This house was maze-like for sure, but up here, the gorgeous day outside easily penetrated. A continuous run of skylights brought both Catalina warmth and sunlight into the heart of the otherwise secretive villa.

A lazy afternoon so far, Doris had given Gordon a set of tennis whites, and now my boy and Lloyd were playing on the clay court surrounded by cypress trees on three sides.

I had just popped up the servants' stairs to fetch a book before heading back down, where I'd sit on the terrace and watch like a dutiful boyfriend.

It was the day after our awkward dinner at the Casino, and I have to say I felt somewhat guilty for being in a mood like that – like I was – practically spoiling Doris' outing, no pun intended, lol. But it helped no one for me to sour my Gordon's high spirits either, and so later, in our room alone, I was able to explain a bit more about that creepy vision I had in the woods, and although he seemed concerned, he made me see it'd just been some random thought anyway. "Overly tired" he explained, and I had a weird feeling that he knew I was with Doris when the smelly, primal face flashed before me. Anyway, I laughed at myself for letting it get to me like that, and more importantly, my boy forgave my pissy-ness with a hug.

Now I've flipped the leaf and vowed to relax and have a good time at Lloyd's considerable expense.

I snapped out of my thoughts all of a sudden and realized I was thoroughly lost. Somehow I'd passed out of the sunlit public spaces into a darker, more intimate section of the house. My light-fingered ways came back to me with a prickle; private spaces meant secret nooks where valuables could be subject to pilfering. A little stealthy scouting was called for.

I came to a door which appeared different from the others, but in the dim light, it might have been my imagination.

A quick scan up and down the passage assured myself I was alone, so I reached for the knob.

As quietly as I could, I twisted it, and to my surprise, it opened.

The room beyond was like a converted dressing room with red walls and no windows.

Again I looked, and seeing yours truly remained unobserved, went in.

On one of the side walls was heavy drapery, but I could see a faint pool of light puddling at the curtain's feet. Slowly, one hand drew a fabric panel aside.

Astounded but calm, I opened the other one too.

What I saw was a shrine of some kind. A pair of red-bulbed candle lamps cast a crimson pall on a painting in a gilt frame. But *WTF!* Who was this guy...?

He looked like a slick-haired accountant, thin mustache and all. He wore a ranchero shirt in white with black pocket flaps; wrapping his neck was a black and white scarf arranged like a tie; the expression on his mid-forties face was placid and saintlike.

There was a kneeler in front of the picture, and a sort of garland of silk magnolia leaves, pink roses and bright sunflowers. This draped the area between the portrait and the place to worship.

I leaned in closer, because pinned to the wall all around the man's painting were passport-sized photos. Most were black and white, formal studio shots, but all were of young men with dark hair and determined expressions.

Before I got nervous and retreated, I noticed there was a placard attached to the main icon's gold frame. I didn't know what it meant, but it said: *"El bandido generoso."*

Drawing the curtains closed so nothing was out of place, and leaving this shrine as worthless to my goal, I had my sticky-fingered instincts raised.

An impressive piece of furniture stood against the opposite wall. Sort of like a secretary in highly polished rosewood, the lower half had drawers and cabinet doors. The upper portion contained four slender panels hinged together like shutters. Flanking these intricate accordion doors, on the far end of each side, fancy Roman columns rose up majestically. They supported a small-scale temple roof in the form of a jutting pendant.

I went there and delicately worked the hinged panels between the Corinthian pillars.

Slowly, my heart rate accelerated; bit by bit, a glimpse of gold met my covetous eyes. 'Lotto!' I thought.

Inside this shrine, a marble pedestal supported an old-as-fuck statue of a naked man. His rippling muscles were shown with a jeweler's precision, while a three-pronged fishing spear rose from his right foot up to his hand.

I picked it up. It was not attached to the base, but heavy nonetheless. The gleaming surface of 'the god,' and the pound or two of weight for such a portable, pocketable treasure, told me this was made of high karat gold.

Itching to nab it now, I placed it carefully back as it was before and closed up the timber tabernacle just like it had been.

'Later,' I thought, 'when the time is right, I'll be back, my precious....'

I hurriedly left the room, shut the door to the hallway as quietly as a rat, and then headed back the way I suppose I'd come.

Rounding a blind corner, I ran squarely into Trọng. We jumped for a second in surprise, and I quickly scanned him. He was also in tennis clothes with a fresh towel around his neck, a Dolce & Gabbana headband was in place, and the man held a racket and Gucci gym bag in one hand.

"What are you doing here, in me and Lloyd's private—"

"I got lost," I laughed. "This place is too enormous!"

The Vietnamese guy smiled, unguarded. "I know. It's great, huh?"

I nodded my head, happy he suspected nothing. My relieved thoughts were truncated though, for with his white polo shirt being open as it was, I spied a heavy gold chain around his neck for the first time. By the lump in the fabric over his chest, I could tell there was a weighty pendant at the end, but I couldn't see what it was.

"Going back outside?" Trọng asked.

"Yep. Lead the way."

"Sure, handsome. Follow me."

As he started to walk, his tone dipped a bit seriously. "And be careful where you wander, Kohl."

I was silent.

"Dangers lurk."

"Oh, really?" I asked.

"Yes. I'd advise you to be wary of stray mountain lions."

I was astounded. "There's some on Catalina Island?!"

He paused just as we re-entered the sunlit public corridor. "Yes, Kohl. There is at least one thirsty cougar in this house for sure."

After a moment or two of just staring at one another, we both burst out laughing.

Trọng re-shouldered his bag and led on.

"So, that part of upstairs is for you and Lloyd. What about—"

"Doris has her own domain on the other side of the house – her fortress of solitude – where she's welcomed to stay, as far as I'm concerned."

"I see, but don't you two come into conflict?"

"What's life without a little spice?" He smiled wickedly.

Chuckling, I admitted, "That's true."

"She has her interests, and I have mine."

We neared the grand staircase leading down. I stopped him at the top step. "But Doris does not mind you living here – so close to Lloyd?"

He sailed on down the steps, tossing back a flip reply. "Why would she?! Better to keep your rivals close to hand, where you can see them, as the old saying goes."

I followed and caught up with him at the first landing.

He continued with his original line of thought. "Don't feel sorry for her. She makes out all right in this fucked-up world. She doesn't suffer in her role as lady 'beard.'"

We arrived on the ground floor's marble tiles. "But, still she must be lonely."

That statement made him chuckle.

"She compensates herself freely with Lloyd's money and political connections. She's no Little Bo Peep lost her sheep. As I say, she's more a female predator than anything else."

I laughed. "You warning me?"

We stopped at the glass doors to the terrace overlooking the tennis courts. "Advising you, and you're welcome to the advice, as it's free. Any favor she asks you to do for *her* may not come with the same guarantee."

He winked before pasting on a grin and sallying forth into the sunshine.

I trailed, going with my book to a table shaded by an umbrella. In a few minutes, I was settled and watching Trọng 'tapping out' Lloyd from the match.

The sexy man spotted me and made his way over. Meanwhile, Gordon and the Vietnamese guy started to play. Whacks, from tennis rackets and tightly-wound spheres of rubber and neon-green felt bouncing on the compacted clay, wove a background tapestry of sound.

Lloyd pulled out a chair and sat across from me. The front edge of his hair was moist from perspiration, although the expression on his face remained cool.

Youthful grunts were added to the ambient noises of smacking sounds, and blended with them to transition into regular beats like a heart; me and Lloyd just observed one another without words, frowns or smiles. None of them seemed necessary.

A bead of sweat rolled down his throat and collected in the sexy tanned divot below his voice box.

He inhaled and gestured to a servant. The uniformed woman brought over a silver tray, from which Lloyd lifted a box and dismissed her again.

Drawing his seat closer to the table, he cocked his head like invitation for me to come and see.

I did just in time for him to open a dark-green case with a gold crown logo embossed in the lower corner. Out came a heavy Rolex watch.

"Hold out your hand," he said.

Swallowing, I did.

He slipped it on and brushed the most sensitive part of my inner wrist as he closed the latch. Lloyd looked up and held my eyes. "Feel that?"

He meant the weight; I did.

"It's 18k. Solid gold, diamonds around the face." He pushed the empty box towards me. "And it's yours now."

The reverberations of the game faded far into the background. I was dizzy and hoped Lloyd assumed it was from emotion. In truth of fact, I was assessing how much I could get for it back on the mainland – the 'no questions asked' price at the 'no receipt required' pawnshop.

My eyes filled simultaneously with alligator tears and dollar signs.

I suddenly realized I must have been grinning too, for I could see Lloyd's hopes were up. Deciding to play into them, I rose halfway up from my chair, leaned across the table and took the man's clammy cheeks in both hands. I kissed him, with tongue.

The heartbeat sounds completely stopped.

When I opened my eyes, Doris was standing there with a tray of icy glasses and a pitcher of lemonade.

She set the tray down with equally frigidity and waited. "Am I interrupting?"

I flopped back in my seat, and the sounds of the game returned.

"No, dear!" Lloyd leapt to his feet and turned her cheek away from me to smooch it, loudly. At the same time, behind her back, his free hand made a broom and dustpan pantomime towards the tabletop, and I got it.

While she was distracted, I swept the *Rolex* box into my lap and lowered my wrists to remove the watch out of sight.

"You sit," Lloyd told his wife. "I'm going to shower and change. I'll be back in a little while to join you in some of your sweet lemonade." He left her to silently turn her wrath on me.

I smiled and gestured to the seat.

While Gordon and Trọng continued to play, she poured me a glass, eventually sitting across from yours truly looking rather suspicious. "What was that about?"

"Um – just showing some appreciation. It's been such a lovely stay so far."

Silently, she dispensed a glass for herself. "Good. I'm glad you feel you're one of the family." Her glance wandered to the court and landed briefly with a frown on Trọng.

Maybe I shouldn't have laughed, but I couldn't quite help it. Under-table, I popped the watch into its box.

Doris sipped, then picked up my paperback. Sarcasm rolled along her tone as she read off the title. "*Shifters in the Dusk...?*"

"Yeah. It's a really cool take on high school were-panthers and their hot chick girlfriend cheerleaders who are a coven of were-witch-owls."

She rolled her eyes. "God. What next – shifter-frogs and vampire mosquitoes?"

I half chuckled. "Well, if they are teenage alphas and their straight fuck buddies, folks will pay to read it." I shrugged. "It's our escapist age, I suppose."

"Yes. Reality is getting more and more unbelievable by the day, so we run away to only slightly more outlandish fiction for relief." Again her gaze shifted to Trọng, and I started to feel uncomfortable.

She must have sensed it because Doris smiled and invited me to drink.

When I set my glass down again, she was holding a wrapped gift. It took me a moment to realize it had been lying on the tray the whole time.

"Here, Kohl. A little something for you."

I took it. It was rather thin and about the size of a piece of loose-leaf paper. "Are you sure? You don't—"

"Please. I want you to have it."

I turned it over in my hand. It was surprisingly heavy for its size, and tastefully wrapped in Asian-style gift paper.

I released the bindings, and held up a brand-new electronic tablet.

"I do a lot of reading these days," Doris informed me, "so I took the liberty of uploading my ebook collection of about a thousand titles – everything from *The Satyricon*, to *Bound & Bound* – which is a great gothic novel, and one which might suit your tastes. I hope you enjoy."

I depressed the power button and watched the screen come to life, thinking how this item would be easy to liquidate at a swap meet. "Cheers, Doris. It's thoughtful and handy. I'm – speechless. Your gener...osity...."

I looked up, and the woman was tapping her cheek for a kiss.

When I leaned over, Doris quickly turned and planted a wet one on my lips.

She said, "I have another gift for you as well."

"Oh?"

"It's one you'll find laid out in your room when you return."

"All right. Can't wait to see it, and thank you."

She pulled me down for another kiss, with tongue, positively purring, "You're welcome."

The bright light of my cellphone screen made me wince in pain: 2:21 AM, it said.

I turned it off and snuggled down on my pillow again. Gordon thought I hadn't noticed him rise from bed and sneak out of our room more than an hour ago; he thought he could engage in his extracurricular activities without me being any the wiser – but he was wrong. So, I'd been biding my time, waiting to catch my skanky boyfriend red-headed, or handled, whatever it is.

In the meantime, I tried not to fume, told myself it would be unwise to make a big scene in our hosts' house in the middle of the night – especially the house of our hosts so liberally sprinkled with goodies to lift.

Instead, I rotated my head to the right and watched the moonlight inch across the carpet. An ironic thought crept into my mind, one that made me chuckle softly in the darkness.

I didn't want to sleep with either husband or 'wife' – not with Lloyd, because I assumed he was a total top like me – not with Doris, because... well, because she's female. Yuk. However, there was a delicious thought in knowing she was the type of woman my ex would love to 'slam.' I laughed to think how Assauer was getting his schoolboy uniform torn and his backside beaten right now by Hojax, while all the while I had this hot lady I couldn't use. He'd be so 'sore' and jealous – downright upset, I guess – I'd have to make sure and feed him all the sordid details, lol.

I'm cruel, I know...but he's the same. It's part of what makes me and my ex click so well together. Years ago, when we were late-teenage roust-abouts on the mean streets of Braunschweig, when we were both at university going after our teaching degrees, I grudgingly had to accept Assauer's Bi inclinations – habits, tendencies, proclivities, fetishes, 'choices,' whichever is most PC – and realize he couldn't help it; the poor fuck was born that way. I mean, like it or not, we have to accept shortcomings in the ones we love, right…? Even if it's something as emasculating as a hoo-ha addiction.

I shuddered.

Anyway, we had our good times – me and Assauer – and he did help me out of a giant jam…staying true to me, or to our love, for what it was worth. But we'd had our bad times too, and I suppose there were nights just like this one where one or the other of us would be in bed, alone, waiting and on the verge of inciting 'a scene.'

As far as my boy and Assauer, they did have one thing in common though – they could both drive me to total distraction! Another chuckle accompanied a sigh and a changed view as I counted shadows on the ceiling.

Dinner intrigue! *Gott im Himmel*, that had been more than a scene: more like a whole Comedy Act for sure, as it seems eating with people in my life has come to be these days.

Once I re-entered our room that afternoon, I found a brand-new Armani suit laid out on the bed. The perfumed note on top said: "Kohl, I thought you should look nice. Lloyd never wore this, but I think you should. Doris."

The slick fabric of the trousers gave me a boner as I accompanied my boy down to our evening meal; the suit fit well, and I knew I looked sharp with Gordon on my arm. I could also feel the weight of Lloyd's 18-karat gift on my wrist, out of sight, and below a stiff French cuff.

A dining room of sea views, with open French doors and gauzy curtains, looked stunning in the summer sun of late evening.

However, as the meal progressed, I felt like the painter invited to sketch the Last Supper. While Lloyd sat next to me, Doris, Gordon and Trọng were all arranged on the long side opposite us. And the two rivals engaged in shocking behavior: Doris fixing my boy's napkin under his chin and indulging in other sick motherly stuff to the point of making me want to toss my salad. Hell, I'm surprised she didn't cut the boy's meat and spoon feed him.

Trọng, literally on the other hand, was flirty and touchy-feely. Frankly, if I didn't know any better, judging by the Vietnamese guy's groping, I would have thought they were boyfriend and boyfriend already.

To divert my hot tendencies, I complimented our hostess on the décor of the room, the fineness of the Ginori dinner service, the luxe of the food, and told Doris she had "angry skills."

The others puzzled a moment, but Gordon laughed his ass off at me. "He means 'mad skills,' and Doris, I agree."

The smile he gave me then – like a little boy in his mommy's kitchen in front of a rack of cooling cookies – made me sick.

After I had had my fill of this sticky display, I'll admit it, I resorted to the tactics of jealousy. To Doris, I openly thanked her for the suit, pinching the lapel fabric, and enjoying the slow recognition in both Trọng and Lloyd's eyes that the 'Lady of the House' had given me some of her lord and master's best attire.

It was also the first Gordon had heard of the woman's gift.

Then, to really drive home the mistrustfulness in my boy, I pulled up my sleeve and pointedly looked at the time.

"Thank you so much, Lloyd," I said, lifting and kissing the back of his hand. "It's the nicest gift I've ever received."

Ha-ha. Now no one was happy! Trọng fumed at the extravagance of his partner's bauble to win my affections – or ass, as the case might have been. Doris ground her teeth to know her own present had been effortlessly bested. And Gordon looked stunned to see me indulge in PDA with our sexy-ass host, which was how the boy himself had described the sea captain.

And what of Lloyd? Unlike the pot-boiling, steaming-mad vibes coming from the three across the table from us, the man by my side appeared calculating and turned on.

But now, 2 in the morning, I was half-tempted to get out of bed and go to the room Lloyd had showed me after dinner with the words "Come to me later, if you want."

Did I want? Maybe he'd be happy just to suck my dick, but I doubted it. 'What was that sound...?' I wondered.

There was a shadow beneath the door to the hallway. I quickly turned on my side facing the window, prepped a waiting finger on the lamp switch, and pretended to be asleep. I'd catch my guilty teen-*Engel* red-herringed....

The door opened quietly as a whisper. It closed again in the same manner, and after a few moments of silence, I felt the sheets move as someone climbed into bed next to me.

I flipped the switch, lurched to a sitting position and yelled at the top of my lungs: "*SLUT!*"

Doris blinked back at me with innocent eyes.

I leapt out of bed wanting to apologize, but covered my nakedness instead.

"Not you! I thought you were Gordon."

"He's busy with Trọng."

"But what are you doing—"

"I thought you'd be pleased...."

Looking around and not seeing my boxers anywhere near to hand, I grabbed the corner of the sheet and carefully slid back into bed.

Doris, who was wearing a frilly black nightgown and robe, kneeled and reached out with unflappable ease to stroke my arm. "You looked so fine this evening, Kohl, and word got to me that you were on your own tonight – well, I thought I'd stop by for a visit."

I gulped down a lump. "A 'visit,' at 2:30 in the morning?"

"And to give you this." She sheepishly pulled a dark red box from the pocket of her dressing gown and placed it in my hands.

It was surprisingly heavy – a familial theme in Lloyd's household – and Cartier was emblazoned in the lower-right corner. "Are you sure?" I asked her.

She appeared slightly hurt by my inquiry. "Yes, I'm sure. When I saw what Lloyd had given you...I, well, I wanted to let you know, I *care* too."

'*Scheisse!*' I thought. 'Rich people only know love via a price tag.' But, I grinned appreciatively and cracked the container open.

At first I couldn't tell what it was. It looked like a black billfold, with a huge diamond and platinum clasp and corner guards, but opening it up revealed an 18-karat gold cellphone case – the windows for the camera and flash were also encrusted with diamonds.

"Wow," I said, fumbling over the worthlessly precious item; a Faberge egg for the Trump epoch.

"I hope you like it."

"I do. You don't have a use for it—"

"No, it's yours now, Kohl."

"Thank you." And although it seemed ludicrous, considering I was trapped in bed with a rich and beautiful woman at 2 in the morning, I shook her hand, much to her bemusement.

Doris suddenly let out a burst of air, and collapsed like a Hollywood starlet, arms draped across my scantily covered legs.

I tugged myself to sit fully upright with my back against the headboard.

Her beautiful brown eyes peered up at me. "I'm lonely, Kohl. None of this is easy."

I was not sure what to say.

"That day in the woods," she went on sadly, "you wanted to ask me how I came to be married to Lloyd, didn't you?"

I nodded. She clearly had understood even then.

"Well, I'm sorry to say, you were right. I am a slut too. Not for eggplant or peach, as you kids might say, but for other things. A good life, a suitable position—"

"But you don't have to stay married. You've done your duty to stop the rumor mill."

She sat more erect, gracefully kicking her legs out from under her frilly coverings.

"It's worse than that, Kohl. You see, Lloyd and I signed a prenuptial agreement. He agrees to support me financially throughout the marriage as I see fit, and I agreed to accept nothing in a divorce settlement if I initiate a split – a non-equal disposition of the nuptials, as the lawyers called it."

"Oh. So you'd be broke."

"But..." an oddly inappropriate sparkle attached itself to her. "There is another clause, one that benefits me, if it's ever activated."

"Which is?"

She inched her way up my body. "If Lloyd ever outs himself – for whatever reason – the 'dutiful wife' gets a cool hundred-million, tax-free."

I got goose blemishes, and she noticed.

"You see, Kohl. I *am* a generous soul. If that little, itty-bitty clause"—her fingers caressed the skin around my belly button—"ever comes into effect, I'll gladly peel off a million or two to show gratitude to a helping hand."

'Wow,' I thought. 'Trọng's warning about a cougar-crossing had been a good one.'

As I was seeing more dollar signs in my eyes, she launched herself at my mouth, all lipstick and tongue.

Just then, wouldn't you know it, Gordon walked in. "What. The. Fuck!"

We paused, as we were – caught red-handed – and looked over to see him still standing in the open doorway, fingers gripping the knob.

"Oh, dear," Doris said, as she climbed off of me. "Looks like I climbed into the wrong bed."

Me and Gordon watched in silence as she stood, arranged her teddy and robe, and then mussed her hair back into place with a great deal of dignity – all of this before making her way to the exit.

My boy stood aside.

"Silly me," she said to him, but smiled like the least silly thing in the world.

As Doris closed the door behind her, she said, "Night, gentlemen. And Kohl, do remember what I told you about that little contractual matter, all right…?"

Click. She was gone.

"What was that about?" my boyfriend asked.

"Some scheme she's got with Lloyd to get a shit-load of money—"

"No! I meant her being in our bed, her face-sucking out your soul."

I stood up and went to him – it looked like the scene would be coming after all, but not the one I envisioned. So, I hugged him, pressing his lower back into me.

"She's lonely – stuck in a loveless, passionless relationship. Thank God that's not us, huh?" I kissed the nape of his neck, raising his desire there and making him moan as he gripped onto me for support.

"Poor sad bitch," he mumbled.

"Yes." I kissed around to the front of his throat and up to his chin.

He pushed me back a bit, using his sweatshirt sleeve to rub it across my mouth with a frown. He held it back so I could see it smeared with lipstick.

"I'm sorry, baby," I pleaded. "I *am* sorry…."

The moment I bit my lip in genuine remorse, he kissed me, grabbing the side of my head and making me know instantly I was forgiven.

I pulled off his shirt and lowered his pajama bottoms. A moment later we were cuddling in bed, my boy's head resting against my heart.

"Let's not quibble," he said.

And I stroked his wavy locks in agreement. "We've been through so much together."

"Hard to believe eighteen months ago...."

"Yeah. Things have moved so fast since Aptos High."

He paused. I felt his body tense up. Nudging his chin so I could see his eyes, I asked, "What is it?"

"Um. Nothing. I just got lost in a moment thinking about the night we ran away, and about my father."

I hugged Gordon. "Don't fret about him, or your mom either."

"Her I don't worry—" He halted mid-thought and started again. "That is, I have faith that they're all right. As for bringing a scandal down on their heads, they're not the type to spread rumors concerning their own flesh and blood."

I knew how my boy felt, at least partially. We shared the pain of a sudden separation from *den Eltern* – the family.

"Did I ever tell you...?" Gordon's voice had slipped into storytelling mode. "It was hard being the youngest Sanchez boy at the nursery. They all saw our dad play favorites with me; they all got yelled at, while I got patted on the head for my screw-ups. They didn't want to stay there; maybe never felt invited to, and so, off they went to college and careers outside the family business – leaving the nursery and Dad far behind."

I felt a tear on my chest. "Oh, honey—"

"You know the story of Joseph, right?" my boy asked.

"Mary and Joseph, Joseph?"

"No, the other one in the Bible. How the teenage Joseph was the youngest brother, and the Queer one too; how his brothers beat him and left him for dead at the bottom of a dry well because their dad gave him a coat the bros thought was too 'gay.'"

"Ah, yes, that one. Why...?"

He wiped his nose and let out a single laugh. "Cuz that's how I felt. My dad looked to me to be the *one* anyway. The one who'd take over and run the operation someday. And, now...."

I slowly swiped a precious tear from his eye, and then brushed his hair back. "Sometimes I'm not sure what we're doing in life."

He used my chest for support with his hand. "But I don't regret it, Kohl. Just so you know."

"I know, baby. I don't regret it either, not for a moment."

He settled down again and I continued stroking his hair.

I inhaled and spoke with new resolve. "Let's just stick to the plan and look for opportunities to escape with some of these top one-percenters' good stuff."

"Yeah," he agreed.

After a silent moment or two, my calm was fully restored, so I could tease him with a slight chuckle, "You sexy little throt. I've seen the way you've been flirting with Trọng."

He defended himself with an easy, carefree grin. "The same thirsty way you've been acting with Lloyd and his wife, you mean?"

"Yeah. I guess so." I don't blush, so I know I didn't right then. "But the sea captain's our host! I have to string him along."

"Well, Lloyd's partner is our almost-host. I have to do the same."

"So, did you get tired of Trọng?"

He snickered and climbed on top of me, sitting in my lap with hands on the headboard. He knew I was defused, starting to get hard, and could speak truthfully.

"Yeah. He's an indifferent bottom – just lays there like a carp, mouth open. Plus, he's got this pendant that kept distracting me."

I rumpled my brows. "A pendant?"

"Yeah. A weird one – like a winged dick in gold. He said it has meaning to him, but he wouldn't tell me what."

Queasiness rose in my gut. "He has, one of, those...?"

"Yes. Says he never takes it off. Why?"

"No reason." I changed the subject with a smirk. "An indifferent bottom, huh? Not like you, my little power pathick lover."

Gordon smacked me, then laughed. "I never should have taught you that word."

"Why? I love it. Love it when you are under me; love it when you moan my name and lock eyes on mine."

"Love it when I make you cum, saying you'll love me forever."

"Yeah. And I will, you know."

He leaned down and grazed his mouth across mine. "Good."

We wound up hugging, and I was glad he couldn't see the dread concern on my face.

Chapter 7: Hot Heads Explode

New Message
To: Assauer4U2@gmail.com
Subject: ...get your shit together...

We've had a crazy week with the sea captain and his extended *familia*. Breakfast this morning turned into a shambles. You would have loved the sight of it: Lloyd pissed at me because I wouldn't put out; Trọng mad that Gordon dumped him; Doris fed up that her house is full of her husband's boyfriends! lol

The situation got tense around there, so before hot heads could explode, me and Gordon plotted our escape.

While we were alone, we checked the ferry schedule, packed and helped ourselves to some choice souvenirs we felt *sure* our hosts would want us to have. Anyway, we slipped away by calling a car and telling Doris and Lloyd that me and my boy wanted a day alone in Avalon. They reluctantly accepted our pseudo-romantic mood, but didn't know we'd already stashed our bags by the side of the garage, where we loaded up once the driver arrived.

Anyway, I also found out Trọng has some connection to the donkey dick people, which Gordon confirmed seeing the guy wearing the flying penis mark on a pendant. I'll give you details later, but it's all the more reason me and my boy didn't stick around until I asked the Vietnamese guy about it, or worse – he brings it up on his own.

We're on the Catalina Ferry now, so get your shit together, cuz we'll be back to Hojax's house by this evening. We'll need to decide what to do in a hurry.

But for now, me and my boy are looking out across the sea, sky and sun and enjoying ourselves.

Wish you were here, not. lol

Tschüss, loser.

The boat bounded on a wave just as I hit the 'Send' button. Finished and satisfied, I snapped the case shut on my brand-new iPad. Of course I'd be selling it, but I might as well get a few emails sent on the ferry's free wifi.

Apparently coming back *from* Avalon to the mainland was not regarded as a romantic voyage, because the few dozen people on our afternoon trip were mainly inside, on the two passenger levels below us. Which was okay, for me and Gordon had most of the top deck, light, ocean views and air to ourselves.

We stood on the starboard side, facing the sun, and near to the open door of the bridge. Occasionally, a uniformed sailor would come and go.

I turned to lean my elbow on the railing and watch my boy. He looked so sexy with his brown eyes casting glances over the waves, the breeze rustling his chestnut locks from time to time. He wore his blue and white Aptos High letterman jacket with the 'A' and anchor logo on it, and had his gym bag by his feet.

A tall and swarthy sailor – or junior officer? – came out and stood with a clipboard in front of the wall to the bridge. He was focused on his paperwork, but peered up and shed a sexy smile as a younger, redheaded sailor appeared with a sweep-up broom and pan; this second sailor also had a soft rag in his hand, with which he began to polish the ship's bell.

"You hungry, Kohl?"

I shook my head, more intent on feasting my eyes on my boy than putting sustenance in my belly.

"Suit yourself." He extracted a ripe banana from his coat pocket. It's bright yellow contrasted sharply with all the blues around us, and I even noticed the redheaded sailor seemed to startle at the fruit's appearance. He stopped polishing and watched us with hands locked confrontationally on his hips.

Gordon peeled and ate, splitting happy glances between me and the vastness of the ocean. I liked it; I felt a growing happiness in me as well.

My boy tossed the spent peel behind him with a grin. It landed making a dull thump on the deck.

Then I noticed our young observer go up to the older man and draw his attention to us.

Now they both glared our way with some pissed-off vibe, which was only interrupted as the redhead grabbed his dustpan and broom and came towards us.

All my attention to the front of the boat eventually made Gordon turn just in time to see the sailor sweep up the peel, and glare at us from close range. A clicking sound of disgust erupted from his closed mouth before he walked his frown and himself back to the other man.

"What's up with Gilbert Grape?" Gordon asked.

"Who the fuck knows," I said without playing.

The boat bobbed again, and I latched onto the railing, having my attention totally recaptured by the environment surrounding us.

After a few moments of wordless contemplation, these lines to a Rubaiyat appeared to me:

'Homer chanted of red-wine seas,
and of tempest-tossed Ulysses,
but on The Main, success or naught,
each criminal or saint she frees.

Her eye of glass broods on one thought –
to drench each errant Argonaut
and *be* their own mortalities,
seeking no more for what is sought.

Thus, Poet or reverent Sailor,
to the shroud the Deep-One's tailor
when our final hour is aught
and the salt of our blood flows to Her.'

When I looked over again at my boy, Gordon had retrieved clippers from his bag and was now standing back from the railing cutting his nails and whistling a pop tune into the wind. He gyrated his hips to the beat, his trimmings flew back and scattered on the deck. After a moment, I realized the song was that old sentimental classic: *I'm Bringing Sexy Back*. And he certainly was. My boy looked very content and happy, which was always a huge turn on.

I crept up to him, turned his face to mine, and we leaned on one another. Our hugging session lasted a minute or two, until that pesky redheaded sailor came grunting by with his broom. He actually made us part, knocking at our tennis shoes with his bristles to pick up Gordon's clippings. By the nasty glares he shed on us at close range, we could tell more than just 'littering' was on his mind, but who knew exactly what.

While this guy was still watching, I latched onto Gordon's beautiful rosy cheeks and drew him into a loving kiss with both hands.

I guess Popeye moved on, because, quite frankly, with our eyes closed as they were and us melted into a blissful unity, we only opened them to find ourselves alone again.

My boy brushed my hair. "You hungry now?" Kiss. "Doris packed a few things for us. Want a banana?"

I laughed. "Oh, *that's* what's in your jeans right now."

He ground against me a little tighter. "Nope. Want it?"

"If you mean *it*, yes. If you mean Doris' banana, then no."

He chuckled and broke away. In another moment, Gordon squatted on haunches with a sun-drenched grin up at me. He unzipped his bag and pulled out something small. While he was down there, I gave him my iPad to stow in his ratty old gym bag. The rest of our stuff was downstairs in the bins with the other passengers' luggage.

He stood again, and I saw the small thing he'd grabbed was a hard-boiled egg. "How about this?"

"Nah, I'm good," I told him.

Gordon shrugged, cracked the thing on the railing and peeled off the shell in large shards. They went skittering on the deck to the rear of us.

We usually did not litter, and we're not such bad people. Proving it to myself, I remembered how we returned that little Bangladeshi custard plate.... Oh wait, no. I left it in our motel room the night we had to flee West Hollywood and a sex-crazed Assauer. Oh, well. What's one dessert dish and a few misplaced egg peels? We're busy fellows on the go, lol.

A sudden crunching sound made us look. The moody Junior Joe Officer from the wall was standing next to us; the other was tidying up right behind the man's shoulder.

He spoke with a pronounced Caribbean accent, lilting in a pissed-off way, "Tis cracked enough, Tanguay"—he meant the redhead—"that we 'ave to go-a sailin' on a Friday, but in addition, we go and get dealt a pair of land-lubbers actin' the fools."

"Yeah, Hesus," affirmed the equally irate younger seaman. "This here wessel is cursed enough already."

"It is?" I asked.

"Aye," Hesus said curtly. "See, de boat owners are never supposed to re-christen sea craft, but dis one did."

Gordon asked, "Why, what was it called before?"

"Da *Ellea-ner Roosevelt*," said Hesus.

"And now?" I enquired.

Tanguay supplied the answer. "The *Mrs. Jared Kushner*."

Molten laughter spilled from me and my boy. "Don't worry," I said, "It won't stay that way for long!"

"Good one, Kohl."

After we'd had a good belly-buster, and another hug, we realized our unfriendly observers were not even slightly in a yuck-yuck mood.

"You don't get it, do you? How you wandalize—" The redhead was suddenly so spittin' mad, his shipmate actually had to hold him back.

Gordon got hot under the collar. "Get what?"

Hesus explained, "Good lord, man – you fellas' sea manners! Dey're cracked enough to draw the ire of Poseidon 'imself, I tells ya."

"Poe-sigh-who?" Gordon aped the older Caribbean's accent.

"You know who's I mean."

"Look," I said, "I guess we're sorry for, whatever—"

"It's not vhatever!" The redhead was proving to be something of a hothead.

"Hey, now," Gordon said, trying to control himself, "I don't know if you got a problem with guys showing PDA, but you can be on your way now. Kay?"

"Typical," the younger sailor exclaimed, slapping hands on top of his head in frustration. Then he paced around in a tight circle.

"No, young man," said the older sailor. "You gets it all wrong if ya tink homophobia—"

"We're partners too, you idiot!" Tanguay yelled. "Just because ve actually verk for a liwing you think you can disrespect us—"

Hesus cut him off. "It's awe-reet, nug. Dey be ign'rant cusses, fa sure."

"If that's what you do, then work," scoffed Gordon in Tanguay's direction, "and stop being as amenable to the passengers as Ignaz the brick-hurling mouse – and quit being just as pretty too, ya ugly Krazy Kat."

"Take it easy," I said. "I don't know what everybody is getting so upset about."

Suddenly Gordon scuffled, poking Hesus in the chest. "Well, take your bottom-boy and go drown yourself for all I care. Good-bye and good luck!"

Tanguay was stunned into salt-like stature. "...But, ve're werse...."

Hesus ignored that and explained very calmly to my boy, staring him straight in the eye, "Der be but only one way to appease the god of da sea now."

He hauled off and punched Gordon in the nose.

"Was zum Henker!" I yelled and took a swing at Hesus. He ducked and I connected with Tanguay. As he stumbled, Gordon latched onto him and landed a few choice uppercuts to the redhead's freckles.

Hesus lurched and grabbed at Gordon's jacket. I stuck my arms around his beltline and fell backwards to pull the older sailor off my boy.

With the wind knocked out of me from the weight of his body, I barely acknowledged the voices and hands coming at us from other crewmembers.

In another moment, me and Gordon were inspecting one another's faces for blood, which thankfully there was none to be seen. In the meantime, their fellow shipmates had restrained Hesus and Tanguay.

The captain walked up. "What is going on here?"

Tanguay blurted, "They got wocal and disrespected—"

"I was asking the passengers."

"I want to press charges," Gordon said passionately.

"No police!" I said. *Gott im Himmel*, what was my boyfriend thinking?! I glared at him, and he snapped out of it, realizing the 'Law' was the last thing we needed.

"Let them go, Captain," said Gordon. "It's all a little misunderstanding."

"Are you sure?"

"Yes," I added, "this little car-buffle was just a storm at sea, but it's all clear sailing from here, right, boys?"

The sailor couple reluctantly nodded, and the captain signaled for them to be let go.

Even before the crowd of uniformed men broke up, I had Gordon in an embrace, and eyes shut so we could re-group in the proper way. The sights of the sea drifted from my mind, and silence replaced all concern.

It turned out a bit of concern would have been warranted, for when we finally opened our eyes again, we were totally alone, and pulling into port. Shockingly, my iPad was sitting on the deck behind us, but my boyfriend's ratty old gym bag was gone.

Gordon asked in a stunned way, "You think that Ignaz swiped it because of the nail clippers—"

"And bananas and hard-boiled eggs, yeah."

We thought it best to rush downstairs and make sure the rest of our things were still there, but – even though they were – there *had* been another reason why my boyfriend's gym bag was on deck with us....

"I still can't believe it's gone." Gordon fumed as he paced our room at Hojax's house. It was dark outside, about 10:00 PM.

"Can't believe what's gone?" Assauer asked.

"His mousy old gym bag," I explained.

"What's the big deal?"

"It's a link with my past!" Gordon stopped. He looked adamant and hurt.

I chuckled a bit. "You know it's more than about some moldy old piece of high school kit."

My boy sat on the bed, away from us, and I guess pouting.

"*Was geht?*"

I told my ex, "What's up is...well, Doris – Lloyd's moustache of a wife – told me all about this contract the two of them have. She wants me to help, and I sort of said okay."

"Help with what?"

"Outing Lloyd."

"Dude—"

"Don't worry. It's all about money for the both of them anyway. See, she got this clause put in the marriage contract that if Lloyd outs himself, she gets a poop-load of cash."

"So?"

"So she wants me to help with that. Promised a cut of the fortune if I can figure out a way to 'assist' the sea captain opening the closet door, but of course, I don't want to out the poor bastard. But either way, it's *whatever* to me what they do."

"Sea captain, my ass," Gordon muttered. "Pot king more like it. If he dealt in importing meth, his yacht wouldn't be called the *Mary Jane;* it'd be called the S.S. fucking *Tina Marie*."

"Honey…" I entreated.

He whipped around on his ass to face us. "Tell Assauer the rest."

"Well," I continued, "to show me good faith, or whatever they call it, Doris slipped me about five grand in Lloyd's bearer bonds. She said it was a down payment, but I didn't commit to anything—"

"And what did *you* decide to do with them…?" Gordon was pissed, and it made me a bit lambish.

"I – ah – well…. My smart boyfriend said we should stash them in our clothes, but I was worried we'd lose some or get them robbed, so I picked at the lining of Gordon's gym bag and sewed them up in there."

"For *safe keeping*." Gordon scowled.

"Babe! How was I to know we'd be assaulted by a pair of lunatic sailors. Who can predict that kind of *Scheisse?*"

"I think your boyfriend is right. You should have carried them."

"It don't matter, Assauer," I said. "We couldn't liquidate them right away anyway because of the 'heat' of Doris freshly stealing them."

Gordon said, "Still don't think it was worth the effort of sewing them in my bag. It's not as if Lloyd is going to the police about his wife's scheme to have him out himself via a pair of lowlife hustlers."

I grinned and got to my feet. I went over to his side of bed, asking, "Who you calling a lowlife?"

"You, hustla." He stared up at me, looking sexier than ever.

I belly-flopped on the sheets next to him, letting my weight pull him merrily into my arms. I hugged and kissed him, and in a moment, he was helplessly giggling like the teenager he was.

We wound up with our heads hanging off the edge of the mattress, panting and watching Assauer looking at us as he sat on the floor.

I drew my boy's lips to mine for an upside-down kiss. "Two lowlifes enjoying the highlife. That's you and me, baby!"

We heard Assauer's "Gimme a break," and after I had righted myself on the bed, I caught my ex's weird look for the moment it lived. Was it envious…? Was it angry…? I don't know.

"Oh!" I almost forgot. I jumped up and went to my jacket, which was yoked on the back of a chair. I reached for the inside pocket and pulled out my wadded-up hankie.

I returned and sat on the floor in front of my ex, using the bed as a back support. "This is something I had on me the whole time." I unpeeled the covering as soon as Gordon slipped down next to me. I held up the little gold statue for them to see.

Assauer plucked it away. "It's heavy," he marveled.

"Yeah. Pure gold, I think."

My ex turned it over in his hand. "It might be ancient. I'd say it's a cult object for Neptune or somebody."

"Lloyd had it set up like in a shrine. We should pawn it tomorrow."

"Not so quick," said Gordon, reaching out for it.

Assauer agreed with me. He said, "We should get rid of it right away."

"Yeah," said my boy, "but we have to get a fair price. We can't pawn it or dump it at the flea market."

"Ideas?" Assauer asked.

"Yep. Neil Campbell."

I rolled my eyes.

"Neil can fence it for us. He knows a lot of rich collectors and can get us a high dollar amount."

"He's right," Assauer said.

"Well okay, but we can't hold onto it for long, lest Lloyd comes looking for it and we still have it in our possession."

"Agreed," my ex said, placing the heavy chunk of precious metal back into my handkerchief.

I nodded at Assauer. "And how did you make out here?"

"First off, my *Arschbacken* are really sore and red – so thanks for that."

Gordon slapped his knee, laughing. "I guess old Hojax is a real pedo-perv, the way he makes you dress up."

Assauer was serious in his reply. "I'm surprised at you. We of all people know not to get judgy-judge on a person's ass just because of their kink."

My boy shook his head slowly. He was skeptical.

"Look," Assauer continued, "if the Captain was into little ones, he has a steady supply, but he's not. Like most guys, his fantasies can involve role-play, and he's into that – but with adults only."

For half a moment, the sincerity of his defense made me think there was something personal in it for my ex, but then I brushed it aside, grinning. "So your first point was how sore your ass cheeks are getting. What's the second one?"

He stood up, going to a drawer. "Secondly, I located most of the valuables in the house." He sat on the bed, squeezing his legs between me and Gordon. In his hand was a shallow wooden case. "But I did manage to snag this already."

We sat up on the mattress with him. Then he slowly opened the box.

"Oh, geeze…" sputtered Gordon.

Star-struck, I reached in and lifted up a black pistol. Sleek bullets were fitted in velvet around the inside of the case. "What is it, exactly?"

"A Luger, from World War Two."

"Kohl, put it away."

I ignored Gordon, picking out a choice bullet. "How do you load it?"

"Kohl!"

I looked over. My boy was highly agitated.

"I don't like guns…."

I waved it around, holding it up to my eyes to peer through the sight.

"It's all right, Gordon," my ex said softly, and reached out to lay his hand across the top of the pistol. In another moment, the Luger was back in its box. Assauer shut the lid.

I shrugged. What was the big deal?

"I say," Gordon went on, "we leave right away. Tonight."

Assauer explained, "Tomorrow is Laguna Beach's big street fair. We can slip away unnoticed then, and it gives me a chance to sneak the captain's most valuable items in my bag in the morning."

"There's another reason to stay too."

"What's that?" Gordon asked.

I turned to Assauer with a grin. "You need to go 'back on duty' for one more night."

"Why?!"

"Simple. So you can get Hojax firmly on our side, and the sooner the better. Because pretty quickly Doris, Trọng and Lloyd will figure out they've been conned and we're not on the island anymore. Time's ticking until one or all of the inmates of that madhouse reach out to the captain and bitch about us. When they do, we need him to say something to protect us from the lunies. And he'll do it too, because he's sweet on you."

"Oh, God," Assauer sighed, but I could tell he'd seen the logic in my scheme.

"So," I concluded, "slide in your little boy uniform and go mince it up with Hojax."

Gordon suddenly laughed. "You mean 'chop it up'!"

"What'd I say?"

"Mince it up."

"Englische Sprache!" I bellowed. "Is that the same as 'hash it out,' or 'in,' whatever? You know your language is *verrückt*, right? Just insane."

My boy chuckled. "Sorry, I guess it is."

Assauer was back to being dubious about my plan, because he double-checked on our haul. "Anyway, Gordon, what did you get from your stay on Catalina Island?"

My boy smiled and picked up a beige-colored lump from the floor. "This. I swiped Trọng's Gucci gym bag."

I laughed, then joked, "See! Fate stepped in. You lost your old piece of tat, but now you have this one!"

"Hell no." Gordon, disgusted by the notion of actually using it, tossed the bag aside. "I'm selling it ASAP."

"But"—I turned to Assauer—"nice attempt at flipping the subject. You still have to get changed, little boy."

"Yeah, yeah, I'm going. Don't worry. You two can shag your brains out in privacy."

I suddenly felt a pang of concern for my ex. "Are you really okay?"

"No, dude. My bum's completely red from that pervert's spankings – ugh."

Gordon laughed. However, I thought I spotted some gesture of sympathy and caring pass between them. Swallowing it down, I tried not to lose my head.

□ □ □ □ □

Captain Hojax was our guide to the sun and fun. We'd parked Assauer's car on the main drag, but several blocks south of the beach, and walked our way amongst the merrymakers north.

The Pacific Coast Highway – just a four-lane street in town – was blocked off to traffic and now the toughest little wheels pounding the pavement came from baby strollers.

There were lots of Gay couples with their kids, and seeing all the smiling tots riding their daddies' shoulders made me reach out and take Gordon's hand. The sky was azure; the water, a deep lapis; and everywhere, palm trees and unapologetically red flowers greeted the fresh air and folks out for a good time.

From the beach, still about a quarter-mile up ahead of us, some live music of the salsa variety put extra pep in everyone's step. The smell of fair food – deep fried, what else? – also wafted toasty and inviting from that direction.

"Remember the malt shop?" Hojax suddenly asked Assauer. The man was gesturing left, or to the ocean side of the street. A narrow storefront, made to look like a tropical shack with thatched roof, had a long line of patient folks waiting for ice cream treats.

"Sure do. Best banana shake I ever had."

Hojax squeezed his shoulder for a second. "And I know how my little Ass-Hour loves his bananas."

Me and Gordon chuckled; the captain was having such a good time, and so was my *Exfreund*.

At the next corner, young guys in shorts, no shirts at all – or skimpy, 'muscle man' tank tops – stood under the wrap-around awnings of a bar. All the windows were open and dance music spilled out onto the sidewalks to make the patrons bob sunglass-wearing heads.

"I remember *that* place," Assauer said.

The logo on the building had a cartoon leviathan in blue with white letters on top spelling out The Beached Whale.

"Gay bars," Hojax explained, "used to be our Community Centers, but now that LGBT-xyz folks are being priced out of their own enclaves, these watering holes have been drying up quicker than the Republican sense of decency. And that's fast!"

"Well, on your first point," said Assauer with a cynical edge, "I'm sure the abundance of hookup and dating apps has nothing to do with the disappearance of these 'Community Centers.'"

'*Dieser Arsch*,' I thought, 'can't keep his mouth shut for one more afternoon?'

Hojax's response was to grab and plant an aggressive kiss on my ex. That made Assauer giggle, little-girl fashion, and re-eased the mood again.

After the intersection with the bar, the street narrowed. The sidewalks were still passable, but two long rows of food trucks were parked along either curb. Canopies stuck out. They partially shaded standers-by, while tables and chairs were filled with folks enjoying their food.

The smells were incredible as we passed along one stall at a time: powder-sugar-sweet from funnel cakes, biting citrus from the limeade, smoky molasses from the barbequed ribs, and last but not least, deep-fried goldenness from treats as diverse as tempura asparagus to battered Mars Bars.

Near the end of the line, one truck appeared particularly busy, and the central shaded eating area had been replaced by a dozen folding tables shoved together to make one long one.

We had to proceed single file through this section with me in the lead. Near the end, an attractive middle-aged woman – with strawberry blond hair and a fearsome spring in her step – raised a bullhorn.

"Hear ye! Hear ye! The corndog eating contest is about to begin. Plenty of room at the table. Haul up! Haul up!"

Lowering her horn, she reached out to latch onto my arm. "How about you, handsome?" This was followed by a wink and a lip-lick as her fingers assessed my bicep. "Want to join the fun? Prizes will be given."

"Um—"

Hojax took command and my other arm. "Maybe next time. We're on our way to the main stage."

The rest of our little troupe trudged past, but I turned as I went. The corndog lady was standing akimbo – bullhorn by her hipline – still licking her lips and eyeing me up and down.

In a couple more minutes, the good smells and bustle of the food truck area were behind us. We descended the steps onto the beach and headed towards the source of the salsa music.

Hundreds of people were fanned out like playing cards in front of a large stage. Colorfully dressed young couples were dancing on it, and a blue and white archway of balloons provided a gently swaying proscenium arch of sorts.

"Oh, shit...." Hojax stopped in his tracks.

"What...?" I asked, following his eyes over to an enormous banner. It said:

The Neptune Line,
Official Sponsor
of the Laguna Beach
Street Fair.

"Oh, no," Gordon said, grabbing my arm, and apparently not listening to Hojax at all.

"It's Lloyd's company," the captain said. "Oh, my God. How could I have forgotten—"

"Never mind that," Assauer clipped shortly, seeing what Gordon saw. "They're here."

And sure enough, at the bottom corner of the stage stood Lloyd, Trọng and Doris, scanning the crowd like they'd lost someone.

The three of us began to back away in slow motion, eyes locked forward, and then, we were spotted.

Trọng raised his arm and pointed right at me.

"Oh, *Scheisse!*" I turned, and we started running.

"Hojax?!" Assauer pleaded, wanting to know what happened.

"Lloyd texted me this morning, asking to come over to the house. I told him the truth, that I'd be out all day."

"You could have told us they were in town!" Gordon called from up in front.

"He didn't say he'd be here, so – sorry."

At this point, we'd just gotten back on the sidewalk, and could look down over the beachgoers' heads. The crazies were forcing their hot and heavy way through the crowd, and they knew where we were.

We ducked behind the food trucks, thinking it'd be quicker, but plastic piss booths lined the way, and lots of people waiting in line slowed our progress.

Now we could hear Lloyd and Trọng shouting something like "stop thief" over the heads of folks behind us, then suddenly we were in the clear again.

"In here!" Gordon shouted and took my hand.

We had to dive through the sidewalk crowd to get inside the Gay bar, but the interior of The Beached Whale was a sea of people as well.

Hojax stayed behind, saying something about "...talking reason with them."

We hankered down and tried to blend with the bar patrons.

Hojax was attempting to stop them, but Lloyd, Trọng and Doris stormed past him, the sea captain leading his little pack of lunies to the D.J. booth. While they headed to it in the center of the space, we inched our way along the front of the bar, back towards the open doors.

Lloyd scratched the record to a halt, and amid loud groans and screams from the guests, the strong man grabbed the mic.

Forcefully, he spoke straight to us, but it was clear, not any one of the three of them had spotted us yet. They kept scanning the crowd. "Give me back the statue, Kohl, and all will be forgiven."

'Yeah, right,' I thought. 'As if....'

Doris took the microphone. Her act was one of the dutiful, pissed-off wife. "Give back my husband's bonds that you stole."

'The bitch, acting like *we* thieved what she took from him.'

Trọng grabbed the mic next with genuine fierceness. He copped a 'Oh, no she better don't' attitude with his sideways head movements. "And Gordon, you little shit twink, my Gucci gym bag better still be in trade-in condition." He clicked his tongue. "Ok-kaay?!"

We slipped out the door.

"There they are!" Trọng shouted.

'Scheisse...!'

We were on the move again, running behind people waiting for food-truck fare. I glanced back, and now, The Three, plus Hojax, were hot on our tailbone.

When we got to the Corndog Wife again, I latched onto her arm and pleaded, "Help! Those maniacs are after us!"

"Sure, sugar britches," she said coolly.

We ran on, but I turned to watch her raise her bullhorn and command Trọng and Lloyd to sit down and eat a deep-fried footlong.

She blocked their way so effectively, the last I saw, Trọng was starting to climb on the contestants' table to run down the center of it. Hope he didn't slip on any mustard, lol.

Now we were back where the chase started, on the sands of the beach.

Assauer pointed, and we made our way to the far side of the stage, which was mostly hidden from view.

The music ended to warm applause, and we acted like we were there to play fangirls to the salsa dancers as they flounced gaily off stage.

The MC whooped it up, and more applause rang out. I peeked around the corner but could not see the lunies or Hojax, much to my relief.

The announcer sangsong, "Welcome back to our livestream broadcast. And now it's time to hear from some random fairgoers."

More clapping, and an organizer with a headset pushed the three of us on stage.

The sea breeze cooled my brow suddenly, and I could see me, Assauer and Gordon's faces on the giant monitors spread out along the beach.

'Shit.'

"So, tell us," the MC chirped, placing a hand on my boy's shoulder, "are you enjoying the acts appearing on the mainstage today, the one so generously provided for us by the Neptune Line LLC and its multinational subsidiary companies?"

"Yes, sir."

"Good, good." He moved on to my ex. "And you...."

I tuned them out, for all of a sudden, I saw Lloyd, his wife and partner climbing the front steps of the stage.

I lurched for the microphone. It crackled and squealed in protest as I said much too loudly, "And here is the man of the hour himself!"

My elaborate hand gestures caused all of the TV cameras to swing and zoom in on Lloyd. And he stopped in his tracks; Doris and Trọng pooled around him nervously.

I looked dead into my camera, seeing the sea captain's face on the live-feed monitor behind his head. "We all owe so much to this man's generosity. Without him, the world would be such a colorless place."

A smattering of applause greeted that, and Lloyd took a step towards me.

"And so"—I wasn't giving up the mic till we were free—"I owe a personal debt of thanks to him, to his lovely wife, and charming boyfriend...."

The crowd gasped. Time stood still. 'Oops. I swear I didn't mean to do that....'

The TV cameras zoomed right in on Lloyd's face.

"Um," I said, "I mean his enchanting *partner*, in life...Sang Trọng...."

To say all the eyes of the world were on the cryptic businessman would be an understatement. Pin-drop silence aurora'd all around us. We waited to see what he'd do.

The man, not master of the situation, but in perfect control of himself, stood as still and dignified as his little gold statue. I could see him calculating his options, but then Lloyd glanced at Trọng and decided.

I surrendered the mic to the MC and stepped back.

The sea captain took Doris by the arm and strode as self-assured as any faking-it Conservative could to the center of the stage.

Once the microphone was in his hand, he said, "Good afternoon. Today, I stand before you with my lovely wife to announce that, yes, I am a Gay American—"

A flurry of reporters' flashbulbs went off as the reporters themselves erupted into a pyroclastic flow of questions.

During this tumult, me, Gordon and Assauer slipped offstage again. As we made our way to the top of the stairs, I could glimpse Doris' face in the monitors. If I had to characterize her expression, I'd say she looked to be about the happiest woman on earth.

I waited for my companions to go down ahead of me, and just as I was about to descend the steps myself, the soon-to-be ex Mrs. Lloyd turned and blew me a sincere kiss. Truth was, I did not mean to out her husband. I really didn't even think about it – but now that she'd come into a windfall, I hope she'll be true to her word.

On the sand again, we rounded the corner of the stage, and Hojax was there. "Run now. I'll take care of Lloyd and company and throw them off your tracks."

We started to go, but Assauer went back and took the sad looking man by both cheeks, planting a genuinely affectionate kiss on his lips.

"Thanks, Hojax. Always an adventure with you, Captain."

As we made our way back to my ex's car and freedom, I thought again, maybe there really was more to the Assauer-Hojax relationship than my former boyfriend let on, maybe even to himself.

"...dum vivis, sperare decet..."

— Part Three —
Passion in Pasadena

#mastodon-memory, #inexpiable,

#hot-schlock, #fun'ed-to-death,

#Double-duh, #stagy-laughter,

#how-bad-could-it-be, #pet,

#monetary-scream, #Eros,

#wet-horse-smooches,

#Psyche, #debris,

#Mr-Devil-chin,

#pro-war-crap

Chapter 8: Rose Bowl Flea

"So what?" I chuckled, unpacking a pair of Imperial rising-sun Japanese chopsticks from the Hojax's collection. "We steal from the rich to give to ourselves. That makes us honest thieves, unlike those politicians who get working-class schlubs to vote for them, then rob those very same people to pad the lifestyles of the money-fat and flabby-famous."

Gordon laughed. He was next to me, unpacking a few of Lloyd's silver chess pieces from Trọng's bag.

People passed, slowing to look, on this Sunday one week and a day after the Laguna Beach Fair.

As Gordon laid stuff out on the table, he said low, under his breath, "I wish Assauer had brought that stupid pistol to dump here as well."

I was amazed. "We couldn't sell it out in the open."

"So? Half the sales at flea markets like this are done round the side of the car, out of busybodies' eyesight."

"True…. But, why are you so nervous around guns anyway?"

My boy stopped laying out things. "Why aren't you? They're dangerous fucking things."

I shrugged. That answer didn't satisfy me. "You Americans, you grow up with guns on the brain, seeing and talking about them all the time, so I thought you'd…. Well, at least in Germany we don't think about guns, and don't see them around, other than a few hunting rifles in the country. To me, they're interesting, mysterious, powerful—"

"Damn it, Kohl."

He'd said this so calmly, I paused and reflected a moment on his withdrawn attitude.

"So," I eventually repeated, "why is it you're *this* nervous around guns, again?"

"Let's just say, you know better than most what a hothead my father can be. Anywho, let's finish unpacking so we can get the hell out of here as soon as possible."

I did know, from firsthand experience, what type of man the senior Sanchez was, but my boy was withholding details. However, as it was, now was not the time to get the truth out of him. Eventually, I would. My memory was Mastodon-like, unfortunately.

Ignoring my boy's moody altitude as a passing fancy, I reached in my paper bag and pulled out a bunch of captured mini flags from the Far East – thank goodness Hojax labeled everything. And these particular items had been individually graded by some collectors' authority. The same ones who'd permanently slapped them inside a hard acrylic case, like a comic book. Seemed an odd thing to collect, but then again, the whole area of collectable Militaria just leaves me scratching my head and thinking it's macabre. Celebrate war…collect the debris of its aftermath like Beanie Babies or Hallmark ornaments…? Ugh. I don't get it.

Assauer came around from the side of the car with his duffle bag of loot. The Pasadena Rose Bowl Flea Market was as good as any to 'fence' our 'gifts,' stolen or otherwise. We'd arrived late – at about noon – so had to take a parking space and set up near the end, which was okay. We were here to get some much-needed liquid assets, dump the evidence, and continue to enjoy our time in this sleepy, leafy suburb of Tinseltown. Hard to believe it now, but Pasadena got its launch more than a century ago by – wait for it – yes, its very own cult leader! A man who just like Joseph Smith had been driven out of Missouri by those hard-hearted, rational-only residents of the Show Me State. [5]

Anyway, the day was gorgeous, the crowds milling, and we were planning on being out of there by three in the afternoon. Our fingers were crossed, anyway.

Assauer had more of Hojax's blood-and-guts knickknacks, and laid out helmet badges from ruthless empires past – chief among them, British ones. These got placed right next to the strangely personal Japanese items of everyday utility, treasured as war booty by lots of people. Warped people, but lots of them, lol.

"Hope somebody buys this shit."

"You and me both, brother," said my ex, and then suddenly grinned. It was his signal that I was in for my own round of shit-taking. "Of course, we don't need to sell anything now, do we, Kohl?"

I scowled for a second, puzzled. "Well, we pawned my iPad, that jewelry phone case—"

"Not what I meant."

Gordon sidled up to us. "He means the fortune we'll get from your girlfriend, the soon-to-be-single Mrs. Doris."

"Oh. That."

"Yep," Assauer laughed with a backslap for me. "On easy street any day now. Right…?"

"Yeah." Gordon joined my ex in playing the little grinning shit. "Now that Lloyd's had 'his truth' revealed, when's our check arrive?"

"Doris—" I started.

"Yes…?" They both knew better.

"—Hasn't returned my texts."

My boy laid out a pair of cufflinks he'd lifted from Trọng's dresser drawer. "Typical. As the old saying goes, 'When you got it, flaunt it.' But nowadays, it should get updated to say, 'When you got it, keep it!' Just because the rich have everyone else's money again, they don't want to share, cuz they know it's not theirs. Greedy fucks."

"It's a shame." Assauer shook his head in genuine disgust. "There are dishonest people everywhere you go these days. Even our betters are beneath us."

"True. But, her betrayal still stings," I said, setting out more Nazi crap – a set of little swastika butter dishes, to be exact. "I thought better of Doris, but turns out she's just like the usual politician's wife: as untrustworthy as her party-drone husband limiting women's health from behind a desk in Washington. Sad."

"More like dictating her pap-smears from behind a pew in the Vatican, you mean." Gordon zipped Trọng's precious Gucci bag and placed it proudly front-and-center for sale. "Well, cheer up. We still have Lloyd's little statue."

"What'd the pawnbroker say about it again?" Assauer asked.

"I showed it to him the same day I got the 'back-room price' for the watch and Cartier phone cover. He drooled, turned it over in his hands, but then dished it, saying it was 1960s Italian tourist-trade schlock."

"But," scoffed my boy, "why'd he offer you $5,000 for it then?"

"Don't know. Must be hot schlock, but I followed your advice, Gordon, and Neil Campbell's already lined up a buyer for twice that amount. The client's a real 'kind of sewer,' he says."

"A *connoisseur?*" asked my boy, puzzled.

"Yeah," I confirmed, smiling. "One of them, but filtered through an Aussie guttersnipe drawl, lol."

The two of us did laugh out loud.

"*Idioten,*" muttered my ex under his breath.

"You know, I like Pasadena." My boyfriend stretched his arms up into the sunshine.

"A bit quiet," I said, arranging the last of the fascist tchotchkes from my satchel.

"That's why I like it." Gordon smiled, and I kissed him quick; he was irresistible.

"But here's the *piece of resistance,*" Assauer announced, slowly withdrawing a sword from his duffel bag. It was black, looked to be plastic, but had some scrawl in silver marker across the scabbard.

I wondered out loud, "What's that?"

"Some TV-used Kung Fu prop, signed by Keith Carradine himself."

"The *Kill Bill* guy?" Gordon asked.

"No...I think that was his brother, David Carradine."

"Ohhh."

"Yeah," Assauer affirmed. "And that's the same guy who had too much fun in a Bangkok hotel room one night."

"Oh, yes," I said. "Fun'ed to death – but what a way to go."

The three of us nodded with reverence and mis-matching sighs of envy.

An opposite-sex couple, a man and woman in their thirties, began looking over our product offerings. Even though the female tossed me a grin, there was something about the demeanor of the two that put me on guard. Maybe it was the man's beefy size, or the sideway glances he shed on me. One rule that's always true of the game of graft is: It's hard to con a conman....

The lady swept her long brunette hair aside and bent at the waist to inspect Trọng's cufflinks.

"Ah, yes," Assauer chimed, sounding hollow. "Excellent taste." He scooped them up and placed them in her hand. "They're Hermes, brand new, and on sale today."

The woman showed them to her strong-but-silent-type man.

She inquired with no particular interest of Assauer, "Set up here often?"

"No, our first—"

"What about Olvera Street, in L.A.?" the man asked.

"Um. No, never set up – never been – there," I insisted, casually.

The woman bounced the links in her hand. "How much?"

My turn to spring into action. "Oh, *those!* You couldn't expect to get them for less than—"

"Twenty and they're yours," said Assauer, jumping the gun.

Gordon suppressed a guffaw at my astonishment.

"No, no. My friend here misspoke," I told the mark – I mean, woman. "We'd have to have at least a hundred."

"No, no, no..." Assauer schooled me with a painted-on grin. "Twenty will be fine."

"But—"

"Take it to the sides, boys," Gordon said, stepping up to the table and getting between us and the clients.

I dragged my ex around to the car door. "I want top dollar. We can't give our crap away for free."

"You always do this! What normal person wouldn't think about getting rid of"—he paused and said under-breath—"*evidence* before squeezing out a few extra pennies instead?!"

"*Gott im Himmel* – I always...." I noticed the couple had left. Gordon hadn't closed the deal. "You're a fine one to talk about *always*—"

"Oh, shut it up, why don't you."

We went on like this a bit, my words getting hotter, but my brain got distracted, for my boy had started acting visibly weird. He was craning his neck, scanning down a few tables and into the slow-moving crowd.

"Oh, yeah?" Assauer's snark brought me back to present with him.

"Yeah!"

Gordon tugged on our sleeves. I ignored him with a "Just a minute, honey."

The teen socked us both in the gut. When we glanced at him from our slightly stooped position, he said, "Look!"

I did. "O...M...fucking *Gott.*"

"What?!" Assauer demanded to know.

"It's them, right?" Gordon asked me.

"Fuck yeah, it is."

"Who, goddamn it!" Assauer was mad.

"It's that Caribbean sailor and his batty boy," Gordon said.

And sure enough, Hesus and his redhead pathick, Tanguay, were strolling around, picking up stuff two tables away from ours, and miracle of miracles, the younger of the two was carrying Gordon's gym bag!

I explained to my ex. "It's those two water-on-the-brain sailors who picked a fight and swiped our money!"

"No...shit?"

"It's them," Gordon said, pulling us deeper along the side of the car. "They're coming this way too. What'll we do?"

"You do it," I told Assauer. "They don't know you."

"Do what?"

"Check the bag to see if the lining's ripped open. If not, it means the bearer bonds are still in there."

"And if they *are* still in there?"

"Then get that bag by any means possible," my smart boy said.

I shoved Assauer forward, to go back to the table, while me and Gordon crouched by the front fender to watch.

"Hi, guys!" The sailors approached, and Assauer was fake-ass friendly to them. "Nice day, huh. Stop and have a look at my merchandise. Lots of good stuff."

They did, especially the pimply Krazy Kat, whose attention was caught by the shiny helmet badges.

My ex, the well-tutored hustler, started flirting with the boy, licking his lips and leaning one hand on the table to draw his face closer to the lad. "Nice retro bag you've got there. May I?"

Without any kind of permission, he reached over, unzipped it, and – before even a word of protest could erupt – was feeling up the inner shell right to left, top to bottom.

"Vhat the.... Hey," Tanguay said, turning the tote out of my ex's reach.

Hesus came back to them from the next table. "What'd you playin' at, mate? You get ya jollies coppin' feels of young mans' sacks, eh?!"

"No, no," Assauer laughed brightly. "I just like it, is all. But it is a little worn out." He picked up Trọng's Gucci bag and shoved it into the redhead's arms. "This one is only $10—"

I bit my lip to prevent a monetary scream from escaping.

"—Or, we could do a straight-up trade." He slid his oily leer on Hesus. "Your boyfriend might like an upgrade. That designer 'sack' is worth two grand, at the very least."

Even from our lowly position by the car, we could tell the men were kind of shocked and silent. They began to move on, after Tanguay put the Gucci bag down in revulsion.

Assauer rushed back to crouch with us. We had a quick and loud conference.

"Well?!" I asked.

"Lining's intact. Even felt the bonds in there."

I chuckled from sheer relief, slapping his shoulder. "Don't you see, brother, our treasure flown the coop, has come home to roost!"

He rolled his eyes around his smile. "Oh, the wonderful vagaries of fortune."

"Holy fuck, you fools!" Gordon exclaimed. "We gotta get my bag."

"No shit, Shylock, but what are we going to do?"

My boy blankly blinked in non-answer to my question, and then, half a second later, took off.

He dashed at the sailors, snagged the ratty old gym bag, and yelled at the top of his lungs, "*THIEF!*"

Naturally, a crowd assembled like gnats at a picnic, so me and my ex jogged our asses over there.

In an instant, the hothead sailor with the freckles assessed the situation – Gordon standing there, clutching his bag – and then recognized me.

Tanguay leapt for and grabbed the Gucci tote as 'hostage.' He drew out his sailor's knife and told my boy with whites-of-the-eyes menace, "Hand it over wery slowly, or the quality stitching gets it!"

I gasped softly, "Two grand...."

Assauer barked at Hesus, "You know you stole that gym bag. Just give it back to the rightful owner."

"Uh uh, there's no vay!" Tanguay welled...um, yelled.

"Why?" I asked.

"It's da bag," explained the older sailor, "from which da defilements came."

Me, my ex and Gordon exchange a WTF look.

The redhead continued yelling, "Vhat he means – the *banana*, the nail *clippers*, the *hard-boiled* eggs – don't you see? All the things the god of the sea hates, and he's wiolent."

That kind of empty rhetoric reminded me of the bible-humpers screeching 'Obama-Nation!' every chance they get, but wearing cotton-poly blends and going to Red Lobster for shrimp scampi – two other things apparently a really PMS'd 'god' hates with all his pretty-lame might. No difference at all from the nail clippings, if you think about it. Just more human foolishness of a different flavored 'faith.'

The crowd around us had grown large. Murmurs of "Call the police" were heard.

"Okay, okay." I held up my hands to the younger of the two sailors. "Let's say everybody is sorry, everybody did what they thought was best at the time, but now Gordon has his gym bag, and to show there's no hard feelings, you two can keep the Gucci. Okay...?"

At least the crowd around me agreed, sending up a general chorus of "Yeah."

"I'm no-so convinced. Sounds pretty cracked in da head," Hesus said like a conniving bastard. "We got scheduled dis week to go for a disciplinary hearin' – all because of all your antics."

My fucking blood boiled. Our antics – is he nuts? They assaulted us, their passengers on the boat.

"Take it or leave it," Gordon suddenly announced, relaxing his stance and shouldering his bag in a natural way.

After a tense moment of silent debate between the seamen, Assauer closed the deal. "Neither party wants to involve the police, so take that bag and be happy you got the sweeter end of the deal."

While the seamen couple thought about concluding the negotiations, an odd tingle arose on the back of my neck – you know the kind. I glanced around and saw that freaky couple, the ones who'd asked the weird questions, standing out in the open. They were watching our whole little scene. The woman was talking on her cellphone, but by the way she kept glancing up and straight at me, it was obvious, I – or rather, me, Gordon and Assauer – formed the topic of conversation. Goose dimples rose on my skin.

"Take it or leave it," Gordon repeated himself.

The sailors finally nodded, and just at the point where it appeared the tension was broken, wouldn't you know it, our luck struck again, and not one but *two* lawyers stepped in.

A balding man in a cheap suit rushed through the crowd, business card outstretched and leading the vanguard. "Hold on; hold on there, in the name of the law! I'm Seymour F. Stammer-Hanky from the attorneys' firm of Grubb, Grubb & Grouse, and I demand we take things slowly."

"Wait a minute; wait a minute." A second ambulance-chaser emerged from the assembled like a maggot from meat. "I too – William S. Slipcause, firm of Jackleg, Soreback & Piepowder – demand justice be served!"

"What possible business is this to you, or you?" Assauer asked them in turn.

They cried in unison, "What business?!"

"An alleged crime has been alleged." The man from Grubb, Grubb & Grouse strode up to the expensive piece of luggage, nearly salivating.

"That is most astutely correct, my somewhat-distinguished legal associate," chimed William S. Slipcause as he formed the other half of the 'we've got you surrounded' noose around Tanguay.

His boyfriend stepped closer, speaking reason – for once. "Lookie here, you two addle-pates, whoever da hell ya be—"

They were on the verge of repeating both names and titles, but Hesus shut them down with a half-eye glare. "Da parties of da first part in dis here dispute, and da parties of der second part"—he gestured to us—"'ave worked out all our differences. Capeesh? So den what makes ya dink you have da right to step into da middle of dis here settlement not involvin' you directly?"

The legal beagles thought it was obvious. After a momentary consult, they both cheeped in harmony, "The Law!"

"What is it you want, gentlemen?" Assauer was slipping back into the negotiator role.

The schemers fingered the fine Italian leather, growing dreamy as they counted the printed Gucci marks like hundred-dollar signs.

The Grubb, Grubb & Grouse man said, "This needs to be collected as evidence of a crime—"

"Alleged theft," the Jackleg, Soreback & Piepowder doyen corrected his colleague, while he caressed Tanguay's leather strap.

"I propose, gentlemen," said Master Stammer-Hanky, Esquire, "that we take this aforesaid-mentioned, and precious, merchandise up to the Rose Bowl Flea's front office."

"Yes," concurred the 'honorable' Counselor William S. Slipcause – no doubt his S stood for *Scheister.* "Take it up, log it in and allow one of us fine officers of the court to hold the item until such time, as warrants, the true ownership of the afore-stated valuable hunk of merch can be positively identified—"

"Assuming it can ever be positively established..." added his lustful associate.

I got inspired. Fast on my feet, I latched onto the strap and shoved Gordon's smelly old gym bag in their faces. "But this is stolen property too. Don't you want to confiscate it, take it to the front office, tote it home with you...?"

Sarcasm had dripped from my tone, but the men seemed shocked nonetheless.

"No," I said in victory. "I didn't think so. See, it's an old story – maybe older than your profession itself – but the so-called 'Law' is there to advance the agenda of those who already got all the good stuff anyway. Don't act like anything anyone ever does in the public court of opinion isn't motivated by what's in the best, monied interests of the powers that be."

After my stinging rebuke settled in their heads, the crowd rallied behind me, cheering and saying stuff like "Word!"; "Ain't that the truth"; "Yes, God"; and "I hear that all right."

The lawyers got nervous. I guess the public *could* change things if they spoke with one voice and did the obvious – however, that's unlikely to happen on a societal scale, so the legal profession is safe, for now.

"Kohl's right," Assauer said as I gave Gordon his bag back. "You two lawyers scram before we really do call the police. On you!"

That put the fear of God in them and they toddled away, exchanging cards and pleasantries about "past-due billing" as they went.

After the commotion settled, and both our side and Hesus and Tanguay too, received handshakes and 'job well done' backslaps, the people who had been watching us spread out and continued shopping under the bright and cheerful Southern California sun.

This good feeling was not matched by the sailor couple though. The older man glared at us, but put his arm around his partner to reluctantly lead them away. They departed with hostile stares, and the hothead redhead seemed thoroughly disgusted by his new Gucci gym bag. He spat on the ground with daggers in his eyes for Gordon.

Seeing that made me hug my boy, and turn him towards the car.

In a moment or two, the three of us peered into the lining, and sure enough, a loose thread was yanked to reveal the pile of Lloyd's bearer bonds, safe and sound.

We smiled, and Gordon said, "Fuck yeah."

"That will make it easier for a while."

We zipped up and stowed it in the backseat, turning to see our table still full of Hojax's junk.

"What do you say," Assauer suggested, "we pack up, get out of here and look for something to eat."

"Yeah," my boy sighed. "We don't need the sunburn and hassle of the Rose Bowl Flea anymore."

We grabbed boxes and our bags and started to pack. As we did so, that unwanted feeling of a static charge against my skin returned.

I looked around again, and after a minute of searching, found that man and woman watching me from about fifty feet off.

I wondered which route we'd take to drive back to the motel, and knew my ex *would* believe this tightness in my chest was real. The question was, would my boyfriend believe it too.

As I threw the last of the pro-war crap in a box, I suddenly recognized this particular queasy feeling was identical to the one I'd felt with Doris on Catalina Island. The one I'd experienced it in the dark, foreboding – dare I say, unforgiving – depths of the woods.

Chapter 9: Wonderful Vagaries of Fortune

I had rarely seen him so happy. You'd have thought Gordon loved his ratty old gym bag more than the money sewn inside.

'Whatever,' I thought. The weight of it – and the two other bags I hefted – made me adjust the shoulder straps. Assauer was equally burdened, but he also carried the file box. This was all the loot we were trying to picket-fence at the Rose Bowl; I think that's the term Gordon had used.

We'd sent my boy off to get carry-out food for us to eat back in our motel room.

But we'd been careful, and not parked my ex's car anywhere near the Saga Motor Hotel, in case someone, anyone really, came looking for us. And this time we were semi-lucky to park about two blocks away, on a side street bordering Pasadena City College. Currently we were walking through its twilight setting, admiring the leafy green trees all around.

I told Assauer with a grin, "Not bad parking tonight, brother. Beats that night we had to park all the way by Grant Park."

"Yeah, that was a bit of a hike, but we never would have seen *it* otherwise."

He meant a building, another college in fact – The California Institute of Technology. "Why. Bring back memories?" I laughed, but he did not. Of course it brought back memories to the both of us.

We'd both grown up in the German equivalent of the Midwest – me in a small town in the Hartz Mountains, and him in a slightly bigger town to the southwest. We arrived on the same day of orientation at *TU Braunschweig*, or The Technical University of Brunswick.

I still remember it. He was so carefree, or so it seemed, laughing with the class coordinator, so I went up to him and asked about his major.

"Mathematics?!" I scoffed, half-joking.

"And you, Mr. Wiseguy?"

"Ah, I'm studying the far superior subject of English."

Then he really laughed, grabbing onto my arm, and I joined in, thinking I liked the feel of him on me.

We both quickly found out our goals were to slide by with the minimum work required. "Why stress out when all we want is a pair of teaching certificates," he told me, and he was 100% right.

So, we started slacking together. First after class, in his rented attic room while we smoked weed and dashed off our assignments. But later we'd wind up going out for *döner kebab* late in the evening and prowling the tough thoroughfares of Braunschweig looking for trouble – usually with an ice cream in our hand. More often than not, we found none, but sometimes drunk kids would stumble out of bars and we'd 'help' them to the tram, while also helping ourselves to a few Euros from their billfolds for expenses, like our *Jägermeister* and pot.

One night, when we decided to stay in and indulge in these alcohol and THC-laced luxuries, I let slip that in high school I'd had a string of boyfriends, but only really kept them around until the sex became predictable.

I didn't think anything about my statement until I took a shot and glanced up to see a pall had come over his face.

"What, Assauer...?"

"Um.... So, you're—"

"Yeah. Thought—"

"No, it's cool. It's just that I'm Bi. Broke up with my longtime girlfriend when she saw me kissin' on a boy last summer."

"Oh," I chuckled.

Slowly he then revealed that although he'd fucked several girls, he'd never felt much for any of them, so was holding out for the right guy to try it the other way.

"Whoa, brother. I'm flattered, but just so you know, you won't be fucking me. I'm strictly a top."

I was the only one laughing.

"Who said I wanna top?"

"Oh. Okay. If I see a nice, strapping boy, I'll send him your way."

"Yeah. You do that."

Truth was, I liked Assauer. Even though his outlook on things was a bit too positive and upbeat for my personal taste, he was mellow and we clicked naturally enough together. However, I wasn't ready to shift quickly out of the friend zone. Sure, his good looks and taut physique caught my attention, but how much of a spark was there really between us…?

"Hey, *Idiot*."

"Huh?" I looked over at my companion.

"Where have you just been? In your head?"

I felt myself grin, adjusting the shoulder straps again. "In our past."

While I wasn't paying much attention, we had walked through the campus and come out along the side of the college's palatial main building.

We turned and started to stroll under a canopy of trees. These were planted like a unifying allée, while off to our right, a block-long reflecting pool with water jets provided cooling sounds and moistened the air.

"Our past, like when we met?"

"Yes," I said. "When we first got into trouble, and first got together too."

"Ha-ha," he chuckled so softly it struck me as unlike him; it was tender and nostalgic. "When I first played Hercules to your son of Neptune?"

"No…. When I first played Muscle Man to your Antaeus and slew your heart."

He was silent, looking away, and I knew I had gotten to him.

"Come on, Kohl! I'm starving."

"You're drunk," I replied, grabbing his jacket and tossing it to him standing by the door. "It's late. You need to wear something, *Schnapsdrossel*."

He slipped on his coat, laughing freely as I slid past him to get to the door out of his flat.

He kissed me.

Assauer had just reached out, placed a hand on my cheek, and kissed me on the lips with loving ease.

He left me there and called me a slow poke as he jogged down the steps without a care in the world.

Maybe for him the kiss had been brotherly, but for me – judging by my internal compass – I suddenly had a new course to follow.

Later, after another set of piping-hot *gyros* wrapped in foil from the best of the center-city stands, we walked, joked and ate. It was late, so we were pretty much alone, but with each step, with every bit of shared mood and happiness, that something new in me grew.

By the time our wrappers were tossed aside, we'd come to

the plaza where water sloshed and played at the feet of "The Wrestlers," a neo-postmodern statue of Hercules and Antaeus grappling.

We stood and admired the beefy acres of naked man-flesh – after all, this image of the ancient strong-man lifting an equally fit stud in his arms had been a staple of homo-erotic tastes since the Renaissance.

The debate whether the pair represents a couple at the moment of *la petite mort* – or conversely, of the actual ex-tinguishing of life via ecstasy – has been debated for centuries. Obviously, the queer-honest mind knows there has never been a real question that this is Queer Art generated for viewing by Queer smarty-pants, lol. But the existence of the so-called point-counterpoint discussion in the first place presents one of those fake hetero-enforced myths used to suppress or deny same-sex artistic expression is all around them, or indeed, that Gay people can be as abundant as we so evidentially are. They keep working at it, although the truth gets harder and harder to mask all the time.

But none of that mattered to us, for the night we stood under them, the moon was projecting a shadow from the defeated man's arm over the top of our heads, as if the surrender of one man to another was the paramount form of bliss. And, it was.[6]

I took Assauer's hand in my own, and his jolly grin faded.

He drew into me, and this time, I kissed him. There was nothing fraternal in my tongue forcing its way in, nothing brotherly about how I felt – except in the Classical sense of lovers.

He panted and gripped onto my ass.

It was after midnight. We were alone, young, drunk and randy – and on the verge of love – so I tugged on his hand and led him to a narrow alley just to the side of the fountain.

"Kohl...."

I shushed him.

"I'm – I've never—"

I stopped up his mouth with kisses as I undid his jeans, compelling them to fall around his ankles.

He moaned into my mouth, so I slipped my hand between the white cotton briefs and his smooth-as-a-baby's ass.

Not quite the novice he pretended, he had meanwhile unzipped me and brought my hard dick out into the night air.

As my finger toyed at the entrance to his hole, he slid his hand around my cockhead, making it long to get inside of him.

Moments later, he had me pushed against a wall, on his knees, taking my dick halfway down his throat. He may not have fucked with guys yet, but he sure had played flutist with them.

I closed my eyes, letting the sound of the fountain and the sensation of Assauer's lips overwhelm me. There was no doubt about how I was going to cum tonight, and I felt it was time to take someone's virginity.

After pulling him up, and kissing him thoroughly, I turned him around, spread his hands on the wall, kicked his ankles apart, and pressed my dick along his ass crack.

I leaned in close to the back of his ear. "Want this?"

"Yes."

"Want it...now?"

"Oh, God, yes."

I spit on my fingertips and worked it into his hole, which dilated greedily while he cried out my name in pleasure.

More lube from my mouth went to my cockhead, and then I was positioning it straight for his inexperienced heart.

I slid in and waited, expecting some resistance, but Assauer straightened his lower back and drove his hole on my dick to the balls.

Instead of him sighing like a doe in heat, it was me doing it; he felt so amazing. Tight, yes, but also giving and needy.

It turned me on so much, I latched onto his waist and fucking pummeled him good.

My eyes had to close, partly from the adrenaline in my blood, but mostly because of the fullness of my emotions.

I barely was able to get out "Cum.... Okay...?"

He replied by grabbing the base of my thighs and forcing me to go as deep as I could.

That's when I lost it, and took his man-on-man maidenhood to the nth degree. We were bound now, by blood, and would be to some extent forever.

After we had fucked like wild tomcats in a public midnight alley, within earshot of the Hercules and Antaeus fountain, Assauer took me back to his flat and dragged me willingly into his bed.

Late, and tired as we were, we lay still there chatting in each other's arms until it turned into a make-out session for an hour.

I could hardly keep my eyes open anymore, but his sucking of my rock-hard dick, and pleading for another 'bedtime load' made me climb on top and fuck him like every good-wife deserves.

He kept watching me with his intense blue eyes, and although it was a grudge match – had to really fucking slam him to coax my cum to the forefront of my dick – he loved every moment of it.

In the end, I seeded him twice because I came and just kept going; it felt that good. I couldn't help myself, and when finished, felt weightless as I drifted into his arms.

We became fuckbuddies after that, and within a month, I had moved in to fuck him nightly.

Soon after, we both referred to one another proudly in public as our boyfriend, and it was all due to that wrestling match in bronze and moonlight.

"You okay?" he asked.

I realized, by following his gaze down, that I had a huge erection in my jeans. He must have been thinking of the same scene, because his hard cock was very evident too under denim.

I told him the truth. "I did, you know."

He knew what I meant. "Why do you think I've done all the things I have for you, Kohl? Yeah, I know you did."

In my mind, a silly equation presented itself: Gordon's love of his ratty old gym bag was analogous to Assauer's affection for me. 'Both worn,' I considered, 'and a little threadbare, but once you're attached, I guess condition doesn't matter.'

We continued walking on with a smile. It felt good to still have my ex in my life.

Scents of cilantro, lime and *carne asada* surrounded us.

The TV was on, playing some soft-o chick-on-chick porn that Assauer had found on the motel cable. Even though halfhearted girl-grunts provided the white noise of the background, me and Gordon barely cared, as the three of us had our burritos and were happy.

"What do you call a girl," I joked through a mouthful of rice and beans, "who goes down on another chick willingly?"

"Dunno," my ex said.

"Well-paid!" my boyfriend explained, and me and him burst out laughing. Gordon got where I was going.

"Yeah," I said. "You couldn't bribe me enough to even touch one of those with a ten-foot pole."

"As if you've got even a ten-centimeter 'pole.'" Assauer was proud of his witticism.

I turned to Gordon, smirking. "He sure liked it well enough, and he's not one to talk about massive *schlongs*."

"Shut up," *Mein Ex* laughed, because he knew I was right.

Suddenly there was a rapping on the door. It was so faint....

"Turn that off." I motioned to the TV, and Assauer found the remote. Soon the sounds of commercial muff-diving were on mute.

The knock came again, and the three of us stood. Whatever it was, I was sure it was the last thing we needed.

Gordon stepped close to the doorframe. "Who's there?"

My mind flew to seeing Hojax's pistol, in its box, in the drawer of my bedside table.

A deferential female voice replied, "It's me. You left something at the Rose Bowl Flea today."

My boy came back to us, and we shrugged at one another. Did we lose anything?

Before we could think another thought, the door opened, but strangely, we didn't see the woman's hand near the handle.

I grumbled at Gordon, "I thought we locked it."

"We did," he said in a harsh whisper.

The girl in the doorway was dressed like a dude, and had a hoodie veiling her eyes. She hovered at the threshold. "I will tell you, but may I come in?"

Gordon immediately told us, "I don't think it's a good idea—"

"Yes, come in," I said to her.

On entering, she closed the door and lowered her cowl. As soon as I saw her face and long hair, I had a feeling—

"My name is Psyche. You met me and my boyfriend, Eros, at the fair today."

Yes, that's right. That couple asking oddball questions right before our encounter with the uptight sailor-boys.

"How did you find us?" Assauer challenged her.

Her gaze fell on the women making out on the TV screen. She replied calmly – too calmly, "You may think you're hard to track," she added creepily, staring us down, "but The God has eyes everywhere."

I wanted to laugh; what was that? Some Saturday, late-night B-roll movie line?

Suppressing a chuckle, Gordon asked, "Which god?"

"He of the olive and elder; the Great Blue-Gray One; He of the rustling leaves and sun-dappled blossoms."

'Okay,' I thought. 'At least we know we're dealing with a nut job.'

"What do you want?" Gordon curtly asked.

"To return something."

Psyche held out her hand and produced Trọng's cufflinks. "You left these behind."

My boy grabbed them, muttering, "More like you and your bimbo-rambo escort left them behind in your pocket."

I chided my boyfriend, "Be nice, Gordon."

Assauer laughed at our bickering, the ass.

The religious freak stepped to the end of the bed closest to the window. "I am the personal assistant of Parthia, she whose sacred rite you interrupted that day in Los Angeles. She wishes to have a word with you about your inadvertence."

"It wasn't me!" Gordon blurted unhelpfully.

Me and my ex glanced at one another. I think we both felt this day had been coming for some reason.

The woman continued, "You needn't worry. Parthia merely wants to put things right again, and to learn what nature of daring young men Destiny propelled across her path." A weak grin followed.

"One second," I said to the loon to get her to stop talking. I then gathered my companions' shoulders into a huddle.

"We need to ask her to leave," Gordon suggested firmly.

"I agree," said Assauer.

I poked my ex's chest. "I'm not so sure. They won't quit until we give in, so now's as good a time as any to do what they want and put this incident behind us."

When we straightened up and glanced over at her, Psyche was texting someone, her long hair falling over one shoulder.

"Um…miss," I started. "It's nice you and, Eros, was it, returned our stolen property and all, but we're more than sorry about seeing what we saw that day in the sex club. And we can assure you—"

She held up a finger. Her phone was vibrating, and so without another word, she went to the door and opened it.

A gorgeous woman, indeed the very same one from the sex club stage, stood there in a flowing dress. To her side waited a young teenage girl with a cellphone. That one fingered her blond bob and chewed gum noisily.

"I am Parthia, High Priestess of the Great One, and this is my pet, Lolita. May we be invited in?"

"No!" Gordon shouted, and I reacted by restraining him at the chest.

"Yes, please do," I said. Gordon threw my hands away from his body in disgust.

Assauer appeared ambivalent, but in my mind it was clear. This crap needed sorting. And besides, why be afraid of three women, one no more than a teenybopper of about seventeen?

They glided in, with Lolita closing the door behind them.

The priestess was younger than I had thought. Her long dark hair was pulled back, and up close, it was easier to tell her handsome, almost man-like features were South Asian. Perhaps she was descended from Tamil or Sri Lankan roots. Her bearing was dignified; her voice, deep.

This noble carriage was contrasted all the more only a moment later when she engaged in typically female dramatics. First going on a crying jag, sobbing like she couldn't breathe, and gripping onto her 'pet' for support. After this, the woman gave up and tossed herself like a ragdoll across my bed.

We boys regarded one another coolly. This Parthia person may have been used to manipulating cult-addled brains, but quite frankly her tears – if indeed there were actually any – did nothing for us, so we stood around, waiting for the performance to come to an end.

When her emotional buckets had emptied themselves, she stood with the help of Lolita and Psyche and came to us.

"The aftermath of your defilement of our sacred rite has been a sore vexation onto me personally. That night I took to my bed with violent shaking and chills – I thought it resembled malaria or Tourettes, I know not which – but through my tears I implored The God to show me the way. When I eventually fell into an exhausted sleep, He did, via a dream."

"Look, ma'am," said Assauer matter-of-factly, "we didn't mean to—"

"Have no fear, gentlemen." Parthia intoned her phrases with freeze-dried composure. "I seek no vengeance, only to show compassion for your youthful indiscretion. For unawares as you are, you have no concept of the inexpiable abomination you have committed."

"Huh?" Gordon said.

Lolita, the other teenager in the room, explained through a popping bubble, "She's come to work things out. Duh!"

My boy got snotty in return. "Then why didn't she say so?! Double duh."

"I did, my dear, sensible child," Parthia told Gordon. "I did say it in my own way." To me and Assauer, she continued, "I want bygones to be bygones...."

"*But...?*" Assauer, consummate conman, knew there was more to 'this scene' than hugs and kisses.

"However, it's not entirely up to me," the priestess explained. "With your permission...." She seemed on the verge of fainting, but recovered – miraculously – and went on. "That night, after the corruption of the ceremony, I took masses of Diphenhydramine and slept fitfully. The God appeared to me and showed what I must do. He guided me to seek you out, and have you assuage the onslaught of my malady by a secret method revealed only to me."

My boyfriend put his hand around my waist. "I don't know, Kohl. Sounds shady as fuck."

Lolita burst out, "Watch your manners in her presence." *POP!*

Gordon bowed to the girl with fake deference.

The priestess continued, "And yet, my insomnia and wasting condition are not my primary concern. My main worry is for you. Fear that you remarkable gentlemen, as you so clearly are, will divulge the nature of the ritual you spied upon – in your imperfect understanding of it."

I scoffed to myself, 'Imperfect understanding?! She was about to get Catherine-the-Great'd by a donkey.'

As if somehow reading my mind, she stepped closer and laid a frigid finger on my chest. Her even-keel tone took on a keener edge as she added, "What you've seen in your blindness not even all the members of our society are allowed to witness. We fear you will mock our Faith, and try to deprive us of our holy religious liberties."

'*Gott im Himmel,*' I thought. 'Horse-rodgering is hardly the same as nuns refusing to educate kids on condoms and the birds-and-the-trees, but once you open the door on taxpayer-funded "Religious Exceptions," you have to let all the crazies go on a rampage, no matter what they wear on their heads.'

Parthia turned her attention on Assauer, who now that I looked at him seemed a bit mesmerized. I suddenly recognized that same glazed expression as the one he had that day in the sex club.

The priestess chanted softly, prayerlike to him, while Lolita and Psyche suddenly appeared rather 'devout' at her words too.

> "The wind's blast may rage,
> And the leaves stream away from the trees
> Before the first of the violent frosts.
> It's then that birdsong falls silent;
> Then the randy pulse of the beasts,

So lusty in spring, goes dormant.
'But I,' sayeth The God, 'But I,
The lover of all things holy,
Refuse to bow to the temporal,
The changeable whim of the seasons,
And the mere drive to brute dumbness.'" [7]

So saying, she fell into another crying jag, assisted back to the bed by her attendants.

The girl-on-girl porn still played, but we hardly noticed.

"Time for another group meeting," Assauer said.

We jammed ourselves in the little area outside the bathroom door. We did this so we could keep the room, the women, and our loot within easy eye-shot.

Gordon led off. "I don't know about this."

"Your boyfriend's right. This don't *smell* legit."

"She looks harmless enough," I said.

"What!"

"Calm down, honey. Don't get your noose out of joint."

"That's nose out of joint."

I puzzled a second. "But...noses don't have joints.... Is it flaming nostrils...?"

"Flaring—"

"Will you two. Shut. Up. This is not the time."

"Right. Look, the point is," I said, "this donkey dick thing's been hanging over our head." I glanced at the cult members. "Sure, they're a little coo-coo, but we let them do their voodoo, and then we tell them to shoo-shoo."

"Um..." Assauer was relenting. He could see my point.

Gordon though.... "This is nuts. We need to just shove 'em—"

"All right, ladies," I turned and answered. "We'll help you with your little problem. We are, as you say, sensible after all."

"Kohl!" My boy grabbed my arm.

"It's all right," I reassured him. Also, Lolita and Psyche stared down his protests.

"And you?" inquired Parthia of my ex. "What do *you* say...?"

"Yeah." Assauer shrugged, stepping forward. "Let's get it over and done with."

I was just about to add 'How bad could it be,' when the cult leader's mood turned on a dollar. She rose from the bed like a spirit possessed and approached us while cracking her knuckles. "Who do you think you are? Some Picaresque anti-heroes in a tawdry graphic novel?! Do you think you can just blunder your way into other people's realities without consequences? Without punishment?!"

I wondered, 'Pick-a-who...?'

Assauer chortled. "You might wanna cut down on the coffee, lady."

"But you said," Gordon stammered, "you weren't looking for revenge."

The mad woman cackled *"I'mmm* not," and then proceeded to do a mime performance of laughing at me: one hand over her mouth; the other used to point from an arm's length at my face and crotch.

Suddenly, she was done. She clapped sharply. Psyche went to the door, opening it to reveal 'Eros' – her burly beau from the market – and another equally beefy and pissed-off-looking dude with a devil-face goatee.

They crowded into the room, each of the men latching onto me and Assauer's arms. The gum-popping tart grabbed my Gordon.

Mr. Devil-Chin tightened his grip on me, pulling back uncomfortably on my inner arms, drawing my elbows too far. I winced, but then saw the madwoman step up to me. She opened her mouth and smeared a wet kiss over my lips and tongue. It sickened me, and her lipstick tasted gross.

She pulled back, looking maniacal. She then brushed the hair out of my eyes and pinned it behind my ears. "I'm glad we've struck a bargain," she said, "but make no mistake, if you had not volunteered for the trial, or even failed to let us in, tomorrow morning would have found a gang of Eros and his friends to make you more than regret it."

The dude laughed behind my head and jammed his knuckles in my lower back. Parthia returned for more disgusting wet-horse smooches, and I glanced at the bedside table where the gun was. It might as well have been in Egypt for all the good it could do us now.

Chapter 10: Sweating it out with a Pornstar

I opened my eyes. Stubborn sunlight found its way between the gently moving slats of the motel blinds.

I groaned through my foggy head as I rolled over and patted blindly for the bedside cabinet. Hovering my phone screen over my face, it glowed a nauseatingly cheerful: Monday, 12:03 PM.

Slowly, feeling hungover and bruised, I tossed the light-weight sheet aside and sat on the edge of the bed. I got up on the side facing away from the annoying light. At least I was wearing my boxers, lol.

'What happened last night?' The thought remained unanswered as I rubbed my scalp. I couldn't remember what went on, but I felt wiped and vaguely ashamed.

An impulse made me check, so I opened the drawer. Hojax's Luger was still in its wooden container, all the bullets accounted for and surrounding the weapon like bonbons in a demented box of chocolates. I shut it up again, noticing a couple of things at once.

I had to pee; that was primary. But secondly, Gordon and Assauer were asleep back-to-back on the other bed. It looked innocent enough, but still my jealousy stirred a bit though my morning haze.

Anyway, I stood up and took a leak. Afterwards, I returned to the room to see my two 'logs' had not rolled an inch. So I went to the windows, yanked up the blinds, and went over to kick the bed. "Rise and shine, lover-birds!"

They slowly roused and looked no better than I felt. While they were scratching and rubbing eyes as prelude to sitting up, I heard my phone. It vibrated in the way it does to tell me a new text had come in.

'Where was it…?' Oh, yes. On the pillow where I'd dropped it to go piss.

I grabbed it, and the three of us sat on the beds facing one another.

"What happened last night…?" Gordon stammered, his voice sounding hoarse.

Assauer shrugged, glancing around. "Don't know. We were here. Then those weirdos came, and we went with them…."

"Yeah," I agreed, "but the rest is a blank."

My ex and me looked to Gordon to see if he remembered more. He didn't and shook his head painfully to confirm the fact.

"Well, whatever." Assauer rubbed the back of his neck. "Where's the aspirin?"

While he was doing that, with elbows in the air, I pointed, and Gordon saw them too. Our companion had black and blue marks on the inside of his arms.

My boyfriend stood, lifting my hands and confirming I had them in the same place. A quick inspection of Gordon turned into relief as I didn't find any bruises on him.

The teenager folded his arms and leaned his butt against the night-stand. "I think it's time to fly the coop."

Me and Assauer agreed. I pulled up my phone, saying, "Listen to this text I just received:

> "Hey you pasty-ass losers, it's me, Neil Campbell. lol I sold your statue and got cash like you wanted. I also got us all into a *MAJOR* art event. Come back to L.A. right away or you'll miss out."

"So, fuck it. Let's go." I finished with a hand flourish.

Assauer agreed, standing up and stretching. "As long as we're not around those donkey dick freaks anymore, anyplace is fine."

Gordon nodded, so it was decided, but then added, "You both stink. We better shower before we blow this popsicle stand."

I licked my lips. My boy is so sexy when he's authoritarian. "You go first, Assauer. Me and Gordon will do it together."

Assauer was too sick to protest or make a 'gross, you two' face, so while Gordon climbed in my lap to cuddle, my ex stripped before us.

He turned around, scratching at his navel, and I could feel both Gordon's and my own spine stiffen.

When Assauer had closed the bathroom door behind him, I asked my boy, "Did you see—"

"His cock...?"

"...Yeah...."

"You think—"

"It grew overnight?"

"Yeah."

Gordon lifted his arm and hugged me across my back. His head came resting on my shoulder, as he murmured sleepily, "Looks bigger than yours now."

"You think?"

The boy bobbed his chin, already nodding off.

"Trick of the light," I said, more for myself than my boy.

The shower came on in the other room as I stroked Gordon's locks. I allowed a little wayward thought to intrude on our bliss, a soft specula-tion, really, for my morning wood was a notorious nuisance to my boy, but this morning...? There had been none when I woke up, none to try and piss through, and now – with Gordon dozing in my lap – there was still nothing stirring down there.

'Funny,' I thought. 'Just overly tired, I guess.'

I shrugged and gripped Gordon all the tighter.

A few days later, I felt a little better.

It was a lovely afternoon in West Hollywood. From my position on the sidewalk, I could see the rainbow lampposts, and the people-watchers as the young and buff strode by.

I looked at my phone. The latest text from Neil said:

"We're parking and can see you."

"Where?" I typed.

"Right in front of ya, mate!"

Glancing up again, the only thing I could see moving was a plumbing van parking off to my right.

The side door rolled open and out camped a scantily dressed Neil Campbell. He had on a pair of flimsy nylon board shorts, and a 'surfer dude' type tank top that left nothing to the imagination. You know the kind, loose around the arms and flashing tits and armpit hair at will, lol.

He slammed the door, after nodding in my direction, and came sauntering over. The sun pinged his eyes, so he pulled shades down from the front fringe of his dirty-blond dreads.

Neil called out "G'day" just as another man, a dude in a We-B-Ho Rooters uniform and gray cap came around from the driver's side. Seeing who it was, it took me a moment to re-hinge my jaw shut.

"But...but..." I stammered as he approached.

Napoleon Trueblood had to explain. "My life coaching consulting, and my motivational speaking engagements are my 'porn gigs.' Snaking shitty drains is how I pay the bills."

I shrugged. Assauer was right. We all do what we have to.

"Is this where we're supposed to meet?" I asked.

"Yep," Neil said, gesturing to the glassy building behind me. "Pump Up the Volume Gym – the man-mecca of SoCal."

I chuckled, scanning my hosts up and down. "Didn't know you two were the sports club types."

Napoleon put his arm around my shoulder and led us on. "We're not, but if there's one place to be seen and make contacts in Queer L.A., it's right here."

After changing, and me getting annoyed with Neil's open checking out of my bod – I mean, the guy's boyfriend was right there! – the three of us walked into the main exercise room. Floor to ceiling windows looked out onto the sidewalks on two sides; gorgeous men were on the treadmills facing the glass, all heads down, looking at their phones.

Neil chuckled, poking me in the ribs with his boney Aussie BBQ elbow.

"They're on hookup apps, seeing who's around."

I told him, "You'd think they'd just look up and find a guy the old-fashioned way – by cruising."

The two parts of Neil Campbell that were the brassiest, his laugh and his accent, came to the fore. "Ya' jokin'?! We ain't in the dark ages anymore, busta."

Napoleon pulled us along, bobbing his man-bun at us sagely. "Come on, boys. The eye candy can wait. We're here on business."

The celebrity self-help guru guided us to an interior glass wall. I noted lots of people watching what was happening on the other side. Many of them held phones way up high to stream vids. A few others copped 'gangsta' poses for selfies in front of the action.

Neil used his foreign tones to make room for us at the glass.

Our view was of the long side of a brightly lit handball court. The 'front wall,' against which the ball was bounced, was off to our right.

Two guys were engaged in *very* casual batting back and forth. One of them was a middle-aged, slightly paunchy man in dark workout clothes. His deferential opponent was a long-haired blond twink, who, in his white tennis shorts, was needlessly shirtless. But he was hardly alone, for behind the red serving line on the ballcourt floor, a long row of equally hot and bare-chested studs leaned against the walls. They feigned interest in the older man. One of these hotties appeared to be keeping score, because he made periodic notations on a tablet. However, something seemed to be off about the timing of when he made a note on his iPad....

"Who are those topless guys?" I inquired.

Napoleon told me, "He has contracts with all the best modeling agencies in town. They send over their newest, freshest faces to him for free, and hope he gets the models into the tabloids."

"What...?"

"Christmas crackers!" Neil Campbell blurted out. "Don't ya recognize the bloke?"

I closely scrutinized the looks and actions of the older man on the court. He was not bad-looking, say for a guy in his mid-fifties, but he was far from memorable, with somewhat truncated and ordinary facial features. His hair was not too full, a uniform dark-brown, and suspiciously non-moving as it hugged the top of his head above a soaked sweatband.

The guy suddenly lunged for an easy return and missed; the ball went bouncing out-of-bounds. And then it dawned on me. The recordkeeper dutifully updated the 'score,' but he was only counting the number of balls the older man fouled.

I eyed Neil and Napoleon, and hinted under my breath, "Well, the half-naked boys explain this hungry-tongued assortment of spectators, but who the devil is the old guy? I have no idea."

Napoleon informed me matter-of-factly, "That's Tre-Princely Knight."

I shrugged. The funny-sounding name rang no bells.

Neil proceeded to be agog. "The big man-on-man pornstar.... And I do mean *big!*"

"Sorry, I'm not a size queen," I said, but looked harder at the man all the same, trying to jag my memory.

Napoleon tapped my shoulder rhythmically, explaining, "He was the highest-paid male bottom in porn a couple decades back. He made a fortune and invested it all in hand sanitizers, oil fracking, Big Tobacco, illegal pipelines, Canadian Oil Swamps, modified food engineering *and,* bottled water. So, needless to say, he's insanely rich today."

Neil chortled. "Yeah, even more so now that workin' Yanks put a fox like the great Orange One in the henhouse of oversight. Well, safety and health regulations had a good run, but they've gone the way of the Dodo, thanks to private corporate funding of the GOPs."

Trueblood agreed. "But it's hardly new. We all remember how the Cheney-Junior Administration 'tackled' the threat of Mad Cow disease getting by forbidding the FDA from testing for it."

"Bad for selling ground beef over the 4th of July weekend, huh?" I said.

"Yeah, biz above all else nowadays. So, Big Ag didn't want an encephalitis panic? Therefore, a few dozen Americans had their brains eaten out by a meat-bone parasite instead. That's what happens when 'Progress' itself is turned into a dirty word."

Neil smiled snakishly, glancing at his boyfriend. "Yeah, but you be careful, Kohl. Don't get this guy going on the lil Brush Administration, or we'll be here all bloomin' day!"

"Well," huffed Napoleon. "It matters how people vote."

"Amen," I said, mainly to snap the conversation to a close, lol.

On the court, the long-haired boy was dismissed, and Tre-Princely chose an almost identical one to replace him in the competition. In the meantime, another significantly younger lad with red hair brought the man a white towel and tropical cocktail, complete with parasol and pineapple chunks. The former pornstar wiped his face, and I noticed Napoleon trying to get the man's attention through the glass. It did not work, so after a deep sip, Tre-Princely Knight shooed the red-haired boy away. The game continued, with the man playing notably more aggressive, maybe due to the iron content of his piña colada mix.

"Yeah," Neil said as the ball went back into play. "He was the biggest man-bottom for over a decade, and even though a billion guys have wanked watchin' him get dicked, he's straight."

"What?!"

"Hundred percent," confirmed Trueblood. "Real name's Malcolm Schwartzbaum, from Cheboygan, Michigan—"

Neil interjected, "He's one hot Jew!"

"Anyway"—Napoleon slapped his boyfriend's chest—"he has a lovely Mrs. Schwartzbaum at home."

"A real smart cookie she is too," Neil added.

"And he has a habit of calling her his *Rabbit's Foot* or *Lucky Charm*. You'll meet her at the event."

I was still stuck in amazement mode. "So, this guy's not Gay?"

"Nope," Napoleon said. "But even though he's retired, he still maintains the front of liking boys to promote his tube-site – Nightly with Tre-Princely dot com."

As we made room for a Japanese tourist with a shutter-bug of a Nikon, Neil rapped in a joyful singsong:

> "He was gay-for-pay
> Like Maria Callas,
> Way back in the day,
> Hitin' high notes for dollas,
> But dreamin' bout divas
> While wankin' to bea'vas."

The former pornstar under-glass had tuckered himself out, for his opponent was dismissed, and to my astonishment, a completely different towel boy appeared. This one was just as young and spry, and wearing the same uniform, but African American and toting a margarita glass. The rocks of salt glistened on the bowl as Tre-Princely Knight drew it to his lips. His eyes sparkled in my direction, and I glanced to see it was because Napoleon had finally gotten the man's attention.

In another moment, the player wiped his face and gestured to the side of the court.

Trueblood evidently knew what that signal meant. "Come on, boys. Time to get naked."

Through the sweat and steam, I idly watched two 'professional' masseurs compete. The guys with model-worthy bodies wore only leek-green Speedos and flimsy white vests without shirts. They operated the clinking ice and firm agitation of cocktail shakers from behind a pair of drink carts. It was incongruous to see these portable bars in a cedar-lined gym sauna like this, but me, Napoleon, Neil and Tre-Princely sat companionably enough on the room's wooden ledges.

Naturally, we were all down to nothing but towels, and I tried hard not to stare at our host. He was a bit more pug-nosed closeup than I could see from afar, or maybe it was just a certain way he looked out on the world. It was quite a challenge to keep my eyes off the bald head of the ex-pornstar, which was now slick with perspiration. The toupée was off...possibly getting combed, spruced up – and/or sterilized – in another part of the gym.

"So, Napoleon, I'm very pleased you'll be at my little art happening later tonight.'

"Oh, yes. We can't wait." The motivational-speaker-slash-drain-snaker indicated the beaming Neil with his *we*.

"And who is your new friend?"

The pornstar's inquiry was aimed at yours truly.

"This is a very cool German dude, named Kohl."

"So," Tre confirmed, "you're from overseas, across the mud puddle, as they say."

"Yes, I am."

Neil chimed in, "Precious fuckin' accent, ain't it?"

The retired pornstar ignored that, preferring to murmur towards me, "Kohl; Kohl; Kohl – I've heard that name before. Remind me."

"Hmmm," I said. "Well, 'kohl' reminds me of cabbage, sauerkrauts, kale, soup—"

"No, no. A person."

"OH! Yeah. You mean former Chancellor Kohl. He was a political bigshot back in the days of Reagan and Gorbachev."

"Yes, that's the one." Tre-Princely beamed, proud of his powers of recollection.

"When I think of *that* 'Kohl,'" I chuckled. "I remember how at State Dinners he'd force foreign dignitaries to eat his favorite dish: Palatine Pork Paunch. Pig stomach stuffed with potatoes, root veg, chestnuts, spices and herbs. And then boiled like a pudding."

Neil and the masseurs-cum-barkeeps shook sour-puss grimaces off their noggins.

Napoleon, however, looked contemplative and muttered with admiration, "How positively Roman. A page right out of Nero's school for diplomacy. They don't make politicians like that anymore."

'*Gott sei Dank!*' I thought. Thank the Lord.

"Ouuuugh, Napoleon." His Aussie lover whinged. "The whole pig stomach thing's gross, or just plain feral, as we'd say back home."

The self-help guru's eyes lit up. "Speaking of food, I've extended tonight's invitation to Kohl and his, um…boyfriends. Hope you don't mind."

"No, not at all."

I corrected the statement. "Boyfriend, singular. But, also my ex is coming along."

Napoleon hastened to add, "Kohl here is a poet too. Did I mention that?"

"No," chimed Neil. "No, you didn't."

All eyes fell on Tre-Princely Knight. I didn't know if that information was supposed to mean anything to him, although I knew I didn't like the sound of that tacked-on *too*.

"I dabble," the older man said with a jaded sigh. "But only from time to time, when the muse bites. Why don't you recite something for us?"

I shrugged and coughed up some famous lines every German schoolchild should know by heart.

"Unter allem Diebesgesindel
sind die Narren die schlimmsten.

Sie rauben euch beides,
Zeit und Stimmung." [8]

Again, all gazes settled on Mr. Schwartzbaum. Would he realize I was shitting him...?

"Wonder-bar!" he exclaimed. "And you wrote that yourself?"

"Sure did."

I suddenly noticed the hostile glares coming at me from the pair of cocktail makers.

"Oh, my." Tre-Princely praised me to Napoleon. "So very talented, Mr. Trueblood. Very talented. You know, when the poet laureate of Belize was entertaining me one day at his estate on Trinidad, he said 'Poetry is like the sap of the rubber tree plant – when it oozes, it's all about the flow.' You can't fake that."

The competing Speedos tussled a bit to get their admiring looks for Tre's 'wisdom' acknowledged first.

They glowered hatefully at me again, and I got the point of their jealousy all of a sudden. These two happy-endings boys thought I'd captured their potential sugar daddy's eye.

"Okay, boys," said our host. "Time to get shaking—"

Trueblood interrupted with a disproportionate laugh for the size of Tre's pun.

The pornstar smiled, drinking in the praise, and continued with his original thought. To the rest of us he said, "Order anything you like to drink, gentlemen. But, just so you know, Japanese *mm-umami* karate-kicks have Shanghai'd cocktail trends this season." He put his hands behind his sweaty bald pate, leaning back to relax. "But long as long as my grog gets mickeyed with my old standby, gin, and some of the new canna...diaboli syrup, I'll try anything, twice!"

Me, Neil and Napoleon glanced at one another, unsure what was on hand to order.

Tre-Princely piped up again, instructing the barkeeps, "Run down your list, fellas, of what's hot this year with the celebrity set."

Puffing up for a chance to impress the bigwig bottom, the shaker boy on the left announced with authority, "This month's *it* drink is a martini made with apple-cider vinegar-cider, fermented sour Pu-erh tea vermouth – shaken, not stirred – served with a twist of daikon radish."

'What!' I thought.

The other white-vest would not be outdone. He stepped forward to block the view of his rival. He made precisely two dismissive clicks with his mouth and shook the rest of his head in disdain. "SO not fashion-forward anymore. The *real* trend this week for the discriminating palate is Concord-grape rum on the rocks with a kombucha chaser."

'Yeah, I'd discriminate against that too....'

The first one stepped in front again, raising his voice. "Man-Mountain brand saké, with miso soup and tonic water!"

The second got even louder. "Green whortleberry vermouth, Himalayan-pink salt and hundred-year-old yuzu balsamic‼"

"Boys; boys!" exclaimed Tre, like he was getting a headache. "You both make your best cocktails for all of us, and we will be the judge. But, don't forget to tell them about the special, down-low ingredient, CBD."

"What's that?" I inquired, bemused.

The first barkeep answered, "Food-grade cannabidiol oil. A few drops, and zoom, you're on the floor!"

The second added more info. "You know, canna as in cannabis; weed, pot, mara-ji-whanna-somemore...."

I glanced around the sweaty room, only to discover I was the odd man out in knowing nothing about this syrupy delivery method. Almost whispering, I asked, "Where do you get it from?"

The first bartender looked astounded. "Where else? The pet store. They've got CBD oil right at the counter, just like supermarkets have candy bars and rag-mags."

"Convenience shopping, they call it. Pick it up and go," the second guy in a white vest said.

Stupid me for not knowing Americans these days wanted to drug their pets with the equivalent of canine Ritalin. I suppose parents have settled on there being too much hyperactivity in nature, as evidenced in their own offspring and designer Shitsza-poos, lol.

"Get to shaking, boys!" Tre ordered, and they did.

Soon we each double-fisted a pair of cocktails. I sipped one and tried to hide my pickle-puss reaction. The other was not much better, but by then the CBD was kicking in, so I relaxed and forced it down. And, you know me, I like to loosen up as much as the next guy, but still, call me old fashioned for preferring my weed not diluted with Chinese black beans and acai-flavored cocoa.

Yuck.

Just then, one of the barmen, already busy whip-creaming up a round two, flipped the lid off his cocktail shaker a little too vehemently and splashed crimson slosh on his rival's vest.

That was followed by an angry shove, once the victim had used his hand to squeegee liquor off his clothing.

A full-on tussle erupted between them, and Tre-Princely called out gleefully, "See?! They're fighting over me. It's just the way Nature intended it." Then he told the servers more forcefully, "Come on, now, guys. Splash out some more of the canna-diablo to my guests. Time's a-wasting, and you're thrusting my groove."

Amid the instant clamor of clinking ice and splashing gut-rot booze, I leaned in close to get a translation from Trueblood.

"It means he's sobering up," the naked guru whispered through a wink.

I nodded wisely and leaned back against the sweaty cypress.

When we each had a second pair of elaborate drink-trends in our mitts, a daydreaming look crept upon the retired porn-bottom's face. He recited some verse with a faraway expression:

> "Here today,
> Gone tomorrow.
> In light, what we're paid in joy,
> In dark, we'll pawn in sorrow."

Then, laughing, he lifted his glass to us. "Bottoms up, men. No one will remember us when we're dead anyway!"

A rosy-black smog tinged the twilight as it clung to the stone-veneer walls of the Getty Center. This complex of arbitrarily misshapen buildings sat aloof, disconnect from rhyme or reason, atop its bulldozed-but-lonely hill high over Los Angeles.

After more sweat and awkward poetry from Tre-Princely Knight in the sauna, I'd returned to the motel room and changed. Now we were all here in casual evening clothes.

The museum was closed so the ex-pornstar could have his cocktail hour for about fifty – just him, his guests and the press. Right now, the man was engaged in a kind of red-carpet event on one side of the Modern Art Gallery. Four sexy guys, in sleek Italian tuxes, posed with Tre as their linchpin. I'd say the tableaux was staged to resemble a mob-style night out on the town, because the host himself was arrayed in a rakish fedora, white dinner jacket and buff-colored trousers, which did no favors to diminish his belly bump. The cameras flashed away like birdsong, the cellphones were raised to capture live footage; 'news' voices called out for the group to look this way and that.

I strolled alone with Napoleon, who was munching my ear off while we perused the staid, artificial-colored paintings on the wall. Occasionally, my eyes drifted out of the many open French doors to the terrace, where there glowed natural and beautiful hues in motion. I could catch glimpses of Neil Campbell, Assauer and Gordon leaning on the railing, drinking in the view and chatting easily.

Napoleon put his arm out and stopped us in front of a silly-looking piece of sculpture. The artist had taken any number of cereal box tops and cemented them together to form a sort of whirligig staircase. To 'improve' it

– or to make it artistic…? – he'd taken puke-green paint and spilled it down the run of steps.

Trueblood placed a hand on his chin and looked rapt in apparent concentration on 'the message' before him. However, he said, "You know, back in the day it was Oscar Wilde who coined the phrase 'Art for Art's sake.' But now, looking at emotionally irrelevant pieces like this, I think the new maxim goes: 'Art for Fuck's sake.'"

I copped a similar pose as his, but mainly to mask my smile of agreement. "I see. Go on."

"Contemporary art is in a funk, a malaise caused by a total detachment with reality. Think about it. If it means nothing to the artist, how in the hell is it supposed to mean anything to anyone else? Yes, Kohl, it's a sorry state of affairs, for the freer any artwork is of social commentary, cultural context, or emotional relevance, the more it's praised. For example, freeze, slice and press a marmot kidney between panes of glass, and the movers and shakers will toss a Turner Prize at it, and laude you as *important.*"

We'd started our tour again, but my attention was more and more drawn outside. The ugly canvases and pasteboard dioramas stood no chance against the lure of Gordon's free-spirited laugh.

I remembered the very first time hearing that laugh as I walked down an open breezeway at Aptos High School, which in reality, was not that long ago. That day I saw a beautiful boy loitering at his open locker with his friends – a taped-up picture of a shirtless pop star on the inside of the door – and the sexy owner's eyes trained on me as I passed. Though, naturally, or perhaps I should say, *especially*, alarm bells went off saying 'Danger Ahead,' I knew caution was the last thing on the boy's mind, lol.

Out on the terrace, Assauer laughed too, and like a palm smack to the forehead, it brought me crashing back to reality. My ex's too-lecherous leer on my boy's bright face stirred heat within me, and made me wonder what those two could have been up to today while I was at the gym. They spent the afternoon alone in the motel room, and could that explain why Gordon appeared so flushed when I joined them later on?

I slowly pulled my attention away from them and returned it to Napoleon's nattering.

"…Big Art, Inc., is currently viewed as a mere get-rich-quick scheme. If you're a struggling young artist, the only path to success is finding your *shtick* – one that no one's done before, or at least one that no one remembers. Do that, get in good with the professional critics, and you're set for life."

Rather annoyed, I said, "When has it really ever been different?"

I filtered him out again, because he had no real answer, other than 'ancient times,' which I scoffed at.

No, my attention drifted back out to the terrace and my boy. The beginning of some verse formed itself in my head:

'Are we prisoners to that captivity? –
   jailed by fickle nature and love,
   caged passive to activity,
while freedom we think we have no part of?

No. The key to unleash our liberty
   is a pre-set combination,
   which found, returns our property
And lets us go to our destination.'

I'd have to develop that some more.

Some form of commotion arose. Waiters directed people from the outside areas in, and Tre broke up the photo sesh. The porn-bottom smiled, thanked the Media and walked up to his wife, who had been standing just out of camera range the whole time.

The couple began to lead the way out of the gallery, and just as the rest of our party joined us, Napoleon explained, "The *Event* won't happen here, and only a few of us are going on to the private part of the evening anyway."

We started walking through the building, making our way down to the ground floor.

"No? Where will it happen then," asked Gordon.

"At the Getty Villa, in Malibu. Tre-Princely thinks its much *classier* there."

"Oh," my boyfriend replied.

Neil added, "And our host's arranged for a real V.I.P. procession to get us through all the traffic."

"Police escort?" Assauer asked.

"Nope," replied Neil. "It's better. You'll see."

By now we had made it out the front door, and were ushered to wait on the side while the press continued to snap pix of the ex-pornstar. His wife – a buxom brunette, silicone-enhanced sex toy of a former pornstar herself – stood out of the way again and allowed a new troupe of hot escorts to bandy themselves about our evening's host.

I turned to Neil. "What did you mean by procession?" But before I could complete my own thought, a pair of black Lincolns rolled up with their lights on. Right behind them appeared a stretch Rolls Royce hearse, glinting in gaudy metallic silver.

"Noooo..." I gasped softly, but Mrs. Schwartzbaum and the V.I.P. entourage of guests got into the lead vehicles. At the same time, our host kissed his 'boyfriends,' before the five of them piled into the back of the 'Spirit of Ecstasy' death carriage. Amid that action, the press went nuts snapping photos and flinging wild questions in every direction.

Once this first assembly of cars had departed, and the museum staff began to shoo away the paparazzi, more limos with their lights on pulled up to the curb for the remainder of us chosen few 'main event' guests.

As I gave one final glance to the twilight streaked behind the trees, a sudden rustle of wind sent chills down my spine. For some unknown reason, a micro-spurt of sound and fury burst like a bubble in my head. I saw and felt Doris blowing me in the woods on Catalina; Gordon's mercurial smile as I fucked him after kicking Assauer out of our room; of my ex's newly enlarged dick flopping about as he went for his shower.

And then, like a nasty jolt, the sight and smell of that scruffy stranger appeared, his face hate-filled and close to mine, eyes burning like coal. The shrill bray of a burro raced across my eardrums like a vindictive laugh.

'What's happening to me,' I wondered as I slid into the backseat next to my smiling and beloved Gordon.

"...nusquam currere..."

— Part Four —
"Will there be food at this event?"

———————

#Jeffersonian-hooch, #wolf-boy!

#sexy-boy-Democrats, #Priapus,

#tootsie-rolls, #live-streaming,

#gas-treek-freak! #cricket-salsa,

#toss-her-tripe! #hash-slinger,

#Auntie-Pasto #grubs,

#talk-about-GAY!

#acceptor-amoris,

#Uppity, #Si

Chapter 11: Tre-Princely's Happening

The question just asked about food and our next event was followed by Assauer stating "Because I'm starving!"

'Too much physical activity this afternoon,' I brooded silently.

Neil and Napoleon, sitting opposite us in the back of our limousine, exchanged sly glances. "Oh, there'll be food all right," said the Australian, "but you may not want to eat much of it."

'What did that mean...?' I wondered.

The car took a few gentle curves as it ascended a hillside and eventually slowed. We pulled into a torch-lit driveway just as it was getting dark.

Someone from the outside opened the doors, and the five of us piled out.

The first sight that caught my eye was the guy holding the door for me. He was a dark-haired muscle stud, dressed like a Vegas Caesars Palace extra. A helmet with scarlet plumes glinted in the flame light, while the metal flaps of his centurion armor clanked above the hem of a red tunic – and his hairy knees.

I gave the guy a little smile and nod, eying the plastic sword he held erect in his free hand.

"All hail the guests of Tre-Princely Knight! Welcome to my master's event."

"Thank you," I said, moving onto the sidewalk with my companions.

The building we stood before was generally Mediterranean, but not that special looking. A long set of columns along the ground supported a second-floor terrace, abounding in trellises and flowering vines above. The edge of red roof tiles played peek-a-boo from behind the foliage.

"What is this place?" Gordon asked.

"The Getty Villa," explained Neil. "This used to be *the* Getty before they built their modernist Frankenstein in glass and stone."

"Looks sorta weird," Assauer observed in his typical no-punches-barred manner.

"It's a recreation," said Napoleon, "of the seaside crib of Julius Caesar's father in law."

"Oh, cool!" A wide-eyed Gordon stammered.

The other guests, who had all piled out of similar limousines earlier, were now on the move, slowly being guided by a smiling Mrs. Knight, although Tre-Princely was nowhere to be seen. Because, including our little gaggle of friends, there were only about ten others who had filtered down from the public event and photo-op to this, the V.I.P. happening.

Just when we got under the shelter of the overhang, the pair of massive bronze doors opened as if by magic to our hostess' approach. A large hall was inside, and beyond it, a two-story atrium.

Strolling in, the sound of water appeared for us, for in the very center of the room was a rectangular fountain set in the floor. I glanced up and saw it aligned perfectly with an opening in the ceiling/roof. A couple of stars already twinkled in the heavens.

Motion from deeper in the space attracted my attention, for several women of the party were laughing and pointing phones and tablets at one another. One said "Here we are, live-streaming from Tre's event." Another added a translation for the younger set. "OMG. This is so real. And I think I might die, like dead!"

Together they held devices up for a duo-selfie, asking viewers with matching smirks, "Jealous yet?"

In the meantime, our host's wife was chatting with the male guests and leading everybody through a wide opening at the opposite end of the atrium. I followed, but decided to lag behind a bit. [9]

The second space she led us into was a fully colonnaded garden, again two-stories high, but much larger and nearly breathtaking. Four fruit trees in massive terracotta pots marked the corners of the manicured greenery, while a long rectangular reflecting pool shot up quiet jets in arches between five Grecian goddesses in bronze. Each one was slightly different, but all stared placidly into the rippling water as if lost in thoughts of the timeless. I noted five of them, for a sixth base, the central one on the right side of the pool, was unoccupied.

Something made me turn to my left and enter one of the museum galleries.

It was a rectangular room, beautifully clad in marble panels. On one long wall was a mural. I strolled along it, recognizing the subject was the storm-tossed wanderer, Ulysses. He had to sojourn ten years after the Trojan War as the plaything of the gods...for some reason his plight felt very real to me at the moment.

A sensation like static-cling prickled the hairs on the back of my neck. I slowly rotated my torso to locate the source, and was led through a low doorway into a dimly lit display area.

This room was round and domed. Mosaic tiles slathered the wall, and recessed niches behind glass exhibited smaller-sized, precious objects.

One of these cases gradually drew me to it like a magnet. Some totem-like statues were there bathed in spotlights, but they were weird idols for sure. Some woodland man, with a staff in his hand but no clothes, sported an enormous erection. Another was of the same person but he wore 'city duds': a long tunic, the front hem of which he held up like a skirt. In the basket created by this, an abundance of fruit overflowed, while oddly enough, more produce appeared under his clothes on either side of his engorged phallus, curving upwards and in insistent need of attention.

'Talk about fruit of the loon....'

This case had an information card. "Roman Priapus Cult Objects, 1st Century C.E."

I peered closer, drawing myself almost by compulsion, to examine this nature spirit's face.

Elfin ears stuck up in front of a ribbon wrapping his disheveled bush of hair. His attributes were strength and a commanding confidence in the prime of his potency.

And then inexplicably, those features seemed all too familiar; my skin went clammy; my heart rate, thready. It almost felt as if suppressed recollections were forcing their way to the surface, but what they could be, I did not know.

I knew something had happened—

"Kohl?"

Surprised, I whirled around into a kung-pow stance.

Gordon stood there as beautiful as ever. "You all right?"

"Yeah, okay. You?"

He grinned at me like I was being silly.

My response was to hug him. I mean, really hug him, hoping my trembling didn't transmit through my touch too strongly.

He appeared not to notice, for a moment later he took my hand, saying, "Come on. Wait till you get a load of this setup. You won't believe it."

It was a relief to let my boy lead me away from this Priapus person, god, creature – whatever he was.

I heard the encouraging sound of blenders crushing ice.

Around the garden with the ladies' fountain we went, along the pillared walkway to the other side. A large room waited beyond another pair of columns, but lined up across from the pillars were a dozen reclining chairs from a salon.

Tre's wife directed the activities, taking drink orders and telling us to disrobe our feet.

The other guests were getting mani-pedis by what I took to be Australian Aboriginal young men in skimpy cargo shorts and unzipped walkabout vests over bare skin.

Me and Gordon joined them, kicking off our shoes and stuffing the socks inside before sitting down.

While our toes got manipulated, filed and shellacked, more boys arrived to collect our foot apparel for storage somewhere.

I started to relax once my vodka-cranberry appeared, and the young man working on my tootsie-rolls freely flirted as he went about his flesh-kneading. Normally I'd get in trouble with Gordon by my side and my cock straining to get out and into a handsome boy's touch...but...I didn't have to worry.

'Still overly tired,' I told myself.

The earlier guests were getting finished, and stood up to be presented with golden slippers, complete with Tre's monogram on them.

By the time me and my boy were polished up, we walked into a grand room full of people chatting boisterously.

Three tables formed a 'U', leaving an open staging area in the center. The head table was positioned in front of several columns leading out to an unbelievably immense garden on the other side. It stretched back five hundred feet or more. Another central water feature reflected the freshly emerged stars, and this garden was again completely enclosed by Doric columns.

"This way," Napoleon called, and me and my boy sat at our places with them and Assauer at the table off to the left.

A quick scan of the room told me our dinner companions appeared to be mostly of the crude Tre hangers-on types – middle age douchebag tools for the men; plastic-surgery-marred ex-pornstars for the women – and I could tell few if any of the guys were Gay because they clearly acted 'not interested' in me or my boyfriend when we walked in, lol. Instead they generally eyed our table of 'outsiders' with hostile wondering of what our purpose here could be.

Tre-Princely was still conspicuously absent, but once we'd been settled for a few minutes and enjoying our drinks, weird South American flute music started from somewhere back from where we had come.

A leprechaun-looking Irish dude in chef whites arrived on the scene. As he strode into the central staging area, he was as rough-n-tumble a scrapper as anyone ever was. He sported IRA tattoos and a shocking-red goatee. His head though was completely bald.

He cracked his knuckles and announced through a shimmering intonation, "I'm sure ya know I'm Cory O'Shay, celebrity chef, TV host, et cetera, et cetera, but I'm here because Tre-Princely asked me to serve up you fine lot of people a mess o'vittles. To that end, ladies and gents, the first course will be a real gastro-treat! I've got duck foie gras tacos on a bed of re-fried natto beans and a julienne of raw dinosaurian kale. It's all tied together with a topping of Model Negra foam gastrique. Enjoy!"

He cracked more knuckles and disappeared back into the shadows. I turned to Napoleon on my left. "Dark beer foam, on French liver tacos...?"

"Yep. Go with it, you lucky boy."

Neil interjected himself. "Chef O'Shay is a real gas-treek freak! It's all the rage these days. Anything can be made into a foam."

"But not all foam can be made edible," I wryly observed.

Just then, the flute music grew very loud, punctuated by castanets and tambourine rattles.

To my unbelieving sight, more scantily clad young men – three Thai boys this time, wearing huge sombreros – pulled in a half-scale papier-mâché donkey on casters. The beast was harnessed to a gold-plated food truck, or 'roach coach,' as the locals call it. On each narrow shelf of the vehicle were stacks of tacos, and once the boys hauled up the donkey and truck, they served the food with smiles. The musicians strolled around the room with their portable din.

While all this went on, I leaned back and poked my ex. He glanced over, and I pulled him back to confer behind Gordon.

"Have you remembered any more of that missing time?" I asked.

"From *the* night?"

"Yeah."

"No. You?"

"Nope, but...things seem to be coming back, so, maybe."

My boy turned to me. "It's like some weird alien abduction shit that we can't remember anything."

"I know." I agreed.

Just then, a surly-eyed man from the first table – the V.I.P. of the V.I.P. seating, I guess – cleared his throat loudly in our direction. He was short, dressed in an Italian suit, and periodically ogling the plastic bimbos half his age in the room; but I guess *we* were the ones being rude, lol.

Plates were set before us, on which sat three 25¢ deep-fried taco shells from the bulk box. Poop-colored chunks of meat oozed out the side from under torn shreds of kale. Frothy brown goo was jiggling on top of the raw greenery.

Assauer had already shrugged and picked up the 'taco.'

I smelled one of mine. It reminded me of my grandmother's farmhouse – or maybe her barn.

I caught Gordon biting into his, his eyes soon telling me it was awful.

The South American percussionists traipsed out of the room just as the servers had dished up the last of the first course. The final Thai boy to depart plopped his sombrero on the burro's head...and then a funny thing happened.

The papier-mâché glint in the creature's eye jolted me back to that lost Sunday night.

> While still in our Pasadena motel room, just being led out, Parthia reached for and massaged my crotch. Of course, I didn't get hard.
>
> "Sorry," I told her, "hundred percent Gay here. You're out of luck, lady."
>
> She cackled. "It's you, young man, who are out of luck." Then to her followers, she screeched, "Blindfold them and take them to our local holy prescient. Their passions await."
>
> The words made my heart sink, but not as much as seeing my beloved boy manhandled by that crude, gum-popping teenage airhead, Lolita.

A startling noise made me jump and spill my taco contents.

Mariachis led the way, strumming and bellowing the song *You're So Vain* at full volume, with Spanish-language lilts. Behind them was

Tre-Princely Knight, mouthing a toothpick and humming loudly. He had effected a costume change and now wore a black satin dressing gown, à la Hugh Hefner in the Playboy Mansion. Around his neck was an elaborate aviator's scarf. I guess that was a nod to Howard Hughes, lol.

As the band crescendoed, the man's friends squeaked chairs and gave him a standing ovation – Napoleon and Neil were right there with them. Distracted as we were, it took glares from the pug-nosed throat-clearer to get me, Assauer and Gordon to stand too.

"Ermanno! You old dog." Our host slapped the surly guy's shoulder before sitting grandly in the middle of the central table. From where I sat, his toupéed head was framed beautifully by the water feature in the garden behind him. His wife appeared at his side with a large gin and tonic, which she placed in his hand. Then she smacked a full bottle of the sapphire liquid by his plate and kissed his forehead before stepping aside.

The toothpick came out of his mouth and was discarded. "Have you all met my better-half – my Lucky Charm, my Rabbit's Foot? Prospera Texas-Ivy, ladies and gents. Some of you may have *seen* her before."

The livestream cameras turned on the demurring woman, but Tre forced her to take a bow.

Napoleon Trueblood leaned over and told me under his breath, "Hyphenated porn names were all the rage at one time, don't ya know."

The mariachis struck up again and led the donkey and model roach coach out with an ear-piercing rendition of *La Cucaracha*.

'*Gott im Himmel*,' I thought, already looking around for the easiest escape route.

Tre-Princely Knight drained half his glass and dabbed his mouth with his scarf. "I hope everyone is enjoying their post-Post-Modern experimental theater so far."

The response was lukewarm.

The former pornstar insisted, "It's Performance Art, a marriage of food and mental stimulation."

"Hear, hear," said a man in his thirties opposite us; his tone was slow and Southern for sure. "You're always such a wonderful host. It's absolutely our honor and privilege."

"Thank you, Nicholas, my dear buddy."

Nicholas added, "I am blessed, Tre."

The comment made another one of the man's friends – the one who looked like a mortician and sat at the main table to Tre's left – start a second round of applause. The cameras lapped it up like kittens with a saucer of milk.

This Tre took as suitable accolades and grinned while pouring himself another big gulp. He then spoke as if to the bottle, "Oh, Rabbit's Foot, what would I do without you? You're my boulder."

Tre's wife dismissed the sentiment with an "Oh...."

"See, we are good partners. We both have sweaty pasts – that's well known – but we're different where it counts. She's frugal where I'm generous; she's a book-reckoner where I'm a 'make it rain' kinda guy."

"Now, Tre," she said, glancing around the room, adding a bit sharply, "stop."

"No, it's true," he insisted. "She keeps me on the straight and narrow, no pun intended. But seriously, if not for her.... Well, times are up and times are down; don't they say that? Take my good friend, Gavin Coruptti here." The former pornstar slapped the shoulder of the thin, pale guy to his left. "He was a day trader, energy broker, ETF peddler – God knows what else in the make rich men richer bugger-all Bush years – but then, poof! All gone. And do you know what he does now?"

As the question seemed directed at me, I answered, "No."

"He's better off than ever in the burial racket."

"A funeral director, to be exact, with a lucrative sideline in the monument biz," clarified Coruptti.

'Knew it,' I thought.

Tre-Princely briefly laughed. "If anyone needs to dole out advice to the youth of America, they should remember our graying population and tell 'em to get in the grave business for themselves. It's where our future lies!"

"True," the monument-maker opined with dark pride. "It's the one and only recession-proof profession." A smirk arose. "There's *always* money to be made in death. I'll be handing out business cards later."

Our host clapped his hands twice, shouting, "I think it's time for wine!"

As if by magic, two *quinceañera* servers dressed in bedazzled frockcoats, green britches and sparkling powdered wigs brought in a giant platter shaped like a five-cent nickel. Smack in the center of the third president's head was a dusty old bottle.

While the girls set up the tray on a table in the middle of the stage area, Tre began to ramble in a storytelling clip. "I picked up a few of these at the garage sale Malcolm Forbes' children had after he died. Also snatched up a few *fab* eggs." He paused for recognition. None came. "Get it? A few Fabergé eggs!"

His cronies whinnied "Oogh's!" and "Ah's!"

Another round of non-spontaneous applause broke out, which Tre-Princely soaked up, along with more gin from his glass, lol.

A little Mexican day laborer, in his jeans and flannels – but wearing a powdered wig – entered sheepishly.

Tre gestured to the bottle, and the man stepped up to serve as sommelier.

We were all pretty stunned, but the ex pornstar explained rather nonchalantly, "He's my leaf-blower from back home."

When we guests acted unsure how to react to the entire situation, Tre-Princely Knight added like it was obvious, "If a Latino guy can play Hamilton and earn a billion dollars on Broadway, why not have a real Latin-

American serve our Jefferson wine!"

We were still uncertain, but the man doing the work shrugged and popped the cork. "*Sí.*"

The combination of sounds clearly made our host turn philosophical, for he drank more straight sapphire and called out, "What a fucking shame it is when a wine in this world can outlive a man, and this one we're about to slurp is over two hundred years old. And *this* is real Jeffersonian hooch! I fed a better class of people last night, and not even they got the good stuff!"

The remark made Mrs. Schwartzbaum scowl at him briefly, peeking from behind her phone's live-streaming out to the web.

"Pardon, folks. The ball-n-chain rebukes me. You lot are plenty classy enough." He nodded at his missus, like 'There. Happy now?'

In the meantime, one of the presidential girls had taken off the metal collar from the bottle and was slowly parading the label so all us guests could see for ourselves. Engraved upon it was:

> *THOM. JEFFERSON WINE*
> *BOTTLED IN THE PRESIDENCY OF THEO.*
> *ROOSEVELT*
> *ONE HUNDRED YEARS OLD.*

After we all had a glass of the turbid stuff in front of us, our host said, "You do the honors, honey."

Rabbit's Foot stood, and lifted her glass to the center table. "To Tre- Princely Knight. *Le'chaim!*"

"Le'chaim!" we repeated, and I slowly brought the glass to my nose. If musty ditchwater could cover it, let's say that was the 'bouquet.' The taste, well, if vinegar could be said to be 'girlish,' it was.

The only redeeming feature may have been the hundred-proof brandy used by some Rooseveltian charlatan to embalm the nearly dead wine a century ago and make it still drinkable today. I did just that – drank it – and put on a brave face, which was good, for I needed fortification for the next part of the *happening.*

While the rest were still choking back the ghost wine, oddly sad music arose from out on the peristyle behind Tre.

At the same moment, between the columns at the main entrance to the room, appeared a tall figure, robed and hooded entirely in black.

This Grim Reaper actually freaked me out for some reason as he slowly strode up to the now-empty coin-top table.

He bowed to our host, who had a knowing glint in his eye, and the Reaper slowly opened his robe. He had been hiding a silver skeleton on a set of fishline strings. This marionette appeared accurate down to the tiniest of articulated bone.

The Grim puppet master made the white metal skull of his toy look at each and every single guest in turn without the man moving his cowled head an inch. He then slowly placed the skeletal feet on the tray like it was a stage.

The music started again from outside, and the marionette performed a hair-raising dance of the macabre.

It was hard to describe how something so un-lifelike could act and move in a way that seemed more naturalistic than any living thing.

Transfixed, Tre began reciting. "As the great William Burnaby once wrote:

> "Unhappy mortals we,
>   Who on so fine a thread,
>   Find our lives but depend,
> Know like this puppet man
>   There's no time to pretend
>   We won't soon be dead,
>   Therefore, live ye merry,
> Or fake it while you can." [10]

The wine, the music, our host's voice, the sight of Death himself working our strings, it all cast me into a blackness of memory and lifted a horrifying veil.

> I gasped for air, suddenly coming to, but I was still blind. In another moment, rough hands ripped away my blindfold.
>
> I was lashed with my wrists behind me to a wooden post, and what I saw was weird. A mass-market bird-bath trickled, below which congregated toadstools colorful gnomes; shelves were piled high with bags of fertilizer and soil; houseplants and potted flowers were everywhere; checkout counters were off to the side – was I in a...Pasadena garden center? How nuts....
>
> Looking up, I saw a skylight open to the night air and stars.
>
> Motion drew my attention. The husky devil-chin guy who had just ripped off my blindfold went to the column to my right and did the same to Assauer. My ex was bound to a post just like me.
>
> I was tugged by a different sound, for under the ripples of moving water was a softer, sadder riffle. Gordon was sitting on some steps, his forehead in his palms. Was he crying...?
>
> Just at that moment, he glanced around like he wanted

to come to me, and tears *were* in his eyes. He jumped up, but the muscle-bound Eros slapped a hand on his shoulder and pinned him in place. "Stay put," he told my boy, which made me flush with anger. Gordon in physical distress crosses the line.

"Let me go!" I commanded. "You've had your twisted fun. Time for this to end, now."

The two goons, who currently stood next to one another by Gordon's side, said nothing. They did sneer however. Suddenly, emerging from the shadows, appeared the three females in charge.

Parthia strode up to me wearing some sort of Dominatrix-slash-Nurse-Diesel bustier in black, garter, fishnet stockings and high heels.

Behind her right-hand side was Eros' girlfriend wearing a teddy and a long, gauzy robe with faux trim.

Lolita, I guess as the madwoman's pet, was attired more modestly in a short-short cheerleader's outfit – and bunny slippers.

The cray-cray cult leader paused in a position where her sight could access both me and my ex.

I repeated myself calmly, "You've had your fun frightening us. Now let us go."

Parthia said, "You two volunteered to work The God's physic upon me. There's no backing out."

"Then do it so we can get out of here!" Assauer blurted.

I wanted to know something more important. "Why is my boyfriend crying? What have you done to him?"

"Nothing." Parthia farted a laugh. "In fact, as he was not a witness to our sacred rite, and thus not a defiler, he's free to go."

"I'll stay," Gordon immediately affirmed.

My heart swelled with pride.

Assauer guffawed. "Touching, but will you two shut up and let the woman get on with it?"

Lolita nodded, and added, "Gordon's in no danger." Her

lingering look took on an edge that made my boy uncomfortable. She popped her gum.

Parthia walked to Assauer, stroking his cheek maniacally as she explained, "The God relayed to me the process you must endure to work my bodily cure. First, the pair of you must be offered a shot at redemption."

"And if we fall short of this 'shot'?" I asked.

The woman came and stood before me with a glazed expression. "Then I pity your youth. Existence on this planet is burden enough if lived short and fancy-free, but woe betide one long and saddled with the Blue One's displeasure." She glanced at Psyche, gesturing to me. "Him first."

The priestess stepped aside with Lolita following.

Psyche undid the tie from her long hair, coming close to my face in order to shake the locks out seductively.

Afterwards, I did a *'phut, phut'* to spit out a stray follicle or two.

Then she opened her robe, thrusting her boobicles out and started smearing them on my chest and tummy. The whole time her hands rubbed me up and down and she had this 'come hinter' stare in her eyes.

It was all I could do not to giggle.

After she ground on me for a few minutes, she started forcing her wet tongue in my mouth. Needless to say, I closed my eyes and thought of Prussia.

Psyche relented, and Parthia ordered something I did not hear.

Next thing I knew, Eros was roughly grabbing my crotch and hate-squinting deep into my eyes. He turned and responded to his boss, "No good."

Parthia, pissed, barked to the men, "Hold him down on the floor."

I was untied, then carried hand and foot to the very center of the space where there was a massive metal grate in the floor.

Eros restrained my hands above my head, while Satan-

Stubble pressed down on my ankles. Oddly, I stared up and realized what a beautiful starry night it was.

"Now it's his turn," Parthia said.

I rotated my head and watched as Psyche went into super sexy mode, sloughing off her outer covering and slinking her way up to Assauer.

I could see my ex swallow hard, a breath hitching his Adam's apple.

He began to moan as the woman did the old bump and grind on him, and then panted excitedly as she Frenched him.

When she pulled away, he looked hungry for more, and Psyche's hand on his privates easily confirmed for Parthia that Assauer was game.

This reaction pleased the cult leader, but only for a moment. She directed Psyche back to me, and horror upon horrors, the nearly naked chick straddled me, forcing me to glance up into her crotchel region. I wanted to scream, but I couldn't....

She squatted, hands landing on my chest to caress me, her ass rubbing my trash.

Again she kissed me, and this time, believe it or don't, I recognized the taste of Assauer's saliva. The absurd nature of the whole thing caused me to peal off sheets of uncontrollable laughter.

"Enough!" screeched Parthia.

Psyche retreated away from me, and the priestess turned to my boy. "You, strip him."

"Me...?"

"Just do it," Assauer said.

Reluctantly, Gordon came to me and kneeled.

"It's okay, honey," I told him.

He slowly unbuttoned my shirt, and Eros ripped it off me – I wasn't wearing any underwear.

Gordon stroked my belly, making his way to my fly, and

undid my jeans. Chin-Hair Guy yanked them down, revealing a tent pole in my briefs. I could not help my reaction to my boy's touch.

"All of it," Parthia commanded, and Gordon tugged my shorts down to my ankles.

I glared at the madwoman. 'Was this what she wanted?' But it was not. Seeing my erection for my boy made her furious.

"You dare to defy The God?!"

Assauer laughed, most unhelpfully.

"Tie him to the post again!"

Parthia's order caused Eros and his biker buddy to lash me back in place next to my ex. In the meantime, Lolita and Psyche had stripped Assauer down to his socks too.

Something I hadn't noticed until right then was a red curtain straight in front of Assauer. I didn't notice till Parthia went up to it and drew it back. Inside the little niche stood a weird statue-column. The upper part was a wild man's bust with elfin ears, a be-ribboned head, curly hair and handsome face.

But starting below his chest, his 'body' was a square plinth, yet square was not the enormous and fully erect dick and balls sticking out from the column where it would proportionately be on a man.

Parthia mumbled something foreign and picked up a small bottle of olive oil. She greased her fingers and did obscene hand-job things to the marble member. And she didn't neglect the stony *orbs* either!

Trancelike, she turned to me and my boy and approached us. "Your lots have been cast. The God forgives me and heals my malady, but has more in store for you."

She walked up to Assauer, latching onto his goodies with her slick hand. He stiffened right away again, in fact got really super large, for him....

"For you," she said, "The God has these words to impart:

> "For as long as you thrive, live in hope:
> I, the Rustic God, will stand by your side

To gird your loins with priapic favor." [11]

She stroked his member like it was the statue's. "There, young man, blessings from The God, and soon you will be endowed with his full bounty."

The priestess left him and came to me. Parthia took ahold of my stuff too, but I naturally stayed limp. She grossed me out.

"And for you, He says:

> "*ut subiceres imperium meum,*
> *condicio fixum est,*
> *tuos omnes misirabiles dieres.*"

She released me and stepped back, filling the Pasadena garden center to the rafters with her shrill cackles.

Glancing at the cold stare of the statue, I felt a chill seep right down to the very marrow of my bones.

Chapter 12: *vivamus, dum licet esse bene*

Waves of clapping snapped me out of my flashback. First thing I saw was the wife of the undertaker-slash-day-trader filming my reverie with her tablet device. My mood was livestreaming on www.NightlywithTre-Princely.com.

I applauded too, watching as the skeleton marionette took a final bow and disappeared beneath the Grim Reaper's death shrouds.

Meanwhile, I nudged Assauer, desperately waiting to confirm my memory was not a twisted fantasy. I hoped he'd remember going through that fucked-up torment as well.

Fresh bottles of 'new' wine were opened and the corpse of Jefferson's vintage removed, thankfully. My first sip of the supermarket-grade California Merlot was like spring water to a desert-wandering man.

Tre silenced the crowd, saying, "I hope you enjoyed my little *dios del los muertos* panto-mime. When I was a kid, I loved those creepy puppets Mr. Rogers fisted on his little kiddie horror show."

No one knew how to react. Was he serious? Yes.

He added solemnly, "Makes ya think."

Others agreed with befuddled "Uh-huh's."

People drank their wine in contentment for a while, staring at, or daring to eat their first course, and then something sounded in the hallway. It was an off-key version of that old free-love tune *Age of Aquarius*. In trooped a bunch of tie-dyed hippies playing kazoos and blowing police whistles while pushing a gleaming medical gurney. The entire top was mounded with stinking sod, with the exposed dirt falling away from the edges.

Tre rose to his slightly wobbly feet. "Salad course! This one is self-serve."

The tie-dyed young people stood back as guests gathered around the hospital bed on wheels. Tre explained, "Chef Cory said we should forage."

No plates, no forks – the former pornstar started picking stuff and munching on it.

Amazed, I inspected the offerings closer. Amidst the grass was a wild assortment of micro greens of every hue. They had been 'planted,' and we were to graze like sheep on them.

One of the women screamed.

"Ha-ha-ha, Aurora," Tre laughed. "You found the salad dressing!" The man reached in and plucked a fat earthworm off the grass. He held it up. "Our chef is a molecular genius. Can take a liquid and turn it into a solid – and vice versa."

He ate a soily clump of baby kale shoots, then bit off the head of the worm. "Oh," he mumbled with a mushy mouth, "it's Thousand Island!"

While people swallowed down their honest reactions and started to pluck, I yanked my ex aside.

"You sure you don't remember anything…?"

"About that night? Um—"

"About being tied up, in a garden center? How that mad Priapus woman made her personal assistant, that nympho-bimbo, grind all up on you?"

"Oh…." Light seemed to dawn a bit in his eyes.

"It was some sick *Psycho-Scheisse*," I added.

Gordon joined us with a nightcrawler dangling from his mouth. "What's up?"

"Kohl is remembering what went on last Sunday night."

"How about you?" I asked my boy.

He shrugged and chewed.

"How you were forced to strip me while I was held down on the floor?!"

"Oh." Now light began to shine in his eyes too.

"Chef Cory!" Tre-Princely called out.

We turned to see the leprechaun-looking cook return. All of a sudden, the shape of the 'salad course' seemed clear to me; it was mounded like a freshly covered grave.

Our host continued talking with a wink and a nod in his tone. "It's great, Chef, but don't you think it's a little plain? Shouldn't this be the bed of something fabulous served on top…? You chefs are always laying out beds of this and that."

"Funny you should ask, Mr. Knight." The chef strode up to the head position of the grave and reached down.

Freakily, he pulled open two doors covered with sod and micro greens. A platter slowly rose from the hidden depths.

Everyone drew near to have a look. The serving plate appeared to be full of…deviled eggs…?

"Chihuahuan eggs *diablo*." His Irish pride shown through his quaking accent. "The buried treasure of some long-lost hiker. I believe they're stuffed with cactus candy, ancho chili, and mixed with a goose fat aioli."

"Yum," his former-pornstar boss said while taking one. "Just like Mother never used to make."

Assauer ponied up to try one, but my boy sensed I was troubled and led me back to the table.

We sat.

"Are you remembering more, Gordon?"

"Well, what you said sounds real familiar."

"I'm not…." I stumbled in my thoughts.

"Not what?"

"I'm not so sure I want to remember the whole night."

"Aww." He moved his hand under the table and stroked my thigh, high up. His action should have caused a reaction, but….

I noticed that surly friend of Tre's, that Ermanno guy, sitting at the head table and swirling his cocktail glass. He glared at us, clearly suspicious.

"Nevermind." I grabbed and held my boy's hand underneath the table. "We'll get through this."

Our host drifted back to his seat with a burp, once the novelty of the salad course faded among his guests and live-streamers. Ignoring the glass of wine there, Tre drained his bottle of gin to the dregs, letting it drip morosely into his highball tumbler. "Get me another one!"

"Darling—" Prospera started.

"I'm thirsty, Lucky Charm." He signaled one of the hippie boys wheeling out the deceased salad. "Sapphire, boy. Bring me one."

"Yes, sir."

"Good lad." He wiped his mouth on his increasingly dirty scarf, and muttered under his breath, "Gin is my first missus." Tre-Princely settled in again, shifting his attention onto a guest seated at the table opposite ours. "Say, Dana, I'm glad you and Cynthia could make it."

"Wouldn't miss it for the world," the guest's wife said, training her phone on Dana's nose.

"Yes, Tre," he added.

"How was that auction you attended?"

"Oh, the blowout of that guy's estate?"

"Indeed."

"It was good. Picked up a '76 Aston Martin. Needs a whole new electrical system – they always do. Don't ever trust a Limey to rewire your home." He laughed.

"Who is this?" Rabbit's Foot inquired. "Someone we knew had to sell out?"

"Yes, baby doll. It's the stalled economy."

"It's a typical riches to rags story," said Dana. "But don't worry – they're on the Gop welfare program, and'll receive a taxpayer get-out-of-debt-free card. That's because they're 'the right sort of people,' meaning 'rich' no matter how negative their bank balance."

Prospera chuckled. "Oh, *that* kind of welfare! Lord knows Mr. Orange Sherbet financed his six bankruptcies on the backs of honest taxpayers to fob off his debts. Naturally, 'honest taxpayer' never included him."

"Yeah," Neil added. "The only tax that Yank ponies up is sales tax, and even that he deducts as a 'business expense.'"

"*I* saw in the papers," prattled Cynthia, "the guy who had to sell out claimed to have too many investors. The Feds are sniffing all around his assets to see how many of them they can grab."

"Yes, well…" Tre felt the convo was wandering too far away from him. "My old high school teacher warned us about being adrift in life. He'd say 'Malcolm, you'd do best to remember that old Greek Ulysses guy, and don't float around so much!' Such profound words, and I took 'em to heart."

He seemed to pause for applause, but none came so he went on undaunted.

"One thing I've used over the years to stay on track is Astrology. Prospera will tell you. I had Nancy Reagan's woman once tell me my Venus was ascendant up Jupiter's…arc, or some such. I even had one write down my exact date of death—"

"Tre, don't." There had been real urgency in Prospera's voice, and her former pornstar husband took it as an affront.

Fortunately, the tie-dyed minion returned at that moment with two fresh bottles of gin.

"Ah, my boy! Come here." Tre fished in his robe pocket, pulled out a donut-sized roll and skinned a hundred-dollar bill off the top. He pushed it into the smiling teenager's chest.

"Thank you, sir."

"No, thank you." He gripped his bottles by the neck in both hands and recited another 'poem.'

> "Whosoever plays this life in the open,
> gets the gift of a homerun from the bullpen!"

He suddenly remembered me.

"Our new friend, Kohl here, is a poet too. Why don't you recite something?"

All eyes inched my way, including the envious guy who now had reason to fear I *was* after Tre's attention.

I drained my wine. "Truth is, I'm too sober right now. Maybe later."

Tre-Princely Knight chuckled a bit. "I'll hold you to that. I never forget anything; remember that."

Just as he twisted the cap open on a fresh bottle, Tre got a funny expression on his face. "Um, you folks talk – honey? Where is the…? You know, *baño de maison?*"

Mrs. Schwartzbaum stood and led her man off to find the closest museum toilet.

Thirty seconds after they were entirely out of sight, we all released a collective sigh of relief. Every personal device got set down, and the conversation started to flow naturally.

Gavin the mortician patted his lean belly. "Up to his usual snuff."

"Are you enjoyin' the fare?" Neil Campbell asked me.

"Well, to be truthful – I couldn't possibly eat another bite."

"Ain't that the truth," Dana said seriously, as if I'd uttered something profound.

"Actually," I said, "I'm not sure what to make of the last course. I mean the whole concept: a mound, shaped like a grave, on a gurney – and salad with hippies?"

"Go with it, or get out," barked Ermanno with a scowl.

Napoleon, kind-heart, split the explanation between me and the sourpuss blowhard. "Who ain't a slave? The only way we come back as equals is through the great equalizer."

"Ah." I nodded at his reasoning of the artistic conceit, but realized since I can't follow the logic of these 'sane men,' I better keep my crazy mouth shut, lol.

"Let's have more wine," Dana called to the waiters, and then swelled up sadly. "Celebrate while you can. Afterall, what's a day? You get swept up into one, spun this way and that, and then, before you even know it, it's night again. Ain't that right, Sal? You know what I mean."[12]

This man was sitting next to Gavin's wife, Aurora, and he nodded. "I do. That's the problem with the young. They think they can cheat time, but they can't. This life will be done before they know it. To put a nail in the coffin of the truth of it, I had to go to another funeral just today."

"Oh, yeah," Cynthia asked. "Who?"

"Jack Daria, former governor of California."

"Oh, I know," said Coruptti, "I wanted his corpse...um, his 'trade,' shall we say. But for the sake of my own reputation, I couldn't underbid the lowest estimate. So how was my competition's 'Costco' wake?"

"Sad, and not because the funeral was for an eighty-nine-year-old, but because he's just another of the real generation of GOPs fading into memory. What passes for a Conservative today is actually a Retrogressive – not keep what we have for ourselves, but positively take from those who have nothing to begin with."

"Oh, don't I know it," agreed Aurora. "Today's toadies must make the old vanguard sick. No wonder they're dying off so quickly!"

"Used to be the satire you'd see on TV," Dana said, "seemed outrageous, and then they started using the so-called politicians' actual words to make audiences laugh, like that quitter Sandra Pale-Heart's 'I can see Russia from my trailer!'"

We all laughed, and then he added with a sober shake of his graying head, "Yes, sadly, yesterday's parodies have become today's realities. And oh, my God, that woman's so-called foreign policy *experience* can be summed up in one little ditty. 'I see Moscow, I see Gdansk; I see Putin's underpansk.' And now we're supposed to believe *that* was too scary for the American voting public, but Mr. Indebted-Up-To-His-Orange Glo in Russian Mob money isn't?! No one believes that, not even the few members of the Coalition of the Coerced who actually held their nose and wasted a vote for that man to take a Dump on our country and have the Gop leader of the Senate wipe the So-Called's backside with the Constitution." Dana indulged in a drink and then muttered with sour slowness, "We won the Cold War, my ass.... History will be the judge."

Gavin ventured agreement. "Yeah, things have changed, and they don't make Gops like they used to. Never mind how Old Governor Daria was an diet-pill junkie – at least all his bribes from the lobbyists were sorta on the books! He never took strings-attached 'loans,' especially not from the Kremlin, for God's sake."

"From what I've heard," Neil added slickly, "the hoary ole devil died raunchy right up to the end. Liked his boys hotblooded for sure, and remained hard as a horn, as we say Dow'Undda." [13]

All the middle-aged men in the room – including Napoleon – bobbed chins in amazement, hoping for the same Viagra-fueled destiny in old age.

"Yeah, he was a quote-un-quote 'good man.' So what," said Cynthia, "if Governor Daria was a notorious lush."

"Yes," agreed Gavin. "So what if he screamed at his beard-wife in public...?"

"So what," added Sal, "if he beat his staff where it wouldn't show?"

"Indeed." Aurora nodded. "So what if he proposed anti-gay amendments regularly – lots of them...?"

"That's right," trumped Napoleon. "So what if he drowned kittens and kicked puppies at press conferences...?"

Ermanno grudgingly confessed the moral of the story. "He was still a more honorable man than what passes for a Grand Old Partisan these days."

A nostalgic "Amen" went around the chamber.

Sal stood and offered a toast. "To the mean old S.O.B. bastard. To your health, Jack! They don't make 'em like you anymore."

We all drank to the dead man's irascibility.

After we sat, the undertaker looked pensive. "Still, the men of his time would never put up with the tax-payer-funded shenanigans going on in today's world. People now had to pay a million dollars a day, for Secret Service details, just so the Orange One's wife didn't have to sleep in the same bed with him. Him in D.C.; her in New York, and all on public welfare."

"I heard," Cynthia intoned confidentially, "the excuse of her son finishing out his school term in New York was total bullshit. The real reason she stayed was to apply public influence while her lawyers worked behind the scene."

Rabbit's Foot frowned. "Behind the scenes to do what?"

"Up the amount in her pre-nup! She never agreed to be Putin's fake-ass First Lady, so demanded the 'salary' she earns putting up with the Orange Glo's humiliation be raised to match her elevated actor's position. It's all the Kremlin's money anyway, so who cares."

"It ain't all Russian money," Nicholas corrected. "The Dumpster himself has made tens of millions billing the taxpayer for everything from three-hundred-million doses of a fake drug – made by a foreign company he just happens to own a stake in – to new carpet at Mara Lago because the Chinese dictator is stopping by for lunch. It's a slap in the face to working Americans who actually still pay taxes here, unlike the rich."

"Yeah," Dana added, "and real men like Governor Daria would never prolong recessions, as congressional Gops always do now, just to profit from them politically."

"And profit literally too," Nicholas interjected, leaning forward with his hands together on the table. "They've been exposed using classified information to do insider trading of stocks and other investments for their personal hedge funds."

"Recessions is all the foreigners' fault anyway." Ermanno's glance landed squarely on me. "There are too many of them in this country already. I echo the President's awe-inspiring words: 'Sorry. We're all filled up.' That's why we need a fifty-foot-high border wall. And I'll go farther and say build two of the goddamned things! Then we'll see the good times return."

"Speaking of *I-lie-gulls*," my ex chimed in, "anyone ever seen the 'papers-please' on the current Mrs. Dump the Third? Seems she overstayed her tourist visa. From what I heard, overstayed it till her shopping for a rich codger was succes—"

"He's joking," I said, slapping across Gordon's chest to punch Assauer.

"Yeah," my boyfriend added. "Totally joking."

"Well, anyway," Dana clipped on at a merry pace, "we need more bootstrapping, more hope-filled, can-do spunk, but the so-called man who was shoe-horned into the White House by foreign leverage knows nothing about that. He is angry, deeply insecure and reactionary. He can't tell the difference from being a schoolyard bully to a staid and confident leader on the world stage. He lashes out in all directions with gloom and doom, and that's the very opposite of optimistic. It's downright Un-American, is what it is."

"It's true," Gavin affirmed. "But, what can you expect. He's a millionaire today because his indulgent daddy was a multi-millionaire who didn't really teach him much about how to be a proper slumlord like himself. Jesus, no wonder this unloved son of a bastard had to make do with Manhattan office dumps and New Jersey gambling dives. Sad."

"Speaking of teaching," said Sal, "the public schools are going to pot. Hurray we got the private school tax-giveaway-vouchers, thanks to the Gops syphoning off public funds for private use, cuz now we've hired a young guy to live in the house and teach our teen boy."

I drank some wine and moodily thought to myself, 'Yeah, *teach* him more than the three R's. I would know.'

"But," Gavin asked, "you think he's only a paltry millionaire? Hell, the way people are price gouging today, even my podiatrist is a multi-millionaire. The Cheeto Duché claims he's a billion—"

"Oh, please!" Dana chuckled, after taking a hurried sip of wine. "If that man finally paid each of his debts, parking tickets, and back taxes – liquidating all his red-ink holdings to do it – I doubt the repo man would reckon him worth much above a low, low, low seven-figure mark."

"Ha," exclaimed Aurora, "that was *before* he got ahold of the government. Who knows how much money he'll make out of 'public service.' I say, make sure to check his pockets for White House silverware before they haul him away to Leavenworth."

Our laughs were short-lived, because we heard Tre coming back to us whistling that antique pop tune – *All Star,* by Smash Mouth – and drying his hands on his aviator scarf. Prospera Texas-Ivy followed close behind with a bit of embarrassment showing.

"Sorry, folks!" our host announced, heading for his seat. "Been blocked up lately; my docs are stumped. But things are movin' now!"

The missuses picked up their devices again. The show was back on.

"Tre," his wife said, "I bet they're thinking *too much information* right now."

"Pee-shawl! As if I don't get occasional rolls of thunder from your belly at night in bed, darling. None of us come to this life with mortar and concrete blocks down there. Things gotta shake, rattle and roll. Nothing natural should make us ashamed." He took a seat, shakily pouring himself another. "Holding it in ain't good. It's like those poor schlubs, I've always thought, slamming themselves in the closet. So my dear friends, you have permission to fart freely here. Let it rip, because if you don't, the sick vapors go straight to the head. And believe me, I've known plenty a blowhard who died, suffocated by breathing his own fumes instead of airing out his noggin."

"More wine, everybody?" Mrs. Schwartzbaum busied herself and changed the subject at the same time.

Tre-Princely drank deeply and then turned his smile on Napoleon. "So, self-motivational guru, what moot points have you been hammering home in your lectures these days?"[14]

"Oh, the usual things, Tre. Stay focused; commit to a plan of action no matter the number of folks talking reason to you; love yourself as you your neighbor – the usual."

"Oh, wow!" our host admired. "You could work in Washington!"

General laughter circulated the room.

Tre continued, "Lots of smart people in the capital, but unfortunately, the smartest are not. Take me for instance. These rich guys in Torrance wanted to put me up as their Gop congressional candidate, but I told 'em, after a hard life of getting fucked on camera for a living, I don't want to get screwed behind closed doors by The Party. I said they should get Sonny Bono, because he was used to that sort of thing with Cher, you know. They said thanks and called him."

"Oh, wow, I didn't know that," Neil said, and his eye-roll made my ex bust up.

Ermanno placed an 'I told you so' curl on his lips and raised his eyebrow in our host's direction. Tre-Princely caught it and shifted on his seat slightly.

"I'm smarter than most men," our host said, "and I can prove it. I may not be a certified intellectual, but I've got quite a library – all on DVD. I've got every type of show, and I know about being trapped and so forth. Like that poor Cyclops fellow who had Jason do some unnecessary cataract surgery on him and lost his sight because of it. It could happen to any one of us."

When none of us knew how to react, Tre added "Makes ya think," and we could all nod.

A lady in a frilly Mexican dancing dress entered playing an accordion. Behind her, little girls made up like bullfighters – right down to painted moustaches – pushed in a giant saguaro cactus with far too many arms. At the end of each limb was a plate holding some dark, glossy substance on plates.

"Ah!" Tre exclaimed.

The accordion lady stopped playing, referencing a notecard in her hand, and read: "Chef Cory proudly presents agave blossoms…in a dark Belgium chocolate *mole* sauce…over a bed of cactus paddle croquettes. Enjoy… he says." She could barely hide her own revulsion.

The little girls distributed the dishes, and the crew rolled out the prop cactus with more accordion music. This 'happening' started to remind me of some absurdist opera; in and out with stage props and improbable characters all night long.

I glanced at Gordon to see if he'd try this new food delight. He stuck his finger in the sauce and tasted it with a sour face.

Drunk now, Tre gulped down the food and mumbled something.

"What's that, darling?"

"I said, *ex omnibus in unum, nec hoc nec illud.*"

Napoleon translated for us, apparently recognizing the quote. "Neither this nor that, but all one and the same."

"Yes," our host said, holding his tumbler of gin to the light. "Water to clean our bodies, but only firewater to bathe our core. The innards – that's where our darkest humors lie."

He woke from his reverie suddenly, smiling and looking for his wife. "You men, won't any of you take my Prospera for a turn on the dance floor? There's no one better equipped to lead a hoe-down, I can assure ya."

"Oh, you," his wife chuckled.

Tre-Princely pushed on the table a bit, rattling dishes as he stood wobbling. "All right, old stick in the mud. If you won't, I will. I studied ballet as a boy, or *bal-ey*, as my mush-mouth Limey dance mistress slurred it. Took me a while to realize I wasn't studying belly dancing…but who could tell with her accent. Shall I dance for everybody?!"

Prospera had quietly gone behind him and placed a hand on his shoulder. "Maybe later, dear. They're still trying to eat."

He surveyed the room, and slowly deflated into his chair again like a balloon.

"Sometimes I wonder if…. Oh, never mind, because in these uncertain times," Tre mused darkly, "wealth is the only safeguard a man can have. I for one worked hard for it – never mind my old man telling me I'd never amount to beans and disowning me when he found out what I was doing in Hollywood – cuz now, you know, I'm so rich, I have my head of security shelling peas."

That was a real head-scratcher.

Nicholas was brave. "What do you mean, Tre?"

Our host laughed. "I mean I'm so rich and powerful no one would dare break and enter me and mine, so I send my security chief to the kitchen where he can be put to some sort of useful work, like shelling peas or stringing green beans."

After a round of laughter and some handclapping for Tre, we all sat in silence for several minutes, trying to digest the rhetoric and sour-smelling agave blossoms.

Suddenly, a clamor of whoops and hollers arose from the corridor. An old man and a little boy in circus silks came running in carrying a short ladder.

Tre-Princely's face lit up like the birthday boy at a kids' party.

Now I realized the child was not wearing dark makeup on his arms and face, but was covered in wolfman fur.

"Welcome, Señor Aceves and grandson." Tre quickly explained to the rest of us, "Acrobats from Mexico, famous for the werewolf gene."

And then it hit me. I did hear something about one family in Mexico with a genetic predisposition to having hair grow on all parts of their bodies. Nevertheless, the boy was attractive and bright-eyed as he leaped onto his grandfather's back. They provided their own musical accompaniment in the form of more grunts and shouts.

Tre applauded loudly.

The boy sprung into an upside-down handstand, head to head with the older man, each using their fingers to steady one another.

More hoots and hollers; more jolly clapping from Tre.

We guests were more unimpressed than our host. To us it appeared like more of that Circum Solum stuff, and everybody hates a mime, as some wise someone once observed, lol.

Tre-Princely picked up on the vibe, remarking rancorously, "The *Arts* can't get no respect these days." He lifted his glass with an acid chuckle. "You know, I once hired that Metropolitan Opera Company to do Benny-Hill-style goosing skits and 'sock-it-to-me' cream pies in their lemon-pusses for the night. But they did it though, cuz money speaks louder than honor, that's for damn sure." He gazed through the crystalline gin held up towards the ceiling light. And then, lost in joyful memory of the Met divas' misuse, said, "To crown it all off, I had them sing the final chorus of *Porgy and Bess* – in Spanish! I can still hear them now." Tre started a wistful, but choppy, singing.

"O, Dios Mios,
¡VámAH-ahahaha-nos!"

He drank down his clear liquor, then grunting through the throat-burn said, "Talk about cultural appropriation!"

Once more, we, his guests, were unsure if the former pornstar were serious or not. In any event, a round of "Bravo!" and applause went 'round to greet the man's enigmatic grin. [15]

As for the floorshow, the hairy boy did a somersault and landed on the floor gracefully. The ladder was picked up, and the child started to climb it at the same time. Señor Aceves gradually slid it up along his chest into the air.

Next, the boy did a somersault and landed on the floor gracefully. The ladder was picked up, and the child started to climb it at the same time. Señor Aceves gradually slid it up along his chest into the air.

We were all holding our breath, wondering what would happen next.

The old man kept lifting as the boy got to the very top. Eventually, the grandfather kicked his head back and placed the bottom rung on his chin.

Slowly – oh, so slowly – he moved his hands out to the side, while the boy did the same.

Then, just as the child was in mid-celebratory *whoop*, the ladder began to fall forward. The old man tried to grab it, but the kid was flung right onto Tre's fat belly. *Thump!*

After a moment of shocked silence, not knowing if this was all part of the 'performance,' his wife rushed over with a fresh bottle of gin. "Speak to me, sweetheart...."

I saw her fanning his face, saw the boy bound up unharmed, saw other guests pour our host a stiff one, but there was something in the voice of Prospera – the genuine shimmer of concern – that slipped me out of the moment.

I jolted awake back in the garden center, naked, but me and Assauer had been moved to a greenhouse.

Above us arched the rustling plastic of hot-house roofing, and our hands and feet were bound next to strawberry plants.

The door opened. In strode Parthia, with Psyche and Lolita behind her. A sheepish Gordon trailed in last.

The cult leader's PA held some sort of drinking bowl. Parthia told me and my ex, "Your first trial is here, young men, to test the strength of The God's wishes upon you." She turned to her secretary. "Administer the *satyrion*, Ms. Psyche."

She moved and pressed the chalice to my ex's lips, making him swallow about a third of it.

"What's in that cup?!" I demanded to know.

Parthia came close, picking a red strawberry and smearing it on my clenched lips. "A concoction of ground Viagra, the root of an endangered wild orchid, and Cialis – a goodlier provocative to love does not exist. And now, seeing as I am cured, we'll begin your trials by female; one of you has been sanctified, one of you has been bound; can you guess which is which?"

Her leaden chortle soured the air, and Psyche pressed the cup to my lips. I had no choice but to choke back the bitter fluid, yet the girl still left some in the bowl.

By the time my eyes stopped watering and my heavy breathing slowed, I glanced over to see Assauer look like a man possessed. This pleased the horny Psyche, who immediately gave his stick a handle and worked it up into a powerful pose.

She untied his hands, and to my surprise, he pulled her into appalling kissing, undoing her teddy at the same time.

Soon she mounted him, riding and bucking like a cowboy heading out on the range. Assauer was beside himself with unnatural lust, and I pitied the poor bastard.

My inspection of the disgusting display drew Psyche's conniving attention, for she slid off of my ex like a snake in the grass and slithered over to me.

Her sweaty, insistent palms were all over me, stroking this and that, gripping and releasing here and there, but I had no reaction of a physical kind. My privates, on public display as they were, felt as chilled as fast food patties before cooking.

The depraved secretary gave up when Assauer called out, "Come back, baby. *I* got something for you."

Psyche grabbed the bowl and lay on her back at my ex's feet. He mounted her for missionary work.

Parthia and her demented assistant laughed at my discomfort, and even Gordon began to chuckle too – but more at the possessed nature of Assauer's animal grunts.

I watched in horror as Lolita popped her nasty gum and

walked up to my boy, forcing an ugly tongue-kiss onto him.

When she started groping him, I shouted, "Oh, evil priest-ess. Kill us now, for the punishment is far worse than the crime!"

At that precise moment, Assauer's choked-up moans let everyone know he was ready to burst. Psyche backed off of him, and held the love-potion bowl for him to ejaculate into.

After he was spent, and falling backwards with a notice-ably enlarged schlong slowly growing flaccid, Psyche got up – careful not to spill the contents of the cup – and came to me.

"What are you going to do with that?!" I asked, getting lightheaded as I resisted against my restraints.

"This," she said and drizzled it up and down my chest and belly. Female cackles in three different pitches erupted all at once, pinging my poor ears from every corner of the greenhouse. Gradually, I let my breath go, and passed out with the maniacal acolyte still rubbing the mess all over my clammy skin.

Chapter 13: Escapism

"My dear friends, feel free to simply be!"

Tre-Princely was all right and had dismissed the Aceves family acrobats with thanks and hundred-dollar bills. The wolf boy had smiled at him warmly and shook his hand…um, paw, lol.

Now our host sat back at his old place, devouring Chef O'Shay's disgusting agave blossoms in Godiva sauce.

Napoleon, who had practically licked his dish clean, asked, "You don't like it?"

"I'm…I'm already stuffed to the grills." I smiled to show him my teeth, even though they were not gold or diamond studded.

"Then, do you mind…?"

"Nooo." I gave over my portion and watched him scrape the brown goo between himself and Neil.

The motivational speaker said under his breath, "It may not taste good, but it's the latest food trend, so you know it has to be in good taste."

"No matter what," I laughed.

"Yep," Neil chimed.

"I'm lucky he cooks for me," Tre suddenly announced. "Chef Cory's got a huge, A-list celebrity waiting queue. He's the current real-deal Mex-*gastronomique* hash slinger in L.A." Our host took a bite, barely hiding the grimace as the flavor assaulted his palate. "He studied under an Asian master of Oaxaca cuisine, for *six months!*" The man swallowed audibly. "And that was in La Joya, so you know it's authentic."

We, I mean they, ate on in silence for a few moments, but Tre-Princely Knight – apparently like Nature itself – adored a vacuum cleaner and spoke up about the recent presentation.

"It must be a hard profession to be a performer-*artiest*, but then again, I'd know all about that. Porn is still in business, but the circus is officially dead in this country, and worse yet, replaced by geeky twinks in blue body paint. I ask you, is *that* art? Is that 'experience' meant to move the mind and heart? That escapism? I don't think so. No, for my taste give me Larry, Curly and Moe slapstick, or give me '*You're fired!*' types of scripted reality TV shows. Now those are food for thought."

No one seemed to agree or disagree.

"Tell me, Napoleon," our host went on with more earnest intent. "Who would you say has the harder calling: a great trial lawyer, or a pop songwriter?"

Trueblood was confounded, the first time I'd seen the self-help guru look dazed.

"You mean," he asked for clarification, "between, say, Clarence Darrow and…Stephen Foster…?"

"Well, I don't know who those two are, but I mean put Gloria Allred up against Burt Bacharach; Justin Timberland against that so-called Attorney General Barr; or – oh, oh, oh – that O.J. lawyer, versus Paula Abdul. Who's got it rougher?"

"I'm not sure I—"

"To me it's pretty easy. The pop-star songwriter has the harder job because they have to convince us the unnatural – mushy lyrics – are real. A good shyster legal-eagle just has to convince people the unreal is halfway plausible, and boom, they're famous, or on their way to a political career – even without a catchy tune to back 'em up."

Actually, maybe it was the wine, or the long exposure to Tre over the course of the day, but I partially saw the logic in that.

He noticed me nodding. "And you, Kohl? You're a poet like me." He paused and took a swill of straight gin. "I still haven't forgotten you owe us a bit of verse."

Tre was right. "Okay," I said. "But in my native German:

> *Das Leben gehört*
>   *Den Lebenden an,*
> *Und wer lebt muss auf*
>   *Wechsel gefasst sein."*

I glanced to Assauer, who smiled, recognizing it.

I explained, picking up my glass as a toast, "It's Goethe, and means in English:

> "Life to the living,
>   For we to it belong,
> And while we breath draw,
>   Change is our only song."

Applause came up – all except for Ermanno, who glowered at my ex with even more of his brooding Sicilian contempt. I guess Assauer showed too much enthusiasm for my ditty.

"Bravo, Kohl," cried Tre. "You are better than a poet. You are a *writer*."

"I was quoting—"

"It don't matter! Hell, you could be channeling some two-thousand-year-old piece of pulp fiction, but what matters is if it connects with people or not. And your stuff does. Like I said, escapism is all the rage today – comic book zombies, S&M vamps, toothy aliens – as long as they're hella unbelievable and full of teenage angst, they'll be a hit with folks feeling too stressed and unhappy about the mess of a society they were too busy escaping to go out and vote for sanity and decency." He suddenly turned sad. "Nobody wants what's real anymore, that's why the old crap is best, if you ask me, like my real Jeffersonian wine. There's been such a slide in the arts, and all done in the name of the mighty buck. Reminds me of a poem of mine:

> "Two chickens in the pot –
>   A promise way-long unwrought –
> But instead, look at what we've got,
>   A diet of talking-points & junk food for thought."

He paused for ovation, and somehow, I found myself leading the rest, smiling straight into the live-stream cameras.

"Thank you, thank you, my friends," he said, touched. "I've been down recently, and your good efforts warm me. But like I started to say, after pop-song-writers-singers, the next hardest job is doctor cuz he must look at a man's true heart, then hedge fund manager-slash-pyramid-builders, because just like a cardiologist, they have to assess the true heart of wealth." He glanced at Gavin Coruptti. "No offence."

The newly-minted mortician gave his best, professional-grade nod. "None taken. I'm more fulfilled building houses of death than houses of cards anyway." He crossed himself with a question mark.

Tre-Princely continued, unfazed. "But after them, the poor tollbooth operator has it about the worst."

None of us knew what he meant.

"Think about it. All day long with the coins, but still they have to know – like the doc and banker – when a flash of silver is enrobing a core of base-metal worthlessness."

Ah. That sort of made sense....

"But as I was saying," our host exclaimed, "the *very* hardest job of all is being a writer. They have to spot 'rotten at the core' people and situations and call them out like the others, but God forbid they can't do it in a way that makes people roll in the aisles with laughter, cuz if they are too serious, or fail to entertain while exposing the truth, then they are crucified by the everybody's-a-critic mentality, or worse yet, pushed over a cliff like some closeted Cat-on-a-Hot-Tin-Roof Tennessee Williams character. They either succeed or have to die with their art."

The mood had grown a little dark and my wine seemed to sour. I guess no one feels comfortable with the idea of puffing up authors' egos....

As if reading the vibe of the room, Prospera Texas-Ivy jutted her chin at her ex-pornstar husband.

The man clapped his hands pertly several times.

A moment later, a dozen attendants appeared from the flanks of the peristyle behind him. Young women and men – some with full beards – were dressed like Paris Hilton wannabes with short skirts and oversized sunglasses. Each 'girl' skipped in swinging a large blue Tiffany & Co. shopping bag.

"Red-carpet takeaways!" Tre cried giddily. And while each shiftless-heiress- impersonator placed a bag on the table before a guest, he continued collectively, "Don't mind the sacks, people. They're just leftovers from last B'uy and Buy'not Mitzvah season. I swear none of Tiffy's mass-market junk is inside. You'll find only the good stuff in your grab-bags."

Like greedy kids on Christmas morning, there followed the sounds of rustling paper as we dug in, deep.

Me, Gordon and Assauer compared identical Patek Philippe wristwatches, and vials of Himalayan jatamansi cologne. And there were many more pawnable things in the bag too.

The women had strings of natural pearls – fat as garbanzo beans and white as Ivory Soap – Hermès mouse pads, and something that looked like diamond-encrusted pill bottles.

When I remembered my manners, and looked up to thank Tre-Princely, he had a weird expression on his face.

He held up his hand to stop me. "I'm pleased with all my guests' sicko-fancy. It's the way it should be – toss a dog a chunk of red liver and he'll love you as long as you have more. As they used to say, money always keeps the best society."

"But still," growled Ermanno, "you are too generous, Tre, to strangers and hangers-on like these foreigners." He was a drunk, a mean one.

"So what, Ermie?" Tre-Princely retorted. "You know – I know, everybody knows – the current so-called First Lady is a wetback illegal just as much as my leaf-blower. Everybody knows she escaped from a sightseeing tour bus, so if she's cut some slack, then everybody deserves the same – Golden Rule, my friend."

"Sure, no one's shouting 'Lock her up,' Tre. But look at that intellectual, goon-faced Kraut over there." He pointed past me to Assauer. "He's probably laughing up his superior Euro sauerbraten panties at you."

"Heeeyyy..." Assauer stammered.

"I'm sorry, Tre, but goddamn it, I'm mad, and you of all people know I'm slow to anger, but look at 'em! Lord knows it's easier to make a cartridge loader for an AK-47 out of a sow's ear than get invited to one of your events, and yet there they sit like judges at Nuremberg, long noses and all." His confounded ire turned on Napoleon. "It's bad enough you let that leech of a motivational sham and his Aussie banana-bender use your good name—"

Here, my ex could not keep his damn mouth shut. "Hey, way to play the ugly American card, *Ermie*. We've never seen that one before." He chuckled out loud.

"You laugh...? You great gorbellied blockhead. And that's just a smart way of sayin' you're full of shit. What?! Tre's hospitality ain't good enough for your overseas taste? Don't sit there gaping at me like a nanny goat playing king of the hill on a pile of garbage. You think you're hot shit: young, pretty, on top of life, huh? Well, I got news for you – it won't last. Someday soon you'll have to stop being a foreign parasite on our welfare system, get a job and actually work. Then we'll see what you're made of. All I know is I've never been hauled in court by lawyers shouting 'pay up,' but I bet you have, you scoundrel, or worse! You $100-a-night mintboy hustler, you—"

"Hey," asserted my ex, "I charge more than—"

Gordon elbowed him to silence.

I tried my hand at peacemaking. "Well now, we're all having a good time here. We're really appreciative."

I appealed with my words for Tre-Princely to rein in his crony, but our host simply smiled and folded his arms in enjoyment. It reminded me of his attitude in the sauna, liking to see others compete for his attention.

"*Appreciative*," mocked Ermanno. "Now the other *bosch* coughs up a three-dollar word to impress us. You're like a fella pickin' fleas off another guy's coat, all the time not seeing the ticks crawling over your own flesh."

At this, Gordon lost it, totally. He laughed himself to tears, because I could tell he'd been holding it in for a long time.

"And you," the hater snapped at my boy, "chucklehead – jailbait – you even legal to transport across state lines? Well, nevermind. I got your number, sonny boy. You think you can get into anyone's pants with your hot-shit act. Well, I got a riddle for ya.

> "I come long,
> I come wide
> And I come
> to adjust
> your attitude.

"Solve me, punk. Know what I am?!" He gripped himself.

Gordon stopped laughing.

"Yeah, thought so. You just wait one day and see if I don't come up behind you in some dark alley – then you'll know who's your better, let me tell ya."

"Ermanno, please," Dana pleaded.

My blood starting boiling. Did this ass-swipe just dare to sexually threaten my boyfriend, in front of me...?!

"Yeah..." Aurora tried peacemaking too. "Let's calm down."

My fists clenched on the tabletop, and Gordon saw because he laid his palm over one, drawing me out of my anger a little bit.

"Listen—" I started.

"When you get a job, then you come back to me and talk as my equal, cuz I care and stuff the mouths of twenty family members, and a god-damned dog. So, till you can say the same, just know I wouldn't trade my sterling-plated reputation for a million. Shit, I don't even have a credit card! You, on the other hand—"

"All right, Ermie," Tre said at last. "You've made your point, and quite sharply too." The former adult film bottom had been prodded into action by Mrs. Schwartzbaum and her all-seeing iPad camera lens. "We're friends here. Let's act it, okay?"

The nasty-heart grunted and reached for his cocktail.

"And," our host continued, "you were once a hot-blood like young Gordon here. Don't pretend otherwise." The man laughed, and I suddenly wondered if this straight-guy Ermanno had his own VHS catalogue of getting dicked for cash. Could this explain his paranoia for thinking others were looking down on him all the time? Whatever. He was a surly loser for sure.

"Think of modern politics, and give it up now, Ermanno. Forgive these guys because in a situation like this, it's the defeated who win the day after the dust settles. There's only sham victory in being victorious over the unarmed. Think of the Brits' disgrace shooting thousands of spear-wielding Zulus. History always shames the bully, always – just remember that." [16]

Again, I wondered if my so-called sanity was slipping, for Tre was making more sense by the hour.

"Anyway..." our host clapped his hands with brief animation. "On with the show. What's next?!"

Spurred by that prompt, more eerie music sounded, this time on pan-pipes. Female dancers spread out their gauzy robes, shuffling in like a cocoon around something hidden.

It turned out to be a gorgeous man of a ballet dancer, completely naked, but also completely covered in black body paint. On top of this, bones – in fact, every bone of his figure – had been painted in stunning white detail. He was also handsomely endowed with one 'extra bone,' highlighted with a lickable candy stripe from tip to base.

A living representation of the silver marionette, the girls did a dance of seduction. Each maiden in turn tried to lure the dancer with her femininity and cunning, but each time he refused. One by one, as they failed, they exited in dejection until the skeleton was alone to perform his lonely pantomime.

While the sad music continued, he eventually 'died' by himself, crumpled on the floor like a pile of neglected ashes.

Tre-Princely Knight jumped to his feet, clapping loudly, and we all rose in agreement, applauding heartily. This had been macabre but beautiful.

The maids returned, 'swept up' the bones in the cocoon of their gowns and exited again while we were still clapping.

Suddenly, I noticed Mrs. Schwartzbaum had her arms folded over her chest and was glaring at Tre with a 'really?' sourpuss.

He teased her. "Come on, sweetie – my Lucky Charm – rub some of that luck on Tyler. He deserves the props."

"Who's Tyler?" I whispered to Gordon, his shrug telling me he didn't know either.

She slapped her hands together in mocking slowness. "Talk" *clap* "about" *clap* "sycophants" *clap*.

"Aw, honey pot..." he tried to laugh it off, but whatever 'it' was, made him mad. We were in the weeds of some husband-and-wife realities for sure.

Chef O'Shay showed up out of nowhere, and I nearly fell back into my seat, for right behind the cook was a life-size statue like the ones I had seen in the gallery: Priapus in his Roman incarnation, with lifted tunic, erect phallus, and fruit of the loins on either side. Only this statue was made entirely of pieces of pastry – like an erotic croquembouche. At the statue's feet were a dozen little dishes containing the next round of food.

"Are you all right?" Gordon asked, worried and sitting down to take my hand on top of my thigh.

"I—"

"Ladies and gents," announced the scrappy cook. "Our semi-sweet course is a special one. For you I have prepared quinoa tamales stuffed with raspberry-guava chutney, and topped with a cricket and hominy salsa. Enjoy."

"He okay?" I heard my ex ask my boy.

Still in shock at having this effigy brought before me, bigger than life, several things happened at once: other servers dressed like beekeepers doled out the dishes, but Chef Cory picked one up and came to me with it personally. Gordon in the meantime had stopped massaging my leg and inched his way up to my cold-as-ice crotch.

Just as he grasped onto my limp noodle through my clothes, the cook put the plate before me with a devilish wink for my boyfriend. The chef made sure he flashed his wrist tattoo at me: a winged cock about to take off. He was one of them....

The sight of that wink, the notion that Gordon was under threat, shocked more memories of that suppressed night out of me.

> In our garden center of shame and torture, I suddenly jolted awake from my Cialis induced coma. Confused at first, I soon realized we'd been moved again, this time to some caretaker's shack, for a peek out the windows showed all the long row of plants for sale beneath the Pasadena night sky.
>
> I was dressed in – horrors of horrors – a giant Hooter's tank top! The orange and white vestment barely came down to cover my trash. As I rubbed the cottony fabric over my aching skin and muscles, I saw I was on a cot. Across the way, Assauer and Gordon lay arm in arm, curled up on a wide bunk. They slept peacefully, draped only in lightweight robes.
>
> I sat on the edge of my bed, pressing my eyes and feeling exhausted.
>
> The cult leader and her pet entered from the cabin's other

room. Lolita held a tray of cold water bottles. I took one, snapped it open, and only after downing half, wondered if it could also be drugged.

In the meantime, pernicious Psyche had traipsed in. She produced a sharpie marker from the folds of her teddy and began making obscene cock doodles on Assauer's sleeping face, neck, chest and shoulders. Only after the initial few did I realize they were all Priapic marks of the god.

When I came up for air, finishing my bottle of water, Parthia stroked my hair back behind my ears.

"You look tired, dear boy. Would you like a treat, some antipasto?"

I glared my response. *I'm not hungry.*

By now, Gordon was awake and taking water for him and Assauer.

Parthia clapped her hands. In came a hideous old drag queen in a vulgar green miniskirt and halter-top. Her midriff was bulging, and navel jewelry jangled as she snapped her fingers and did a lewd Madame Curie dance – or, was it Mata Hari? I always get them confused....

Anyway, I crawled up the cot and jammed myself into the corner as far as I could go, but the thing kept approaching with lust-ridden leers, and chanting obscene verses, like these:

> "Roses may be red,
>   But I won't be happy
> Till this violet's fed."

And:

> "Love for sale, boys –
>   Ooey gooey, butt'try
> Love that cloys."

She crouched and started to climb on top of me, a huge winged cock pendant flopping in my face. Instinctually, I grabbed the flimsy afghan under me to shield my privates.

"Lieber Gott im Himmel!" I cried. *"Warum?!"*

Parthia hooted. "I asked you if you wanted some, and here is your treat, young man – the one and only, Auntie Pasto."

The drag performer slathered wet kisses on me, smearing her blue lipstick everywhere and massaging my forcibly exposed groin. The view was gruesome. Her caked-on foundation began to melt in her exertions as sweat boiled from underneath. And being this close, I could see just how spackled the rouge was in the furrows of her ancient wrinkles.

In my gasps for air, I could hear Gordon trying to choke back howls of laughter.

"Any luck?" the mad priestess asked.

Auntie turned from me. "Limp as a boiled cannoli."

"Well, try the other one."

Gordon leaped up and stood out of the way.

With that, the queen slithered off of me and kneeled between Assauer's legs where he sat on the edge of his bunk.

She stroked his body, opened his robe and showed the big boner he sported. I could have sworn it was considerably larger than its normal size....

Auntie gave a thumbs-up to the cult leader and went to work, smearing lipstick on more than my ex's tummy.

As he closed his eyes and let his head loll back, I wiped the blue grease from my face with the back of my hand. "What is going on? Why are we still here?"

Lolita circled around, watching Auntie Pasto's technique like a clinical case study.

"Easy, my boy," said Parthia. "I mentioned you must endure three trials to confirm my cure has been wrought, and The God's will has been done."

"But for heaven's sake, why a drag queen?"

"That's simple. They devote themselves to the art of femininity. Few women can match the studied womanliness of a truly great drag queen."

'Truly great?' I thought. 'She's no RuPaul.... Lady Bunny... maybe....'

Assauer's breath began to draw up short. He latched onto

> the pleasure-giver's head and looked to be on the verge of pain.

> As he climaxed, Gordon lost it, erupting into sheets of laughter which echoed off the small chamber's walls.

I snapped out of my flashback with an utter sense of dread. Although I couldn't yet remember, I knew the mentioned 'third trial' was going to be the most ghastly of all, and it somehow involved danger for my beloved boy.

I took his hand from my lap and kissed it. It was weird to know he was okay, yet fear for something in the past that had put him in jeopardy.

"Kohl?" Gordon asked.

Other guests were eating.

"I remember more of that night. They tortured us, honey."

"Oh. I do think I remember some of it...."

I whispered, "I want to get out here as soon as we can. I don't feel safe."

"Don't know how, with all these people—"

I distracted myself by catching our host's eye ogling the nude pastry.

He rose all at once, rather teary in his drunken way. He lifted his glass to Priapus and said, "I'm feeling rather patriotic, dear friends. Let's all toast George Washington, Father of Our Country!"

We rose in accordance and saluted the baked-goods effigy, but as I drank, I wondered about the irony of a naked guy lifting his skirt and showing an enormous phallus making our host think 'George Washington.' WTF, but clearly the former pornstar knew more about the National *pater noster* than I did, except I remembered they never showed Martha smiling...lol.

We sat again.

"Nicholas!" Tre-Princely turned his attention to his unobtrusive guest at the table across from us. "It's not like you to be so quiet. Cougar got your tongue?" His wicked glance split itself between Aurora and Cynthia, who had been monopolizing him all evening.

"No, no, Tre," he said in his affable Southern slowness. "I'm having a right royal time, as always."

Our host told the rest of us, "Nick here is a world traveler, a lost-generation soul, I think they call it. Been everywhere, seen a lot he shouldn't've, and can talk for hours about his close calls and escapes."

"Ah, shucks, Tre."

"Oh! Oh! Tell us about that 'hair-raising' experience you had. You know the one I mean."

"Really? Here and now?"

"Absolutely. By all means."

Nicholas bathed his good-ole-boy tones in some spirits as prologue, and settled back into a comfortable storytelling position.

He gestured to my boy briefly. "This here happened before young Gordon was yet born, but every last word of it is true. Swear on my life it is.

"Anyway, I was about this young man's age, in high school, and pretty good buddies with this particular Black stud on the varsity football team.

"Wolfgang DeWitt was his name and he was pop-u-lar! As tall and handsome as a movie star, we'd spend long hours sorta together after class. Sorta because I was on the cheerleading squad, and we shared the football field and locker room, joking-off now and then.

"I should say I was only semi-gay till I laid sweaty eyes on the naked Wolf – which is what his teammates called him; never 'Wolfie,' cuz he'd flare his fists and tell a body not to call him that. Said it made him feel like Eddie Munster's golliwog doll.

"Anyway. I say DeWitt was hot and filled my nights with plenty of jack-off material, but if he was studly in his football gear, the effect paled in comparison to his manly beauty in his R.O.T.C. uniform. It was seeing him like that, in his gung-ho, do-gooder mode – with his cloth cap angled on the side of his head – that first switched on my Gay gene. I don't care who you are, no one can resist a man in uniform!

"Anyway, one day we was all getting showered and changed after practice when things changed, totally.

"After getting' clean, me and Wolf stood side by side, pissin' into the trough urinal. I had a peek, as I always did, of his beautiful BBC, and then caught a smile in his eye as he 'noticed' me.

"'Not a goddamn cocksucker, by any chance, are you Nick?'

"He stroked himself a little.

"'Fuck no! No fag tendencies in me. You...?'

"More stroking. 'Nope.'

"Anyway, I better say first off, we were teen douchebags, and secondly, I wasn't technically queer yet, so a little homo-bashing was okay, right?

"The few out guys in Beaumont High weren't like Wolfie and me, so I didn't know any better, I guess, anyway.

"'Hey,' Reggie said, coming up to me and Wolf with his phone. He had it open to some Facebook page. 'You dudes see this?'

"We read it, shocked. Some group calling themselves the Beaumont High Clean-Up Squad had posted a hitlist. Our little redneck school had only six Black students – including girls – and this hate group had listed each of them by name, how they got home after class, where they lived, etc. The page encouraged 'patriots to take 'em out.'

"They had used the N-word, and Wolf said, 'That kind of bigoted language against the way a person was born is totally unacceptable.'

"I agreed, 'Totally!'

"Wolfgang then looked at me, and I could tell his high-school action figure, superhero persona wasn't going to take this crap lying down. But what could your average, red-blooded American werewolf do?

"Well, so, okay, I jumped ahead a little bit. But about an hour later me and him were walking home together, and I asked him if he wanted help with whatever he was planning on doing.

"'You'd do that, Nick? Stick your neck out for us?'

"'It's not your fight alone, Wolf. Decent people gotta stick together, no matter the fight needed to defend a good cause.'

"He seemed moved, but said nothing.

"'So, what are you planning on doing?'

"'I know who the ringleader is. Time to pay him a visit and scare some tolerance into him and the rest of his loser crew.'

"'When?'

"'Tonight.'

"'And you don't need help?'

"'Better not involve you, buddy.' He put his hand on my shoulder. 'You may not like what you see.'

"I went home and felt queasy. It was more than just my friend was going to try something risky, on his own, but – fuck – it was like I was in love with the dude or something.

"So, about 10 o'clock, I slipped on black jeans and a hoodie, and snuck out my bedroom window. I went over to Wolf's house and waited in the bushes.

"About an hour later, he came out and started walking briskly. I followed just out of sight, thinking I knew where he was headed anyway.

"I was right. Wolfie went to the center of our school's football field. I could see him perfectly from where I was hidden beneath the bleachers.

"And what a sight too! The sexy-ass kid started stripping. Then buck naked, he carefully folded his clothes by his feet and grabbed his cock.

"Believe it or not, he started takin' a leak in a circle all around him. He had been mumbling something too, but I'm not sure what.

"And then, right before my eyes in the cloudy moonlight, he started to shift into a big black wolf. He crouched down on all fours, sleek and menacing, before bounding away into the woods – howling once before he disappeared.

"Stunned, not believing my own eyes, I went to where he had been. His clothes had turned to stone, and I couldn't lift them.

"A second howl told me which way he was headed, towards the north side of town.

"I took off and followed, thinking again I knew where Wolfie was going.

"About a mile later, I hauled up to the cabin in the backwoods of one Ricky-Cooter McGee, an incorrigible redneck bully racist. I'd half suspected he was behind the 'hitlist' anyway.

"Seems I was right, cuz him and his crew were in the midst of a white sale, if you know what I mean: torchlight, hoods and the whole nine yards.

"While they were fixin' to burn a straw-man effigy of Dennis Rodman – who was accurate right down to his basketball jersey, stiff-as-a-board tutu and 'I ♥ North Korea' jockstrap – I crouched down in the woods to watch. I guess it's all these dirt-poor, homespun extremists could afford; store-bought crosses cost money, even down at Floor Mart.

"Soon one of 'em got knocked down by a lightning-quick shadow. He was dragged off into the woods just as quickly, screaming.

"The shocked group stood still for a moment, and then a second bigot was dragged kicking and hollering until he got knocked unconscious amidst the trees.

"At this point, Ricky-Cooter shouted for his rifle, and a toady raced to his pickup to get if off the gunrack.

"They were scared shitless, some saying it was God's revenge for their dickhead ways, others that a liberal-media-biased panther come down from the hills.

"All doubt was put to rest, because Wolfgang DeWitt, as a frickin' giant werewolf, strode into the circle and growled for them to take the hit-list down from Facebook.

"Stunned, the wimps started bawling and saying they'd comply, but then, when Wolfie turned to leap away, Asshole McGee shot at him, making the lycan yelp in agony as he ran off.

"I was in a panic and booked it full speed back to our high school. But I managed to call 911 and have the racist delinquents arrested and charged with hate crimes.

"When I got to the school, I ran onto the field. Wolf was unconscious, laying in his human form again right next to his clothes, which were fabric once more.

"Tearing off my own shirt, I dropped to my knees in the moonlight and cradled his head in my lap. At the same time, I ripped a bandage for his bleeding right shoulder.

"As I tied it, DeWitt opened his eyes, and time seemed to slow to a languorous crawl.

"'How much did you see?' he asked.

"'All of it, and you were amazing, Wolfie.'

"'I said'—he stated flatly, eyes locked tenderly on mine—'not to call me that.'

"'You're some kind of superhero.'

"He chuckled. 'And you? You my Lois Lane?'

"'I could be....'

"At this point, both of us realized I was firmly gripping his junk.

"'You sure you're not even a little bit Gay, Nicky Boy?'

"'Um—'

"'Didn't your pa warn you about wolves in sheep's clothing?'

"'Maybe, but my ma didn't say nothin' about superheroes in lycan attire.'

"I scrunched down and kissed him. 'You sure you don't like it when I call you Wolfie? Tell me true now....'

"His hand came up and kept my face close. 'When you do it – yeah, Nick, it's okay.'

"He hauled me down and we made out like mad rabbits.

"Afterwards, we became a pack of two – him my alpha, me his beta – and we never heard about 'the list' again."

Nicholas paused for applause. None came. Nick added, "And swear to God, that's exactly how it happened too."

Aurora asked, "How did he change? Did you learn to do it too…?"

"Can't tell you that. It's a secret."

Cynthia ventured, "But what happened to Wolfgang? Is he still out there someplace…lurking?" She glanced over her shoulder.

"Oh, he's out there, all right. He married this hairdresser dude in Brooklyn, and now they run a hipster barber shop together called 'Wolf Whiskers.' I get Chanukah cards from them every now and again."

This seemed an unsatisfactory ending, but when we looked over to Tre-Princely Knight, he was the only one not showing astonishment. He told us, "I know Nicholas, and if Mr. Reliable says it happened in such and such a way, it happened!"

Chapter 14: Chocolate Covered Coins

The evening progressed to the point where the happy buzz of the liquor had morphed into the loquacious testiness of a post-high stupor.

Worse yet, the cricket-covered tamale lay challenging me on my plate, making me wonder if this recreated Roman villa was accurate right down to the vomitorium.

I shoved it aside after hearing Tre's comments on his buddy's werewolf account, realizing I'd be starving if not for the general anxiety in my stomach; it'd been induced and maintained by the flashbacks of our passion in Pasadena.

Cynthia suddenly swooned, pointing her phone camera right at Nick's face. "Oh, I just love a good M/M Romance!"

"Me too!" exclaimed Aurora. "Nothing beats them for – I don't know – sheer sexiness."

"M/M?" questioned Assauer.

"Male/Male," our hostess explained.

"Really?" demanded Cynthia. "I thought it meant Man on Man!"

"Anyway, *poTAYho-paTAHoe,* it's sexy as fuck."

Dana inquired of his wife meekly, "And what's so appealing about it, dear?"

"Oh, my!" Cynthia practically scooted out of her seat. She was hot and bothered. "It's a bunch of things. It's—"

"Double the cock," said Prospera, cutting through all the BS. "It's about raunchy, sweaty studs, doing the nasty and not letting anybody know."

"That's your idea of romantic?" I asked.

Assauer put on his best math-teacher tone and inquired, "So this category of so-called 'M/M Romance' is about guys who don't date, but only fuck on the side, and who don't kiss unless it's part of the climax...? Is that the general picture?"

"And they don't hold hands, ever!" added Cynthia helpfully. "And never attend Pride events, never-ever!"

"Well, those things are true," mused Prospera with further deliberation. "But it's more how these men hold a secret that's dark, dangerous and tragic. The forbidden aspects, and – twice the dick."

The woman chortled themselves into a screechy trance, the live-streaming shots going wonky, temporarily

My ex waited for their nattering to end, for he wasn't done with them yet. He said what the rest of us were thinking, "Ladies, no offense, but that is such an insult to Gay men. Maybe you don't even know it, but it is."

"How so?" asked Cynthia.

"When you toss out a phrase like 'M/M' instead of same-sex love, you are totally sanitizing the experience of any meaning, and censoring Gay men out of their own histories."

Prospera echoed her friend. "How so?"

"Easy. Most of these pieces labeled from the outside as 'M/M' are written by straight women for straight women. So, they avoid the obvious: that LGBT people have to fight for every goddamned thing hets take for granted. Like civil liberties, for example."

The women steamrollered the point and went right on clucking amongst themselves.

"You know, Cynthia," said Aurora, "I first got intrigued with 'M/M Romance' in an old chat room online, Lusty-Dudes.com. We'd chew the fat all day in there! It was so much fun."

"Oh, I know. I used to haunt Studly-Men-in-Lust.org. We'd coffee-clutch for hours on end. One guy in there, who said he was straight and doing research"—Cynthia winked elaborately—"had this thesis he was working on. I remember it was all about the attraction we women feel for guys who let themselves get dicked. He said it stems from the fact that we are alike. 'Passivity Ideation,' he called it."

"Oh, God!" I cried out. "What a load of BS."

Now the women looked awake. Their phones pointed to me.

"Explain it to them," said Nick.

Assauer took over. "First of all, this guy doing research sounds like a real douche. If he thinks women are passive in anything, that means he's a misogynist. Period. His opinions of females as a subordinate underclass to men, is what he's saying, and in his personal homophobia – probably a closet-case himself – he sticks Gay guys in the category of 'less than' men, just like he thinks of women. It's pretty obnoxious, and his opinions should have no credibility among any thinkin' person, for a perjured view is never a fair one."

"Yeah, agreed Gordon. "It'd be like listening to some old constipated white guy lecturing on why African American literature speaks to other minority groups: his theory on 'Uppity Syndrome' would probably be the equivalent to your guy's 'Passivity Clause'!"

Assauer added, "It's insulting to both the creator of the content and those who want to read it."

"Well, maybe," Prospera admitted, "but still, what's wrong with stories about guys on the *down low*? The tragic, the illicit nature, and secrets, secrets, secrets? It all plays into the fun of a tawdry 'M/M Romance' for us."

Assauer told the ladies, "I don't know, maybe there's someplace on the net where tall people go to read and gossip about 'the tragedy' of 'the shorts,' cuz that's what you're sayin' about straights reading about us reduced to nothing but figures worthy of pity, quite frankly."

Gordon picked up the ball. "Look, I know the het 'lifestyle choice' is boring as hell, but so are most of your so-called tragic same-sex couplings. We just get on with it, like everybody else."

"But still for us fangirls.... Well, I guess you'd just have to be a man-loving woman to get it." Cynthia chuckled.

At this point, I realized their safe, sanitized, soft-ball porn version labeled 'M/M' – devoid of any of the realities of the actual Gay Struggles – was just another form of escapism. "My ex's right about us having to fight for everything, even recognition. What Assauer said struck a chord in me; remember what happened in your Supreme Court when seven couples finally got the chance to prove the Constitution means us too? Ruth Bader Ginsburg said from the bench that separate and unequal marriage for Gay people is like skim milk. And now I get your 'M/M' stories are just like that – remarkably *lite* on any actual Gay content: 2% at most, guaranteed. Don't want to fill up on it, I guess."

Cynthia to my eyes looked very unsettled, like the crickets disagreed with her tummy all of a sudden. "You know, now that I think about it, on *Man Humping Twink-Sluts.biz* we did sometimes wonder why our chat rooms never had any real Gay guys in there. You think that's the reason?"

Assauer fielded that one. "Yep. Could be."

Now the ladies suddenly seemed to comprehend it.

"Like I was saying about Tennessee Williams characters"—Tre re-established his dominance over the conversation—"all this talk of secrets and tragic types makes me think of *Suddenly Last Summer*. Talk about GAY! Tennessee Williams: Gay; Gore Vidal, the screenwriter: Gay; Montgomery Clift, the star: Gay; Elizabeth Taylor: well, Gay by marriage and fag hag by inclination."

"Which movie is this now, Tre?" asked Gavin Coruptti.

"You know that one! Monty Clift is pushed off a mountainside in Spain for being queer, while Liz Taylor is forced to watch helplessly. Drove her insane in the flick, but in real life, she was every Hollywood Gay guy's shoulder to cry on. She knew all the dirt back in the day when a secret was a secret and could get you lobotomized, just like her movie character." He shook his head in slow disappointment. "What a waste."

"What is, darling?" his wife asked on her way to the restroom.

"Liz went to the grave with so much Gay History locked in her head." Tre took a drink. "If you ask me, there ought to be a law. No Hollywood fag hag can die without first writing a tell-all book so the truth does not march un-willingly to the grave with her."

"Amen," Coruptti muttered, perhaps from professional force of habit.

"Damn right," concluded our host, "selfish to pass on and not set the record straight – so to speak – for later generations. Should be a crime, in my opinion."

As several of us nodded gravely in agreement, loud voices, command-ing footsteps, and laughter erupted from the statuary-garden-side of the room.

To my utter shock, a uniformed policeman strode in lolling on the shoulders of a fur-wearing woman.

I panicked and thought it was time to bolt, but Napoleon must have read my mind.

He put his hand on my wrist to steady me. "Relax. It's just a late-arriving guest."

I settled down again, and looked closer. The cop was a higher-up; his uniform was decorated in tons of showy brass.

"Ah!" shouted Tre-Princely, doing a fake-ass salute. "Lieutenant Nasser, nice of you and Sofia to join us."

The self-help guru leaned in and whispered in my ear, "This cop's on the down low too."

Napoleon looked sly, as if this man's ingrown homophobia was the issue making me uncomfortable. I just grinned.

Drunk, Nasser grabbed a chair and sat himself at Tre's right-hand side. It's where our host wanted him, much to surly Ermanno's chagrin.

In the meantime, Sofia shrugged off her wrap and cheeped merrily with the other women about 'things.' She gave the impression of being just as well lubricated as her husband.

Nasser announced in a voice too loud, "I could use a drink, Tre."

"Of course. Of course." Tre-Princely clapped pert hands, and a server showed up. To him he said, "Mix up a pitcher of 'Sex On The Beach' for Nasser and his wife. Wait! Make a second for me too. In fact"—his attention turned to the rest of us as well—"you order wine and booze as you like, people – let's pretend the sun made a full circuit and it's cocktail hour all over again!"

With that, more waiters came around and took orders, but I watched with curiosity as the dark-haired and fit Nasser glanced at my ex. There was real attraction there.

Sofia finally made it to the main table and air-kissed Tre. "Lovely as always to be at one your events."

Our host play-frowned and tapped the imaginary wristwatch he didn't wear.

While his wife sat down at Prospera's empty position, the L.A. police officer said, "I'm sorry, Tre. You know we wouldn't be late except for Force business."

"Where were you?"

"At a wake. One of my token officers died over the weekend, and we had to make an official appearance."

"How was it?"

"Oh, you know," said Sofia, "homey."

"A front-room viewing – I think I might like that when it's my time."

"That won't be for a long while, Tre."

"Where's Prospera?" Sofia asked.

"In the crapper," Mrs. Schwartzbaum's husband said.

As if on cue, the 'crapper' herself appeared, with rattling cocktail carts right behind her, lol.

"Sofia! OMG, you're here!"

The two hugged, and then eye-raisingly sat together, Texas-Ivy on the police lieutenant woman's lap. They immediately became intimate, with Prospera trailing a fingertip across the neckline of Sofia's pendant, down into the soft folds of her cleavage. They chatted quietly, privately, only pausing to do shots with the freshly mixed Sex On The Beach.

Tre-Princely Knight drained his own and then told the new-arrivers, "Chef Cory will sling you up some grub—"

'...Oh, God,' I thought, 'will there be grubs too...?'

"We ate, Tre," said Nasser. "It was one of those Black wakes, so there was food on top of food on top of food."

"Soul food," corrected Sofia momentarily before returning full attention to Prospera.

"Yes, and what *soul* it had too." By the sour expression on the lieutenant's face, it was clear whatever *it* was did not suit his palate. He suddenly chuckled. "You should have seen Sofia! One taste of the chitlins made her wanna toss her tripe."

The two men's wives were now stroking each other's hair and starting to make out. I thought I perceived another wistful glance from Nasser towards my ex.

The rest of the women-loving guys were mesmerized by the lesbo affection on display. It went live-streaming too.

"A wake is all right I suppose," the cop said, once taking another swig. "But too much of this PC, interracial sensitivity crap is not good for unit cohesion, if you ask me."

Napoleon muttered under his breath for me, "Yeah, the LAPD is famous for its tenderness."

"I think *too much* and *sensitivity* are words that don't belong together," Nicholas said rather bravely.

Nasser threw down the gauntlet. "Oh, really?"

But the guy with a werewolf boyfriend in high school didn't back down. "I'm not sayin' nothin' you don't or shouldn't already know. You stand up for my rights, I'll stand up for yours. If you don't, then—"

"Who's talking *rights?!*" the cop demanded to know.

"You are, sir. You're talking about the rights of your dead officer to be honored by more than just 'his kind.'"

"Nicholas..." attempted our host.

"Well, you know it's true, Tre."

Now the officer glinting ceremonial brass relaxed, deciding it was all a joke anyway. Clearly the other party was being unreasonable. "When you join a Police Academy, or get tossed in jail, let me know if you think too much fraternization is still a good idea."

"Well, I don't know about all that," Nick said calmly, "but this talk reminds me how people do have to fight for change – political and otherwise – but often come up against an irrational fear. Like those bigoted burgomeisters who kept empty busses running in Selma, Alabama, after Rosa Parks was arrested, and kept running them through the boycott. The city dug in and bankrupted itself with 361 days of riderless service. They did, and chose to do it all like little kids refusing to eat their peas. They preferred pride over sanity, and sadly, we're not much better today with Trumpeteers running around, shouting all manner of fear-mongering and lies to get idiots to excuse criminal behavior. And why? Pride over sanity, the niche where the closet bigots keep their hearts."

I glanced around. Most of the room was not even listening. Prospera and Sofia were in full make-out mode while their hands roved freely over clothed breasts, torso and shoulders.

Neil Campbell mused in metallic tones, "Puts me in mind of the LGBT fight of the future."

"Which one?" Napoleon asked.

"The struggle for Gay people to even be allowed to exist."

"What?!" I exclaimed.

"It's true. This whole anxiety-based politickin' the Gops are playin' Russian roulette with – pun intended – is extended right down to the fertility clinics and DNA collection. We've all seen the commercials. 'Send in your DNA today for free analysis.' And what do they do with this most personal of personal information – your genome? Well, if you're an out person with a social media profile they can check lickety-split, then your 'gay-tainted' genes are sold off to the highest bidder."

"Why?" Assauer asked.

"They go to secret labs, to not-so secretly find the 'cure' for the h-word. The company that makes the first queer gene screening test for reproductive labs to use will make a trillion dollars in a week."

"Ya think?" Nick said.

"Hell yeah, I think. Right now, in any abortion place, hospital, or test-tube baby-makin' center, the number one question asked is not will my darling baby be healthy, but will this 'it,' the fetus, be queer. Will it be a family disgrace. So, once they have the test, whole trays of eggs will be disregarded, and abortions will be selective based on the findings. But my point is, it will be the uninformed people of today mailin' off their DNA to private companies, signin' away their rights to use the most personal of personal information, that will mean untold repression and suffering for the next generations of rare and isolated same-sex loving men and women. Mark my words."

Again, few in the room acknowledged Neil's lesson because they were too busy agape at Prospera and Sofia's tongue kissing.

Deep reverberations sounded from the hall. Hard to say what it was at first, but in came a long line of the handsome foot massagers from the start of the evening. Following them was a man blowing in a didgeridoo, and a second one pinging a mouth harp.

"Ah!" cried our delighted host. "Dear guests, time for foot rubs! Enjoy."

In a matter of moments, a smiling lad was under the table in front of me, massaging my toes with eucalyptus oil and making me relax involuntarily.

The music seemed to take on a soothing tempo as well, or at least slowed a bit. I glanced to my ex, and now he was openly returning the lieutenant's flirting. Assauer, never being one to turn down the advances of a mark, particularly a rich one like this cop, appeared to be having a good time at it.

I felt a bit of coolness surrounding my left ankle, and when I looked, my sexy foot-boy had slipped a silver anklet on me, one with Tre's monogram.

Just as I wondered if this night would ever end, our host pulled up his personal masseur and called out, "Bring chairs! I want the servers to be served wine and cocktails too. And if any refuse, pour it down his collar! Now is the time to live."

Commotion ensued as a dozen stacking chairs were wheeled in and the waiters and foot-boys squeezed in at the tables. My own handsome one practically sat in my lap, much to Gordon's dismay.

The dusty outback music continued.

The previously observed little bout of Tre's sobriety was completely gone now, and he slurred words freely. "My God, wife, don't get a room. Go out there and do a dance for us with your girlfriend so we can all see."

Intrigued by the notion, the two exchanged coy smiles and fingertips pressed to lips.

"Dance, Rabbit's Foot, dance!" Tre-Princely repeated.

Prospera stood, took Sofia's hand and led her to the central stage area, which moments later turned into a dance floor for two.

Focusing on one another, they dipped knees and rubbed each other's flanks with sweaty palms. Sofia turned backwards, and Prospera gripped onto her fleshy ass.

Their dirty-dancing of kissing and suggestive thrusts made the unfulfilled men of the room loll out tongues, but began to lead to a queasy feeling in me.

There was something about it which made me fear for Gordon....

> After the drag queen blew him, my boyfriend's unguarded, unwise laughter over Assauer's ecstasies drew the attention of Parthia.
>
> Without a word, she tried to zipper his lips with a series of pricking kisses. Her hand slid down his front, towards his crotch, which made Gordon arch his back away from her and push with his hands.
>
> "Hey!" I reminded the madwoman. "He's *not* being punished, remember?"

The priestess latched onto Gordon's shoulders so he could not get away, then turned a greasy leer on me. "Oh, I know. *You* are!"

In the meantime, Auntie Pasto had stood and licked her chops while my ex and his ever-enlarging *Schwanz* lay drained and exhausted on the bed. He had stupid dick graffiti all over his face.

Psyche got an evil twinkle in her eye and went to whisper in her cult leader's ear. While talking, gestures and leers passed from the women onto my boy and Lolita.

"Ah, yes," announced Parthia, now holding Gordon by the scruff of the neck like a puppy dog. "Brilliant idea, one to surely please the god of lust."

"What is?" I asked.

"This night is as good as any for my darling pet to sacrifice her maidenhood to the Great Blue-Green One. And for you to watch."

She shoved my teenage boy to the center of the cabin.

I stood and went to him. "No, no," I told the woman. "Gordon is a good and decent queer boy. He's not up for this kind of perversity!"

But he licked his lips towards the bubblegum-chewing tart.

Parthia laughed and explained, "It's your third trial. Weather it, and you can go."

Gordon suddenly said "I'm game," horrifying me, but a peek at his face held out hope he had a plan so we could all get out of this garden center from hell.

An hour later, we were dressed and back in the main area before the curtained pillar-statue of Priapus.

A mockery of a 'wedding' procession was led by Auntie Pasto, who had tossed a saffron bed sheet over her shoulders and marched along in the vanguard with two lit tiki torches. These she held in a way so the points came together below her navel, and the tall flames flickered high above each shoulder.

Gordon and Lolita – each with a ring of flowers on their heads; the girl's on top of a flame-colored veil – followed the drag performer. And then me and Assauer walked slowly behind them, with the rest of these motley nut-jobs trailing us.

Parthia stood before the phallic column again and oozed more olive oil over its stony trash, chanting some junk in Latin.

The two men, Eros and Devil-Chin Guy, made my boy and Lolita stand facing one another.

Parthia turned and spoke to them. "Do you each undertake to fulfill the god's ardent desire and spread your bounty upon the earth?"

They nodded.

"Do you, Lolita, give your ventris to fruitfulness?"

"I do."

"Do you, Gordon, lay your seed where it may multiply?"

"I...do? I mean, I do."

Well, for one, yours truly was thoroughly disgusted. 'How dare they disgrace the sanctity of non-traditional marriage like this! There ought to me a law!'

"Then"—Parthia cracked a wicked leer—"by the power of lust invested in me by the *acceptor amoris,* I pronounce you ready for bliss."

While Lolita assaulted my boy's mouth with gum-popping kisses, Auntie Pasto shouted something Greek to me and extinguished her flamboes. Simultaneously, she ushered the rest of us towards the sliding glass doors to the potted plants outside, and Parthia took the teens by the hand to lead them to the cot, which had been moved and set up under the open-air atrium and stars.

My heart was sick. If Gordon had a plan, it better not involve knocking up some random cult bimbo! *Gott bewahre....*

Parthia, an apparent adept at lecherous peeping, joined us outside and made everyone crouch down to watch through the glass. She had turned off most of the lights inside, so we could just barely see the teens in action. Agog, she turned an ape's eye to the spectacle and wantonly robbed me of kisses from time to time.

First Lolita sat on the bed and drew the standing Gordon into her embrace.

"God, woman," I told the cult leader, getting angry. "This is madness."

"Is it?" she snickered. "It's hell on you, right?"

"You know it is...."

"Then watch."

It looked like the slutty teen girl was fumbling with my boy's zipper, when he suddenly gripped her hands and climbed on top. He started rubbing her clothed body, and the virgin slag writhed in moaning ecstasy. He scooched her up, sticking her head and shoulders off the far edge of the cot, and got behind her legs.

'Is he into this?!' I wondered, sick to my stomach.

He slowly lifted her by the underside of the knees, and the girl's back continued to slide on the cot. His feet landed on the ground, off the other end for better leverage, and the folding bed flipped, sending Lolita ass over tits. A dull thud sounded with metal, fabric and wood clanking after her descent.

"My pet!" Parthia screeched at full volume and raced in, followed by her panic-stricken cult goons. They removed the cot, fanned the unharmed girl and made a tearful fuss.

Me and Assauer stood off to the side in the near-dark, and Gordon slunk up, pointing to the garden center's main exit.

Assured the crazies were occupied, we booked it.

Out the sliding glass doors, we ran through the parking lot, heading for the street.

Just as we got there, I could hear the madwoman's cackle from far behind us. "Let them go. They'll not remember this night anyway...."

I snapped out of it with a jolt, accidentally knocking elbows with the Aboriginal pedicurist to my left.

The women were still doing a soft porn dance, the guys still salivating, but Tre noticed me and misinterpreted my actions.

"You know," he said between beats of music. "Some of you may not like the idea of servers being your table companions, but I know that old Roman, Senokot – or whatever his name was – said don't think you're better than them. They sucked the same milk, pooped the same excrement, breathed the same air as you did as a baby, so it was only Bitch Fortune who later raised that person up on the backs of all the rest." [17]

Thoroughly chided but misunderstood, I decided to remain silent.

"Oh, Tre," Prospera said from the lips of her lover, "loosen up."

"Oh, I'm loose, Lucky Charm. But maybe if I called Tyler in here, he'd show me a better time."

Tre-Princely's wife stopped dancing. Statue-like, she stood on the dance floor, casting a stunned look on her man.

The music ground to a twangy halt.

Tre ignored her to tell the rest of us, "That boy, my protégée, knows all the ups and downs of Fortune, just like me, and he's ambitious too. A modeling and dance career – which I help along whenever I can – is tough for the young. But he's learning, and he's taking my advice about stockpiling his pennies and investing wisely. Why, on my advice, he bought a punchbowl ladle." Tre-Princely then added with pride, "Silver plate from Gorham."

By the time he'd finished, the 'F/F Romance' on display was over. Texas-Ivy had gone back to her seat, and Sofia pulled up a chair next to her cop spouse.

"God, Tre," clipped his wife, "What's a kid need a punch ladle for – jeesh!"

"Investment. Tylor can get a whole set that way, piece by piece." Then our host laughed, drunken and vindictive, informing us, "My wife thinks I fuck 'im too, as if. Isn't that right, dear?"

The goaded woman remained silent.

"It's good to work hard at something, even if you don't like it. I did," said Tre, "and it made me rich and set for life, even though money seems a two-edged sword: it cuts both the self and the one it's used on."

More silence followed from his wife.

"See," he went on, acting unfazed, "I believe in Astrology and one gave me my exact date and time of my death. Wrote it on a piece of paper for me, and I keep it in my wallet so the coroner can find it—"

"Tre, please."

"Yes, Prospera? Something upset you?"

"Don't go on about your death."

"Why not?" he asked her pettishly. Tre added for the rest of us with more sentiment, "I've got more money than I can ever spend. I spread it out now so my family can love me as if I'm already dead."

None of us knew how to take that. If serious, it was sublime; if he was burlesquing, it was outrageously ironic and funny. None of us knew. I decided this was ultimately how anyone came to view Tre-Princely Knight.

Prospera poo-pooed the whole notion with a stiff belt. "That's just a prediction. Don't live your life making it come true."

The mood had darkened.

Tre stood up, sloshing on his sea legs for a moment. "It's too goddamned morose in here. Time to move out – up, up, up – and get some air. Chef O'Shay has a treat for us." He gestured behind him to the garden.

We all stood, and Prospera's mood turned on a nickel. "Follow me!"

She led the way, out onto the colonnaded peristyle, and down a few steps, on either side of which stood breathtakingly real statues of deer in bronze.

Prospera gathered her ladies to her, and they walked on slowly, alongside the massive central pool. Their jolly live-streaming devices tried to catch it all as they went.

The men who were Tre-Princely's good friends followed secondly, with the Big Bad Cop forming a nucleus for their chitchat.

After them traipsed Napoleon, drawing Gordon and my ex with him and asking some questions about the event so far.

That left me alone with Neil Campbell, and just as he got to my side, our host joined us.

"I hope you gentlemen are having a good time?"

"We are, Tre," I said. "You're a wonderful host." Just then my tummy grumbled from being empty....

"Provocative ev'nin' as always!" added suck-up Neil.

We walked on, and I'm not sure, but as I glanced around, this might have been the most sublimely lovely garden I'd ever seen. At the end of the pool where we'd started, a large flattop rock sat in the curved end of the shallow water feature. On top of it was a recumbent, full-sized stature of a bronze man. He held his index finger up to the stars, and I followed his pointing line straight to Venus, the bright star rising through the early morning dark.

As we crunched the gravel alongside manicured rows of low boxwood, arbors would spring up on our left with living rows of grape vines. Here and there along the long flanks of the pool, more bronze figures of young men sat on their own rocks and gazed at the heavens reflected in the water.

After a while, Neil said cryptically, "Now that the three of us are alone, I can properly intro you."

Me and Tre were puzzled.

The Aussie beamed. "Tre, may I present the supplier of your newest golden bauble. And Kohl, this is the connoisseur who bought your Poseidon statue."

Tre-Princely perked up. "Ah, your treasure is now mine, and I 'ask no questions' about where it came from, like any good Conservative of antiquities."

"Good," I said, half-chuckling. "Because I tell no truths, like any decent Retrogressive officeholder."

We slowed our pace and stopped, because my comment made Tre laugh and laugh, and then cough and cough.

From up ahead, we heard "Wait here," and his wife came back to collect him. My gang trailed back to us as well.

In a moment, Prospera was leading them away, but I snagged Assauer and Gordon to stay behind. We were right on the pool's edge when I told them through a hoarse whisper, "Let's get the hell out of here. I've got stuff to tell you. Plus, I'm starving!"

Right then I turned to lead us to the nearest exit, and ran smack into a security guard with a German Spitz on a leash. The dog yapped viciously at my ankles and stepped me back into the fountain.

"Where do you think you're going?" the uniformed dude asked.

"Back the way we came," said Assauer.

My comrades helped me out of the drink, while the guard informed us with bedpan seriousness, "No one exits the same way they enter."

We looked at one another, thanked him – and his furry hell muffin – and scurried along to join Tre and company.

When we caught up, our host had ensconced himself on a bench to the side of a life-size naked wrestler boy in bronze. Across the water, I could see his opponent in similar 'engagement' pose.

"Gavin, my good friend…" Tre was slurring his words again. "You get those changes?"

"For your monument, yes."

Our host explained, "Coruptti and Cousins Co. is making my mausoleum: all marble and gold-plated shit. Ain't that right, honey?"

"Yes, dear." Prospera patted his arm.

"Oh, Gavin's plans are beautiful. There are arches and places to sit by a reflecting pool, marble dog houses for my dear dead pooches, and oh, oh, Prospera will have her own en-suite for after she croaks too."

"Yes," Prospera murmured, upset all of a sudden. "I suppose Tyler will have a niche of his own – after all, he's another one of your bitches."

'Wow,' I thought. 'That was kind of acid.' It pissed me off, but our host restricted himself to a cold glare.

In another instant, he was back talking to Gavin. "Oh, oh, tell 'em – what's that class-eey Latin inscription thingy you suggested…?"

"The epitaph?"

"Yeah, the swanky one. Recite it."

Coruptti stood tall, placing his folded hands by his bellybutton, opera-singer fashion. "LECTOR, SI MONUMENTUM REQUIRIS, ASPICE 'Nightly with Tre-Princley.com.'"

"Yeah…." The future house of the dead occupant sighed. "But I think

I'll stick with the plain old English one I've been tinkering with for years. You wouldn't want to...hear it, by any chance...?"

We all coughed that we'd like nothing better. I actually had something better to do, so used the chance to wring fountain water out of my gold Tre-Princely slippers.

Our host puffed up on his bench and recited his epitaph from memory:

"HERE R.I.Ps TRE-PRINCELY KNIGHT

(née Schwartzbaum)

Former Porn Star, Businessman, & Art Patron,

With Honorary Degrees from U.C.L.A. & Bryman College,

Passed in Absentia:

He Might've Pick'd-n-Choosed Any Job in Washington, D.C.—

But, Refused;

A Mover, Shaker, Kind-Heart,
Who Began with a Buck, but Left Billions,

WHILE NEVER ONCE LISTENING TO A

PSYCHIATRIST!

So long for now, Tre-Princely,
And peace out to thee, fellow traveler."

It was getting real around here, so thankfully, while we sniffled a few times and wiped our suddenly blurred vision, the police lieutenant and Sal helped Tre to his feet. From there, we progressed to the end of the garden. [18]

Here, the columns marking the narrow end of the enclosed garden were matched stone for stone by others – twenty or thirty feet away – on the other side of an open terrace.

The breeze was cool and salty, and I could hear the sea not too far off.

"This is where we'll have *dessert*," Tre announced, but there was nothing set up: no pastry-lined tables, no ice cream machines.... The only thing I saw out of place was a hook hanging from a rope on the ceiling.

Suddenly, Prospera Texas-Ivy froze. I followed her eyes and saw a handsome young man – sleek and sexy – dressed in slacks and a sports jacket come on to the terrace with us.

He went straight to Tre and kissed him, exhibiting nothing but smiles and clearly elated tones.

All at once, I recognized him, although the attire threw me for a moment because the only other time I'd met him, he was naked. This was the body-paint skeleton, and he was even more attractive in flesh tones and clothes.

"Tyler, my boy! You were wonderful tonight. A real joy to behold."

The young man kissed our host again, but it was clearly more out of appreciation than red-hot rut.

Prospera lost it. "You. Piece. Of. Filth!" She was talking to Tre. "You dare flaunt *this* spectacle in front of me? And oh, I know who's fucking who between the two of you."

'Wow,' I thought. 'Jealousy is so unbecoming in a person.'

Poor Tre blinked at his wife in shock, then did a little hop of anger. A moment later he ripped the toupee off his head and wagged it at Prospera in rueful frustration, shouting, "Oh, yeah? If that's what you think, then guess what. You're out of the mausoleum, baby!"

Instantly, his fury abated into an emotional breakdown. He pleaded to the rest of us for understanding. "You see that? Well, I'm used to it, not only from her, but from everybody. Oh, there's no respect for a pornstar who spent his career getting dicked for cash, even big money like my ass commanded. No one relates, but I try to make everyone respect me, but like the classic song goes, haters gonna hate, no matter what, but I don't have to sink to their level." He placed his hand rather paternally on Tyler's shoulder. "I want to matter and so does this young man, who I see a lot of myself in. Now, he may be Gay and me straight, but that's no reason to think he's in my pants, or verse visa. We have mutual respect, Prospera, cuz he knows what it's like, and I know what it's like. We want to matter. I know how normal it all is, so unworthy of comment, except against those manning the glory holes along the Interstates, and then going out and voting for repression and stuff for those who dare to be out. But, hypocrites shouldn't matter. Hypocrisy makes me sick.... Just...sick—"

"Tre...." His wife was sorry.

"No. Don't tell me now – you know, folks, I owe it all to her. Do you, any of you, know how down and out I was when I met her? She saved me from myself, took what little I had left and made me 'a brand,' and a valuable one at that." He stumbled to the handrail and stopped, contemplating the out-of-place hairpiece in his clutches. "We make the best of teams. The very... best."

"Oh, Tre."

"You know," he told all of us, "I lied earlier. It wasn't an astrologer who told me I'm gonna die. It was my doctor."

Prospera went to his side. "You don't have to tell—"

"See, folks"—he slowly turned and faced each of us in turn, one by one—"I've got the bug; the one pornstars are most vulnerable to. I won't be around for very much longer."

"Oh, Malcolm." She lovingly took his toupee and arranged it correctly on his head, cooing, "Don't think about it. We'll get through it, together."

To the rest of us, he said, "So now you know, every day I live reminds me I won't be around for as long as I should."

"The doctor says you are fine and will outlive him, but still, I know, baby. It's in you, in your mind as well as in your blood. You can't help worrying about it."

He hugged her. "I'm sorry about this silly fight."

"It was my fault. I know you're trying to help Tyler. Truth is, you're a princely man, Mr. Schwartzbaum, and I love you."

"I love you too, honey, and guess what – you're back in the mausoleum."

She laughed, whooping sardonically, "Hooray for that!"

I suddenly noticed color from the approaching dawn beginning to streak over the hugging couple's shoulders. Our host repeated his quote from the start of the night.

> "Unhappy mortals we,
>   Who on so fine a thread,
>   Find our lives but depend,
> Know like this puppet man
>   There's no time to pretend
>   We won't soon be dead,
>   Therefore, live ye merry,
> And love others while you can."

His wife kissed him and directed his attention down the length of the terrace.

"Dessert! At last," Tre called out, and we turned to see quite a spectacle.

Four studly young men, wearing only skimpy blue briefs and papier-mâché donkey heads, led a giant Trump piñata between them coffin and usher fashion.

The streaming cameras were lapping it up again.

While the crowd gathered around, the underwear models lifted the clay and crêpe paper effigy onto the ceiling hook. Then they picked up baseball bats waiting by the columns.

As Tre signaled with a laugh, the young men beat the living hell out of it, sending chocolate coins flying this way and that. These treats were oddly enough without wrappers, and at the same time other guests yelped and delightedly hooted with each sexy-boy Democrat smack, I bent down to pick one up. It was heavy, really heavy.

Tre saw me, and told everyone, "Look closer, people, like Kohl. The dark chocolate covers $20 silver coins. The white chocolate ones are gold-centered Krugerrands."

We all dropped to our knees and scrambled like kids for candy.

Tre-Princely Knight laughed good-naturedly. Genuine emotion shimmered through his voice as he said, "Groveling in the dirt before me – just the way Nature intended."

"...condicio fixum est..."

— Part Five —
'The Split,' Take Two

#Bucca-Bucca! #tainted-flesh,

#useless, #Kacke! #ice-cream,

#Cool-as-a-zucchini, #pissed,

#crushing-silence, #pump-you,

#feminizing-influence, #YOU!

#shoot-a-kid? #dead-end,

#throtty-clutches, #foggy,

#angry, #blue-pills, #beer,

#not-so-tidy-whities

Chapter 15: Cursed

The three of us entered our motel room with loud "Shooshing" of one another; we were still tipsy as hell. Napoleon had given us a ride in his We-B-Ho Rooters van from Tre's event, but we'd stopped for 99¢ hamburgers – lots of them – because we were all hungry as strays after the 'art happening.' Now I knew what they meant by starving artists, lol.

We closed the door, kicking off our shoes and starting to strip off socks. "Shut the blinds, Gordon." He was close enough, and twisted the rod to block out the morning sun. We needed to crash…or wreck, whichever it was.

I pulled down my trousers and whipped off my confining dress shirt, watching my boy train his eyes to my movements. In response, he opened the door again, hanging the 'Do Not Disturb' sign and making me smile as I climbed into bed.

Assauer went to the bathroom.

From my perfect view, hands locked behind my head on the pillow, I saw my beautiful boy take down his dress slacks, then come up and off with his undershirt. In another moment, my arms were open to him, and his warm skin was sliding against mine. We were in nothing but our drawers.

Tucked under the sheets now, a contented me started groping, spooning and hugging. With each caress of my experienced hand, the excited sighs and moans Gordon sent into my mouth told me he was whetted for desire. Sleepily though, my mind went to places less urgent, perhaps because his attempt to rouse me down there were returning no results.

"You know…" I pulled away from his lips for a moment. "Being with you is worth a million nights like last—"

He grinned sweetly – like saying "shut up" – and dove in for more tongue-on-tongue action.

Groggily, some verse assembled itself on the scaffold of my overwrought senses.

I stroked his curly locks, and caressingly pinched his blushing ears and cheeks.

> "When all is said and done, my dearest boy,
> No moments great will ever be recalled
> With half the flush of pleasure to enjoy
> As when limb-to-limb, enlaced we were sprawled."

My final few words may have been a little mushy, for although I still gripped and massaged his throbbing boyhood, my eyes were drifting closed and his touch began to feel less ardent to my shutting-down brain.

I fell asleep with little improvements to be made to the verse drifting across my mind, and the sensation of Gordon's hand still trying to get me hard.

Tre-Princely laughed and spilled his drink.

A moment later, he slipped the papier-mâché donkey head over his toupee and got down on all fours. The Grim Reaper threw open his coat, and the godlike Tyler stepped out in flesh and body paint as an animated skeleton.

He mounted the former pornstar and slapped his steed's backside. When Tre reared up, shaking his mane in defiant pleasure, the handsome young rider cried out, "*Bucco, bucco* – cheek by jowl – how many fingers can I get up your ass before you howl?!" [19]

When he reached back to fist the creature like one of Mr. Rogers' puppets, the light shifted in the painted glint of the donkey's eye, and the scene changed.

Inky darkness swirled then, from which, with maddening slowness, a sound emerged. Rippling and without form, the atmosphere against my eardrums gradually took on the frightening reverb of Parthia's laughter.

I lay lashed to the floor grate of that Pasadena garden center, naked, and with the evil cult woman's face hovering above mine. "See?" she said, gesturing.

I rotated my head. Gordon was lying in our motel room, also naked, with his back to me. His body trembled a bit, like it was being racked by barely suppressed sobs.

"What have you done to him?" I asked the priestess. Her face floated in the void between the cold bite of the metal I was strapped to and an even colder glimpse of sky beyond filled with stars.

"I...?" she chuckled. "Nothing. But see your boy there, prodded by your selfishness to a state of expectation, a desire for release, and yet you do nothing but drift asleep."

"I'm overly tired...." I suddenly realized through a molasses haze it had been one week and a day now since I'd had an erection. "...I'll be all right soon enough."

Her cackle split my ears. "Self-centered youth! What does

your pleasure have to do with his?!"

I glanced again at the turned-away figure of my boy in our L.A. motel room. Would my lack of...ability...make Gordon seek relief elsewhere?

"You could," chanted the woman, "keep him unteased, un-brought to the pinnacle of lusty want, *OR*, you could take care of those desires you raised in him yourself."

"But I'm a top, only."

"Ha-ha!" she said. "Your hands were not tied earlier; your lips not stopped up with a muzzle. Those pieces of your anatomy know neither top nor bottom. They should know only love and reciprocation."

What did that mean...?

Suddenly there was a gag in my mouth. Before the Priapus statue-column, Gordon and Lolita were flower-decked and taking one another's hand. The priestess, now moved to the teenagers' sides as officiator, pronounced them "ready for bliss," and the couple came to me. But, they seemed not to see me at all, for they were Frenching wildly, Gordon re-moving her veil and top, and groping her like a wild beast.

I tried to scream, but it was useless. My boy settled the gum-popping girl on my chest like I was the cot. They started making love, and I wanted to die, seething with a jealous rage.

Without warning, light filled the room. I turned to watch Assauer emerging from the motel bathroom. He was wet from the shower and wore only a white towel around his waist. My ex walked the straight line from the door to the side of the bed where Gordon was still crying. He crouched for a moment, whispering soothing words and stroking my boy's hair. When Assauer rose, he moved the bedsheet with him, uncovering my boy and scooping him up into his arms.

Assauer took my boyfriend over to his bed and laid Gor-don down on his back. He removed his towel and Gordon's shorts. Their erect manhoods came into contact. They kissed, passionately, before Assauer lifted Gordon's legs, rubbed a big wad of spit on the tip of his enormous dick, and fucked my boy.

Gordon moaned and gripped Assauer's arms like he was in love.

"See?" Parthia said. "Yours is useless now. Only Assauer's blessed cock can quench the thirst you have raised in your boy. Your Gordon craves The Blue One's member, and will get it from now on."

"*Bucco, bucco – dunderhead,*" Tyler laughed, the donkey eye coming back to focus on me. "Chin by cheek – how many fingers do I need to count all the fools both dumb and weak?!"

And then I was conscious of seeing and feeling no more.

Hours and hours later, I woke with only the weary sensation of knowing time had passed by very unkindly.

I rolled out of bed, scratching my belly and heading for the john. I barely kept my eyes open as I pissed and recollected what a crazy night it had been with Tre, and what an awful dream to boot.

A few minutes later, I was crawling back into bed, intending to snooze for a while, but just as I settled down on my pillow again, I sprang up, fully awake.

Gordon was not there.

With steady and deliberate movements, I stood and stalked over to the other bed. My boy was sound asleep on top of the sheets in Assauer's arms. Both were naked as bluejays.

Rage drew a sheen of spots before my vision, but, dispassionately, I went to the desk drawer. As quietly as an assassin, I pulled the lever and brought the box into sight. In another moment, I had Hojax's stolen pistol in my grip.

I walked back to the bedside, cocked it and placed it next to Gordon's temple.

I spoke softly, more to myself than them. "Maybe," I said, "it's time for you to really fall on your swords. Maybe I should help you stay like this, transfigured to death...."

Assauer awoke, hearing me, and slowly climbed over Gordon to shield him. An unusually frightened tone crept into his voice as he asked, "*Was tust du? Komm mal runter und beruhige dich.*"

His question and statement of "What are you doing? Calm the fuck down" had no effect on me.

Seeing that, Assauer rose out of bed, pushing me and my gun back away from the boy.

Gordon woke up then, blinking in disbelief at me pointing the gun at my ex.

I grunted once, stormed over to the window, and jerked up the blinds to let the afternoon sun bleach their tainted flesh.

I told Assauer, "Pack up and get lost."

While the two of them got dressed, I went to the closets and pulled down our bags and loot. I dumped all the contents, including the gifts from Tre-Princely last night, onto the sheets and started making two equal piles. I told my ex, "After we split our things, our divorce is final. I never want to see you again."

"Feeling's mutual," Assauer said. *"Arschloch."*

He stuffed his two bags with clothes and pawnable merchandise. After he shouldered them, a changed expression crept over his face, becoming conspicuously darker.

Assauer walked over and 'found' the gun right where I had left it sitting in its box. He pointed it at me. "Now, let's divide the boy too. Why should you be the only one to benefit from that particular ill-gotten gain? Time to divvy up that booty as well."

"What?!" I scoffed. "You're crazy. You're no Solomon about to rip our baby apart just to make a point."

"Share and share alike," Assauer said through a maniacal grin. "Those are your words, brother. Your. Words!"

Gordon threw himself between us, tears in his eyes. He pleaded, pushing on our chests, "Don't risk doing something foolish that will get the cops over here. Besides, it's all my fault. Why fight each other like common scrappers when neither of you are to blame?"

Gordon finally fell on his knees and dramatically hugged Assauer's shins. "If you want to shoot somebody, then it's me who deserves to die. Don't you see that?!"

My ex softened, and when he reached down to pick Gordon up off the floor, my boyfriend rose skillfully, in a way which allowed him to be in possession of the Luger by the time he was on his feet.

Cool as a zucchini, Gordon un-cocked it, went to the box, shut the gun up and slammed it in the drawer.

We stood around for a moment more, until I told Assauer, "All right, you can go now."

"Not yet," he said. "We still have one piece of unfinished business." Assauer meant Gordon.

"He's staying put."

"Is he? You own him, do you? Like a slave."

"Um—"

"You stay out of it, honey."

"Let's give the boy a chance to decide for himself." Assauer touched Gordon's face. "It's only fair he tells us who he wants to be with."

Cocksure about my boyfriend's love, I said, "All right. Let's do that."

Assauer went to the motel room door, opening it with the 'Do Not

Disturb' sign still flapping. Fresh air assaulted our stalemated condition as he stood there and waited. "Well?" he asked Gordon, extending his hand.

After another tense moment, where time itself seemed to be hostage, my boyfriend glanced at the drawer with the gun and then me.

Gordon went to Assauer and they left together, my boy closing the door quietly after him.

Alone, in crushing silence, I crumpled to my knees on the floor. Racked by sudden sobs I felt I couldn't breathe. For the first time, I knew I was truly cursed.

Chapter 16: Kohl's Lament

I awoke beneath a curtain of sweat, groaning and painfully rolling onto my back. It seemed not even troubled naps were going to be allotted to me, because the midday laughter and sunlight of Venice Beach inveigled cunningly between the closed slats of the closed window. They could all go to hell, as far as I was concerned, and join me in my waking, dreamless sleep of the damned.

Rubbing sore eyes, I became conscious exactly how much I hated that soiled spot on the ceiling of this cheap motel room. I hated that I've had to look at it for three days now, ever since the afternoon my slime-bag ex walked Gordon out of my life.

Frustrated, I heaved over with a sigh and sat on the edge of the rumpled sheets. They hadn't been changed since I got here, but the little bit of moving air licking the moisture on my back felt somewhat refreshing. I'd been forced to relocate – to this beachside dive – because, as someone once told me, the Gay Grapevine is even faster than Dummy J. Dump's Tweets – and mostly just as destructive. Word spread instantly to Neil Campbell that I was 'available,' which made me flee West Hollywood and his throtty clutches.

I stood and stretched, rotating and cracking my back in a few places. Then I fingered my not-so-tidy-whities. They have been the only thing I've worn since I locked myself in this cell.

A few minutes later, the toilet seat went up and I coaxed my useless Judas out into the air. Normally, peeing feels good in its way, but now it only made me think of the lengths I'd gone through to wake him up. On my exiled flight that afternoon, I scored a few street pills of the blue and yellow varieties – the kind old men look for from their hustler dates, lol. I'd also picked up a pack of 'sure fire' herbal supplements at the corner market. After checking in, I had gone to the store briefly to stock up. I needed jarred pickles and energy drinks for my purges.

None of those treatments had worked, either alone or in combination, and the only rewards I got for my attempted 'cure' were a thready pulse, blinking white spots before my eyes, and blinding headaches. It all left me stewing in my anger and not wanting to leave this room. So, I'd just drunk my pickle juice and nursed the last of my Red Bull, hoping against hope...that.... I started to cry thinking about it. I simply hoped my boy would send me a text saying it was all some misunderstanding, that he didn't really run out on me just because I can't get it up.

I flushed and willed the tears to stop by beating my chest, as sick as it was. These teardrops had been no use, just like my three days of fasting and torment. No amount of prescription pharmaceuticals or caffeine; playing, coaxing or fantasy; or streaming porn on my phone had made a bit of difference. Except to drive me closer to utter despair.

Moving as if in a trance, I gradually found myself standing by the closets, in an area with a vanity, sink and mirror. I dared to turn on the light.

What I saw shocked me. Tired and thin, I kicked my hands out on the plastic 'marble' to lean in closer. When did I get those puffy crescents under my eyes; when had my fair hair become such a tangled mess; when did it get cowlicked, sticking up on one side?

"*Kacke!*" I called out. "Land or sea – I don't give a fuck which – punish me. Tell me why am I not drowned in a dirty sinkhole opening beneath my tired feet this very second? And you, great Oceans, you who do not even spare the innocent, whirlwind me down through a maelstrom free of conscience, knowing the soul you smother in wetness is not blameless. I'll never be counted among the acquitted. But, enough—"

I whipped out the offending member and addressed it in the mirror. "And you, limp noodle, *are* you really of the vibrant earth? Part of the soil, alive with sprouting life, rich ground for all things verdant and self-generating? No, inert as clay, you have betrayed me too, and lost me my boy.

"But you should belong to the swelling tides as well, you who course with the strength, the same salinity as the world's vast oceans. You who provide stars as abundant and life-bearing as the cosmos – but not if you are weak. Not if you simply hang between a man's legs like a useless ornament."

And yet this sad state had not always been my lot. Certainly not the night I fucked Assauer in the shadow of Hercules' club, the fountain in Brunswick where we first let down our defenses. No, then it had been my prowess, my dick itself, that had advanced me and Assauer from mere fuck buddies to partners in crime, boyfriends – and yes, lovers too – feeling and sharing in full communion.

Such a thought of deep connection caused my mind to drift back to a pivotal night in our relationship.

"You got what, where...?" I asked in disbelief.

"A liaison position at Ramstein."

"The U.S. Air Base...?"

"Yes. And you're coming with me."

It had been six months since me and Assauer graduated from the Technical University of Braunschweig – just barely – and become underemployed and way-underpaid civil servants of a kind. We had two years to endure before we could take our final exam for full certification. Assauer was restless, but still, restless enough to move halfway across the country...?

"What will I do? Peel potatoes for those Yankee French

fries?!"

"No, Dumbo. Look."

He held out his phone, and on it was the website for the Ramstein-Miesenbach School System. They were recruiting part-time teacher apprentices to be on standby as substitute teachers.

I glared at him, pretending to be incensed, hoping I didn't actually show how sad I was to be the one reduced to needing to take such a job. "What's the difference? They'll only give the minimum ten hours of work a week, plus eight more of lectures."

"The same as here, right? Think about it. There we'll have a chance to stand out more."

He had a point. Since the university was in this town, apprentice teachers in Brunswick were cheaper by the kilo than even the famous braunschweiger.

"Come on, Kohl. Think of the adventures. Me, on base, sneaking you in, so we can have fun hunting down corn-fed Midwestern guys—"

"Sex?"

"Well, of course that, but I also meant fun as in doing a little harmless sob-story ripping off. And who knows, we might get a few good contacts in America this way too."

I hated being poor.

"We can try it."

Truth was, I felt I owed it to my boyfriend. In our second year of university, I got restless and forced a reluctant Assauer to open up our relationship. At first – and maybe for a solid year – we'd worked together to get freshmen out of their pants and into our bed together, but then one day, a sexy boy on the tram caught my eye and I went back to his flat to fuck him without my boyfriend.

Unfortunately, news got around, and Assauer sought revenge in a cruel and unusual way. Yes, he found a freshman girl to seduce and later told me all about the sordid details.

It made me crazy with jealousy – caused a huge scene –

ending with Assauer saying, one, it was my fault because I never let him have my ass, and two, he was Bi and had no problems being faithful to me but if I was seeking dick elsewhere he was going to find and…. I can't even repeat what he said, it was so gross.

And so our relationship became completely open. But we were upfront. I'd tell him which guy I was going after, and he'd name which bimbo-chicklet-tart he was 'slammin'.

"Are you sure, Kohl?" Assauer asked me about moving to Ramstein.

"Yes. You're special to me – plus, I owe you. You know that, and I think we make a pretty great team."

Over the last two years, possibly because of me, my boyfriend had toughened and learned how to hide his cards well, but now his old smile returned as he hugged me. However, I couldn't help wondering if he loved me more than I did him….

Months later, Assauer rolled into the flat one night with a drunk 'troop,' and we fucked the hell out of him. As the contented man lay between our arms sleeping that night, we talked.

"What's the matter, Kohl?"

"I'm fine."

"Something's on your mind. The school's okay?"

"Which one?" Not only was I on call for the district's 'sick list' to be ready for any school, subject or grade as needed, but I'd been making ends meet by teaching nights at a cram school.

Assauer was not amused. "I don't know. You tell me, *Idiot*."

But…how could I tell him about Rolf…? How could I tell my boyfriend that I was developing feelings for one of my regular cram students? A teenage one at that….

I lay myself down in the tub, briefs still on, and turned on the water.
I didn't know, maybe I intended to drown myself in this landlocked disgrace of a Venice Beach motel room; maybe I intended to mitigate my own stink; or maybe I just wanted to feel something other than hurt and powerless anger.
The cold crawled like insect legs of ice all around my skin as the tub

filled. As bad as I was in Germany, I never betrayed my ex like he'd done to me in L.A., and my dalliance with guys was to be expected. On the other hand, his character was disgusting! Whoring himself out like that on the air base, taking all-cummers, being handmaiden to their behind-the-mess-hall hungers – their PX parking lot proclivities; their parade field fornications! For all I know, he might have worn a skirt for some of them, to kickstart their propellers. As for 'his other side,' the dark one, Assauer's tolerance of slit had a severely feminizing influence on his otherwise manly soul. *Gott im Himmel!* I pitied his weakness, because it put him in the compromised position of straight guys. They're all eventually enfeebled and driven mad by a sad subservience to hoo-ha juice. The hets themselves can't help it – poor bastards – because somehow or other, they are born 'that way' {they claim}, and no amount of shaming, name-calling, deprivation of liberty and civil rights – not to mention simply calling on God to pray-the-straight away – can help them overcome their sore affliction. But for a strong Gay man like Assauer to knowingly be effeminized by dependence upon *it,* like he contracted an infectious itch for *it* through vaginal sex, made me quiver in revulsion and fury.

Plus, it's gross!

I slid my head below water and left it there. Through open eyes, I saw my ex on that horrible night we had to flee our homeland. For all his faults, he stuck with me when no one else would.

I rose from the water confused. Had my *anger* drawn forth more tears…?

But still, he stole my Gordon. How could I not hate my ex for that?

Shutting off the water, I lay back and realized I hadn't taken off my shorts. Oh well, but if my boy saw this, he'd bust his sweet gut laughing at me.

Yes, sweet Gordon. How I remember that day too. The one where the boy literally led me on, even though I had sworn off jail-bait temptations.…

"How was *your* day there? Mine was okay, I guess."

"The kids are better behaved than I expected."

"Well," Assauer told me as we ate our dinner, still in our substitute shirts and ties, "Aptos is a pretty rich town."

"It's sure out of the way."

My ex nodded as he spooned mashed potatoes.

We'd been traveling around the States for about ten months, picking up teaching certificates in various places and subbing. Mostly, we'd kept ourselves low and out of trouble.

"There seems to be a lot of healthy, young athletes at this new school—" I was already thinking of one in particular....

"Must be the sea air," he joked, but maybe there was something to that. We'd been here a week or two, and slowly acclimating to the cycle of warm, sunshiny days being followed by foggy, bracing evenings and nights. It put a spring in the step and a smile on the face—

"What are you thinking about?"

"Nothing. Just how the kids have lockers outside, that's all."

He let the subject drop, and I vowed to forget all about the sexy young man I'd been seeing every day at his locker as I passed along. Usually the boy would be laughing with buddies – or sometimes standing, grinning-and-bearing the fawning awkwardness of a pair of infatuated girls – but no matter the situation, the tall kid with the longish curly hair and a devil-may-care cant to his full rosy lips, had a smile for me, had a lingering turn of his head as he traced my progress with his eyes.

But today had been different, or more accurately, my so-called moral resolve, weaker. For, obviously knowing 'the game' better than that young man, I continued on past his position – three steps: one, two, three – and glanced over my shoulder, back at the lad.

He nodded to me, licking his lower lip and letting a knowing smile shine.

'Oh, fuck,' I thought. 'Not again.'

"Kohl?"

"Yeah, Assauer. I'm okay, really. I think I'm going to like Aptos."

"Okay," he said skeptically. "Just stick to the plan and don't enjoy it too much."

I ate my minestrone in silence, letting the sweetness of the boy's thought course through me.

I tried, I really had. After that day with the glancing eye-contact, whenever I saw this kid, I headed the other direction. I avoided asking who he was, who his people were, what his interests were. As I say, I tried.

But one day after several months of the schoolyear had gone by, I was alone in my classroom tidying up at the end of the day. The bell had already rung, and the final thing I needed to do was roll the overhead projector back to the storage room. When I turned around, there he was.

"Mr. Kohl?"

"Um – yes." I couldn't help smiling.

"Gordon Sanchez. I'm a junior here." He shifted the strap of his heavy gym bag and held out his hand.

"Um—" I shook it, growing hot at his touch.

"Need help with that?"

Before I could say anything more, the sexy boy was wheeling the cart out of the room. I switched off the lights and followed.

"This one?" he asked, stopping in front of the correct storage room with a wickedly delicious look on his face.

"Yes. You know your way around, huh?"

That was the first time I saw him blush.

He stood aside as I unlocked the door and stepped in. Gordon Sanchez followed, pushing the projector cart forward and closing the door behind him.

A moment later, his bag landed on the floor with a mighty thud, and he was guiding me with his tongue in my mouth to stand against the wall.

Eyes closed, his roving hands on my clothes felt like fire. I was instantly hard, as he was without a doubt an experienced and expert kisser.

He released me and slid down to his knees, undoing my slacks and taking them floorward as he went.

Just before he took me into his mouth, I fingered the front of his silken hair and made him look up at me.

"You sure?" I asked.

He held my eyes and went down on me, moaning his consent loudly enough that I felt it along every inch of my spine.

Even as I gripped onto his head and began to enjoy it, I knew part of the thrill was the sheer danger of it all.

I wound up back before the vanity, leaning on it, a towel around my waist. Perfect droplets of moisture dotted my skin, except on my cheek. There they had a different shape and flavor....

My sweet Gordon, I thought you loved me. But maybe you only loved my cock. Could that be? Could Assauer's freakishly enlarged donkey dick be the thing that led you astray?

I spoke to him, as if I could see him over my shoulder in the mirror. "Everybody looks at us and assumes the worst of me – figures me to be a cradle-robber – but they don't know, can't see through your beautiful looks how sultry your boy-heart really is."

I pounded my fist on the sink.

"Oh, God!" I cried. "Like a cheap G.I. groupie – a soldier strumpet; a troop trollop! – my beloved boy sold out my love for a romp in the back of the barracks."

I sunk to my knees, these lyrics forming on my lips:

> "On my craggy outcrop, alone,
> the roar of vengeance is as loud
> as the whole sea upon a stone –
> laying me on her flinty shroud.
>
>> Do I deserve such a cruel fate;
>> is my 'sin' any worse than his,
>> the one who escapes without harm;
>> the lying one who steals from me;
>> the scoundrel without compassion;
>> the lover with no love in his heart;
>> the ex with only malice in his?
>>
>> No, too cruel is the punishment
>> to live with what I don't deserve,
>> to be forced to suffer endless
>> rebukes from within my own heart
>> while they go on free to enjoy
>> the illicit bliss of their crime.
>> So earth below, open and swallow;
>> so sky above, part clouds and smite me.
>
> On this heartless cliff-face copestone,
> my voice cries for mercy aloud,
> but Death will not let me atone –
> for cruelty is much too proud."

That's it. A concept had come into my head, making me stagger to the desk drawer. In another minute, I had Hojax's pistol loaded and in my hand.

I ripped up the blinds and stood blinking and paralyzed by the sun.

Regarding the handgun slowly lifting to my temple, I wondered what possible use is a Gay man who can't get it up.

I cocked the piece, murmuring, "Take me, O ye gods. Here, in this hell-hole, let me end this, my – mis...er...y...."

But slowly, the motion of people outside – walking, riding bicycles, cruising on skateboards over the roadway fronting the beach – made me angry. They were having too much fun. Too much goddamned 'life' ran through their veins.

I demanded to know, "Why should I be the one to do it?!"

I un-cocked the gun, digging in my bag for some clean clothes. And while I got dressed, the afternoon noise and animation just outside my window caused me to grow angrier and angrier.

Chapter 17: Teardrops, or Hell-Bound on Venice Beach

I hated it.

The afternoon crowds on the Promenade were thick and annoying. Visitors, overdressed and deeply shaded in near-black sunglasses and ridiculous hats, ambled along in nothing-to-do tourist gaits. Shirtless Gay twinks roller-skated between them, ducking in and out, bobbing and weaving, drunk on fresh air and the possibilities offered by being young and desirable.

I hated the stage-set architecture trying to be a plaster-cast mockup of the Doge's Palace; hated the pastel colors; despised the long line of palm trees edging the sands of the beach to my left; resented how every other storefront was filled with a souvenir shop, hawking sweatshirts and squeaky racks of postcards. These stands littered the sidewalks. I hated the locals too, the young toughs come out to strut and cause trouble with rival testosterone-soaked delinquents; hated the other visitors just moseying down here to lounge *al fresco* at the sidewalk bars and burger joints; hated the fact everyone around me was here to have a good time in their own way.

I prowled the Promenade for a different reason. Like one possessed, I scowled at each and every person who dared make eye contact with me. Young, old, rich, poor – it didn't matter. I moved along with purpose, feeling Hojax's Luger pinching and scraping my pubic region from where it was stuck between my tee-shirt and the band of my jeans.

I was hell-bound to make something happen; wanted to get into an argument; wanted someone to take a swing. Then, like the plot to some old black and white 50s teen-movie rumble, I'd take out my gun and make those who have hurt me sorry.

In other words, slowing my pace, my wild and distracted countenance – I'm sure – showing nothing but thoughts of blood and slaughter, I began to notice the long line in front of a salmon-colored ice cream parlor. Leaning against the low wall opposite the place, the one separating the Promenade from the drop-off to palm trees and beach, were a gang of Latin *cholos*. Tattoos abounding on their bare arms, they conformed to their profession's uniform of saggy-ass, puff-daddy jeans and white tank tops. Heads and foreheads were wrapped in various folds of bandanas, and glittery studs shone from every young, manly earlobe.

I hated them.

I passed by, making sure to look more pissed than ever, and had a hard time suppressing the notion of how sweet and innocent they actually looked: quietly enjoying their own company, the sights, the sounds, and the creamy cones they licked with boyish grins.

In fact, they were so content and self-contained, they missed my bad-ass confrontation entirely. I went on a few paces and circled back, more pissed than ever!

On the second go-round, the biggest, baddest of their group – a twenty- or twenty-one-year-old with a goatee, expressive eyes, and white durag – nodded at me in a bemused way.

I kept a leer locked on him as I moved passed and glanced back. He still observed me and elbowed a couple of amigos, like he wanted to share a joke.

Third time around, I was sure all of them watched as I pretended to fan my tummy with the flap of my tee-shirt, but was really showing them my peace-maker.

I turned back to gauge reactions, and to my horror, saw those young thugs watching a pair of bikini-clad girls roller skating from the other direction.

I gave up on them and walked on.

After another hundred paces, a white sign like a traffic indicator rose on a metal pole. I followed it to one of the best-known features of Venice, California.

However, Muscle 'Beach' turned out not to be a beach at all. In the middle of what by rights should have been a parking lot to an ugly building in orange, a concrete curb and tall blue handrail enclosed a patch of asphalt. In this cage, there was evidently a dress code, or a non-dress code, as all the tanned muscle-bounds wore knee-length shorts, flip flops and no shirts.

A crowd of pasty tourists blinked in the sun next to pimply teen-boy ninety-nine-pounders with skateboards kicked into their palms. They stood two and three deep to watch the profoundly homoerotic, and thus deeply homophobic flexing, 'spotting' and grunting on display like a zoo exhibit. If there were a placard it would have said: "Meatheads in their natural environment. Please do not feed."

I hated them.

I sidled up to a bare patch of fencing, by the rack where the dumbbells – and their weights – were stretched out on a bench. An African American guy was extending his arms, while his white companion lay on the bench and lifted his metal rod up in the air.

I elbowed a geeky kid to my right and said in a voice way too loud: "Hans *und* Franz – careful boy, they may want to pump you up, if you know *vhat* I mean." [20]

The teen looked aghast; the muscle-heads turned to stare.

"You never know with these types," I added.

The boy pushed up his glasses and informed me, "He's my uncle, you pervert."

"As if," I laughed needlessly, but suddenly the wimpy kid cracked his knuckles, and his buddies – all equally scrawny – stepped up to his defense.

"You got a problem with Gary's uncle and his husband, man?" his friend asked me.

"Phaw," I coughed. "Yeah. And with the rest of the world too."

"Get lost," another teen voice called out.

"Oh, yeah. Who's gonna make me?!" I flipped around.

A seven-foot-tall boy with no-baloney written on his face had been the one to tell me to spam, so, despite feeling like a *Hosenscheisser*, I did. I mean, I couldn't shoot a kid, could I...?

I hated all of this. Nothing I plan ever seems to work out.

Kicking loose sand on the pavement as I went, I left the Muscle Beach muscle-heads and plodded back along the Promenade. All the colors were beginning to be intensified by the angling sun headed towards the western waters, but my heart was more troubled than ever. If I allowed my *adagio* pace to generate any thoughts at all, they would have conjured Gordon's smile, Gordon's laugh, Gordon's sweet taste as I kissed him – and what good would that do...? Only make me feel like dropping to my knees in the middle of the slow surge of humanity and burst into tears.

In other words, no good at all.

Something made the skin prickle on the back of my neck. I looked around to identify the source. Continuing to walk casually, even bothering to thrust hands in my pockets, I pretended not to notice the ice-cream *cholos* from earlier following me intently several yards behind.

I might have gone looking for trouble, but now that it was returning the favor, my heart pounded and my wrists perspired with concern.

Past an annoying souvenir kiosk, with plastic keychains in one of a thousand names, I dodged behind a gaggle of Chinese tourists, using them as a visual shield, and took off.

The gun really hurt me now, but I ran close to the buildings, hearing thick-soled sneakers squeak in pursuit behind me.

Nearly out of breath, I ducked into an alley and dashed into a dead-end niche for trash cans.

It was dark here, and I straightened my spine to still my respiration so I could tell if the thugs knew where I was.

They did. Like slow motion, they lined up one by one in a semi-circle outside the opening until the guy in the center reached in and dragged me out by the tee-shirt.

Before I knew it, he'd shoved me across the alley and up against the brick wall on the other side. It took me a non-focused minute to get the wind back in me, and after I had, the men had reassembled their half-circle around me, only now their leader with his white head covering and sexy goatee was dead center in front of me.

A lopsided grin appeared. He took two steps forward, and then I really freaked out. This guy wore a fairly small gold pendant – but without any mistake at all – I saw it was a winged cock: the mark of 'them.'

The young man's advance did not stop. He leaned in really close, only inches away, driving my back and extended hands along the wall so deep, I wished I could melt into the mortar.

As tenderly as a lover's touch, he moved my shirt aside and extracted the gun. His rich brown eyes never left mine.

The young tough held the weapon up between our faces, just below the level of our lips. When he spoke, the deepness of his voice echoed in my chest.

"Until you submit to My control—"

Somehow, through the thready pulse pounding in my ears, the guy's tones blended....

"—This state you are in—"

With Parthia's Latin the night of the garden center....

"—Will persist all the miserable—"

The young man's face merged with that of the maniacal woman's visage as she placed her curse on me....

"—Days of your life."

His silence snapped me fully back to reality. Slowly, he rotated his face and brought a teardrop tattoo under his left eye into view.

The cholo raised the gun and used the tip of the barrel to trace a line from the inky blob down his cheek, chin and chest. It ended up pointing to the pendant. I got the message: the Priapus cult was watching me at all times.

With that, the leader straightened up, tucked Hojax's pistol in the back waist of his jeans and slowly walked towards the Promenade. The semicircle peeled off one by one to follow him.

Alone, I swallowed down my panic and stayed put. I felt stripped... nay, I felt robbed of my revenge.... But I used the couple of minutes to decide what to do. I'd go to the motel, pack up and beat it. Yet, where would I go to...? That I'd figure out along the way.

I stayed still for another moment or two, but then my boy's face intruded on my misery again. I'd be damned if I cried in such a stinking Venice Beach garbage dump. I wouldn't give the fucking nature god the fucking satisfaction.

I bolted and took off, not minding anything or anyone as I reached the full sunlight of the public thoroughfare.

I should have though, for as soon as I got free of the alley, I ran smack into a tall guy. His stature knocked all the momentum back through my body and sat me flat on my ass.

Stunned, with the ever-organizing light behind his head like a halo, the man bent down to pick me up.

"Kohl? What the hell—"

"Oh, my God…. Bertram?"

"Yeah, buddy." He started brushing me off; it was my tall friend with the nose ring from the Flying Dutchman.

"Bertram Hammerick, what are you doing here?" I suddenly felt very weak.

His strong hands reached out again to steady me, by both the chest and back. "I just got done with a client, and I need to decompress a bit before I head back home. You all right?"

"Um—" Through my foggy head, I remembered now that my buddy was some kind of racial kink leader, with a community of followers. "I'm okay, just – had a shock, that's all."

"Ah, man. Neil told me, and I'm sorry to hear about Gordon and your ex."

Neil Campbell. Of course the entire artists' compound would know of my personal misery by now.

He went on, sensing, I guess, I didn't want to talk about my boy, "I'm just about to grab a beer and a bite to eat. Wanna join?"

At the mere mention of solid food, my stomach answered for me with a loud roar. "Yeah." I'd suddenly come over all hungry.

"Want another?" Bertram held up his empty lager glass.

I nodded. What the hell. We'd been here for about an hour, and this would only be my fourth, lol.

I polished off the rest of my burger and settled back on my sidewalk café chair to leisurely peck at my fries. The crowds had thinned the nearer the sun got to the horizon. Perhaps they'd all moved to the sand to sit and watch it set.

My stomach contentedly reminded me this had been the first real meal since before Tre-Princely's horrendous *cena*.

"So," Bertram said, after ordering two more Pilsen, "a few of us from the Flying Dutchman are heading out to the Burning Man arts festival in a couple weeks. I have to leave beforehand – tomorrow in fact."

"Why's that?"

"I'm needed in Vegas for a week."

"Work?" I chuckled.

"Work, work, work." He laughed.

I suddenly got serious. "Is that Neil Campbell going to Burning Man?"

"Hell no. No one likes Aussies – they're riddled with love-hate complexes. Yuck."

I had to smile. Clearly Bertram was a man of discriminating tastes.

Our beer arrived, and I toasted him for that. "What you said, I couldn't have put it better. Cheers!"

After we clinked and drank, 'The Hammer' licked the foam off his upper lip and said, "Why don't you come? You can be my assistant for the Vegas stay – field phone calls, keep my appointment book, keep me fed and hydrated, etc. – and we can unwind at the desert festival after. Seems like you need a little distraction."

"Phut..." I sputtered, "do I. But you're serious. You'd want me along?"

"Yep. We click, and we're two tops, so there's no sexual tension."

"Yeah, getting away would be nice. We wouldn't fight over any of your cult members anyway, that's for sure."

He chuckled. "Don't want any alt-white ass?"

"Nope."

After a bit of drinking and snacking on the last of our food, I glanced out to the waves once more. The inward-coming motion of the surf somehow almost made me want to cry again. It conjured my boy's beautiful face.

What was wrong with me? How could I—

And then, I don't know how to describe it – the way the orange orb of the sun burned my retina and caused pleasant spots when I looked away; the manner in which the voices of visitors all around me suddenly assumed a normal, holiday-making lilt again; the fresh feel of sea breeze on my pallid skin – it all blended into a new concept for me.

Why mope? Why stay in L.A. when it's for sure the one place Assauer and Gordon are not? Why not look for him – win my beloved back, or die trying?!

"You sure, Bertram? You'd let me come with you?" I tried to suppress a smile as I waited for him to take a bite of chocolate cake. 'Why it gotta be chocolate?' I laughed to myself.

"Sure thing."

He was a man of many statements in few words, and I could have kissed him in newfound hope and determination. Instead, I nodded my gratitude towards his grin, and let my sight again drift westward.

I did not want the ground or ocean to swallow me up. I wanted to find and win Gordon back, no matter if I needed to move earth or sea to do it. I'd suffer all embarrassment and hardship just to have the boy I love back in my arms.

I told Bertram, "With your help, I can follow the breadcrumbs, or chalk marks like Theseus in the maze of the Minotaur. The ones left by other kink cults, so I can undo the damage wrought by the donkey-dick freaks."

"That's great, buddy. A positive outlook makes all the difference."

I realized I'd have to tell him more, but there'd be time tonight or on the flight tomorrow.

Now I stood up, wanting to pack.

I turned to the fading starlight from the sun and knew I'd just taken the first step of a new journey. And for once in my life, I had purpose.

"...deorsum fluens..."

Part Six
Ostriches in the Sand

#WITH-nitrates, #silly-cone,

#fisting-dummies, #kitschy,

#lower-than-low, #Arrrrr!

#Chicken-man, #corndog,

#Little-Stevie-Tinn, #chill!

#one-smart-biscuit,

#the-Ohio-dream,

#fake-black-lady,

#beef-cheeks

Chapter 18: A Tool of a Toady

I flicked it with my fingertip. Bertram's tablet screen shot straight to his calendar, and I saw his 3:00 PM appointment was a guy code-named 'Uncle Tommie.' He was booked for an impressive four hours.

We'd been here for several days already, and my racial kink friend was right about needing help. It had been non-stop since the moment we'd checked into this Bellagio penthouse suite. Sheepish men, and those with red necks and shaggy beards, trouped in one by one for 'atonement' with the Master. They arrived in sunglasses and blushing hues, but left with springing steps and relieved smiles in their eyes.

As I glanced out the window and over Sin City, I was glad for this suite – we each had our own bedroom, while two more cycled through penitents and chamber maids, who were on stand-by 24/7. The women from House-keeping shrugged, apparently used to this sort of thing, and did not ask about the racks of flogs, shackles, and knotted lengths of rope each 'penitent chapel' contained.

After the hotel staff had cleaned and tidied, and after Bertram had escorted a man to one of the rooms, I could be alone. Even though these chambers were dedicated to the paying of racial transgressions – and were kept fairly dark and sound-insulated – I could still hear the near-continual bevy of smacks, soft pleadings for forgiveness, and grunts of sexual release. On long appointments, like the one coming up, I could peruse Las Vegas on my own. But I always came back for Bertram's scheduled downtimes to attend to his needs.

Ding! Dong.

Speaking of which – I sprang to my feet – the boy was right on schedule.

I popped over to the door and opened it, immediately stepping back so Room Service could roll in his cart. It rattled cheerily, laid out for high tea – plates on a metal rack with cake and sandwiches, and pots of coffee, cocoa and tea. I made sure Bertram wanted for nothing this time of the afternoon. He needed his strength.

I closed the door and watched the teen-boy booty work under his trousers. He pushed the mobile tray into position by a pair of sofas facing one another.

He'd been the one to come every time, and I'd taken notice for sure, which was his intent, no doubt. A guy doesn't fantail his ass like that by accident.

He set the coffee table for two, knowing the routine, and I inspected the perfectly cut nature of his black slacks and bowtie against the crispness of his white shirt. Eighteen or nineteen, the boy had sandy-blond shag atop his head and a slight bit of lip fuzz to match. Judging by the way the clothes gripped his body, I'd say he'd done some amateur Floor Exercises in high school, and I drooled a little to think about the gymnastic onesie still in his closet at home.

The kid called himself C.G., and now his eyes glanced at me sideways from his task, knowing his ass was sticking out just right.

In another moment, he pushed the empty cart to the suite's kitchenette and came smiling towards me at the door.

"Will there be anything else, Mr. Kohl?"

"No, we're set." I slipped him a twenty, my hand briefly on his shoulder. "See you at seven."

"Yes, sir." He paused, grinning like only a straight boy on the hustle could, palmed the cash as I watched his fingers sink close to his bulge, and then surprised me.

The same hand came out of his pants again with a hotel card. He gave it to me with a ratcheting down of his smile to lecherous.

"I put my number on the back. Call or text anytime, and I'll be here, sir. To serve you, in any way that I can."

He left quietly, and I looked down. Handwritten appeared: "Claude Germaine," followed by a cellphone number.

I regarded it, feeling a real affinity for this ambitious kid at my beck and call. I was sure he thought nothing special of me, but was on the make with all of his suite guests – picking up spare hundreds as they came his way – and why not. I'd have him pinned down in a second, if.... Well, and despite how popular his ass must be on this top-floor bastion of affluence, I can't perform, and I'm not a bottom.

The door from his bedroom opened and Bertram came out wearing a bathrobe, toweling off his short hair.

"Good nap and shower?"

"Yeah, Kohl, thank you."

He immediately made a beet line for the sofa and sat. I poured him some coffee while he selected sandwich slices. I glanced at my watch as I served him his beverage; we had a little while before 'Uncle' showed up.

He said "I'm famished," but I couldn't help laughing.

"Whaaat...?" Crumbs came tumbling out of Bertram's mouth.

"I guess I've never seen you in your full kink vestments before." For indeed, The Black Hammer's robe had slipped open, revealing a harness and waist belt above a leather jock – long cuffs covered his wrists.

Far from shy, he kicked the robe off his thighs and lounged back so I had a full, sumptuous view.

He smiled while chewing. "I got suited up right away. Next penitent is on his way."

"Yeah, but you can relax a bit. Still got ten minutes."

He took a sip of coffee. "Been slammed. My yearly week in Vegas has always been like this. You've been great arranging things for me, Kohl. I really appreciate it." He ate some ham and cheese.

"I don't mind helping out as best I can, and well, let's just say it's been a real eye-opener. I've learned a lot."

"So far, what have you done today?"

"Went to the Liberace Museum."

Bertram laughed.

"I went there to ask around about my doucheball ex – if anybody saw him with Gordon there, as it's the type of tourist spot Assauer would want to check off his list."

"List?"

"His bucket list of kitschy places to say he's been to."

"I see. You have any luck?"

"No."

"Don't worry, still a lot of cheesy places in this town you can go and ask around."

"I guess so."

He lifted his juice glass. "Cheer up. Only rule here is to enjoy yourself."

He toasted, but I was struck by the irony that if I'd been able to enjoy myself with my boy, then Gordon wouldn't have thrown me over for my two-timing *Exfreund*.

"Anyway," I said, "don't worry. I'll clear out of here and head out before your next client – um, pilgrim – arrives."

"You don't have to with this one; especially not with this one."

"How come?"

"Uncle Tommie is an exceptional case. He's all about vocal atonement for his racial sins, and gets off knowing there's an audience to hear his pleas for forgiveness."

"No…. No, shit?"

"I shit you not. He likes an audience, especially a white one, and you will do nicely. In case you haven't noticed, you're white."

I chuckled. "I don't have eyes for such things."

"Well, let me assure you, you are. And so is his 'celebrity' assistant for that matter."

"Fuck. This guy's messed up, huh?" I took a sip of tea.

"Yes. He's my only Black client."

I nearly did a spit-out, swallowing down my *"No…!"* as best I could.

"Yeah."

"So what's he got in his past he needs to do penance for?"

"Oh…" Bertram was suddenly very serious. "A lot. You'll probably recognize his face. Little Stevie Tinn – former token head and laughingstock of the Retrogressive Party."

"Don't think I've heard of him."

"Then you're lucky. Little Stevie was the Chaney-Junior Administration's lackey whipping boy: sent him out to tell African Americans it was all for the best their Social Security was being privatized and turned over for speculation by brokerage-house *Massas* who know better about their money than dumb negros, like 'dem'.'"

"That's dark. He really did that?"

"Fuck! He did much worse. During the fight for The Affordable Care Act, Tinn hushed up a woman telling a town hall meeting about going bankrupt – losing savings, 401k, home – just to try and save her mother's life from cancer. Uncle Tommie, up there, strutting the stage like a cock-ass rooster, one hand on his hip, microphone cord in the other like Cher in her *Half-Breed* phase, told the working mom something like: 'Okay, sista. You done had yo' five minutes of fame in front of them der cameras, so sit yo' black ass down before I be calling the po-lice!'" [21]

I felt sickened to the point of chuckling nervously. "That's so horrible."

Bertram finished his coffee and set the saucer rattling on the table, then, with authority, he cracked his knuckles.

"Most of the poor white bastards coming to me for humiliation raise a spark of pity in my breast. Their sins are at least partially societal. But not so with Stevie Tinn. When I beat him to propitiate flesh for his soul's trespasses, we both know it's for true crimes and misdemeanors."

Bertram finished his last bite of sandwich, adding, "He's a real token tool of a toady – the Gop's wet dream of white-power 'Yessums, boss' politics."

"And you say his PA is some sort of celebrity too?"

"Angekwekwa Umfume-Kintay."

He paused, like that should mean something to me.

"Wha-what?"

"That's her so-called name, although she was born Maggie Smythe III – rich, privileged and white."

"She's not white now?"

He laughed. "Not according to her. Oh, come on, you must have heard about the disgraced woman masquerading as a strong Black Female and heading a Malcolm X activities club before being outed as a closet cracker."

Come to think of it, that did sound somewhat familiar. "And now the Uncle Tom and this culture-appropriator have teamed up?"

"Yeah. I guess they're both social outcasts, pariahs to African Americans – one Black but marshmallow to the core; the other Beige but feeling all hot cocoa on the inside – both ashamed of who they really are."

I shook my head. For this day and age, that was truly sad.

Ding! Dong.

I jumped up to get the door. Bertram dabbed his face with a napkin and stood regally, his beautiful ebony flesh glimpsed through a slit of terry-cloth.

I opened the door and let two people in, a mousy male, and a taller, beefier female tapping furiously on a personal device.

Tinn appeared to be a caricature, or several, really. As a man in his mid-fifties, he looked like a cartoon 'one of the good ones' effigies from a box of instant food – dough-boy expression, wire bifocals, bald head with a monkish fringe of gray-white hair curtaining the back; monkey's foot mustache.

He was also the visual parody of a corporate-owned 'conservative,' with a discount department store suit in gray and a brocade tie that must have cost him all of $20 at the airport. Speaking of airports, no doubt this guy was a true Grand Ole Partisan, and thus an expert toe-tapper under the bathroom stalls.

Angekwekwa Umfume-Kintay was about my size and stature, dressed in a black pantsuit, and mean. A surly snarl inhabited her upper lip as she typed, while a mass of twist-style locks sprung in front of her eyes and forehead like mattress coils. A part of me knew she could not have grown that hair herself, so I suspected a fair portion of actual Black Lady hair had been woven in to 'augment.'

Gathered by the sofa, Bertram did the honors. "This is Kohl, a friend of mine helping out with my trip."

Little Stevie Tinn flashed subservient pearlies at me. "Ah, how do you do, sir? Such a pleasure to meet one of The Hammer's honorable friends and colleagues." He forced a clammy handshake on me.

We paused, glancing together at Uncle's personal assistant.

She eventually looked up from her screen to bark, "'Sup."

I cocked my head in surprise. "Not much."

"Now," Bertram said to Tinn, "have you been practicing your self-abasing punishments, like we discussed online?"

The former RNC Chair turned on a penny. He lost all the squishy deference he'd slathered me with like mayo on white bread and got short with his fellow Black man. "Maybe, maybe not, brotha. You got somethin' you wanna say about it?"

Cool as an arctic 4th of July, Bertram latched on to Uncle Tommie's ear and led him to the bedroom.

As he went, stooped over as he was, the toady still made sure to turn his face back to me, bury his pain in a fake-ass smile, and say, "A pleasure to have made your acquaint—"

Bertram slammed the door behind them.

After a moment of awkward silence, I said to the PA "Help yourself" with a hand gesture. Soon after, I was back at the sofa, loading up my plate with a delayed lunch.

Umfume-Kintay, née Smythe, came around and sat on my left, pretending she was not checking me up and down from behind the anonymity of her tablet screen.

I chewed and started to hear odd things from the Black Hammer's atonement room. First, there were orders to strip, and then Tinn's vocal refusal.

"So, you a queer too?"

Angekwekwa's question startled me; she'd barely even made eye-contact with me.

I swallowed. "Yeah, I'm a real *Gay* – you Black?"

She set down her gadget with a sigh. Now she held my eyes like a schoolmarm going over a lesson she'd rehearsed her whole, tired career. "Just like you queers carrying on these days about 'hetero-flexible' this, metro-sexual that – not to mention poly-wanna-experiment in collage and 'Don't-label-me-bro' – there's broad fan deck of Afro-tinted mores, attractions, culture, and forms of expression in this country. So...think of me like this: I'm just one of the darker spots on the great African American fan deck." As punctuation for her bit of sham sophistry, she smiled smugly.

'*Gott im Himmel*,' I realized. 'She *is* white!' I mean, how pastier could a person get, except for occasions where they're lucky enough to have backup vocals from the Mighty White Chorus, lol.

We were both distracted; more muffled sounds of the penance-in-progress drifted out to us. First, Uncle's refusals, followed by smacks and yelps from the cowardly kowtowed. Then Bertram's strong voice telling the supplicant what a disgraceful streak of toe fungus he was, followed by more smacks and moans of pleasured resistance.

"Sounds like a load of white-wash to me."

"Hey, now, I ain't got no beef against quee—"

"Use Gay, for God's sake."

A new light dawned. "You a foreigner too?"

"Yes. German."

"Ku-ool."

She warmed to me a bit, unfortunately, and tucked a knee under her as she rotated on the sofa cushion to gape at me with a power scowl. I ate and slowly came to realize this woman was 'black' in the same studied way an angry, bitter drag queen is 'feminine.'

"I ain't got no problem with you people; look who I work for," she said, casting a disgusted glance at the door from behind which Tinn's whipping sounds emerged.

I set down my sandwich. "Is Uncle Tommie out...?"

"Oh! Fuck no. He follows a long line of closeted Milkmen – RNC flunkies required to give head as part of 'the position.'"

"Uh." I was learning more than I wanted.

The sounds from the other room had transitioned to Tinn agreeing with Bertram on what a worthless traitor to his race he was and needing re-education.

"I don't mind you being queer, you know. As you're fly and all, and you are, so you must be gettin' lots o'booty in Vegas."

"No..." Something made me hesitate. I didn't know for what reason, but I somehow felt I had nothing to lose, so I confessed. "Actually, I'm here with Bertram to try and track down my ex and current boyfriend. They ran off together because...well, because I can't get it up."

"Shiiiiiitttt...?"

"Yes, it's true. See, back in L.A. I ran afoul of a schizoid sex cult, and the mad leader put a hex on my dick."

"No lie?"

"Weird things happen, huh?"

Speak of the devil, sounds of 'weirdness' from the other room punctuated my point. Now Little Stevie Tinn was practically begging for big black *Gockel* to wash away his sins.

"I guess you could say that. You lookin' for a cure or somethin'...?"

Angekwekwa's power-salute attitude was slipping. She continued a bit more sheepishly. "Cuz, word on the street says there's a Vegas underground cult...to, well, to the Cock God."

My heart lurched. "Not to Priapus?!"

"Who? No, no, to the Holy God—" She stopped herself short, readjusting her 'ku-ool.' "Um, if you're serious about finding a cure – you know, for your gay limp biscuit – I could maybe see about an intro to our...I mean, to their leader."

I shrugged. "You think they could help?"

She winked. "Oh, I know they can."

Sounds of full-on sex interrupted us again. Tinn was grunting and yelling at top volume, pleading for Bertram to "Fuck this sissy negro ass like it deserves – by a real back man!" He settled into a rhythm and continued to sing out, as if they were the words of an old spiritual, "Oh, yes – yes indeedy, Lordy, yes!"

Uncle Tommie, surly little penitent, was now a full-on penetrant, and in the thralls of sheer atonement ecstasy.

"Alone, newly alone –
Counting the characters of love
For my lost boy.
My heart aches for you –
Alone, yet not alone."

I rechecked the character count before posting; 110, that was all right. I'd been uploading lovesick tweets for Gordon since I'd resolved to fight and win him back. It was like a new poetical form all on its own, and it gave my broken heart an outlet to keep my mind fairly constructive.

The pipey fanfare of Mendelssohn's wedding recessional sounded yet again.

I glanced up from my back-pew position in the Holy Rollers Wedding Chapel, Pai Gow Parlor and Skate Rink. I'd first come here a couple of days ago, asking about my ex and Gordon on my tour of Vegas' kitschiest marriage venues, knowing it was right up Assauer's cul-de-sac.

The happy newlywed couple – a pair of middle-aged bikers in black leather and bandannas – stomped down the aisle in their wedding dresses and boots. The six or so people watching as guests trailed out after them for a night on the town. I'd seen half a dozen weddings so far this evening, including being called upon to be an official witness at the union of male and female plumbers from Bemidji – wherever the hell that is, lol.

Thus, right now my heart was heavy. No, broken. Oh…. A new tweet….

> "Like a crystal shattered,
> I grieve a loss, but know
> Yours is the only glue
> To mend this broken heart."

Nothing worse than trying to reduce my heartbreak to 140 characters. It made me sad. I wanted my dick back; I realized now it was the worst curse a cruel god could inflict on a Gay man – worse than death, that's for sure.

I remembered an unpleasant scene from years ago. Thinking, with dread in my stomach as it were, that my ex deserved the truth in Ramstein-Miesenbach, no matter how painful it was to the both of us.

"You what…?"

I had floored Assauer.

"I – um— I've fallen in love with another. A boy named Rolf."

My boyfriend approached me with fiery eyes. "Rolf…? Rolf?! The boy you are tutoring. That boy?"

"Yes. I'm sorry."

"Sorry about which part? That you are tossing me over for a piece of twink ass; sorry that you've deceived me for weeks and months now; or sorry for the boy, the one getting conned by a man five year older than him? Hmmm. Which. One."

"Look, it's not a con. I didn't intend to…to even like the kid. It just happened. I know this is unfair to you—"

"That's it. Pack your bags and get out tonight. We're over."

I stood there.

"What?" Assauer demanded. "What are you fucking grinning at like an ape?"

"I can make it up to you."

"What...?"

I had astounded my boyfriend – um, ex-boyfriend – again.

"There's money too."

He was speechless.

"I can't tell you how I got it, but it's a windfall for us, provided by Rolf's rich daddy."

"Kohl—"

"I'm saying, half of it is yours when we decide to cash it in. I'm still willing to be 100% 'share and share alike' with you, brother."

His tears started to fall. "Is this what you think will make it better? I lose my boyfriend to a snot-nose punk with a rich daddy.... And you think I want cash?"

"No, no." I put my arms around him. "I know you are hurt. I know you deserve better than me, one who's a whole lot better. But I'm saying I still love you in a way, and what's mine will always be yours because of it."

We cuddled for most of the night. Sometime before morning, we indulged in our last 'goodbye' sex.

Then, I packed and moved fulltime into Rolf's house.

Fate had stepped in and wrecked my relationships with both Assauer and Rolf, but I resolved if I ever got Gordon back, I was going to make it official somehow and never let him go again.

Someone plopped down next to me and snapped me out of my stupor. I couldn't believe it; it was CG – Claude Germaine – the Bellagio bellboy.

"Fuck, kid," I said. "Did you follow me here or something?"

The boy sputtered with laughter. "Shit man, that's my line. What are you doing here?"

I held up my phone for a second. "Sending out lovesick tweets, and watching folks get married."

"Ah. You got dumped?"

"Sure did. So, what are you doing here?"

"Me? Oh, I come here sometimes, just to daydream."

I sensed a sob story about to come my way.

"Oh, yeah," I said. "You okay?"

He shrugged and turned adorable as he explained, "This town is okay; 24/7 whatever you want; wide open; anything goes. I should know, was born and bred here – so to speak – from old school Vegas 'royalty.' You think the mob ever controlled this city?" He glanced over his shoulder, adding cryptic-ally, "Think again."

"Who then?"

"It's always been run by the magicians and ventriloquists"—he glanced around one more time—"but you didn't hear that from me. Got it?"

A new couple entered to the strains of Wagner's wedding march, so we popped up to our feet. I leaned sideways and whispered to the teenager, "Got it. Cross my heart and hope to lie, I won't say a word."

"Good."

We sat down again and waited for the preacher to start.

"But," I continued in a low voice, "it looks like you do all right for your-self in Sin City, if I understand your setup on the top floor of the Bellagio."

He blushed a bit. "Even though I prefer to run with girls, and I'm essentially straight, I don't mind a bit of fun and getting tipped with stray Benjamins here and there."

Something about his earnest tone made me ask, "You're saving them, huh?"

"Yes." He appraised me quickly, deciding I was all right. "See, I've got big plans – part of why I like to hang out here, I guess. I want to get hitched and run away from Las Vegas for good. We have dreams of settling down on a farm in Ohio."

"Um—"

He was lost in his own world as he continued. "Imagine it. That would be the life. No partying till all hours; no easy access to liquor, drugs and sex – and best of all, only spotty cellphone reception! Ah, Paradise."

At first I wondered if the kid was pulling my leg, but his glazed, starward glance told me, yes, this was the guy's most fervent desire. Then it hit me: 'We're all the same. Raised in quiet, we long for the fast life. Raised in non-stop "temptation," we crave wholesomeness. Each want is equally rebellious.'

I felt my phone vibrating with an incoming text. Pulling it up, my heart skipped a beat. Maybe Gordon was answering my tweets.... No. It was that crazy black-face lady.

"You're in. I'll pick you up at 10am tomorrow and take you to our...um, *their* leader. Wear loose draws. Peace out."

As the recessional fan-fave struck up again for the humpteenth time, I stood and prayed with all my might for a cure. I had no other way to win my boy back to me.

Chapter 19: Abraca…. *Who?*

I wasn't liking this one bit – tied 'X' fashion, hand and foot, to a pair of stripper poles, like a modern-day Samson about to get a buzzcut.

I almost wished for Angekwekwa's blindfold again. She'd collected me at 10 from the Bellagio, as promised, but covered my eyes in the limo. We didn't go all that far, so I had an idea we were on The Strip someplace. Still blinkered, I wondered if I'd made a mistake, for this procedure bore too many cloak-and-dagger similarities to the crazy donkey dick cult's *modus operandi*. Taken to a room after an elevator ride, my blindfold was removed and I was told to strip and change.

So now, here I stood, wearing only a string-type bottom with fabric front and back panels, and watching these new religious nuts perform their 'ceremony.' Ms. Umfume-Kintay was there too, in her white robe and hood – the same thing they all wore dancing about me and chanting some mumbo jumbo. Weirdly, some had old-fashioned magician mustaches – extra-long and thin – while others carried ventriloquist dummies – each little wooden man dressed in his own white robe.

They marched around my stripper poles, every cowled figure holding one of several inexplicable cult objects: some with long-stemmed poppy pods, dried and used as rattles; some with small whips; some with a round shield on one arm; and others – most oddly of all – a hen tucked in the crook of their arms. One thing they all had was a wand, even the little wooden hands.

I was like '*WTF…?*'

The chants and movement stopped.

From my left and right, two young men cloaked in red hoods and floor-length capes stepped up to me.

The gathered assembly before me parted ways, and an older man lowered his head-covering as he approached. His salt-and-pepper hair was slicked back in the style lots of men in their 60s preferred, and when he spoke, he had an insufferably British mush to his mouth, lol. It was similar to those Americans who affect a decidedly Parisian plonk to their *à la Française {éclat de rire!}*

He raised his hands, letting his sleeves slip, and lifted his eyes to the dim-lit ceiling tiles. "Oh, Blessed of the 365 Heavens, you of each day of the year, hear our beseechment for assistance." He looked down, lowering the hand with a large signet ring towards me. "This young man has been cursed by a false god, and needs the Cock in his life. You, oh, Great Snake-for-Legs, The Anguipede One—"

'Oh, boy. This seemed like a load of—'

"Hear our *voces magicae*. Oh, Lord, cure him."

The leader pressed the cold stone of his finger-jewelry to my forehead.

> "Abraca, speak unto this boy
> That which is sacred and profane;
> Life wrapped in death –
> Light in darkness –
> Questions in explanations –
> Speak the word existent
> At the beginning as well as at the end,
> In the same moment of creation and destruction.
> Abraca, be both terrible and wonderful
> And work your mysteries." [22]

The man stepped back, and simultaneously, the red-hooded boys flanking my sides lifted the front skirt of my loincloth. Angekwekwa produced a long rooster tail feather from beneath her robe.

The cult leader took it, and shocked me by what he did next. Tickling my privates with it, he tried to mutter mystically, "Abracadabra."

It was all I could do not to burst into giggles. Every person's religion is their own, but ultimately, each is just as ludicrous as the next.

And that was it. I heard drinks carts rattle, and the cowled assembly exposed their faces with chatter and self-congratulations. The lights came on, the leader drifted off with his feather, and the two red boys untied me.

A couple of minutes later, the three of us were back in the withdrawing room, where my clothes had stayed the whole time. As I was pulling on my briefs, I noticed one of the boys locked the door to the ceremony chamber and lowered his head covering. "You following me or something?!"

It was Claude Germaine, and he was half-laughing to get a chance at using my line from last evening.

"You have some connection to the—"

"The dude who used the feather, that's my old man, Guy Germaine."

The other boy revealed his head as I slipped on my tee-shirt.

"And this," Claude said, "is my fiancé, Domingo Klaassen."

"Hey." I shook his hand. Ignoring the inconvenient fact that Claude was straight, I took off my cult 'string bikini' and put on my jeans. "You part of this too?"

"Sure am – Claude and me were both born into it."

"Yeah," agreed Germaine, "that's why we want to get hitched and get out of Vegas."

I scanned the pair of them up and down. Domingo was just as shaggy-haired as Claude, but of a darker hue. He was also more open with his assertive smile.

"And you're both hetero...?"

"Yep," they replied unanimously with shy grins.

"See," Klaassen explained, "we want to get gay-married to fuck the whole patriarchal system of oppression, file joint taxes as two dudes and then buy our girlfriends cool stuff with the refund."

"Yeah!" The espoused boys high-fived. "But mostly," continued Claude, "we want to do it to piss off these Abracans."

"These cult people, why?"

"They don't approve of joint marriages," said Domingo.

"Same-sex unions...?"

Claude sputtered like I missed the obvious. "Nah, bro. Two Abracans gettin' hitched. They only want members to marry non-members so we can convert more people on the down low."

"Yeah," Domingo chuckled with an inside joke. "As if by magic."

"But what is it exactly you need to get 'hitched'?"

Both laughed.

However, Claude thought for a moment before he said, "About $4,000 to clear tabs and dump our cell accounts. Then we can get out of town."

"Yes! Did he tell you?" Domingo was animated by excitement. "We want to get to Holmes County, central Buckeye State. We hear Amish girls are easy."

A bro chest-bump followed Claude gleefully telling me, "Yeah, they're real fag hags!"

A knock sounded on the door with a voice asking from the other side "Is he ready?"

"Yes," Claude called out, unlatching it. "He'll be right out."

A couple of minutes later, I was wandering about the ceremony room a little dazed and confused. It was the same space but now the blinds were up and the harsh desert sunlight streaked in.

"Well?" Angekwekwa strode up to me, her corkscrew curls bobbing. "How's your gay pecker-wood feelin'?"

"Um, good, I guess." I didn't know if she expected an insta-boner or what.

"By now I thought you should be cold-stone hard, my little fruity friend."

I simply grinned awkwardly; she did envisage immediate results. To distract my feelings of possible failure, I glanced around our environment. All the freaks had disrobed and now stood in street attire in small groups. They had cocktails – the drinking kind – and their wands dangled from wrist scrunchies like suburban soccer moms' minivan keys. They were all older bastions of vintage Vegas: scotch-swilling, tobacco-slamming, sharky types carefully cultivating the mystique of a vague mob connection à la Sinatra, but with a Slytherin vibe.

"Oh, here he comes." The woman gestured towards Claude's dad heading over to us. He too now had a dark-as-night wand bouncing from his wrist.

"Ah, young man, Guy Germaine. A pleasure to make your acquaintance in fully dressed form."

More of his affected accent grated against my eardrums, but I shook it off. "Likewise. I'm Kohl."

He held out his hand, the one with the ring.

We shook, and then he turned coldly on Umfume-Kintay to dismiss her. She departed, and the cult leader placed a palm on my shoulder to lead us on a stroll, his wand caressing my backside as we went.

"Abraca is a much more powerful god than that crude redneck, Priapus. *His* followers are nuts, as I'm sure you know. But now that the Cock God smiles upon you, your John Thomas will be right as rain in the morning, I guarantee it."

"That's a big promise."

He leered with a lopsided grin and touched the side of his nose. Just at that moment, I noticed the shelves along one wall for the first time. These hosted the chickens the cult members had been holding, and now they brooded in baskets while quietly clucking and watching the proceedings comfortably. "Are you a magician, sir?"

He was flattered, and his wand came up with his hand to pat his chest. "Why, yes. *Guy Germaine the Germaine!* That's my stage name – my *nom de scène* – and I take pride in being an old-school magic-man from the days when magic was feared and honored for its greatness."

"The days of Houdini?"

"No, no."

"Days of David Blain?"

"Greater yet! The times of *Humphries the Humanist*, or those of *Matilda the Metaphysicist*."

"Oh."

"So, you've heard of me...?"

Expectation shone in his voice, so I lied. "Yes."

"Naturally," he gloated. "Quite right that you have."

This guy, with his nearly painted-on mustache and slick demeanor, made me wonder '...what if Vincent Price and Criss Angel had had a baby....'

I glanced around from nervousness as we continued to stroll. This room, full of other, old-time polyester-clad magicians and ventriloquists, was creepy to say the least, especially because of the latter, who kept their dummies' eyes trained on me the whole time. Their little wooden necks creaked as they followed my motions.

Suddenly the room shook with booms – a fireball shot past the window outside.

"What the—"

No one in the chamber even batted an eye. Guy led me over to look out. To my surprise, we were not high up in a tower, but on the third or fourth floor. Right outside the window was a decorative balcony, with ship's rigging beyond. A pirate show was in mid-progress, for a crowd in the plaza below whooped and hollered, and I recognized where I was: Treasure Island. This casino and hotel on The Strip had a full-scale sailing vessel in its fountain next to the building doing squash-buckling events several times a day.

Another cannon went off and pirate actors went swinging by with shouted *"Arrrrrr's!"*

"Let me show you something special, my boy. Our cult objects."

Guy was on the move again, this time heading us towards a wall with lighted niches. I have to say, I felt like I was back at the Getty Villa.

"How much do you know about the Great One?"

We hauled up and stopped. Behind sliding glass door was a stone relief.

"Nothing, Mr. Germaine."

"Look here. This is a North African altarpiece, circa 150 A.D. See the god's attributes?"

How could I miss them! This 'god' of theirs was an utter freak to gaze upon. Some kind of chimera with the armor-clad torso of a soldier, the head of a giant rooster, and most strangely of all, a pair of fat-ass snakes for his thighs, legs and 'feet.'

"See what this representation of the god holds?"

It was the medical wand with the double-helix snakes of Medicine on it, plus two dried poppies like the people used here as rattles.

"This is Abraca in his purest medicinal incarnation – The Healer."

"Oh." What else could I say....

He gestured us on to view another display case. Once there, I felt the painted eyes of the dummies following me from the crowd, and observed the Abracans had a cultish interest in each other's wands.

"You know," I chuckled towards Germaine. "This all seems a bit *Deathly Hallows* to me, what with the capes, and—"

He cut me off testily. "Oh, don't go coughing up more of that Hairy Pooper phenom rubbish."

"Not a fan...?"

"We *despise* all of that riff-raff tit-tat meant only for boobs and imbeciles. It gives real Magic Inc. a bad name. It makes us look silly, not to mention how it confuses the public."

I suppose I saw the logic in that. It was the same as MDs hating doctor shows on TV because the programs got the 'medicine thing' wrong. And no one really needs external help looking silly, lol.

The cult leader caught me watching the act of wand-admiration amongst his followers. He pulled up his own and ran it under my nose like a hotdog at the fairgrounds. "Our zealous interest in our neighbor's staff – learning the timber species, age, maker, and wood varnish like a Stradivarius – is all attributable to a hopeless condition called *wand envy*." Germaine chuckled at his own witticism, if you could call it that.

Again, I was reduced to a simple "Oh."

He stroked his dark member lovingly. "This one is made of the rarest and most prized of all – elder wood."

My eyebrows crinkled involuntarily. Two things popped into my mind at the same time. The first one revolved around the 'Hairy Pooper' phenom.... But the second...that one raised a goose bump or two.

I mentioned the first one to Germaine. "In the series of books whose name shall not be mentioned"— I winked at him—"elder is the wood the devil himself chose for the wand in Snape's possession...." I came to a faltering halt, for my host looked pale all of sudden.

"Rumors, boy. Rumors – and slander against, well, just slander!"

The seriousness of his reply instantly caused the other allusion through pop in my mind as a forced moment of re-play. I saw Psyche standing in our Pasadena motel room, saying in enchanted fashion, "...He of the olive and elder...." She'd meant Priapus, of course.

"Besides," Guy suddenly added, "Draco Malfoy was the Wand of Destiny's true master. Everybody knows that, about that particular horcrux."

With *that*, we moved on. Cannon fire boomed outside, and the new case he showed me seemed filled with jewels sparkling in the firelight coming through the windows.

"Ancient intaglios," he said as I bent down to look at some of the details. Carnelian stones, and large garnets in red and brown were shaped into flat-fronted ovals. Deeply cut into the surface were images of Abraca, all cock-headed and snake-legged, but instead of medical implements like the large relief, most of these representations of the chimera bore a round shield on his left arm and a raised whip in his right hand – an oddly short implement, like a crop for horses.

"What are these?" I asked.

"Very valuable gems, collected over several lifetimes, and carefully guarded by our religion." He drew down his hand that I might admire the matching intaglio on his left ring finger. It was the one he'd impressed onto my forehead earlier.

I stood up fully, and he continued. "In ancient times, these amulets of protection would have been sewn into the underlining of garments, because the Cock God loves to be rubbed in private, next to the privates, under the clothes."

I thought, 'This cult object likes handies.'

The wicked leer Guy shed on me made yours truly not venture to speculate what type of underwear he had on currently.

We continued to stroll, this time to where the two temporary stripper poles were still up. There was another lighted niche behind them I hadn't noticed before. Something oddly familiar and out of place was on a golden shelf there.

"You know," I told Germaine wryly, "I've met your son Claude on a few occasions, and today, Domingo Klaassen, his fiancé too."

The boy's father stiffened; grew agitated. "The recklessness of youth! I raised him right, to enjoy the high life, go out every night if he wants to, run around as much as he can stand, not think about the consequences, but he breaks my heart by talking about settling down and throwing all of this away. Can you imagine, Mr. Kohl, the wicked selfishness of homesteading on a farm outside of Canton? Ohio! The shame of it all.... Oh, children are a great trial unto their parents."

"Yes, they are sometimes indeed."

"And this..." He pulled up short and stopped us between the two stripper poles to look at the contents of the alcove. "This is our most sacred cult object."

"This rusty old souvenir...?" For that's all it was. A vintage tourist-sized model of a rooster weathervane, resting atop a polished marble base.

"Yes," he said, transported. "It used to belong to very important men – two of them to be exact."

"Who?"

"You see, this 'souvenir,' as you termed it, is an exact replica of a weathervane crowning a building in Bern, Switzerland, and sacred because it was bought by Carl Jung to commemorate a romantic romp he shared in that structure with Aleister Crowley. The summer of 1912 marked both men's cult awakening to Abraca's sexual release and power."

"Really? Jung and Crowley were lovers?"

"Oh, yes, my boy! And more importantly, joint lovers of Abraca."

I must have looked dubious, for the old-school Vegas magician and cult leader continued in an 'educational' tone.

"You, young man, should not find it incredible to learn the degree to which Abraca is integrated into the power structures of everyday life. Take the Vatican, for example. One sacred cult object in their possession is a silk weaving from Persia. Dating to about 600 A.D., it shows a proud, sacred cock with a halo. This item is reputed to have belonged to the same pope who in the eight-hundreds declared the image of the cock to be venerated in equal holiness as the cross, going so far as to mandate every church place these two images side by side on the altar. A later pope ordered rooster weather-vanes to be installed on top of all the churches of Europe, in honor of The Blessed One of the 365 Heavens."

"Oh," slid out of my mouth again as another fireball shot past the window. I felt like I had slipped into an alternate reality.

The man concluded his lecture patly. "So in terms of the pope, Jung and Crowley, you see, religion, psychology and magic have never really been divided."

I thought, 'What a damning pronouncement against all three!'

❑ ❑ ❑ ❑ ❑

I knew I was dreaming, but despite the sweat, I didn't want it to end.

Mottled sunlight, sliced into motion through the shifting green canopy high above, strobed on my eyes as I ran. I suddenly had to dodge a rough, fallen log encrusted with moss. I leaped over a second one.

The forest engulfing me was deep, dark and primeval – it represented the heart of my Teutonic soul, if you listen to the myth-makers and head-shrinkers – so I felt invigorated by the pine-scented air.

Gordon ran ahead of me, dashing in and out of the stands of mature tree trunks, and making me chase him. I called out his name pitifully several times, and each plea of my heartbreak simply made him turn to me with his beguiling grin. He'd giggle at my pain.

Leaping over one felled oak, I chanced to glance to my thighs and saw I was completely naked. What was more, I was rock-hard. My energy and vigor had returned.

When I looked up again, the woods were eerily still. Jogging to a halt, and coming 'round one particularly thick tree trunk, I saw my boy's back peeking out as he tried to conceal himself behind another a few paces ahead.

Slowly, watching my footfalls, I kept my eye on the sliver of Gordon's clothes I could still see, and suppressed my joy as I sneaked up to the front of his hiding tree.

I popped around to embrace my boy....

Instead, the snarling face of Priapus was there. As I stumbled back, the woodman's visage maintained hate-filled glances of vindictiveness on me.

I looked down. Around my waist was the loincloth the Abracans had made me wear. Lifting it, my *Schwanz* was as limp as a wet hand towel.

I awoke with the nature god's maniacal laugh still ringing in my ears; it seemed like the bellow of a blast. Tearing off my bedsheet only confirmed the mix of my tears and sweat, and the pathetic state of my manhood.

I beat it, experiencing a moment of clarity. By all rights, the crazy ritual and humiliation the Cock-God fools subjected me to should have triggered a Post Traumatic freak-out in me; but it didn't. Why? Because, despite the outward similarity to my garden center of horrors ordeal, this Abraca-dabra shit was just that – shit! Their so-called god is an excuse for a power grab, and paled in the face of Priapus.

'Fuck them,' I thought. 'This Abraca *Scheisse* is as hollow as the myth of "Conservative Compassion"!'

Angry, I vowed revenge for the squandering of my time and dignity.

My phone said 1:32 AM, but I didn't care. I texted Claude.

> *"I know a way to get your*
> *four grand, and maybe more."*

'Chicken run, part two,' I told myself, lol.

Claude and his fiancé were back in their red robes. They were also currently on their knees helping me complete my look in the cult's dressing room. The boys pinched and twisted and concentrated on getting the plastic souvenir I'd picked up at Caesars Palace on my newly padded body.

I watched them in the full-length mirror, witnessing me become more ridiculous by the minute.

The cult leader's wayward son glanced up at my reflection. "You sure this is gonna work?"

"Yeah. It's risky," added Domingo Klaassen.

"It's easy, boys. Trust me – I've planned and executed worse without a hitch."

They glanced at each other. I guess the word 'hitch' renewed their fervent hopes of a sham marriage and a contented life in Ohio Amish country, chasing good girls for a change.

They went back to securing belts and buckles, and I thought over how this came about.

Burtron checked out this morning, exhausted from all his needy Vegas followers, and went on to Burning Man, where I would join him later tonight. He left his gear behind so I could ship it home to the Flying Dutchman.

Once that was sorted, I paid a visit to a costume shop and the faux Roman casino's gift store, and sent Angekwekwa a text. I told her the Cock God ritual only partially worked and needed a 'booster shot' before I left town. So she assembled the freaks again, and here we were. In a way, I hated to involve her, but then again, she was the one who got me in with this humiliating mess in the first place.

The boys were done with the chest piece and kilt. Domingo helped me slip on the round shield while Claude placed a bullwhip borrowed from Burtron's stash in my right hand.

They slipped on my costume head and raised their own cowls. "Lower the lights," I said and assessed my transformation in the mirror as best as I could see it.

"You look sick, man," Germaine the younger said.

"Yeah, totally...."

"Lead the way, boys."

I toddled along, making some rustling sounds and letting the boys enter first.

As coached, they made horrible moans of fright, and caught the crazies off-guard.

When Domingo shouted "He's here! All bow," that was my signal.

I cracked my bullwhip, and strutted cockily into the assembly room. It was dim like yesterday, and that served my purposes.

Gasps went 'round the chamber, and the faithful dropped like rocks to their white-robed knees. Puppets too lay face down, their mini wands all in disarray.

I walked to the place between the stripper poles, cracking my whip frightfully near Guy Germain's cowering figure. Then I kicked my head back and let out a fierce *Cock-a-doodle-doo!*

I knew the yellow chicken costume, plastic centurion armor, and green trash-bags 'snakes' for legs scared the living shit out of them. Think about it...how would you feel if God showed up at your church cracking a whip?

Through my discreet beak mouth, I saw the boys gather up all the gems from the display cases into velvet bags.

"Oh, Great One," said Guy with trembling voice, "why hast thou shown thyself unto us, all unworthy as we are...?"

'Um,' I wondered, 'why indeed.'

He dared to raise his eyes, so I immediately grunted some mumbo jumbo gibberish – mixed in with whip-cracks and clucking – while the entire time watching the boys finish up and start heading towards the double doors outta here. They ran their arms along the shelves with the roosting hens and sent them squawking and winging it around the chamber.

When they got to the exit, I knew it was time to bolt, but something made me turn and nab the stupid weathervane before I ran.

The crowd, still cowered on the carpet, barely dared look up and see me high stepping it as best I could with these garbage bags trailing 24-inches off the end of my feet.

The boys burst through the doors, and we were in the corridor. They took off to the right, and I booked it in the other direction, weathervane tucked under my wing.

Confused sounds arose amid the chicken squawks from the assembly room, and I knew they'd be after me – me, not the boys.

I hoofed it straight to the end of the passage, trying not to trip over my own legs. I pushed open a door and teetered on the brink of a balcony outside. A fire alarm sounded.

Canon fire boomed, costumed pirates sword-fought, and about a thousand people stood gawking at the show in the plaza four stories below.

This was a dead end.

I glanced behind me. The Abracans had figured out the scam, and middle-aged magicians and ventriloquists ran up the corridor towards me.

I snapped my bullwhip around a loose rope in the ship's rigging and pulled it to me. Pyrotechnics went off, and people in the crowd noticed me. I climbed on top of the handrail, and just as the first cult members got to me, I Tarzanned my way across half the length of the pirate ship.

A boisterous "Cock-a-doodle-doo, motherfuckers!" escaped my beak in mid-flight.

The crowd was amazed, and so were the actor-bandits pausing in their bloodthirst to watch the soaring chickenman and his weathervane.

My rope rotated just right to show me the balcony I'd escaped from moments before. A tumble of magicians, ventriloquists, dummies, and white capes dropped down into the fountain below, releasing concealed doves, bunnies and playing cards as they went.

I landed on the platform halfway up the ship's mast and had a chance to bow for the adoring crowd. They were now chanting, "Chickenman! Chickenman! Chickenman!" Grabbing onto another rope, I kicked off to a second balcony and my ultimate escape.

The whole time, my mind was laughing its German ass off, thinking, 'Abraca...*who?* Suck my limp dick, Cock God!'

Chapter 20: Burning Man (and Woman)

"A wandering singularity in the desert,
Or a human cog in society's machine –
Which is the lonelier position to occupy?

    To place my feet where sands
    Might scorch the very soles
    Attempting to ground me;
    To look out from wastelands
    And see scant sign of man,
    Yet feel no hollowness.

    But from amongst a crowd,
    Where by rights I should feel
    Community's support,
    Isolation appears
    To drive me deep in me
    And instill emptiness.

Thus, now I'm always alone among so many,
At least since you walked away, made me wanderer
In the desert of heart as on the concrete of man."

These pitiable words for my boy filtered through my mind. I was trekking aimlessly, like a lost child, amidst the art tents of 'downtown' Burning Man.

Some seventy thousand people were spangled across the Nevada desert in a semi-circular, temporary metropolis of caravans, RVs, tents, shacks – you name it – but all were oriented to a central plaza where workers put the finishing touches on a fifty-foot wicker man of plank and pallet. 'He' was to be set alight at the climax of the festival.

I looked at it now, letting the happy sounds of hippies playing drums hit my ears as they passed by on bicycles. Other types strolling around were jugglers of everything from balls to chainsaws, flame eaters roaring out an occasional lick of flame as they went, and guys on ten-foot stilts.

The scent of incense and 'burning oregano' was on every scrubland breeze, and so were laughter and good times. They were good times I was not invited to enjoy.

Just as I took a step sideways, thinking I'd pull out my phone and snap a pic to send Gordon, I was knocked down.

Thump. Thump. Two light wheels rode over me, followed by the heavier ones of a kiddie car.

Brakes squealed.

From the dust, I looked up into the long-haired, angelic expression of a guy coming down to aid me. He scooped his dark, slightly wavy locks behind both ears before laying a concerned hand on my back.

"Oh, dude! Crap, crap, you stepped—"

"Yeah, I know. I'm sorry."

"No, no, no. It was me. Dude, I apologize, and so does my daughter, Rainbow." He gestured to the seven- or eight-year-old hitched onto the back of his bike.

By the slight whiff coming off his shorts and tank top, and the faint puffiness visibly rimmed under the lower part of his chocolate-brown peepers, I suddenly knew he was at least half-baked, if not more.

He helped me stand. "Anything broken? I'm Luca, by the way."

I assessed along with him as his hands went roving about my person. Nothing hurt too bad. "Couple bruises—" Then I tried to take a step and faltered, grabbing onto him as my ankle threatened to buckle.

"Oh, dude…. Oh, dude – I knew it."

He was walking me over to his bike.

"Load up here."

He assisted, and I sat on his handlebars.

In another moment, coolish air was stroking my face, and he rode me and Rainbow around the merrymaking crowd. He had to stand on the pedals to get enough traction and see, but Luca told me soft and low, rather close to my ear, "My girlfriend, Skye – Rainbow's mom – she'll fix you up. She works at a hospital in the City."

I didn't ask which city, because the three of us wound up entertaining the assembly too, as if we were just one more mobile art display.

After a few turns, onto ever-narrowing pathways, Luca slowed in front of a raggy tent. Not 'raggy' as in dilapidated, but ragged as in it was made like a kid's living-room fortress of colorful bedsheets, tablecloths, and fringed spreads of every hue.

Luca undid his daughter's seatbelt, then helped me down from the handlebars, gripping me like a fallen comrade in arms.

Rainbow assisted with the tent flap, and her father walked me over to a giant 'sofa' of loose cushions and pillows on a mattress.

"Skye," he called out, "this guy—"

"Kohl."

"This guy, Kohl here, got his ankle run over by me and Rain."

She came over from the wash-up area.

"Oh, how do you feel?"

The lady – who was about thirty, like Luca – immediately felt my forehead. She was pretty; also with long hair, but lighter in color than her boyfriend, and blessed with limpid blue eyes.

"I think my ankle just needs a rest."

I glanced around for Luca's assistance, but he was distracted, setting up a hookah.

Skye was already untying my sneakers. "Which one is it?"

"The right."

She took care, and in a moment or two, I was barefoot and having my swelling ankle prodded.

"I have just the thing." She popped up. "Salve and something to bandage it. Hold tight."

Luca came over with the already-smoking waterpipe and sat next to me. Rainbow pulled up to a little table in another corner and decorated her coloring book without a care in the world.

He handed me the mouthpiece. "It's good shit. Take a good hit of it."

I did. Usually pot makes me want to cough, but this smoke only tickled the back of my throat making me draw in a second deep breath before passing it back to my host.

Skye spread some clear balm on my ankle, and then wrapped it.

It stopped hurting – or I stopped hurting completely, I don't know which. My head lolled back on the cushions, watching beams of sunlight sieve themselves through paisley bedspread roof-segments. They moved slightly, like shards of living crystal.

Luca passed back the pipe.

"What's this?" I asked, sounding mellow.

"Girl Scout Cookies. It's the best, dude."

I had to agree.

Skye gathered up her daughter. "It's nearly time for the Bingo-Bongo Art Parade, honey bun."

Burning Man was a movable feast, and processions and spectacle were a common sight.

"We'll see you boys later."

"Have fun," we called after them.

Once the girls had departed, me and Luca just hankered down and smoked, growing close without much effort.

"What do you do, Kohl?"

"Substitute teacher."

"Ah. You look it."

"I do?" I suddenly chuckled freely.

"Yeah, man, why not. How do I look?"

"Good." His question caught me off guard, but his unguarded smile put me back at ease. "You mean—"

"Job."

"Umm…. I don't know. School bus driver."

That delayed our convo considerably while we both rolled around the cushions in a deep fit of laughter. Finally, after catching our breath and toking on the hookah, we settled back again.

Luca said, "I'm a professional architectural construction manager."

"No shit?!"

"Yep. No one back at the office in San Francisco knows about my Clark

Kent/Super Baked double life."

I wondered if it was more of a Mr. Jekyll/Dr. Let My Hair Down existence, but whatever. He was nice, and he was getting me high, lol.

"Me and the family come out here every year to shed the old inhibitions. In fact, sorta like therapy for me, even though I get paid by the organizers to do some odd jobs around here."

He started cracking up, which became infectious.

"What?" I asked.

"*Odd* ain't the half of it."

"What do you mean?" I couldn't stop laughing.

"You're heard of the Orgy Dome?"

"The little sex tent with people waiting to get in?"

"Yeah, exactly. Well, I work at a rival spot called The Big Tent of
Human Kindness. It's bigger, just one 'room,' but its existence is more hush-
hush. More word of mouth."

"And what do you do there?"

"Promise not to laugh...."

"Dude!" I held the pipe, and we both wasted a minute or two cracking
up. "Okay, Okay," I said at last. "I won't judge. I promise."

"I'm a traffic controller."

My mouth went slack. "A what?"

"I stand on a crate, where I can see what's going on and who is coming
in to join the action, and direct people to vacant 'spots.'"

I sputtered, "Well then, count me out. I'm Gay, so will be steering clear
of any pussy palaces, kitty arcades, beaver dams—"

"No, no, dude. This is Burning Man! The founder's Gay; the organizers,
Gay; at least half the attendees, Gay. Anyway, in the Big Tent there's a same-
sex only area, a polyamorous section, and the smallest one of all – opposite
sex only. That one's almost like a forgotten zone. People come in there to lose
inhibitions, so lots of guys who think of themselves as 'straight' make out
with each other and do a whole lot more."

"Oh. Well, that's cool."

"Yeah, so my job is to make sure everyone's settled in the place they
wanna be. And damn, let me tell ya, after a couple hours in there, I come
back to Skye with a major thirst."

We laughed and smoked a bit.

"That's all cool, but there's another reason I won't need to visit any sex
tents—" My sad emotions halted me.

Luca's eyes grew round and soft; he sympathized with me. "That's
sweet, man." He assumed I was monogamous. "You got a boyfriend you're
true to. I can dig it – I'm faithful to Skye."

I confessed. "Gordon ran off with my ex. Part of why I'm at Burning
Man is to track down any leads as to where they could be now."

"Ah, I'm sorry, Kohl."

"It's not your fault." I took another deep draw of Girl Scout Cookies and went for broke. "He left me because we got caught up with some crazy sex cult in L.A. They put a curse on my dick, and I can't get it up anymore. Now I'm on a hero's journey to find a cure and win back my boy."

"Oh, dude! Sounds awesome."

"So anyway, you know about any sex-kink groups represented at the festival?"

Luca turned serious and started to rattle them off: "There's that tattoo kink group; the underwater underwear folks; the poke-a-hontas cult—"

"The what?!"

"Yeah, dude. Cosplay fetish reality. But they only get in Disney character costumes to boink." Luca shuddered with laughter. "Whatever floats their banana."

"Yeah, I guess."

He dropped his chin while holding the pipe up and smiled. Plenty of the whites of his eyes showed as he joked, "There are so many secret groups out there into anything you can name. Cultish is the other C-word these days."

After we did more rolling around on the mattress, laughing our asses off, Luca bolted upright and appeared suddenly inspired.

"Dude! If you ever want to make a little extra pocket money while inquiring about your boy, you can fill in for me at the sex tent!"

I was confused about why....

"You're perfect, Kohl." Luca was awe-stuck, saying, "No boners means you can traffic control for hours...whoa, dude...."

I was a little upset at the irony of this 'compliment.' I didn't quite know if he was trying to insult me, or just fell over it naturally. Ultimately I knew I could use the cash, as Vegas had been an expensive place to tool around, and I only got a hundred-fifty in cash for that stupid weathervane.

Enjoying my nice and mellow feeling, I'd left Luca, Skye and Rainbow to enjoy their siesta together. Now I strolled down the line of food trucks because I had somehow gotten a bad case of the munchies, lol.

I walked and walked, mostly walking past all the graffiti'ed trucks. These you could count on as being mostly the same: one promoted, or perhaps threatened is the better term, to serve *granola veggie burgers*. Another one a bit further down promised some 'health busting' bean sprout gazpacho. And speaking of heat and treats, a line of young mothers corralled their children in front of an 'ice cream' vendor hawking *Acai-White Mulberry Bars* and *Greek Yogurt Cauliflower Pops*. Poor kids. They were bound to grow into full-fat milk addicts, because, as a wise man once observed, "Repression breeds obsession." Denied these things young, they'd seek them out recklessly as adults.

Good smells coming from a particular direction distracted my musings. They were nice, golden-brown fried food smells, reminding me of being a kid and seeking out the *Weihnachtsmarkt* grilled sausage, especially the *Gourmetwurst*, which are cheese-filled. Yum.

I pulled up at a long, long line in front of the "Sparks Deep-Fried Dog Wagon," which had a corny dachshund in a bun painted along the length of the truck. Unlike the sea of flapping banners preaching about 'free' food – "Gluten Free"; "GMO Free"; "Nuts Free" – the Sparks' banner said: "Beef-cheek franks, proudly served *WITH* nitrates."

I turned and bumped into a middle-aged lady with car keys and a tray of hotdog buns.

"Oh, I'm sorry," I said, and then exclaimed, "Oh, my God, it's you!"

"It's me, sweetheart," replied the woman, "but who are—"

Even before she finished her sentence, she recognized me too. I became helplessly giggly. "You rescued me that day at the Laguna Beach Street Fair by creating a diversion."

"Yes, I remember you, sugar cube." Her eyebrow rose. "And how."

"That was quite a brawl. I owe you one."

The lady flashed a wink and smile on me. "Ah, shucks, 'twern't nothing." She gestured to the crowded truck with her head. "Alisoun Sparks' the name."

"Kohl."

"Well, Kohl, if you're free, come back at nine. You, me and the husband can set out a spell and have some brewskis."

Suddenly, the husband in question called for Alisoun from the truck.

"Sorry, sugar shaker, but we're swamped. See you later, I hope." She winked again before checking me out up and down, and then dashing off.

Just as I was praying the buxom Corndog's Wife harbored no illusions about me, I heard a sharp whistle and "Kohl!" Looking around, I saw Burtron waving me over to the food line he was in.

The racial kink expert was shirtless but wearing cyan-blue grannie sunspecs. I went to join him, despite seeing he was queued up for something called Malted Barley Macrobiotic Raw Falafels.

"Kohl, Kohl, look at this." He fiddled with his phone, hugging me in to watch a vid with him.

Astounded, I saw a yellow chickenman in Roman armor use a bullwhip to bring a rope to him. Then he swung across half the length of the Treasure Island pirate ship with green bags trailing from his legs like snakes. Right after him, robed magicians and ventriloquists tumbled into the fountain, while shouting the whole way down.

"Holy fuck…" I mumbled. "That's ha-lary-ri-ous."

"I know, right. You're a social media star, buddy! Eighteen million hits already, and there are more out there of you sailing through the air."

"That's nuts."

"Look at the re-tweeted news crawl."

He scrolled down to show me. "Media outlets desperate to find the man behind the famous Vegas 'Chicken Desperado'."

Burtron laughed. "You're trending, buddy."

I glanced around nervously. "Not necessarily what I want—"

"Don't worry."

"Any idea if Angekwekwa or the Uncliest Tom of All know where you were headed after Sin City?"

"Nope. They shouldn't know either. I never put Burning Man on my public schedule. This is my time off and I don't want to be bombarded here with atonement requests."

"Okay. Let's hope they don't figure out where we were going."

The food line advanced.

"Don't worry, my German bro. The Abraca people won't go to the cops about being robbed."

"Maybe so." I pulled out a ticket. "Here," I said, giving it to my friend. "Put this in your wallet, and if those bent cock-worshipers come to you about me, give it to them."

"What is it?"

"They'll know what to do with it."

Burtron shrugged. "Okay." He put the ticket in his billfold. "Oh! By the way, I've met someone here."

"Met as in *meet?*"

"Yep." The racial-kink cult leader smiled broadly and let me see his eyes. A new glow was there.

"Congratulations. What's his name?"

"Geoff Bath. He's an experimental artist from San Diego, so we're not too far away once we get back home."

We got up to the order window. "I'm glad for you, Burtron." I couldn't hide the tinge of sadness in my voice.

Smelling the 'raw' macrobiotics, I was also sad I hadn't gotten in line for the beef-cheek corndogs instead.

Fire shot into the air high overhead. The strolling jugglers and flame-spitters on stilts awed the crowds as everyone moved under the stars at Burning Man.

I was slowly making my way back along the shuttered food trucks, and away from the buzzed merrymakers.

As I walked, thinking back on all the smiling faces I had seen today, and the free and easy public displays of affection the couples engaged in, it only drove home just how acutely having no one to share this experience with was getting to me.

I wound up in front of the Sparks' dog wagon. Hearing laughter, I went around the side to the back.

The Corndog's Wife was sitting on a folding lawn chair with an older man. "Sugar cone!" she exclaimed, seeing me. "Glad you decided to come by. Sit down. Grab a brewski." She popped a can of Pabst for me and unfolded the green plastic webs of my own lawn chair.

"Thanks," I said, draining about a quarter of the beer.

"Sit, sit. This is my old man Karl." Alisoun slapped the shoulder of her rather tired-looking companion.

"Nice to meet you, Karl." I shook hands and sat. For some reason, my head fell back right away. The sky above was full to the brim with milky stars.

"Do I detect an accent?" Karl inquired with mild interest.

"Yes." I gave him a smile. "German. I'm sorry."

"Oh, no problem, sugar teat. Your accent's sweet."

I chuckled. "I get comments like 'funny,' 'strange,' 'weird,' but never 'sweet.' So thanks."

Karl drank, then asked, "What do you do?"

"Substitute teacher."

"Oh, that's all right, isn't it?" He had checked with his wife.

"Yes! Teachers are our future. Don't they say that? Drink, drink, Kohl. Feel at home."

Before I took another swig, I toasted them. "To adventure and new friends."

"I'll say," said the Corndog's Wife. "Karl, remember that brouhaha in Laguna Beach a while back – well, this was him. We bumped into him back there. Ain't life strange?"

'Ain't it though,' I thought as Alisoun drank and gave me an overly lecherous look.

"Foreigners," Karl Sparks suddenly mused, "lots of them around these days."

"Oh, Hubby, as my ex Henry – God rest his soul – used to say, 'An alien is just a neighbor who hasn't pissed on your lawn yet.' And now we've met Kohl."

They had an odd dynamic. Alisoun was overt in her likes, and Karl seemed withdrawn, but indulgent of her interests.

"Your ex, died…?" I asked.

"Oh, no, sugar bowl. He just got with a bimbo in Poughkeepsie, and I wish them the very worst, if you know what I mean."

Karl ignored the topic altogether. "You don't look like a pot-head hippy, like the rest of 'em."

"I don't smoke, at least, not much."

The Corndog Husband crushed his empty beer can and expounded sluggishly, "Weed-fueled 'art' – looks like a bunch of junkyard garbage to me. You're not one of those artists, are you?"

"No, sir. I'm a teacher; just here to unwind a bit."

"See, Karl? He's a good one. And besides, these ganja-grungers love our food! They can't get enough of our dogs. Too bad we can't stay to the end, but as Forrest used to say, 'Pack it up to rack it up' – money that is."

"Forrest?" I asked.

"Yes, husband number – hmm, let me see." She mumbled names to herself, the way some people do with their mental shopping lists at the grocery store. "He was number four – well, three-and-a-half at first." She chuckled, and Karl simply reached into the cooler for another cold one.

"But you won't be staying until the end of the festival?" I asked.

"No." Alisoun put on a pout. "We've been short-staffed this whole trip, and we've got another gig to get to."

"The NorCal Renaissance Faire," said Karl.

"It's in Hollister this year, and we've got a long drive, so after the lunch rush tomorrow, we'll pack up and be on the road."

"Yeah," Karl added. "Those tights-wearing, quaking Shakespeare wannabes love our jalapeño popper dogs so much, it's one of our biggest money-maker-stops of the season."

I had to admit that formed quite a sight in my mind. "Ah, but you'll miss the Burning Man."

"Sugar substitute," Alisoun laughed. "There ain't nothing we haven't seen before, including that."

"So, been in the States a long time, Kohl?"

By Karl's tone, the unstated 'you on welfare' question was ice-cube clear. "Long enough, sir, but I've always made my own way here. Land of plenty and opportunity, right?"

Alisoun and hubbie liked that answer, in fact they exchanged impressed, grins and raised eyebrows. I left unsaid the obvious: 'Plenty of opportunity to pilfer from the jobless fat-cats sitting on trust funds and inherited, tax-free wealth, lol.'

I finished my beer and got a little pissed. "But still, I guess I'm one of those foreigners, one of the ones people are so down on now."

They glanced at one another, totally puzzled.

Karl explained as if to a child, "But you're European. That's all right – that's the good kind of migrant."

"Yeah." Alisoun smiled. "You're 'folks,' just like Melania Trump."

'Folks?!' I thought. 'As if we'd all like nothing better than sitting on the back porch with Mrs. Dump the Third, drinking lemonade and chewing the bacon.' Get real.

"Yeah," Karl added with a sour twist, "you're not from Kenya, like that guy who drove this country—"

"All right, hubbie-hub." Alison laughed awkwardly. "We don't want Kohl, lil sugar tongs here, to get the wrong impression about us being racists....."

She said more besides, but I tuned it out, trying not to sigh. I did let my head fall back again however and enjoy the skyward view. The cold vastness of the stars felt like a breath of fresh air, yet also put me in mind of Gordon and my loneliness again. I wanted to do more to locate him, but what...?

Apparently, Alisoun misread my mood because she said brightly, "Reminds me of a story."

I sat up and watched as the Corndog's Wife launched into it.

"Well, way back in the mythical, Camelot days of this country – the Pappy Bush years – or, in an age when hairdressers were butch, and TV celebrities fey, I ran a little afoul of the law. Seems at a wild swingers' party I got a little carried away, and one fella's 'No' was a hard one, but then again, so was his Mrs. Pecker Johnson, if you know what I mean.

"Anyways, I was hauled up on misdemeanor sexual battery charges, and the wise-ass judge bangs his gavel, saying, 'I'll stay your sentence for one year, proviso it that you can tell this court twelve months hence one single piece of information. If you can do that, the conviction will be dismissed and your criminal record expunged.'

"Well, *Mr. She Raped Me Good* was none too pleased, I can tell ya, but the 'court' figured him a fag anyway with no legal rights, so I tells the guy in the fancy drapery, 'Judge, what do you want me to do? I'll do it.'

"Then he floors me with what turns out to be a fool's errand. 'Well,' says he, 'if you can show up here again one year from today and tell me what men really, really want from a woman, then I'll pardon you completely. If you can't tell the court, then your butt's off to jail. Got it?'

"'Sure,' I says, thinking it's gonna be easy. Men are simple creatures, right? Feed 'em, water 'em with beer, take 'em out to socialize with others of their own kind every now and again.... Easy peasy to find out what they really truly want from a woman, right?

"Wrong. Or at least, not 'right' that it's easy to figure out, cuz first of all, I take four months off to concentrate on – oh, I don't know – just stuff, but then I get nervous and start worrying about how to answer this dumb question.

"I turn to the obvious: men just wanna have sex; isn't that how the Cyndi Lauper song goes...? And since I like sex and never get any complaints in that department, 'xcept from puffs, I starts looking for the burliest, roughest, tough-necks I can find: men in uniforms. In our society, it's almost a fetish, ain't it? I mean think about it: put an ordinary guy in tight polyester, slap a meter or a gun to his side, and *BINGO!* Instant stud. Dudes in matching outfits supposed to be 'real men' anyway, at least according to what society tells us in popular science-fiction and Netflix series, am I right?!

"Anyways, I sleeps with mailmen, I sleeps with bus drivers, I sleeps with security guards, G.I.s, cops, dogcatchers – anyone who looks good and can fill out a uniform. Problem is, none of them can agree on a single answer. One is a cry-baby who tells me all men want a career gal who'll bring home the pork chops. Another tells me he dreams of tracking down a genuine madonna-whore type who'll be content locked in the house all day, like a kitten, but who becomes a tigress under the sheets at night. And one sicko – oh, my God – this guy actually tells me what men want most is a woman who'll let *them* take charge! Imagine that…. What a mama's-boy perv. Ick.

"So I look and I look, and I gets lots of sack-time and phone numbers, but I grow more and more disillusioned, because here it's one year later, and I'm only more and more confused. Night before my court date, I go to a bar. At 2:30 AM, closing time, I goes home with a troll – a sloppy, disheveled blue-collar guy.

"Anyways, back at his place, I let him have his fun, my mind sorta pre-occupied, when suddenly I realize this schlub is doing all the *RIGHT* things, lemme tell ya; hitting all the correct buttons, if you know what I mean. And sooner rather than later, he brings me to – well, believe it or not – my first orgasm. I'm like 'OMG, wow, bud…' but looking at his face did nothing for me. I confess my legal jam, saying it was the best sex ever, but I might be goin' upriver the next day. Blah, blah, blah – he asks why and I tells him, omitting the exact question because at this point the whole thing sounded silly.

"'What the judge tell you to find out, Alisoun?'

"He said: 'Find out what men really want from a woman.'

"He smiled, all devious-like. 'That's an easy one.'

"'Well, bub, you might as well tell me your idea too. I've heard 'em all by this point.'

"'Nope,' he says.

"'What? Why?'

"'Information is valuable. I know the true answer, and if you want it, you'll have to 'pay' for it.'

"'Money—'

"'No. Not money.'

"'What then?'

"He picks up my wrist to kiss it. 'You. Your love, your hand – be my wife. That is, marry me before you go to court tomorrow and tell the judge your answer.'

"I looked over this pasty, stay-puffed fella and weighed my options: say 'No' and be nowheres; say 'Yes' and have more great sex tonight, at least, that is, before I have to go to jail and forget all about my new husband in the morning.

"'Okay,' I says. 'Now tell me.'

"He grins. 'After the marriage ceremony. We'll go straight from the county clerk's office to your trial.'

"I shrug. 'All right, whatever. Now, do that thing you did again, you know, with the tip of your—'

"Anyways, I digress, cuz next day, we dash down to get hitched and he brings along a bag with clothes because he'll have to change and go to work right after my sentencing hearing.

"The wedding itself, was, well, forgettable. I didn't have any idea if I was doing the right thing, as marriage seemed so old-fashioned in the late-80s, like what hippies did back in the 60s and such. But anyway, we got done, and pecked on the lips and all, and I asks him for the answer the judge wants. 'In a min, babe,' he says as he dashes into the restroom.

"Alone, in court, I sorta feel hopeless. My case is coming up in a few minutes, and my brand-new husband's nowhere in sight.... And then, wow, in comes my man, and I like nearly swoon because he's dressed super high-tech for the time. My heart went *pitta-patta*, let me tell ya, when I saw him in his light-blue cable TV repairman outfit. No one can resist a man in uniform!

"Judge calls my name, and just in the nick of time, I get the answer I'm supposed to tell him whispered in my ear.

"'Well, miss, have you looked for the simple truth? Have you found out the answer...?'

"'Yes, Your Honor. What men most want from a woman...' I look over my shoulder at my husband for reassurance. He nods gravely, so I turn and tells the judge in a loud voice, 'What men want most from a woman, is to be left alone.'

"Well, let me tell ya, there's stunned silence in the courtroom. All the men in there, from bailiffs to scuzzbag criminals, bob heads up and down in slow-motion agreement. Their eyebrows were sky high too....

"Finally the judge says, 'Well, little missy, it seems you have learned your lesson and found the one true, most correct answer of them all.' He bangs his gavel. 'Case dismissed. You are free to go.'

"I run into the arms of my first husband, Cuthbert, and we are very very happy. The End."

Karl Sparks immediately pointed out, "Yeah, till he choked to death on a chicken bone one month later."

"Oh, Karl – why go and spoil a beautiful story for Kohl with a minor detail like that."

As I sat there, looking up to the stars again – grateful to every single last one of them I was not born straight – I missed my boy and our closeness more than anything. I didn't belong anywhere in the world but in his arms. Everywhere else, I was adrift. He alone understood me...really understood me.

The following day, the relentless sun shone on me as I finally took a pic of the completed Burning Man. It was for my boy, and I sent it, along with a sad selfie and a poetic tweet in the form of a Cinquain.

> "Who says
> Loneliness is
> About being alone;
> In the brightest crowds, I miss you
> ...the most."

The throngs of people were just as half-baked as ever, but now they felt an anticipatory vibe with bleary glances towards the Burning Man sacrifice, supposed to go up in flames tomorrow night. All the efforts of the festival focused like light waves entering the eye: from the temporary city itself, seventy thousand lines of sight were trained on this one retina of purpose.

As always, mobile entertainers wandered around on bicycles and stilts to keep community expectations high – pun intended, lol.

I sent Luca a text. "Where should I meet you?"

Glancing up, I got the goose-flesh feeling someone was watching me. I looked around. All the tie-dyed, hemp-wearing and smoking twenty-somethings surrounding me seemed harmless enough—

My thought was cut off by Luca's reply. "Inside main flap of the Love Yurt."

I made my way to the sixty-foot round tent, which was right near the plaza facing the Wicker Man. Pausing, I glanced up at the rather non-telltale banner. Plain letters spelled out a vague "Big Tent of Human Kindness."

A few people queued up in the sun, and just as I got to it, Luca popped out of the main flap.

He brushed his wavy, long hair behind his ears, smiling. "Training day, eh? Nervous?"

"Um—"

"Don't worry. You'll do fine, but I should warn you, you're gonna see it all. Remember the orgy scenes from *Logan's Run?* Well, the 70s ain't got nothing on us!" He laughed, latching onto my shoulder and parading us into the little reception area. More people stood here waiting to be 'fitted in,' and Luca intro'd me to the receptionist. Her job was to ask a few interview questions to visitors, and based on the answers, hand over a color-coded card.

Fortunately, Luca had sent me an email cheat sheet, so I'd be able to reference it real-time on my phone, but, for example, a purple card with a number 3 on it meant the guests were interested in the opposite-sex fellatio section, and there were three in the party. If I saw room in that section, I was to direct them over to the purple-cushioned area.

In the yurt itself, Luca took me to the big crate near the center, and we stood on it together.

He was right; what a sight. Altogether, the yurt interior was one open space without a central pole, the sections were laid out like a pie chart: narrow walkways separated them, and clients' shoes and clothes got kicked off and left here as they crowded onto air mattresses, each piled high with color-matched cushions, not to mention writhing and moaning clots of humanity.

After about 20 minutes of 'traffic controlling' together, I caught Luca adjusting a major boner.

"You okay alone, buddy? If so, I'll go back to Skye for, um— Lunch."

"You go, Luca. I got the hangdog of this."

"Behave," he joked and winked while getting down from the crate. I watched him exit and got on with placing folks in the right slots, after checking they had openings, lol. It was pretty smooth, for just as often as new cards were held up near the front flap, satisfied visitors collected their belongings and wandered to the designated exits.

Nevertheless, the more and more I saw, heard and 'felt' the carefree happiness all around me, the more and more I wished for a 'cure' so I could win my Gordon back. But still, a part of me reflected on life in general: the sounds of sex, the tingle of pheromones on the roof of my mouth, the sea of wriggling, contented flesh – is this bliss? As much as I missed intimacy with my boy, it was the sharing and connection that made me pine the most. That was the real source of ecstasy....

Without any warning, the hair on the back of my neck stood up again. I traced the source towards the rear of the tent. Two figures appeared way out of place. They were not dressed right, much too old, causing disturbances as they crouched down and searched amongst the bodies, looking straight into faces.

My heart dropped and buckled my knees a bit. It was Angekwekwa and Guy Germaine.

'Oh. Shit,' I thought. I knew they were looking for me.

Making no abrupt movements, so I didn't attract their attention, I lowered myself from the crate, and kept going until I was on my knees. I couldn't use the main aisle because they'd see me for sure, so I was forced to crawl between the sweaty folks in the Red Section of the Human Kindness Tent, and trust me, you don't want to know what these fine people were up to – no pun intended.

My hand slipped on a particularly slick spot, and instantly I was face to face with a bearded, truck-driver-looking fellow. A momentarily pissed-off grimace passed from him to his girl, and then they both reached up affectionately to pull me down into kisses. Stunned, I pecked each one on the forehead paternally, and rolled onto my side to dissuade the truck driver's fingers from continuing to unbutton my Levi's.

"Thanks very much," I said as I clambered over the neighboring couple.

I craned my head up to see where the cock-crazies had gotten to, and saw they were closer than I thought. I hurried and slipped on another patch of lube, crashing right into a woman with long, strawberry hair.

Somehow, my gold chain got tangled, and she screamed when I moved on. Her partner shouted "Watch it, dude!" and I glanced nervously to see Angekwekwa and Guy staring right at me.

"Oh, oh, oh...!" I leapt to my feet and started bouncing as I ran on the air mattresses.

"After him!" I heard the fake Black lady yell.

Soon, I tripped, but stumbled past the waiting, traffic-control-less people at the front flap. I jogged out into the blinding sunlight.

Disorientated by all the noise, commotion and festivities of the crowds, I took off at full speed. I guess I intended to run back into the 'city' streets, but instead found myself in the wide-open plaza surrounding the Burning Man.

As I ran, I felt a breeze and fastened up my jeans again. While doing so, I ran headlong into a five-person bicycle on parade with paper streamers. I sidestepped just in time, but the machine veered and spilled two hippies onto the sand.

They shouted at me, and bystanders got pissed at my running. As I dodged their hands, bobbing and weaving my shoulders into thin blades, I glanced back.

The Abraca cult loonies saw the ruckus-fracas and beet-lined it again in my direction.

I maneuvered a hard right, and started running against the flow of traffic, barely missing a moving pyramid of jugglers.

"Stop, thief!" Angekwekwa called out from behind, mainly to the crowd around me.

As I neared the base of the wicker man effigy, the amount of people was notably denser. They stood around, watching bongo players and little groups of high-as-kites dancers here and there. More performing artists moved in and out, slowing me down.

"Stop him!" Guy cried out, drawing unwanted attention to me as I looked for a way out. They weren't far behind now.

Hippie hands, and mumbles of "Whoa, dude – chill" and "Stop harshing the mellow, man" surrounded me, raising panic within, and just then, as I cleared the last circle of people before the monument, Angekwekwa and Germaine burst through to tackle me.

Body-slammed about the waist amid gasps from the assembled, I stumbled backwards, hands reaching out blindly behind me.

I latched onto fabric and something wooden.

"Oh, oh, oh!" sounded, and I rotated my head just in time from the dust to see the fire-breather on stilts I'd knocked over begin to fall.

As if in slow motion, all of us stopped to watch – like helpless witnesses to Fate's diabolical workings – as the man's bottle of fuel and lit torch made a graceful arc straight into the tinder at Burning Man's feet.

'Oh. Shit....' The figure caught, flames moving from feet to lick ankles, and then crawling up his calves on both sides.

Everyone was stationary. All sound had ceased. The gravity of what was happening was setting in. The crushing disappointment of seventy thousand sunburned hippies – deprived of their 'big moment' – descended around us while their dream was going up in smoke, literally.

In the following instant, this stupor gelled into rage. Pissed-off, blood-shot eyes latched onto the three of us rising to our feet in the dust.

"It was them!" I pointed at the cock-crazies, and fortunately, a dozen witnesses or more agreed, having seen them tackle me.

The noose tightened around them, and I took off.

As I ran, I knew there would be hell to pay, and the loons would have to pony up for what they did to me.

With an arm propped on the rolled-down window of the Sparks Deep-Fried Dog Wagon, I saw Burning Man tumble to his knees. His flames were dull and premature in the desert afternoon sun, but at least I was rolling out of Dodge unscathed.

I was deep enough in purgatory as it was....

Chapter 21: Hollister; Aptos; San Jose

A hundred degrees outside. And I thought the desert was bad!

Worse yet, it had to be a hundred and twenty inside this food truck, parked as it was among a line of them along a dead-grass margin of Hollister.

A name best recognized on low-grade, foreign-built casualwear, the bum-*gefickt* speck of its namesake town in Northern California didn't live up to the marketing attempt at 'cool.'

I whipped off my medieval-style pilgrim's cap to sop the sweat from my face before it splattered into the deep fryer. Why on earth Alisoun insisted the three of us wear Ren-Faire costumes inside the truck was beyond me. She had lent me a pair of black tights, and as I adjusted their grip on my crotch for the hundredth time, the lady's words of "just for fun" rang hollow.

I glanced at Karl Sparks dishing up an order of *Ye Olde Mexican Corne Dogge with Mayonnaise and Cotija Cheese* – you know, Shakespeare's favorite – and suppressed a laugh. Noting he looked cooler, I remembered him telling me "I always go commando in doublet and pantaloons." He must have been wearing a garter belt to keep his stockings up…. No, I didn't want to think about that…but I suppose Alisoun would have one to spare. No, lol. Enough of those thoughts.

I concentrated on my work, and as I lifted one of the baskets and shook out a mess of golden fries, I wanted to leave the confines of this sardine-can of a truck and return to cool desert nights and tossing back a few *brewskis*.

But the reality was, this dogge waggone was busy, and so were all of our rivals – ones that offered deep-fried ice cream, or hibachi-roasted Snicker bars, and especially the ones offering kombucha-infused popsicles.

I crouched down to peek out of the tiny windows as I got more frozen spuds for the oil. We had a long line of people sweltering in duds ranging from 'squire' to 'knight,' to 'dames in da'dress,' and quite frankly, I didn't get the Renaissance Faire appeal. In fact, I didn't get the Ren-Faire type of person. Who'd want to traipse around eucalyptus and live oak trees in Northern California, quaking *thees* and *thous* in hundred-degree heat, wearing heavy curtain-fabric costumes, and eating anachronistic turkey legs…? I shrugged and started frying the next batch of onion rings. 'Just another form of escapism, I guess. Sort of like being a Republican.'

I leaned back, dabbing at my forehead, and watching Alisoun swoosh her sofa-cushion brocade getup around the foot-long sausage roaster. She seemed happy, and I suppose the Sparks were nice enough people, despite their head-in-the-sand Trump tendencies. They sure saved my bacon from the crazy cock fools at Burning Man, but I was getting sick and tired of the Corndog Wife's overtly sexual come-ons.

Pulling at the collar of my costume, another heated situation came to my memory without warning: the tearful way me and Assauer fled our homeland. How does a person launch the thousand steps of a wanderer? I don't know, but for us – at least regarding my ex's love for me – it began as a surprise.

"You did what?" Assauer asked.

"I had nowhere else to turn, so I came here."

All heat instantly left my ex. He hugged me and guided us over to the bed. We sat. "Now, tell me again, from the beginning."

Time seemed like the one luxury in life I had none to spare, but I swallowed down my fear, wiped my sweaty brow, and started.

"Rolf's dad walked in on us. It was clear what we were doing."

"But then, he did what?"

He pulled the boy up by the earlobe and dragged Rolf naked downstairs, into the living room.

I followed, putting on my shoes and pants, and holding my shirt.

Rolf's mother screamed seeing the kid being abused and yelled at by the father.

"I can explain." I held out my hands in supplication.

"He's fucking our boy, Greta! Under our own roof!"

"Dad – I'm the one.... I love Kohl, don't you see?"

"Silence," the mom snapped at her boy, getting it now. She turned her ire on me. "We take you in, and this – this! – is how you treat us, like we're running a whorehouse?! Turning our son into a plaything."

"No, no, it's not like that."

"I love him!" Rolf screamed in frustration and tried to run to me.

Greta grabbed his arms and slapped him.

"Just calm down," I said, getting angry myself. "The boy is over the age of consent. He can choose, and he chooses me.

The money was just a...a—"

I halted mid-thought, knowing too late I'd said too much.

The boy looked sick.

The mother looked apprehensive.

The father stormed up to me. "You've been robbing us too? Speak up, let's hear this."

"Dad, it was me. I gave him—"

The mom cut Rolf off. "I think it's time for you to leave, Kohl."

"No, Greta, no!" demanded Rolf's dad. "Not if he's been robbing us. Then it's a matter for the courts."

"*Dummkopf!*" his wife said, grabbing the father's arm. "You want everyone in town to know your son's been giving his ass away, to...to a...domestic, like him?"

"Oh, my God. What an awful thing to say to you," Assauer said. "I can't believe it. And they just let you walk out of there?"

"Yes and no. I packed, and the father threatened my life when I tried to say goodbye to Rolf. The boy was in tears... but...."

I stopped. My phone vibrated with a text. "It's from – Rolf."

"What is it he says?"

I felt the color drain from my face. "He says, his dad just called the police. Said the money was enough to put me in jail for years."

Lower than low, having just lost the boy I loved – having alienated Assauer because of Rolf – facing a loss of freedom seemed too much to bear. My head fell into my hands as I choked back the tears. Some much in my life had gone wrong.

Assauer stood. "You're packed, right?"

I nodded against my palms.

"Good. Give me a minute to do the same."

"What...?" I lifted my gaze. "What are you talking about?"

He made me stand and held my eyes with his beautiful blue ones. They were determined and crystal-clear.

"I said, I'll pack, then we'll go to the base, and I'll get us on a flight to America tonight."

"Assauer! You'd give up everything to be a fugitive with me...?"

He kissed me. It was once; it was manly and assured. "Yes. No time to talk now. You pull yourself together and I'll pack."

The heat of the food truck came back to me. While I swiped my face, I felt grateful to my ex, but in that same notion was profound hurt he'd steal Gordon away from me. How could the same person do so much for me and then take everything away from me as well?

As my timer went off for the jalapeño poppers, and as I drained them, I realized there was another dramatic scene I could provoke, one that might prove hotter and more uncomfortable than even this truck.

I was in the area, so.... "Alisoun, after the lunch rush tomorrow, I might need rest of the day off."

The ride-sharing car slowed to a stop on the gravely parking lot, and I got out.

It pulled away and left me among the potted roses in full bloom at the "Sanchez & Sons Family Nursery."

My heart hitched nearly up to my Adam's apple. It had been a gut-wrenching ride through the shadowy hollow of Trout Gulch Road once more. I thought I'd never see Aptos again, and certainly never pictured myself back at the place where Gordon grew up.

I moved between rose thorns and parked pickup trucks, along the side of a greenhouse, knowing there was a central path turning off soon. It led me past more enclosed spaces jutting away on either side: the citrus building; the 'creepers' with flowering potato vines, sundial passion fruit, and peppery bougainvillea. I remembered the first time my boy gave me a tour of the ins and outs of this complex, how he'd drawn my attention to secret spots and revealed how much of a true nature boy he was, with a natural green thumb for the plants that had swaddled him as he grew.

The boy's sexual awakening, he told me, had been early and dirty, pointing out to me smaller plant sheds where he'd take "seed-laden" migrant workers to get what he wanted. Always with boys only a few years older than him, always wham-bam and hasty – "¿*Quieres mi leche...dentro?*"; "*¡Sí!*" – and always initiated by the curly-headed lad himself.

Now as I passed these plants that he loved, and that grew seemingly under the magic of his touch, I wondered just how connected to nature he really was.... That line from the *Carpenters'* song, about birds singing and stars falling whenever he appeared, made me revel in my boy's loveliness; a beauty inborn and as sacred as any.

Being here, moving through the quiet buildings, smelling soil and plantings, feeling the muted sea breeze seep through doors and cracks, put me in mind of how difficult it was to go to Assauer, again. But, it was only fair that he hear from me of our resolve – me and Gordon – to be together, even if it meant Assauer would say he was done with me because of it.

It was a hot day in August, some two weeks before our second year of teaching at Aptos High would begin.

Gordon wanted to come with me, to talk to my ex about our plans, but I knew it wouldn't be a good idea. No need for Assauer to hate Gordon if he was going to hate me; we'd do better to keep his ire aimed at one or the other of us, not both.

The fan was on in our little apartment kitchen, and my ex sat typing on his laptop.

"Hey."

"Hey. What's up?" he asked.

I heard my voice crack. "You know that boy...Gordon?"

He glanced away from his screen. "Not Gordon, Gordon Sanchez, my student?"

There was no sugarcoating it. "We've been seeing each other for months now. I didn't want to keep it from you—"

"Kohl...."

The disappointment in his voice made me finally swallow and hold his eyes. "I love him, brother. I can't help it – and he loves me too. His father's a prick, mother's not much better; 'We don't approve!'—"

"Kohl!" He slammed his laptop shut. "Back to your cookie-jar ways, and after that scene with Rolf and the cops, and me giving up everything to—"

"Assauer—"

"No. No, this is unbelievable. You care about no one but yourself."

"I tried to be good, I really did, and with Gordon, age is not really an issue. I'd love him if he was twenty, or sixty—"

"But he's sixteen, isn't he? *Idiot.*"

I added softly, "Nearly seventeen.... But, the point is, I'm telling you this because we're running away. We can't let Gordon's father separate us, and my boy can't let me go to jail now that they know."

"Because you told them?"

"Because he did."

Assauer was silent.

"I know you're angry, Assauer."

More silence.

"But, me and Gordon, we're going to be together, face whatever the world throws at us – together."

"And you're telling me this, why?"

I reached for his clenched hand and took it meaningfully. "I want you to come too. Only you can protect me, keep me sane and safe, like you've always done."

"And *him?* What does he want?"

"He wants you to come as well. He knows we have a special connection, and always will. He knows you keep my temper down and wants the three of us to work as a team."

Silence, but then he massaged my fingers.

"I know it's unfair," I told him softly. "All of it, but please, brother, help us. Please."

It may have seemed so long ago, for all the shit that's happened since, but in a way, it was no time at all.

I blinked. Somehow I'd walked through the whole nursery and arrived at my dreaded destination. I knocked on the Office door and went in.

Gordon's mom held something like a shipping form for her gray-haired husband to read. She was the one to look up first.

Stunned is the only word to describe her eyes.

In another moment, Aaron Sanchez stood behind his desk and whipped off his bifocals. "What the—"

"Um, hi."

"I'll leave you two," Ava Sanchez said, slipping through the door behind me.

Once closed, Aaron began to shout. "You dare to show your face around here?! Where's my boy? Is he with you?"

He started to glance over my shoulder, and my heart sank.

"No, sir. He – he ran away, and I came here hoping—"

"Ran away," he scoffed. "Rich irony. And now you know how I've felt since you, you – I can't even think what you did to his mind."

I persevered, but he was right; this act of penance included knowing exactly how he felt when Gordon ran from him. "Sir, I was hoping—"

"Hoping what?" he said tersely.

"That he'd been in contact."

He stalked from behind his desk to stand within feet of my face.

"My son Gordon hasn't been in contact with us since some foreign piece of shit pervert stole him away in the middle of the night two years ago."

"He's eighteen now, sir."

"You have the balls to remind me of that…. So, he's left you? Well, guess what, I think that's great news. So you can take your hangdog, puppy-dog eyes outta my sight and get the fuck out of here forever."

"But if you can pass along a message if he does—"

Mr. Sanchez grabbed me by the scruff of my shirt and kicked his door open, nearly breaking the glass.

He dragged me along the front area of the nursery, where people with carts and plants waited at the registers. He shouted as he pulled. "How dare you. Don't you ever show your face around here again, cuz if you do, you won't get away without an extra hole in your head."

Out the front door, he used a foot locked against my lower back and kicked.

I went flying, elbows first, along the gravel.

He spat at my shoes and said, "How much can you steal in your lifetime before you have to accept the consequences! Now, get off my property and stay away. Because you are evil to the core – that's what you are."

Ten awful minutes had gone by. Now I sat on the grassy incline across the road from "Sanchez & Sons Family Nursery."

I'd had to take my shoes off briefly, because I need the fabric of my socks to tie around my elbows – to stop the bleeding. But they still throbbed with incredible pain, all the gravel dust being ground into the open sores, and me with no way to clean them.

I didn't mind though. Something physical threatening to make me cry for a change was sort of a relief.

Cloudy as my vision was, I didn't see her cross the road, not until Ava Sanchez folded her skirt and sat next to me. She stared straight across at the nursery. I expected the worst.

"You know," she said, picking up a blade of grass, "Aaron is not a patient man. Gordon, as the youngest, is different from his brothers – his father's temper always frightened him."

She turned to me. "Do you think you frighten him?"

I had no reply.... God, I hope not...

Ava asked very calmly, "How about this: do you love him?"

That I could answer. "Yes, ma'am. More than anything else in the whole world." Now the tears came.

The woman nodded her head and played with her grass. "I thought so. That's what I told my husband. You ever wonder why the cops never came looking for you?"

"I...."

"Well, never mind." She inhaled deeply and sat up straight. "I'm a pragmatic woman, Mr. Kohl. His dad idolized him, and although we parents are not supposed to act human and 'choose,' still, Gordon was his father's favorite. His golden boy, his innocent – well, at least I knew the truth. Mothers always do."

"What do you mean?"

"I knew he was a precocious, sexual teen. I don't mean to shock you, but the truth is, he didn't keep secrets from me like he did with his dad, so I knew – because he told me – about his sexy new German teacher, the one he seduced, and the one he told me in tears he'd fallen for."

Her tone grew stern.

"But I never wanted him to run off, to be 'on the streets.' To live in fear."

"I'm sorry."

"Are you?"

I slowly shook my head. "No. No lies, because you know I'd do it all over again."

"You *are* honest when prodded. He told me you were like that."

Ava stood, seeing my hired sedan pull off the road in front of us. "Yes. I know you'd do it all over again. But you can't help it, right? The two of you are in love."

"Meant to be together." I opened the rear door of the car. "So if he contacts you, will you tell him something for me?"

"Tell him what, Kohl?"

"Just – tell him I'm sorry. Please."

All she said before I got in the car to leave Aptos forever was: "If."

It was after dark by the time I got back to the Renaissance Faire in Hollister.

I mounted the steps of the Sparks' RV and found Alisoun alone in the confined little living area. She'd been tossing back stiff ones, as an open fifth of brown liquor stood on the tabletop.

"Ah, sugar snap-pea," she said on first sight, "what happened to you?"

"I'm a little battered and bruised, aren't I?"

"You sure are." She'd already retrieved a second glass. "Sit down."

She pointed, and I drank, barely registering her words about Karl playing poker with Mr. and Mrs. Bacon-Wrapped Asparagus Sticks.

The stuff burned my throat like fire, but had a sweet aftertaste like caramel.

She perceived my unstated question. "It's Fairfield Whisky. A. R. Morrow and Co – six bucks a quart, and not too bad at that, considering the price."

I didn't care. I poured myself another, topping off her jelly-glass tumbler as well.

After I downed my second, feeling the heat spread to my chest, she laid her hand on my arm.

"What's wrong, sugar cookie?"

"I've had a terrible day, the kind you can predict, but still have to go through anyway."

"Aww." She stroked fingers up to my shoulder.

I asked her plainly, "Do you think I'm evil to the core?"

"Kohl, honey, I can assure you – you're not. And I have known many an 'evil' man in my life."

My phone vibrated with a new text, distracting me from fully acknowledging Alisoun Sparks moving closer to me and licking her lips.

I looked at my mobile's screen and puzzled. All it said was: "Fitness Revolution Gym, San Jose. Tomorrow, 3 pm."

"Won't you tell me what's on your mind, Kohl?" Alisoun asked, and I felt her caress the back of my neck.

"Huh...." I tapped out a reply. "Who is this?"

A second after I sent it, an error message returned. "This device cannot reply to blocked numbers."

I shrugged, for the first time realizing the Corndog's Wife was practically in my lap.

"I can take your mind off of things...."

Delicately directing her back to her seat, I chuckled. "No, no. I'm afraid you've got the wrong idea. See, I'm Gay, and in fact went looking for my boyfriend today. He's run off with my ex."

She scooched closer again. "Who ain't a little gay...?"

"Me. I'm all-in on the Gay thing, as you'll find most of us are. But you see, I'm also impotent because a crazy sex cult hexed my dick and I've been looking for a fix."

"ED?" she asked brightly. "Is that all?! Karl has the little blue pills—"

"No, no, they.... I'm well beyond pharmaceuticals."

At that point I eyed Gordon's gym bag, which I'd been using as a suitcase, packed and sitting near the door; it was there because the sofa in the 'living room' was also my fold-out bed. I always keep my stuff neat and packed up, prepared for any unexpected 'emergency exit' I might need to make.

I decided the situation called for a little flattery. "But, despite the *totally Gay* part of it, I like you, Alisoun. And I'd repay you for your hospitality if I could." Ha. What a farce; there wasn't enough caramel-colored whisky in all of Fairfield to get me to sleep with her. "But you see, I can't. However, if I could – even though I'm Gay – I would."

"Oh, sugar tooth, what in the name of all that's saccharine does that have to do anything? I mean, my husbands numbers three, six and seven WERE gay, even though one claimed I turned him that way, so...." Alisoun's mood changed. Her tones down-geared into sexy lust. "If you're serious, there's still a way for you to 'perform.' Let me corndog you."

"What...?" I slowly rose from the built-in couch.

"Let me show you." She popped up and pulled out the long drawer under the seats. Alisoun turned and placed a shafty nine-inch strapon dildo in my hands, the hip straps dangling.

"I – aaaa...."

"I'm really good at using that too." Her eyebrows flared. "Karl will tell ya. ALL my husbands, God rest their souls – even the living ones – will tell you how much they loved it."

"But I'm strictly a top.... I've never even had a real one in there, so I'm not gonna start with a silly-cone imitation." I shoved the apparatus back in her hands.

She wouldn't take no for an answer and walked me back to the cushion. "Well, if that's true, sugar booger, you don't know what you're missin'." She shoved me down, crawling on top. "It'll rock your world. Guaranteed to adjust your attitude forever."

The cockeye leer of lust on her face was matched by the upward thrust of the rubber schlong in her hand.

"No," I said.

"I know you want it." She forced her drunken kisses on me. Revolted, my mind went to wondering about the topsy-turvy times we lived in; times when a man's body was not his own to decide what to do with.

The door opened, and her spouse walked in.

"Karl. Thank God!" I pried the Corndog's Wife off of me, and she stood there agape with the dildo in her clutches.

"My God, Alisoun, have you been fucking another one of our boy-employees?"

She puffed up. "It's none of your business if I have, Karl. You'd do well to remember you're just my husband! What gives you the right to barge in here, acting uppity...."

I grabbed Gordon's beloved gym bag and slipped out into the night, leaving the Sparks well enough alone, to their own kind.

The next afternoon found me in downtown San Jose, in front of Fitness Revolution Gay Gym.

I peered through the show windows, none too sure of what I was doing. What if this was a ploy by the crazy Abraca people, or worse, by the donkey-schlong freaks.

I hesitated.

Another text came in. "I'm glad you're here."

I went in and found a day pass with my name on it at the front desk.

The main workout room was what you'd expect to see in any place catering to the buff, the queer and the beautiful. Hmmm, mental note: new name for a soap opera. ...*Next time on* The Buff, Queer and Beautiful, *will Adain come clean about his lobotomy to Colton; will Clayton out Dawson to Preston; will Paxton clear the way for Jackson to get a green card...?* And on and on, lol.

Walking around a bit, I got the lay of the land. Treadmills faced the windows; weight machines lined the opposite wall.... Wait. Was that...?

About twenty feet ahead of me, on some dead-press contraption, sat Assauer. Older men stood around and fawned over his every gesture, and then I saw why. My eyes nearly popped when they saw the outline of his cock beneath the silky rolls of his basketball shorts, flopping halfway down to his knees.

I had a sudden realization. If Assauer was here.... Then.... Gordon...?

I saw the boy eyeing me from behind a nearby weight machine.

Swallowing, and making sure my ex hadn't seen me, I went over to him.

He had initially appeared sad, but started to smile. "You came."

"Does this mean—"

"Oh, Kohl. I'm sorry, please – please rescue me?"

I gestured for him to stay quiet, and the two of us quickly headed for the exit. He had Assauer's gym bag, and we were careful my ex didn't see us slip away. I was also careful not to shout out loud in sheer joy!

"…redeant in coniunctionem…"

— Part Seven —
(Not So) Sequestered in San Diego

#pharmapseudocological,

#Art-Inc., #not-loaded,

#sure-flame, #Sadeeq,

#jealous-fuck, #Cortez,

#not-loaded, #burp,

#Gordon's-boy,

#McFearsome!

#rag-mag,

#turkey!

Chapter 22: Facing Facts

I preceded my boy into our motel room, immediately going to pull the curtains on the San Diego afternoon sun. Gordon followed me in and set our bags on the little fold-out luggage stand near the entrance. I watched him going around and turning on the various lamps before I went to the door and locked it.

In the quiet, alone at last, we faced one another. I opened my arms, and my boy walked into my embrace.

I stroked his curls, inhaling the sacred scent I had missed for so long, and raised his chin. Words failed me, so I simply wiped his tears away with my cheeks, turning his one by one, and placing reassuringly delicate kisses on his lips as I went.

Finding resolve, I gently pushed him back slightly and held onto his shoulders so I could step out of my shoes.

I kneeled before Gordon, and let his hand use my upper body for support as I removed his sneakers and socks. Then, hand in hand, I led him to our bed.

I propped up the pillows and lay down first so my boy could cuddle up in my arms, his head resting over my heart.

"Please, no more tears," I said, sliding my fingers down his arm.

He sniffled a bit. Still looking away, he told me, "I've missed them, you know."

"Missed...?"

"Your eyes. I missed looking into your beautiful green depths."

"That's ironic, isn't it?"

"What is?"

"That I'm such a jealous fuck, and have Billy Shakespeare's sure-flame mark of it upon me."

"Oh, Kohl—"

"I will try, Gordon, to do better. To not be *so* jealous all the time. Is that why...?"

"Why?"

"Why you left me."

He pulled out of my arms and sat up on his own.

We'd not had a chance to be alone – to talk – until now. After our flight from the gym in San Jose, we ducked into an alley and called for a car. Then it was on to the Amtrak station and an overnight train to San Diego, because Burtron and his new boyfriend, Geoff, were hanging out here, and with what I knew, my ex had no reason to venture this far south. We'd mainly slept on the fairly-crowded train, with me barely letting my boy out of my arms. I'd asked no questions, harbored no hard feelings, certainly not in public, because having Gordon within reach was enough.

Now we just wanted peace after our trip, and to be sequestered in a nice, quiet room like this to work things out.

"I'll try and tone down my jealousy, I really will. But why, honey? Why...?" It was time to face facts.

He was silent, looking down morosely into his lap.

I pressed on. "Did I justify this? To be shamed by the boy I love taking up with a *Spitzbub* like Assauer? A...a take-a-runner in the night sex-fiend?"

"Kohl—"

"My heart's an open sore, babe, but no callus covers it yet. No hard skin is growing there because—"

He stifled me by letting tears come and reciting my own words back to me.

"Unfair –
How many times
Have broken hearts said that,
Been forced to lay themselves open,
When they just want to hide.
How many times?
Unfair."

After a pause, needed to swipe my own tear, I asked, "You read my tweets?"

"Every single one, Kohl. How could I ignore your lovesick messages? You know how wonderful a poet I think you are."

"And you memorized it?"

He nodded. "And I forgive you, Kohl."

"Um—"

"No one can judge us or our love, so I'm ready to let bygones be bygones, as long as you're truly sorry."

"What did I do, again, honey...?"

"Come on, Kohl, be authentic. Truthfully now, was it I who left you, or was it you who forced my hand? I mean, you were acting nuts, waving a gun around – I was scared you'd do something insane. And what then, huh? You shoot Assauer, and I have to watch you get the electric chair, your ashes deported to Germany as permanent punishment. No, in such dire circumstances, the smart thing to do is go along with the more forceful of the two – to protect the weaker – and that's what you forced me to do, to protect you."

'Oh,' I thought. 'I never considered it...that way...?'

I blurted out, as if it were the main topic, "I got rid of the gun."

"Well, hurray for that." Irony bellowed from the blast of his tone. Then he turned serious. "You did scare me half to death with that damn pistol."

"I, ah—"

"No, let me finish."

I shut my mouth.

"I didn't tell you before, that day at the Rose Bowl Flea when you asked for details, but – but my dad…. You see, when I was around twelve, there was an attempted break-in at the nursery. He got me out of bed to go with him in the middle of the night. In his office, he unlocked—"

"His desk drawer."

"Yeah, his desk drawer and took out a revolver. We snuck around the darkened greenhouses, heading to the front registers. Anyway, there was a confrontation, lots of shouts, then the thief wrestled the gun away and it went off, nearly shooting my dad."

"You can't stand the sight of guns because it puts you back to that dark place."

"Yes. To a moment where I almost lost a loved one because of a fucking gun. And my mom was furious. I mean, angrier than I've ever seen her. She came running and found me so close to danger."

"Yeah. Your mom is quite a…a smart biscuit."

He chuckled. "She told me about your little chat on the side of the road."

"So, you've been in contact with her the whole time? Since we ran from Aptos?"

"Yep."

"And you never thought she'd reveal our location to the police, or worse yet, to your dad?"

"Nope. She and I – we understand one another. My mom is a very special person. I felt awful running from her, but now you know, I didn't really. I've been sending her updates and letting her know I'm happy and safe with you."

"Then I'm glad I went to Aptos."

"You are?"

"Yes. Your father beating me, saying he'd shoot me next time, felt like divine justice, or karma maybe."

He crawled in next to me.

"But Gordon…." I cooed.

"Yes?"

"Just so you know, that day in L.A., when you…when I drove you away, the gun wasn't loaded."

"It doesn't matter. You tried to scare me either way."

"Yes, you are right, honey. I was a shit for doing that."

I lifted his eyes to mine.

"Um – I'm sorry, Gordon. I am sorry, baby. Forgive me?"

He pursed lips like he was considering my sincerity, but a moment later, he let one more tear fall and cuddled down on the pillow of my arm again. My heart glowed.

My boy grew talkative, and I stroked his hair while I listened. "Besides, being back with you will be a welcome change. Assauer's dick grows by the day, and so does his appetite for fucking."

I paused, overcome with sadness. "I'm sorry my *Schwanz* has stopped working, baby. Are you content to stay with me anyway?"

He gripped onto my arm with his right hand. A sly smile rose to me. "I know you're a top, but if you love me, you can think of other ways to let your boy have his pleasure."

A bit of flash on his finger caught my attention. I rotated the gold band. "That's...."

"Assauer's ring – the one you gave him."

"I'm confused.'

"He presented it to me, in fact, insisted I take it. So I took off the cheap one you gave me and slipped this one on, the whole time imagining it came direct from you. You don't mind, do you?"

"I'm glad you have it. It's where it belongs."

An adorable 'I know, right' smirk arose, just before he lifted my hand and kissed it.

I pulled him close and filled him in on the latest. "While I was looking for you two, I also kept running from the Priapus folks, looking for other cults who might have a cure."

"That's not using your brains, Kohl."

"It's not? What do you mean?"

"The smarter approach is for us to run *to* the donkey dick people. As they put the hex on your cock, maybe we can track down a 'good one' to take it off again."

I heard myself say with a total lack of irony, "I didn't think of that." I also never really considered how much smarter Gordon is than me. Maybe I was growing up a little bit in the relationship. Who knows?

He caressed my chest and recited another of my lovesick Skyscraper poems:

> "How could you?
> How could you leave me so,
> Leave me with hapless lovers crying:
> 'I thought I knew you, but it turns out I was wrong.'
> I never imagined I'd be one
> Left to stagger and cry:
> 'How could you.'"

"I still can't believe you saw them."

"I read each and every one in secret, once I knew Assauer was not watching. Anyway, when my mom told me that you'd been there saying you were sorry, and my dad beat you up, I sent you the text about San Jose."

"Well, more like roughed up, but I'm so glad I went now. Something was telling me to stand there and face the music. When I saw you in the gym, I've never been so grateful."

Gordon teased me, guiding my hand to the hard bulge in his jeans.

"How grateful?"

"Very." I took ahold of him gently, lovingly. "From now on, it's just you and me. Remember 'our' song, baby? The words still mean everything to me.... 'They may try to keep us apart.... Think our journey's doomed from the start.... They may try to keep us away.... But we know we're blessed day by day'...."

"Ah, Kohl—"

I pulled him up and stopped up his beautiful mouth with my own.

As his sweet breath mingled with mine, I reinforced my vow to do better – to be better.

I knelt on the bed and undid his shirt and jeans. In another moment, I was on my back, guiding his member to my lips.

He moaned, looked to the ceiling and flung his arms out for balance.

I sucked him, drawing his shaft as far as it could go, making him become a bit weak in the knees. His hands landed on the bedspread on either side of my head. His legs locked – jeans and shorts pooled by his ankles – and he began taking a commanding control in face-fucking me.

I latched onto his upper thighs and realized things were different. I'd sucked him a few times, savoring his fragrant aroma and taste, but now I thrilled deep inside to know his hardness – the amber sweetness of his pre-cum slicking my tonsils – was *for* me, caused, raised and maintained by my pleasuring this boy. I was going to make him cum, and I'd take his precious gift with the true gratitude I'd just vowed to him.

I loved my boy, my Gordon, and I would do better by him and not doubt his love. Why shouldn't I? I can in a very literal sense taste it.

His breaths grew jagged, and I used my hands to push up on his hips – just to pleasure the tip of his flaring cock with my lips and tongue.

"Kohl...Kohl...."

I sucked harder and stroked the back of the shaft with my tongue.

My boy paused. His moan erupted a split second before my mouth filled with his love seed. I let him finish pumping me full, realizing I did have some hope for our future. The future we'd have once this curse was removed.

And then I swallowed greedily, never, never any happier than at that moment. I had my beloved back.

For three blissful days, the *Do Not Disturb* sign swayed outside our motel room door.

Whereas Venice Beach had been a three-day purgatory of pickle juice and purges, for me and my boy in San Diego, it was an indulgence of gluttony and excess, but all aimed at one goal – celebration. Our reunion was meant to last, so we'd have sex, order food, shower, have more cuddles, watch TV or

surf the web, nap, have sex, order more food – you get the idea. I was beginning to think of myself as Gordon's boy, but what did that matter? We were
together and happy, although at this point, I should make clear our actual
activities were limited as far as 'sex' – just me bringing him off with hand
and blowjobs – but the endless making out, the closeness, the reestablishing
of our bond, that's SEX in all-caps! Gordon pleaded to rail me, but my virgin
entry was sealed and off limits even to him, and he knew it.

However, because of all this, the cure pressed itself more urgently on
my mind. I longed for the return of a 'normal' time between us, but we'd
never find the trail of the Priapus cult locked away in our rented room. So, on
the third day, I texted Burtron Hammerick, and he told us to head over to an
artists' commune because Geoff had a friend for us to meet. The Hammer
and his new boyfriend had been doing their own San Diego sequestering –
think love-doves in a cozy cot someplace – but Burtron had not forgotten my
mission and got us all an 'in' to some event the Beauty Cult was hosting tonight. In the meantime, we'd head out and meet Geoff's buddy.

So, that's what we did. Grudgingly getting dressed, and discovering
our atrophied walking muscles were a little sore, we made our way to a
downtown address.

"Is this some kind of mistake?" Gordon asked, for in front of us was a
freeway. Well, it rumbled and polluted the air several stories over our heads,
but at sidewalk level was a gate, which was open now. We could see a compound behind the fence, where neat shacks arrayed themselves around an
open-but-shady plaza below the overpass.

"Nope, this is it. See the sign? Art4arts-sake.com."

We went in.

I sent a text to the guy we were supposed to meet. "Dude, we're here.
Where are you?"

A minute later, I read the reply to Gordon. *"I'm by the soapbox, in a
yellow hoodie."*

"What's that supposed to mean?" he asked.

Noise interrupted us. Folks were gathered by one side of the plaza and
suddenly started hooting and clapping their approval.

"Ah," my boy said. "I think I know. Come on."

He led the way, and soon we were angling ourselves to the nucleus of
the hipster confab. In the center stood a wooden crate, and just as we got
there, the speaker receiving all of the applause stepped down.

"Hey"—Gordon gestured—"that must be him." A middle-aged man,
with dark face-stubble and a ponytail, loitered amongst the front-row of the
standing crowd.

Even from this distance, his appearance marked him as one of those
so-called *literati.* He was the type the rich love to hate – i.e., those fearful
anti-intellectual Dump-heads who hate anyone smarter than them. Thus,
they wind up hating everyone, lol! As for trust, or let's just call it 'respect,'
these same pro-idiot-a-logs unknowingly abide by old Harpo Marx's maxim:

'I'd never belong to a proletariat that would have me as a member!'

But anyway, he had on a mustard-colored sweatshirt, so we went to him.

"American-4-all?" I asked, using the social media handle Geoff Bath had given me for our contact.

He barely looked my way. "You Geoff's buddies?"

"Yes," Gordon said.

"Cool. Name's Sadeeq Amergin, and poet-agitator is my profession." He suddenly pressed burning eyes on yours truly. "Ever heard of me?"

"Um—"

Just as I was preparing to lie and say "of course," the poet's phone cheeped an eagle's cry. It was his message alert ringtone.

"One sec," he said, pulling it out. A moment later, he frowned. "Listen to this, and I quote: 'Your shit is so shitty and Anti-Merica I needed a pooper scooper just to make it three words into your newest so-called poem.'"

Me and Gordon swallowed. What could we say, lol.

When Sadeeq glanced up from the screen, he had a big grin. "I'll yell at this take-it-raw-from-Russia-redneck later, but I love feedback. No such thing as…bad…."

His tone trailed off as he first realized how lovely Gordon was.

"Why, *hello*." He shook my boy's hand, lingeringly.

"I'm Kohl, and that's Gordon, *my* boyfriend."

Fortunately – or not so, depending on your POV – the next speaker approached the pulpit and distracted Amergin.

"Oh, fuck," he said. "This guy's a real douche garbage-bag. Art4arts-sake.com lets any old numbnuts climb the soapbox and spew – well, you'll see."

The assembled quieted, and the thirty-something-year-old white dude with a bandana headscarf started rapping, or 'tossing up' a beat and rhymes.

> "Yo, yo, listen up, ya'all
> Home of the free,
> The Don's the man for me.
> All those fake-newsters,
> Givin' the peeps the bluesters,
> Outta be heading to jails
> And tossed on rusty nails,
> Without bails
> So our *president* – word – never fails.
> That's the real news, ya'all."

He wrapped up with an edgy flourish: a fuck-finger kissed and patted over his heart. After that, the lingering smirk on his face challenged anyone to 'unlike' him or his message.

The crowded plaza erupted with wild cheers of support.

Sadeeq cupped his hands and booed. "Un-American drivel!"

The people around us were not happy at the dissent, so I yanked on the poet's arm. "Give us a tour. It's our first time here."

With another glance at Gordon, Sadeeq licked his chops, walking us out of the soapbox area. As he strolled, he told us, "Sorry about that. San Diego ain't really a part of California anymore. They drank the Retrogressive koolaid decades ago and still like to make believe it's 1985, when the world was a simpler place for simpletons like them."

His phone chirped again, but this time he simply told us while reading, "More haters. Love it. A happy consumer may tell one friend; an unhappy person, ten times as many! Gotta get my share of views up by any means possible."

A couple minutes later we were heading to a tin-plated shack of a building. On it, recycled metal from oil cans, signs and crushed beer cans made up the siding. A continuous row of widows along the tops of the walls gave away the fact this might be gallery space. Once inside, Amergin paused admiringly at an art installation. His hand went to his chin.

Me and Gordon exchanged question-mark looks.

"Is that," I asked, "um – tupperware?"

"Yes."

The 'mural' before us consisted of various sizes and colors of the plastic food storage containers nailed to the wall.

"Makes you question things, don't it?" Sadeeq said.

"Um – yeah."

"Reminds me of a Cinquain of mine."

Without me or Gordon being able to protest, Amergin launched into his verse.

> "I know –
> It's *Art* you say,
> Meant to have no meaning;
> Can't argue with the obvious,
> They say."

Now I knew for sure. This poet was mad, mad as a milliner.

Gordon chuckled. "Yeah, nice 'art,' but does it burp?"

The poet and I just stared at the teenager.

"You know," my boy explained through a grin, "Tupperware, make it burp, like on the commercials."

Just then, Gordon's phone signaled he'd gotten a text. He went pale, reading it quickly and shoving his cell back in his letterman jacket.

"Oh, yes," the social media phenom exclaimed, "burps, belching, passing gas, all of it. It's perfect allegory of the state of Art these days. Shall we?"

He gestured, and we continued on our tour of the galleries.

"Yes, apt metaphor," the poet droned, "because just as in modern politics, those without taste, but flush with funds, can buy down an artist's worth like a commodity – like sow belly futures, or penny stocks. No more than that is Art these days."

"What do you mean?" Gordon asked.

The poet swished his ponytail a few times for good measure. "I mean, my *handsome* lad, in the old days, artists only cared about the advancement of the state of the art. If Van Gogh were alive today, he'd make the cutting of his ear a big social media 'happening,' and auction off the severed chunk to the highest bidder online. He'd still say he was doing it for Art, but he'd really be doing it for publicity, 'views', *and* the cash!"

I inquired, "And how does that play into buying down a person's worth...?"

"Easy. In the 19th century, Van Gogh was a man of honor. Today he'd be a money-slut like the rest of us, at the beck and call of those who would make a brand of him, a commodity to be bought and sold like junk equities on the Art Market. Pay ten grand on a painting today and hope it fetches six mill in a few years."

We were suddenly standing in front of another installation.

"Is that...piss?" my boy asked unpleasantly of the mad poet.

"Yes, urine from beauty queens and celebrity talk show hosts."

"Oh, my...." I was looking at racks of test tubes filled with yellowing liquids, sitting on a table made of wooden tongue depressors, lol.

Gordon's phone vibrated again, and Sadeeq instantly reached for his own.

"Sorry," my boy said after he pulled it out and glanced at the screen. "Give me a few." He walked several paces away.

"Say..." Sadeeq elbowed me and stepped close. "You fellas have an open relationship...?" He moistened his mouth, leering at Gordon.

"No," I told him firmly. "It's tightly shut, as a matter of fact."

He nodded and continued to ogle my boy like he'd barely heard me.

Gordon returned to us, and the lecherous poet led the way deeper into the gallery. "You know," he said pedantically, "the Gop Party is devaluated just like *Art Inc.* today because they let Big Tobacco, Big Gun and Big War Machine, Big Wallstreet and Big For-Profit Healthcare become their corporate owners. They did it just so they could fearmonger and devalue the public's trust enough to let voter scam-artists creep into jobs they have no qualifications for. Just look at that Repub chuckle-n-groan factory they call the 'Senate' today. It's just like *Art Inc.* and reminds me of a little poem."

'Oh, boy,' I thought. 'This guy can bend it like Beckett.'

He recited:

> "Old Petronius once said it best –
> 'The rich feast off the misery of the poor,'
> And though ancient, none better could attest

To the most modern truth we all ignore." [23]

He halted us in front of another art piece.

"Is that—" Gordon started....

"—A reindeer's ass?" Sadeeq finished. "Yes!"

We were looking at a blank plaster wall. The rear-end derriere – get it, deer-ree-air, lol – was sticking straight out, like it was frozen in mid-leap.

Our guide took us around to the other side of the partition, and there was the front half of the plaster Christmas icon, antlers and all.

"Oh, wow," I couldn't help blurting out, "is this...art?"

My musing was interrupted. Gordon's phone went off, *again!* "One second, Sadeeq," said I.

I pulled my boyfriend aside while American-4-all checked his latest hate-praise.

I tried not to hiss, fearing the worst. "What is up with all the texts?"

He looked guilty and confessed. "It's Assauer saying he's going to find us, and a...and...."

"Take you back?"

"Yeah."

"I won't let that happen." I put a protective arm around my boy's shoulder. I was not going to let Gordon out of my sight again, and I had vowed most solemnly to myself that my ex should never get the chance to steal him away again.

Sadeeq strolled up to us. "Come on. That was the soapbox messenger. I'm up next."

A couple of minutes later we were back on the plaza watching the mad poet claimed the raised platform of the public podium as his own.

The crowd looked none too receptive, and several crunched the gravel beneath their feet like bulls with slow-simmering resentment.

"Friends, Lovers, Americans!" Sadeeq called out. "Don't lend me your ears, but your rationales. Let my verse sway your clouded minds back to clarity."

He cleared his throat.

> "Hector twiddles, while falls Troy,
> Nero strums, and feels joy
> While fires his Rome destroy.
>
> But what of us today?
> Will not one stand and say
> Our empire cracks while we look away?"

The assembly started to boo. Sadeeq only raised his voice:

> "Awake, fellow citizens!
> Fiddle not while politizians—"

The mind of the mob grew mental. Now openly hostile, many reached to pick up stones from near their feet. Sadeeq repeated himself:

> "Fiddle not while politizians
> Make you of your nation mortizians—"

They hissed loudly and pelted the poet. He stepped down from the front of the box and stumbled towards us, hands protecting his head.

I panicked and grabbed Gordon's hand to make a run for it, lest the rabble mistake us for poets too!

In a few jogged paces, Sadeeq Amergin caught up with us as we neared the compound gate. He laughed and said, "Well, what can you expect – this is Koolaidville after all!"

Chapter 23: "Ass Cream" – or the Divine Beauty Balm

"What issue?" Sadeeq Amergin asked through half-chewed shrimp toast.

The five of us – that is, me, Gordon, Bertram, Geoff and the madcap poet – stood in the ballroom of a former San Diego grand hotel, mid-event with the Beauty Cult people. This palace built to luxury was now Beauty Inc.'s Cooperate Headquarters, and Bertram had gotten us in, and he's also the one who'd just mentioned tonight was as good as any to track down help for my 'issue.'

I didn't want Amergin to know I was impotent, and Geoff Bath got it right away, sparkling as he changed the subject for his boyfriend.

"Did you get a load of that crazy sign outside?"

"I did. Isn't it spelled wrong?"

Bertram nodded. "Sure is, but that's the way they like it."

The topic was how the fifteen-story-high tower of this 1920's building was capped by massive red neon letters. Taking up several floors in height to do it, in Spanish they read: EL BELLEZO.

Geoff then chuckled. "So, Kohl, Burning Man was a blast, huh?"

I blushed towards the twenty-something with his light brown hair and devilishly good looks. "Oh, yeah – speaking of blast – sorry about burning Burning Man early."

"Yeah," Bertram agreed, holding Geoff tightly in his arms and towering over the younger man's buzzcut. "Folks were sad, and the festival was canceled."

"I didn't mean to. In fact, it was the nutso magicians really. They knocked me over."

The Black Hammer smiled and kissed his boyfriend's neck. 'Bergeoff-tram' made an adorable pairing; Bertram tall, dark and easygoing, and Geoff slight, white and a tad needy in the cutest of ways. They were in the thrall of young love, and Geoff's brown eyes looked up admiringly at Bertram.

"What happened? Kohl…what did you do?" My boy had shown plenty of the whites of his peepers as he asked this. My response was to grin and drape my arm over his shoulder – with the added intent of showing Sadeeq that Gordon was firmly taken.

"Long story, honey. Surface it to say, I made a mess of things and departed, posthaste."

"Oh," Gordon chuckled. "Just another *Wednesday* for you."

I kissed him. God, I loved my boy.

A loud crunch distracted us. The social media poet-prophet had taken an additional bite of his melba toast, while his hungry eyes feasted on my boyfriend.

"Anyway," Bertram said brightly, "Angekwekwa and Guy Germaine got their pawn ticket from me and were 'happy,' well as happy as any cult dolts can be."

"What did you pawn, Kohl?" Geoff asked.

"Some stupid old weathervane with a rooster on it."

"Anyway, they were glad to get it back."

"Thanks for doing it, Bertram. Oh, and speaking of Germaine, I got a text from his son, thanking me and saying Claude and his husband are getting lots of hoo-ha in Amish country. They're happy there, living the Ohio Dream."

"I'm glad," said The Hammer. "We all deserve our shot."

More lustful crunching sounded from the hungry bohemian.

"A shot?" Sadeeq said with crumbs spilling out of his mouth. "Hey, guys, there's an open bar here...?"

"Yes," Geoff said, pointing. "Go help yourself."

"Thaaaanksss." He whipped his ponytail at us and made for the liquor. I immediately mouthed to Bertram's boyfriend, "Thank you."

He said 'you're welcome' by flaring his eyebrows.

Now that I could breathe again, I glanced around the room. Light jazz played and the milling crowd was definitely camera-ready.

Skinny women wearing shift dresses mingled with linen-shirted guys. These bean-pole broads had a default standing position where lips pouted, hands rested on waists, and elbows thrust themselves forward. When they moved, it was either in catwalk heel-pounding, or a pair of mincing steps to place stilettos at uncomfortable angles. I don't know, I guess 'beauty' meant looking hobbled and knock-kneed...? But at such moments, their glazed stares locked on something impossibly far-away, and apparently not so very interesting to them.

The tall boys on the other hand – many with slickened blond tresses; others with wet-looking dark curls – stood around showing admiring blue sparkles in their eyes for one another. When they moved, it was with canted necks, hands stroking hair, and coy smiles peeking from beneath. Suddenly, they'd stop, toss heads up to strike catalog poses. These were meant to impress, but reminded me more of turkeys strutting the barnyard, puffing up to woo anything from a milk pail to a passing truck on the road.

Geoff minded how I glanced at the propped-up people, and added with a chuckle, "You've heard of the three *do's* of real estate. Location, location, location? Well, Beauty Inc. takes itself far more importantly, so they have twice as many pointers to remember. 'Body, yadi, yadi. Face, ace, ace.' Those are the six golden rules of modeling. And they get treated like holy scripture, believe you me!"

"He's so smart." Bertram beamed lovingly.

"But," I asked, "do they need an actual runway?"

Geoff smiled. "Just wait and see."

I looked again at the elevated catwalk, in front which, in the center, was a speaker's podium. It reminded me of how, when we came in, I noticed folding tables with 'product' and other glass cases displaying more precious items near the doors.

"Oh, there he is," Bertram said, gesturing with his head across the room.

Gordon asked, "Where who is?"

"Tyson McPherson, the Beauty Cult's leader."

Casually looking, I saw a tall dude with dark hair flashed with yellowy blond down near the roots. Even from across the room, this white-suit-wearing character looked like a cartoon version of an 'ex supermodel.' "Who's that with him?" I inquired, because a younger, shorter and throtty guy was fawning upon every gesticulated word the dear leader said.

Geoff said, "Wagner Dano, Tyson's common-law PA, and downlow boyfriend."

"Oh, yeah, but act like you don't know." Bertram winked.

"It's true," confirmed Geoff Bath. "You need to be circumspect, for although this place is as Gay as a *Barney's* basement sale in December, you just have to pretend all is het to the max with them."

"But why?" Gordon asked, looking adorable in the suit Doris gave me on Catalina.

Bertram said flatly, "Because they're homophobic."

"Oh...." A lightbulb flashed. "I think we were warned about them at Hojax's house. Remember?"

My boy shrugged. "Vaguely."

"Yeah." The Hammer's gaze panned the pretty fools suspiciously. "Be careful. This assembly is as hypocritical as the Gop caucus recruiting at church. And just like them, they're officially anti-queer."

"Officially?"

"Yes, Gordon," continued Bertram. "Never mind *all* the leadership of this cult is 'gay,' their gospel tells them that beautiful people should be miserable and mate with other beautiful people to make the Earth prettier, even if they have to bat for the wrong team."

We all laughed, then Geoff said rather seriously, scanning the crowd again. "But be careful of the not-so-pretty types in this room too. Beauty draws all manner of weirdos who glom on—"

He stopped, for in speak-of-the-devil fashion, a balding man in a thrift-store suit had suddenly joined us. He was stuffing his face with crab appetizers.

As we all stared at him, he eventually said, "What are we talking about?"

"The strange weather we've been having," I lied. "You are?"

He thrust an oily hand forward, his eyeglasses glinting with enthusiasm. "Sprag Dickson, editor of *Sceptical Non-Enquirer* magazine. Perhaps you've heard of it...?" He aped a grin. "Available on every supermarket checkout rack, right next to *Teen Zitz Blitz*...."

The four members of our group exchanged head-shaking glances.

"We're cutting edge," boasted Sprag. "Yeah. We shoot down all the mysteries of the world with easy-to-spell explanations, no matter how convoluted and laughable."

"Oh," I said, as the mag-man seemed to have eyes only for me. What I actually thought was, 'Wow, an honest editor. How rare is that?'

"Crab puff?" Dickson held out his napkin. The man was several inches shorter than me, and I had an unfortunate view of the greasy landscape of his dandruff-flecked comb-over. His lips were greasy too mouthing his appetizer, and the shaggy monkey-foot of a mustache attracted crumbs to it like lint to velcro.

"No, thanks – where are you going?" My posse peeps were stepping away.

"We're going to mingle, Kohl," said Geoff. "You stay and chat, and enjoy your crab poof."

'Gott im Himmel,' I thought. 'The moment some freak latches on, they head for the hills.'

"So you're name's Kohl, huh?" Sprag munched away contentedly.

I had to admit, despite my attempt to deprive it of oxygen, my jealousy flared a tiny bit. After so recent a reunion, I didn't want Gordon out of my grasp, let alone out of sight, but I trusted Bertram. He's a decent guy, and I'd asked him earlier to shield my boy from the mad clutches of the amorous Sadeeq.

"So, Kohl, are you a member of our little merry band?"

'You? – A beauty cult maven...?' I thought, but failed to ask the snively man.

"No, just visiting. I'm here with my friends, including my boyfriend."

"Oh, I see." Sprag smiled ambiguously – something closet cases are good at, I guess.

"So, you were mentioning the freak weather."

"Um—"

"Yes. In our magazine issues we have to deal with global warming debunking on a monthly basis. That one's getting harder and harder to confuse a distracted public about, what with the world literally on fire and all."

"What do you mean?"

"I mean, that's what we do. Our informal motto – one we borrowed from the NSA, our official black-budget sponsors – says 'RIP truth. Long live opinion!'"

He led the way, and we slowly walked to view the display cases and tables.

"But it's not only in print that we work to curtail people's common sense via the lever of 'beliefs.'"

"No...?" I had no idea what he was going on about, because my eyes were busy scanning the room....

"Since you're 'one of them,' I'll let you in on a little secret. Per our mandate, we have a team of sceptical non-enquirers daily scrubbing The Net of queer content."

That got my attention. "What do you mean?"

"I mean – take Wikipedia for example, because it's the easiest. Anyone can edit the articles there, and *we* do. What's more, the site lets us become draconian 'owners' of the content and veto any alterations we deem as vandalism. Like saying so-and-so was Gay. Hell, even though it was cool for Cher to play Karen Silkwood's real-life partner 1983, you go to Wiki nowadays and there will be no mention that Silkwood was Gay, *or* happily married to a woman. The truth is scrubbed clean." He grinned a shrimpy smile.

"You can do that?"

"We do it every day, young man. We decide content, so if you went on there right now looking for information on the totally out, same-sex-loving, great poets of the world – Sappho, Rumi; Cavafy; Whitman; Tennyson; shit, Shakespeare himself! – you'll find no mention of their true orientations or beloveds. Same with painters – Francis Bacon, Caravaggio, Michelangelo, Leonardo da Vinci, John Singer Sargent." He puffed up with pride. "But our biggest achievement is with Plato's *Symposium*. Look it up, you'll see a reversal of twenty-five centuries of common knowledge that the book is an exploration of all the shades of Gay love, because now on the internet, it's about 'relationships between men and women.' And try it yourself. Go in there and say the obvious – that it's about same-sex love – and you'll be slapped with a warning for 'vandalizing' the entry. Try it, cuz it's our private property, no matter what Wiki says about public content."

I felt sick to my stomach. "Why the hell are you doing that?"

"Money, my boy. The far-right has tons of it, ergo they swipe up content contrary to their 'beliefs,' and there's nothing they hate more than out people. Simple as that."

"RIP truth. Long live privately funded opinion!"

"Precisely." He smiled and cheered me with his wine glass. "But our main mission, per Vaterland Security – um, Homeland Security – is to spread doubt among the masses concerning paranormal matters at the magazine. Few people actually buy it, but the hype pays back our sponsors. And we make up stuff so blatantly untrue, sometimes I wonder, but people today…. It's all part of the War on Facts not many people realize is being waged. Take for example – have you heard of SHC, or Spontaneous Human Combustion?"

"Where people suddenly catch fire from the inside?"

"Yes. Well, we did an air-quotes *experiment* with a lit cigarette, a pig carcass, and some gasoline, but that last ingredient was officially off-record. Anyway, even though we were only able to reproduce 5-10% of the well-documented conditions reported with SHC, we declared our results 'science' and a total explanation of the actually very unexplained phenomenon."

"Um—"

"Peace of mind. People don't want answers to complex questions, only peace of mind that such questions don't matter to their everyday lives."

"Oh." I think I got it. "A case-closed kind of reassurance?"

"Precisely! We did the same with the Loch Ness Monster, inventing a made-up toy submarine 'debunker' tall-tale, even though we knew the famous Dr. Robert Wilson photo was cropped, and actually shows both the near and far shore of the loch."

"Um.... I don't get it."

"It's easy. Since the unaltered picture actually shows the full width of the lake, any five-minute, genuinely scientific analysis of our invented claptrap of a submarine would reveal the 'toy' had to be twelve to fifteen feet high! Nervous as we were that we'd be shut down for going too far, just the opposite happened. Thanks to our 'fake science,' the perfectly good reputation of a dead man – the best kind, because they can't defend themselves – was smeared like roadkill, and now the public believes this real photo is 'phony.' As I said, it's some of our best work to date, because our so-called debunking can be shot down in like this." He snapped his fingers.

"Wow, and you're proud...?"

"Wouldn't you be? It used to be hard to disgrace reality, but thanks to our huge Pentagon budget, and a slow *drip-drip* eroding of common sense, we mangle it every day now. See, we can do it only by tying into peoples' deep fears of the unknown. All of us have a natural comfort level with nonbelief. It's the messy truth that wakes us up from our dream of 'superiority' in a cold sweat. Faith in non-belief, distrust in institutions, hate of the media, doctors – anyone smarter than us – is the tempest in a teapot that put the Great Unknowing one in the oval office. Only thing kept him there too. That and cowardice, but I digress. What I really mean to say is simple: The so-called truth belongs to he who gets there last."

Continuing to stroll, I considered why this strange little man was so open and honest with me. I quickly surmised he was a classic bore, or a windbag who'd dole out his life-accomplishments to any and all drifting within his orbit. However, maybe in Sprag's case more was at play; a something akin to Bertram's penitents seeking to get caught and exposed in their evil machinations. It could have been this rag-mag editor was not looking for flesh to propitiate his soul's transgresses like the others, but to simply get exposed as a charlatan, so that with a relieved sigh, he could move on to other pursuits.

Thinking all this tied my stomach in knots, and a glance around the room did my gut no favors, showing me the mad poet had rejoined our group to stand right next to my boy.

"Look at these," Dickson said. We had arrived at a table full of gleaming, brand-new cosmetics bottles. The man joyfully picked one up. "My personal go-to"—he read from the container to me—"*The Crows Feet Eradicator is the best in the Industry. Guaranteed to pack them right up!*"

"What is all this anyway?"

It looked like I had shocked the professional skeptic. "Why, the *Simply*

Divine Beauty Line, of course. All rank and file cult members are required to spend at least 45% of their modeling money on Tyson's products to sell door to door. It grows his fame, and spreads his brand."

"You too?"

"Me what?" Sprag asked.

"You have to buy it yourself and sell it on for a profit?"

"No, no, young man. I'm management."

'Ah,' I thought. 'Even worse.'

"Don't worry…" he misread my mood. "You'll have plenty of opportunity to stock up after the ceremony."

"Oh. Good. What a relief." I smiled weakly.

We continued on to the glass cases. A few ancient looking artifacts were carefully laid out on black velvet, like a 70s porno shooting.

"What is this stuff?"

"Ah, Mr. McPherson is a collector of ancient beauty aids." He gestured left to right. "That's a Medieval tube of Viking eyeliner. Those are a few of Attila the Hun's hair curlers. And lastly, we see Rameses II's loincloth stuffers."

"Loin. Cloth—"

"Pharaoh's bobbysocks, to boost the size of the royal package. As they say, it's good to be the king, but better to look like you've got balls for the job."

I was speechless.

A sudden burst of laughter made me realize how close we'd moved to the cult leader and boyfriend/slash personal assistant.

"Have you met Tyson – and his, um – Wagner Dano?"

"No, I haven't."

"Well, I'll introduce you, but be warned. Dano can be a bit swishy, but he *is* heir apparent to the cult and cosmological-cosmetics empire."

As we walked, I asked in a low voice, "How did they meet?"

"Photoshoot. Seems Wagner is a former, semi-pro *Sears Wish Book* catalog model, plumbing section."

He walked us right up to the big shots.

"Ah, Sprag," former supermodel Tyson said none-too affectionately. "Who do you have here?" His interest picked up.

"This is a visitor to our proceedings."

"Kohl?" asked the cult leader's PA.

I grinned. "That's me."

Tyson extended a clammy hand. "Oh, yes. My peer – Bertram Hammerick – informed me of your, um, difficulty."

I glanced nervously at the truth-disputing mag slinger. I didn't want to mention Priapus in his presence.

"Oh, oh," Sprag chirped in the cult leader's direction. "I have to tell you how we infiltrated *Stars* this week, the trashy tabloid, and slipped in a totally fake segment about Rock Hudson sleeping his way to the top in Hollywood – with women! Calling him a, quote-unquote, 'hunky bisexual.' Oh, we busted a gut in the office when we read that in print. Someday we are going to go too far, but as long as people don't want to believe in the truth—"

"Thanks, Dickson," beeped the assistant with attitude to spare, "but you're free...to...mingle."

With that dismissal, Sprag disappeared back into the beautiful crowd, like a troll to his under-water hiding place. I suddenly noticed Geoff and Bertram in one corner, cuddling. Panicking, I sought for and discovered my boy's ear was getting chewed off by the hungry poet.

"I'm Tyson McPherson, by the way, but you probably already recognized me – I'm sure." The cult leader had charming, nearly hypnotic Southern sweetness to his voice.

"Yes," I fibbed. "Supermodel."

My smiling lie must have appealed, because these two instantly became 'interested,' or Setting No. 2 on most of your standard Gaydar screens, lol.

"And this is my assistant, Wagner Dano."

The leader's not-so-closet boyfriend presented the back of his hand, hinged loose on a limp wrist. It seems he expected me to kiss it. I lifted it up once or twice and shook it instead. "Nice to meet you."

The assistant was mid-thirties, a bit on the wiry side, with dark close-cropped hair and coal-black eyes.

"Everybody knows Tyson," he lisped. "That's why I call him *McFearsome!*"

I smiled; that was kind of cute.

Tyson in contrast to his partner was about fifty, tall and commanding. This last feature was one not even the bleach-bottle nature of his hairdo could mask. His steely gray eyes burned with cultish intensity.

"Bertram already informed us, as I was saying," continued Tyson, "and me and Wagner will be glad to help you out, later, after the ritual."

His wink threw me for a second, but a more pressing question emerged. "Actually, I wanted to ask you about...another...group. Ritual? What ritual?"

"Yes. These little cocktail parties are rouses. Soon, well, you'll see."

His downlow lover nodded vehemently. If he were a snake, he would have flicked his tongue at me deliciously.

With charismatic flair, Tyson McPherson placed his arm on my shoulder and asked like a father confessor, "Tell me, young man, what are your thoughts on beauty?"

"Um—"

"Do you have faith in beauty, and believe the beautiful among us – yourself included – are naturally endowed by our creator to lead the ugly masses?"

"I can't say I really thought about it before."

The intensity of his steely gaze burned into me. "We believe the Divine Esthetician created all that's good and fierce in the world, and it's our job to put the good looking in control of the world's fate."

I nodded, like a dope, muttering, "Yes—"

The cult leader grabbed ahold of my chin, positioning me to the light as Tyson inspected. "My boy, you have prophetic bone structure. You could go far in our Church."

"Yeah, yeah," cheeped Dano. "And sell our *Simply Divine Beauty Line* of pharmapseudocological religious items for God! Tax-free religious exemption on all the profits, naturally."

"Yes – it all goes to the Church, the money that is, just so you understand. But you keep your soul, and eventually that goes up to the great beauty parlor in the sky."

"Um—" I felt I was getting into the weeds.

"But, Tyson! He'd have to study his catechism, *and* learn how to walk."

"I know how to walk," I protested mildly.

"Walk, my boy – *walk* like a runway model. Wagner, sweetie, um, buddy – show him how it's done."

With that, his 'sweet' personal assistant swept himself along, kicking shoulders and rigid arms back and forth to the clear floor before us.

All eyes turned to Dano as he paused, whipped around with a coin-purse smirk, and punished the floor tiles as he walked back to us.

Tyson mystically whispered in my ear, "The higher the strut, the closer to God."

Not thinking of that at all, I glanced around the room and felt my heart pound. Sadeeq was leaning an elbow on my boy's shoulder and getting much, much too close for comfort.

There was a sudden noise.

"Places, y'all!" Tyson clapped his hands. Before he strutted away, he intoned quietly, "Time for the ritual."

The models gathered closely and locked me into position near the center of the elevated runway. I looked around and saw Gordon with the mad poet to my right about a dozen people down the line.

In the commotion, I failed to notice a substantial number of the cult members had taken up flanking positions on either side of the podium, forming a sort of choir. To my astonishment, Tyson, Wagner and Sprag Dickson walked to the center of the catwalk and stood there. The rag-mag deceiver turned to the chorus and raised his hands.

The lights dimmed. A moment later, a solemn sound erupted – they sang an unusual doxology in canonic fashion.

> *"O! Death, where is thy sting;*
> *Grave, ya think ya got anything?"*

The catalog, internet and fashion models all around me bowed their heads as the choir proceeded to sing the most frivolous pop-song lyrics in Sunday-school seriousness. It started with a Sprag solo:

> *"The old adage has it,*

> *That if you want to keep "IT,"*
> *You suck in a deep breath –*
> *Leavin' unsightliness bereft –*
> *And say, "Oh, my Dear Lord,*
> *Let fall Thy beauteous sword*
> *To ginsu my wrinkles*
> *In your robe's holy crinkles."*

The full chorus joined in, raising holy voices for an unholy subject:

> *"Behold! God loves the beautiful*
> *Who help themselves to the makeup puff;*
> *Who do weight-training dutiful*
> *To beef them up like the Angels buff!*

> *"Because! God loves the cosmetics*
> *Able to banish every blemish;*
> *Able to cover genetics*
> *With hair dye blondish,*
> *Which grants every wish!"*

As Sprag returned to another solo moment – graver than ever – the crowd around us began to part. A weird procession had started and made its way slowly to the catwalk where Tyson and Co. were waiting.

> *"And He loves the silicone surgeon*
> *In-filling the Lord's holy mission*
> *To turn sow-ear and face of sturgeon*
> *To the light of God's great omniscien."*

Sexy, near-naked dudes – supermodels in Halston-cum-Roman-centurion costumes – bore a canopied litter on their shoulders. I thought some grand cult object must be on it, but when it drew near, I had a perfect view inside as the studs set it on the floor below Tyson's feet.

> *"...Always flaunt your stuff,*
> *With stuffing-socks*
> *Or powdered puff...."*

The holy relic rested on a gold lamé cushion, but it was anything but attractive. An old tin canister, it appeared about the size of a woman's palm, and was beat up and tarnished. In other words, it appeared to be something even a charity shop would toss on the garbage heap.

The choir picked up the mag-man's tone, singing in *Row, Row Your Boat* polyphony:

> *"Beware! We all suffer alone*
> *In an ugly cling, when the Lord can bring*

A gorgeous man to call your own –

"God loves the dutiful,
Who make the world more beautiful!"

When they calmed down, Sprag ascended over them with a faith-affirming:

"O! Death, where is Thy sting,
Once ya stick 'im for a diamond ring!

And then it all ended in *soto voce* quietude as Mr. Rag-Mag took care of some of the small print:

"Words and music by
Tyson McPherson and Wagner Dano.
All rights reserved...
Ahhh-Men...!"

In the silence following the music, Tyson addressed his congregants in a commanding voice, "Now, let us reaffirm our creed." He led off with "I believe," and the choir hummed as the head-bowed assembled recited in a Gregorian-type credo:

"...In the Holy Church
Of the Divine Esthetician,
Founded on Earth to beautify
The most ugly heart of mankind....
I believe in Godly cheek bones,
Divinely high with His blessings,
And that high-hoofing it along
The sacral catwalk can bring me
Closer to Supreme loveliness....
I believe in natural beauty,
And of being reborn again
At the hands of His holy priests –
The plastic surgeons – trimming here;
Plumping there, in the name of God....
I believe in brand loyalty,
And in trickle-up franchising
Pyramid schemes for the leaders,
Plus all the sacred dividends
That may flow up towards heaven....
I believe Tyson McPherson
Is undeniably gorgeous,
And for sure, he's *the* chosen one
To lead us closer to Beauty....

I believe the Divine Esthetician
Plopped down to Earth from some space war
Seventy thousand years ago
And then established his home base
In a volcano where he ran
A beauty college to instruct
The chosen how to beautify –
And zhuzh – Man one face at a time...."

The religious ~~bullshit~~ fervor was getting a bit thick in the room, aided by the background chorus, who had grown louder. Now, as if forming the soundtrack for an old Hollywood climax, they started a sunrise-worthy crescendo of *AH's*.

"I harbor faith we might someday join Him,
On his planet, Electrolysisacon,
Where all is lovely, and reigns The Gorgeous
For ever and ever swell, without end...."

Their equivalent to Amen was a cultishly chanted: "Beauty...!"

I managed not to laugh, but glancing at Gordon was dangerous, as I knew my boy would burst out at the slightest provocation.

The study fellows picked up the litter and held it so Tyson could reach for the ugly old can. Once he took it, they proceeded out of the room.

"My followers," Tyson announced, "it is now time for the sacred anointing of the cream."

Dano took the cannikin like it was made of radioactive glass, and his cult leader boyfriend-slash-boss removed the lid. A white salve with two distinct fingermarks came into view.

And then – the odor hit me. Consider what rancid goat yogurt would be like, say, stored for a couple of years in a yak carcass.... That pretty well covered it.

Tyson retched slightly, but said to the faithful, "This two-thousand-year-old face cream, recovered from the bottom of a London well, is made of pure ass' milk, and crafted"—he needed a moment to choke down his gag reflex—"and crafted by the hands of the Supreme Cosmetologist himself."

Everyone in the audience stood taller, at rapped attention, knowing the climax was about to happen. Tyson dipped a quivering finger in the ointment and dabbed some under his own puffy eyes, which immediately began to water – due to the 'Divine Stench,' no doubt. [24]

That was it for me. I moved behind the front row of people to Gordon. I tugged on his arm, and the two of us discreetly made for the exit.

I wondered how skeptical non-belief failed to work on any of these people, but then again, if it didn't work on the voting electorate, why would it on a chamber full of cult stooges?

We slipped out of the room unnoticed just as Tyson was calling for

"The Holy Catwalk" portion of the ritual to begin. I realized my Gordon was right, as always. It was far better to look for the garden-center crazies directly. They're the ones who behexed my member; they're the ones who could un-hex it again. As for Tyson McFearsome and his batch of beauty peddling androids, I didn't want his precious ass cream anywhere near my...my, Benedict Arnold.

I must be maturing. I could have devised a suitable 'punishment' for these dopes like the one I gave the dummy-fisting zanes, but why bother? Live and let be nuts, as my boy would say. I had more important priorities to focus on, and with Gordon by my side, I found it much easier to be 'good.'

A couple of hours ago, we walked in thinking they might be able to help, but walked away again understanding there was a difference between *Cult Incorporated* groups – and their moneymaking, made-up 'theology' – and the ones based on actual living polytheistic tradition, like the Abraca and Priapus folks. Don't get me wrong, because that doesn't mean the cock god and donkey schlong set aren't bat-shit crazy too, cuz they are, but just like modern political 'believers,' some are duped out of their minds, while others are bamboozled out of both cash *and* their powers of reason.

Chapter 24: The Lamp-Stick Battle

Ironically enough, these were the kind of accommodations my ex would seek out as retro-cool – the El Cortez Motel. Rat-pack chic he'd call it, with its perfect 1950s nicotine-stained panache, right down to the vertical neon fins on the saloon windows.

Oh, yes, I should mention its most non-conformist feature was having a biker bar attached to the front office. And the patrons' "choppers" and "hogs" – or *mincers* and *pigs*, whatever is the right term, lol – lined up in the motel's central parking court like dominos.

As for the clients' private quarters, the walls were white, while the pictures of fruit or flowers looked out from dusty velvet. Furniture was minimalistic in style, with abrupt corners and angles. On the countertops resided some peculiar table lamps reaching their shades for the stars. Why people back then liked three-foot-high lighting fixtures, I shall never know.

I had just barely turned on the lights and closed the door to our second-floor room, when Gordon pushed me against it. We made out, blissfully unaware of anything else. We must have been attractive to look at too, as we were still in our cocktail attire.

Knock. Knock.

The bellow rang in my ears. Eyes opened, lips separated, we froze.

Knock!

Me and my boy ducked down to the floor. But when I scrambled my arm up the wall to the switch, Gordon whispered, "That's dumb. The people will see the light go off and know we're here!"

I was about to argue the point with him when my phone vibrated with a text. "Hi, guys. It's Sadeeq, outside your motel room door. Whatcha up to?"

I gave my boy the hush-finger and let him read the message.

We bunkered down and said nothing.

Knock. Knock. Knock, knock, knock, knock, knock…. Knock…knock.

At last they trailed off into parting silence.

After a few minutes of quiet, I gingerly made my way to the window. I parted the blinds and saw no one. Just as I was about to give the 'all clear' signal, my boyfriend got a text.

I watched his face implode with shock. "Oh, shit!"

"What?"

He chirped hoarsely, "Pizza's here."

I peeked out the blinds again and spotted the delivery man coming up the open steps.

Shrugging at Gordon, I opened the door.

Sadeeq Amergin strolled in, saying, "Hi, guys. What kinda peeza-pie we get? I can't eat mushrooms, by the way."

The mad poet stretched out on one of the two beds just as the delivery man arrived. Gordon paid him, and I noticed Sadeeq crack open a small bottle of ghetto hooch – Cisco – koolaid-flavored and deadly strong.

Gordon walked over with the food, and Sadeeq leapt to his feet. "Wanna drink? I'm gonna have one."

He didn't wait for a reply, just started plopping old, half-melted ice from the motel-room bucket into plastic cups. While the syrupy, candy-red liquor slurped in after, he chatted merrily as if to himself. "Funny about that rough and tumble leather bar being attached to the motel. I bet it used to be a typical greasy spoon, like motel guests expect for coffee and eggs, but just like everything in Trump's America, there's more money to be made in sin than sustenance."

He handed out the cups. "Careful. It ain't no wine cooler, and assuming you like cocktails of cough syrup and rubbing alcohol, you'll find the initial taste surprisingly easy to swallow. After that, watch out! They don't call it paranoid-punch, reason-acid or liquid-meth for nothing."

Sadeeq laughed up a storm at his own witticism, and then took out the desk chair to sit. With a sweep of his ponytail, he helped himself to his own cup and a slice of 'peeza-pie.'

"That cocktail party was a bust tonight," he said with greasy lips. "You guys bounced at just the right time. After that it was all struttin' and posin' like their vacant stares off into the ether was some form of speaking in tongues."

While he blathered, I morosely sat on a bed and took my first sip. It wasn't bad, but after I swallowed, I saw Sadeeq slipping lust-filled eyes on my Gordon over the rim of his plastic cup. I fortified myself by draining my drink, despite my boy's warning glare. I just wished the noisome poet would spill down the plughole too.

Gordon took a slice of food, and as he chewed, the poet resumed his chatty ways.

"That Beauty Cult is too much, and *I* know about mixed up religions, let me tell you! I'm half Palestinian and half Irish, so I got faithful 'drama' and pageantry up two ends as a kid."

I could see those ethnic traits in the man, especially in the broad brown eyes but narrow and pale cheekbones. Although the man's scruffy hair was not a common attribute to either cultural group as far as I knew, lol.

"Speaking of drama," the poet continued, "you should have witnessed the brouhaha at my gym this afternoon. Wildfire-gossip spread about this big-dicked guy and his L.A. cop boyfriend scouring dives all around town. Apparently, they're hot on the trail of a runaway teenage boy and the pedo-perv who kidnapped him."

"Big dick…?" I asked, fearing the worst.

"Yeah, guys in the shower said he's a real tripod of a man, if you know what I mean."

I glanced at my boy. He didn't seem too concerned, but I stiffened with a nasty suspicion. Could Gordon have texted Assauer our location...?

"It always pays," continued the poet blithely, "for a person to be more developed in brawn than brains. No one nowadays listens to their betters, and that's because they're too busy talking about their own half-baked theories. But on the other hand, for all who drop pants, the ears open up, the tongues stop wagging and start slobbering. For years I've said if Progressives political hacks want to start getting their message heard: striptease press briefings. Easy; done."

Although fuming, I dared not say a word in front of Amergin. I held out my cup, and the poet refilled it. This stuff was making me warm from the chest outwards.

Sadeeq looked confused. "What was I talking about...? Oh, yeah – Mr. Big-Dick. As I was saying, this guy was so big, he just reminded me of a poem I once knew, by somebody or other, who was famous at one point. I think it goes:

> "For nature had so
> Qualified him for a lover,
> His body seemed but the skirt
> Of the mighty member it bore." [25]

After he poured himself a top-off, the poet added, "Yeah, and his cop boyfriend, who's some kind of higher-up on the force, is even offering a thousand-dollar reward. Man, oh, man"—he shook his head—"I sure could use a cool grand, lemme tell ya."

Me and Gordon played dumb, and I finally took a pizza slice for myself.

Sadeeq went on. "This is pretty good pie, but I bet most of the hoity-toity, basic-bitch conformists of our society would never know it. They never appreciate what they can come by easily. Those folks – with more moola than sense – must be told by tastemakers what's trendy. Celebrity mushed-cauliflower pizza crust with mung bean sprouts growing on top, anyone...? YUK. Give me good old-fashioned American peeza, swimming in pepperoni grease, and loaded with so many ingredients they slide off when you go in for the first bite. You know what I mean? Those Yelping online restaurant gurus, for example, wouldn't know good unpretentious food if it barked 'em, because they never grew up eating honest-to-goodness grub. It's a shame really, but it's our current social condition: we never read, write, watch, enjoy or eat anything wholesome anymore. We're like sick people, only craving that which is bound to make us sicker."

When me and Gordon merely chewed on in brooding silence, Sadeeq held up his cup. "I offer a toast. As William Burnaby, the great poet, put it:

> "Once enjoyed,
> We straight to a new desire,
> For the absent pleasure's
> The only one we admire." [26]

I gave my boy a rancorously sidelong glance and mumbled, "That sounds familiar."

I drank – in fact, drained my cup – watching Gordon become upset. Anger flushed the side of his neck.

Sharply turning to Sadeeq, I said, "Poet, spare us. We've heard it all before. And what do you think those bikers in the bar would do to us if they knew we harbored a poet in our midst?!" I chuckled bitterly. "Just think of it...even the art community stoned you at the commune. Imagine what a regular crowd would do to your type."

"I'm not afraid of the mob mentality. I have to navigate it every day."

Gordon defended Sadeeq. "We're all entitled to our opinions, Kohl. And we all deserve the elbow-room to express ourselves without others saying 'spare me.'"

I felt my jaw go slack, barely registering how the poet's desires for my boy had kicked into high gear.

"Oh, Gordon!" Sadeeq schmoozed. "What a treasure of a young man you are. So handsomely endowed with both brains and looks, and a heart o'gold to boot. You must be such a real blessing to your mother."

"He is," I scoffed. "But not only to her. In fact, you might say he's something of a public-access treasure."

Gordon had had enough. He stood up, grabbed the vinyl-upholstered bucket by its clear plastic handle, and clipped shortly, "I'm getting ice."

Once he'd cleared off, slamming the door behind him in fact, I got in a huff, jumping to my feet. "You're dense as a board, despite your poetic sensibilities." I started shouting. "Can't you see we just want to be alone?! Now, scram; be-gone; vamoose; get out!"

Pounding sounded on the wall from the room next door, accompanied by a muffled-but-angry voice yelling "Shut the fuck up!"

"Well?" I asked Sadeeq at the top of my lungs. "You going to leave, or am I going to have to throw you out?!"

More pounding arose from the wall.

Sadeeq narrowed his eyes and stood. "There's something suspicious about you two, isn't there...? Say, how old is that kid, exactly?"

I was relieved I could tell him the truth. "Eighteen. Now, clear out." I went to the door, opened it and waited impatiently.

Sadeeq wavered for a second, appearing sad and misunderstood, then he grabbed his Cisco hooch and stalked towards me. In the doorway, he paused. "I thought...."

"You thought what?!"

"Oh, never mind. I guess I was wrong about you. See ya."

The mad poet exited, and I slammed the door gleefully after him. The guy next door repeated his wall-banging and profane threats, this time adding something about calling the cops, but I thought 'Who cares!'

I paced a circuit around the room, fuming, thinking everybody judges me. 'Why can't they leave us the fuck alone? What'd I ever do to anyone? What'd…we—'

I stopped cold in my tracks, realizing my boyfriend should have been back by now.

Outside, the chill night air and the lights from the open parking lot below assailed my sweaty brow and eyes. I got to the opening of the ice room.

Sadeeq was pushing Gordon against the back wall, snogging the teenager passionately, the ice bucket still in the boy's hand.

"What. The. Fuck!"

"Hey now…" Sadeeq tried to slip sideways along the front of the ice machine with a slick grin. "The kid was giving me signals—"

"No, I wasn't!" shouted Gordon.

"You can't blame a guy," the poet finished, pausing to make a run past me for the exit.

He bolted and I easily latched onto his sleeve, shouting, "You slime! This is how you act?!"

Sadeeq broke free, walking backwards along the balcony in a defensive posture. His bottle of Cisco sloshed out blood-colored goo as he went.

"As I say, he was—"

"Giving signals, my ass!"

Lights came on in the room windows as we passed.

"Kohl," Gordon cried from behind me. "Keep your voice down."

That slight distraction emboldened the poet, and as Sadeeq got to the pool of light coming from our open room door, he tried to dash inside. No doubt he had plans of locking us out, but I got there just in time and pushed the maniac back into the room.

The door slammed open against the wall, and the walkway began to fill with people coming out to see the fight.

Gordon came in behind us. My anger turned on him. "You're a slut, just like your mother warned me!"

"It's your fucking jealousy!" my boy yelled back. He jabbed a dismissive finger in Sadeeq's direction. "How can you think I'd ever be with a *poet* like that?!"

Sadeeq mumbled, "Poets get no respect." His blasé tone made me look and see he sat at the desk, casually typing out a text message.

Gordon sobbed. Big tears formed under my boy's beautiful eyes. "Your tweets nearly broke my heart in two…you're the only bard I'd ever…I've ever…. Goddam it, Kohl – I tried to kill myself when I was Assauer. How can you now try and hurt me like this?"

I regretted my words of accusation, but I still had one nagging doubt. "Baby, tell me – did you or didn't you tell my ex where we were?"

"Yes, but don't worry! He was texting me a hundred times a day, so I said leave me alone. I'm safe in San Diego with friends and not to worry. I didn't say anything about you or where we're staying. I swear it!"

His reassurances hardly settled my mind.

I suddenly became aware of all the faces peering through our door when a big, hairy-chested man in monogrammed El Cortez Motel bathrobe and slippers pushed them aside.

"What in the Sam-Hell-Houston is going on in here!"

It was the sweaty, unshaven front desk manager.

"Nothing, sir," I said.

Frank squinted, surveying our faces one by one with penetrative hostility. Then his vision alighted on the half-eaten pizza and its greasy box on his floral bedspread. "So, what are you guys anyway? Drug addicts...runaways – both?!"

Surprisingly, it was Sadeeq who got all upset. He pushed past me so he could be the closest to Frank and his perspiring scowls.

"Back off, buddy," the manager warned the poet. By now he was at the corner of the desk himself.

Sadeeq puffed up. "You have no right to suppress folks you look down on just because they are down and out, you...you, Republican pollster you!"

Frank slapped him. "Don't you call me that!"

The crowd outside our door gasped at the severity of the poet's insult. They watched as Sadeeq, no doubt still stinging mad, grabbed one of the tall, ugly table lamps and ripped the pug out of the wall.

"You're trying to oppress me!" said Sadeeq. "Don't come any closer—"

"Or what?" taunted the manager, picking up the empty plastic water pitcher from the counter.

"Or this!" The mad poet choked up his grip on the wooden lamp and took a swing.

The manager ducked, holding up the pitcher as his shield. Then Frank turned on his heels and bolted out the door.

People screamed and stepped aside as Sadeeq pursued the manager down the walkway, swinging wildly. His hysterical shouts echoed around the verandas. "Poets get no fucking respect!"

Me and Gordon scrambled out to the balcony just in time to see the poet catch up with the manager on the steps. I told my boy, "The crazy poet has had too many dips in the paranoid punch."

Gordon gave me a funny look.

"What...?" I asked, while he said nothing in reply.

Looking back to the action, we saw Frank turn and expertly land an uppercut with his plastic pitcher, connecting just above Amergin's eye, and opening a gash there. Touching the blood from his own poetic body, Sadeeq let out a barbaric yawp.

As they continued downstairs, the enraged poet repaid the wound by viciously beating the man about the head with the silk-shade end of the lamp. The cord flew wildly like a whip to strike Sadeeq's arms and chest.

The manager stumbled out onto the pavement of the motor court, shielding his head with both arms and yelling "Help!" He was chased around the parked cars and motorcycles for a few minutes before going almost to the center of the lot, tossing his pitcher aside, and standing his ground. Frank assumed a proper boxing stance and put up his dukes.

By then the patrons and kitchen staff of the leather bar had poured out to stand around to watch the brawl. Shouts arose from the drunk biker dudes and their chicks: some for the punch-tossing man in the robe, others for the lamp-wielding 'artiste.'

A Rottweiler being walked by an insomniac old woman dragged her from the street into the court to join the melee. His angry barks at Man's madness sorely strained the blue-hair's ability to hold the choke collar. Finally, he was able to tear into Sadeeq's trouser leg like a ragdoll, and the bikers started scuffling. I guess they had some old cornbeefs to settle amongst their drunken selves.

The Vietnamese dishwashers, in their greasy white aprons, hauled out pans of cold water, which they gleefully dumped on Frank instead of the mad dog; the motel manager was liked by none.

But the water did manage to scare the dog back to sanity, and the lady quickly exited them the way they'd come.

In another moment, the motel owner emerged from the door of his ground-level home. He was an intimidating sight – paunchy, wearing a wife-beater tank top, holding a lit stogie and looking like an extra from a TV Mob show. He stepped right between the two principal scufflers, but had enough menace of presence to halt all the fighting.

"What in the name of sweet Baby Jesus is goin' on here?!"

Both adversaries shouted: "He started it!"

"What are you," said the owner against Sadeeq, "an addict or a runaway – or both?"

This upset Sadeeq all over again. He shouted, "Nobody appreciates poetry anymore, goddamn it!"

He took the cigar out of his mouth. "Are you a poet?"

"Yes." Sadeeq straightened up his composure. "Online I go by the name of the American-4-All."

"Sadeeq Amergin? The Tweeter, YouTube performer, social media celeb poet?!"

"Why.... Why, yes. You've heard of me?"

"Oh, shit yeah! I've heard you've got a wicked tongue." The motel owner suddenly got friendly, draping his arm across the back of Sadeeq's shoulders, and telling the manager, "Hit the showers, Frank. I got this."

Frank skulked off, gathering the open flaps of his robe and shucked slippers with as much dignity as he could muster.

The owner told the poet, "I've heard about you because my two-timing *goomah* is gone all artsy-fartsy on me. See, this girlfriend of mine keeps bitching at me about leaving my wife and whatnot, so I want you to tear her to pieces in a couple of rhymes. You know, bust her balls, and maybe then she'll learn her lesson on how to be nice to me. Ehhh?"

Sadeeq looked so crestfallen, me and Gordon busted up, big time. This two-bit poetaster was tasting the kind of attention his 'talents' deserved.

Just then we saw the bikers and motel patrons scatter like locusts. Flashing red lights and two patrol cars pulled into the motor court.

My boy and me ducked down to watch from behind the handrailing. *"Scheisse!"* I exclaimed, for out of one of the cop trolleys popped Assauer and Nasser – that uniformed higher-up from Tre-Princely Knight's dinner party. I guess my ex had tricked and slept with him, and then stayed in touch.

"Which one of you's Sadeeq?" Assauer asked.

"That dirty rat poet…" I muttered. But we heard no more of the conversation down below, because I grabbed him, and me and Gordon ran into our room. The boy locked the door.

"Hide!" I said.

"Where?!" he said.

We looked around. The closet was no good. Both beds were still made and draped with ugly 1980s black and flower bedspreads going all the way to the floor. One bed shoved was shoved in the corner, and I went and lifted the skirt. "Under here!"

"No, no! They'll look under—"

"Then…" I lifted the top mattress. The dusty box frame was below. "Lay flat as you can, face down, and don't make a sound or move a muscle."

He did, and I let the mattress fall on top of his grunting body, arranging the bed skirt to be in perfect order again. Then I thought better of the slight lump running down the center and quickly rumpled sheets, pillows and bedspread to hide my boyfriend's form in disarray.

Just then, loud banging sounded. "POLICE!" and the manager opened the door with his key.

Two San Diego cops stormed in and immediately began searching. Sure enough, the first place they looked was under the beds using their flashlights to penetrate every nook and dust bunny.

Assauer strode in next with a sneer on his face. The crowd was back on the walkway, gaping like guppies to see the goings on.

Inspiration struck and I immediately fell to my knees at the feet of my ex. I pleaded, "Please, please, just let me see my Gordon one more time!" This was shouted at enough volume for my audience to hear it loud and clear.

"What the fuck you talking about, *idiot?! Bösewicht!*"

"Is this the way it ends…?" I murmured, digging in.

He reached in anger and pried my fingers from his shins.

I shellacked my tone with misery. "I haven't seen him since he abandoned me to shack up with you – cuz your dick is so freakishly large all of a sudden."

This made Assauer gulp and turn sheepishly to the crowd, who started busting up and passing the intel along the motel grapevine.

"I don't know what game you're playin', Kohl—"

"No games, sir. Just let me see my boy one last time before I kill myself." I gripped his thighs this time, feeling his priapic donkey kong for myself.

"Just tell him to text me, for God's sake, Mr. Assauer, sir. Just one last text before I consign myself to the deep!"

Assauer shoved me to the floor. He was about to start yelling when the two uniformed cops came up to us.

"There's no one here," the one said derisively.

"Yeah. You've wasted our time."

Both men roughly shouldered past Assauer out the door. They shouted to the crowd "Break it up! Nothing to see here! Move it along!"

I stood up and tried to control my victorious leer.

"This is not how it ends!" Assauer walked past me and went straight to the bathroom. I heard him angrily shove the shower curtain aside, doing his own search for Gordon.

"Well, well, well."

I turned to see the lookie-loos had completely dispersed, but now Sadeeq darkened the doorway. Being slow on the updraft as he was, the poet simply stared close-mouthed as Assauer darted from the bathroom and tore through the closets.

My ex then looked under the desk and beds.

"What's he—"

I silenced Amergin with a finger to my lips. The man had a big fat reward check in his hands.

In a rage, Assauer shouted and ripped all the bedclothes off, balling them up and slamming them in the middle of the floor.

He paused, glaring back at me, before inhaling and calmly stroking his hair into position.

"You know," my ex said in desperation and tiredness. "I used to be cheerful and positive. I used to even be 'sweet' in a way. In other words, I used to be all those things Gordon is now, so, I tried to rescue him before it's too late. Before you do to him what you did to me."

Miffed, I replied, "Grow up. We're all free agents in life. You decided to run with me. Accept responsibility at least for that."

"I do. Fuck, I certainly do. But Gordon's decided to come with me. He knows the better man when he sees him, so hand him over."

In my mind, I knew it was over with my ex. Forever. I'd always love Assauer in a way, but for now, it was done. "It's best you go. Like I said, I haven't seen the boy since he dumped me to shack up with a fly-by-night flutist like you."

He walked to the door, pausing there. "Don't turn him into a jade, Kohl. Just don't. Love him better than you did me."

With as much dignity as he could, he walked out of the room, only to come back a moment later and rip Sadeeq's check into a million pieces.

As the mad poet crumpled to his knees, clutching at the worthless confetti, and sobbing "My money! My money!" I leaned out the door and watched Assauer be hugged by his L.A. cop boyfriend in the motor court. Both men got in a patrol car, and after they pulled out of the El Cortez Motel parking lot, I closed the door on the sight, doubting I'd ever see my ex again.

When I turned around, Sadeeq was standing. His expression had turned mad-dog. "What the fuck did you do to my money!"

"I thought artists weren't supposed to care about cash."

"Fuck that." He started stalking around the room. "Where is he?"

"He *is* eighteen, you know." I kept my voice calm. "He can decide for himself where he wants to be."

"Not when there's money involved, he can't!"

"Look, truth is, once he saw the cop cars, he took off running. He's probably halfway to the Naval Base by now, but if you hurry, you can probably still catch up and collect your ransom – I mean, reward – money."

I opened the door and gestured for him to kindly get the fuck out.

He glanced around one last time, and slowly started to leave.

My boyfriend sneezed.

Sadeeq was just passing through the portal when he muttered absentmindedly, "Gesundheit, Gordon."

I tried to close the door behind him, but the mad poet pushed his way back in.

"AH! HA!" he roared. "I knew it."

Gordon started to panic, and said in a muffled shout, "Get me outta here!"

I closed and locked the door before running over and upturning the mattress.

Sadeeq made himself comfortable at the desk chair and resumed pouring a cup of Cisco.

In the meantime, I helped my boyfriend stand, stretch and brush off.

"Well, well, and what do we have here?" the poet said. "I may have to send another text...."

My blood zoomed to dangerous pressure levels, but Gordon looked crafty. He laid a hand on my chest and told me silently 'Let me deal with this.'

He sauntered up seductively to the side of Sadeeq's chair, pressing his bulge on the man's arm. "You're hurt," he said, touching the poet's wounded eyebrow. "Let me clean it for you."

By the time my boy parted from him, the poet was mesmerized. I shoved the pizza box aside and sat on the untouched bed. A moment later, Gordon was back with the small first aid kit from the bathroom.

Sadeeq swallowed hard as the boy went about cleaning his wound, his young lithe body in contact with his own.

After the bandage was applied, my boy told the man "Stand, please," and picked up one of his own shirts from where the cops had spilled it on the floor.

Placing the collar in his teeth, he undid Sadeeq's slowly, one button at a time, disrobing the man from the waist up. After he threaded the sleeves and rested the shirt on the man's shoulders, he began to close it up. "Can't have you walking around in a torn and bloody shirt. You can have one of my clean ones." He ended by lovingly stroking the man's ponytail back into position around the side of his neck.

The song *Smooth Operator* coursed through my mind.

By the time my boy got his index finger in a position to play with the man's chest hair, the poet's tongue lolled out his mouth. Then with puppy-dog eyes, the sexy teenager said, "Me and Kohl have to get out of town. If you really do love your Gordon, like you say, now is the time to save us."

"Don't know...." The devious bard-wanna-be split looks between us. "A thousand bucks is a lot of—"

"We have stuff – stuff, jewelry, money, goods – things you can pawn. We'll get you your grand, won't we, Kohl?"

I was hesitant, but then— "Yeah, we'll get you that, and more maybe, but you've got to help us get out of San Diego."

Sadeeq took a drink. "And in exchange, I can be a part of your gang...?"

Having just finally shed Assauer for good and gotten Gordon to myself, another potential rival was the last thing I wanted, but we were in a jelly. "Yes."

"Okay. I have an idea, and we're lucky enough that the boat's leaving tomorrow."

'*Gott im Himmel*,' I thought, 'not another boat?!' I didn't know if I liked the sound of this....

"...volare non auferetur..."

— Part Eight —
Seaborne ~~Venus~~ Priapus

#polyester-torture-device,

#fembot, #face-palm,

#sequins-tits, #farce,

#green-gills, #folks,

#Possessive-much?

#Miss-Polly-Aenus,

#concord-not, #fist,

#playthings, #gods,

#pantyhose

Chapter 25: What Are the Odds

The boat deck was a perfect place to get away and think, especially late at night like this. I could sit alone in my reclining deckchair on the starboard side and cast glances across the waves. Because it could be a bit chilly, I had Gordon's dark baseball cap on, and was curled toe to shoulder under one of the *Neptune's Ekdíkisi's* black blankets.

Tonight, long panes of wispy clouds, like broken shards of wool bundles, drifted across the pale face of the waning moon. The peaceful swells of the endless sea shifted color from dark indigo to even darker ultramarine. The view was hypnotic and tranquil.

I pulled the cover up to my neck and considered our situation. We were basically stowaways on this Puerto-Vallarta-bound cruise ship, for Sadeeq's "I'm well-known on board" turned out to be among the fey and giggling fellows of the service crew. But anyway, they are great guys and found beds for me, my boyfriend and the mad poet in already-cramped staff cabins. For the two days we've been at sea now, those bunks have just been places to crash. Our daily routine has been to wake early and sneak above deck, as they say, where we spend the majority of our time among the paying passengers, like we belong there. We've blent in – had breakfast early and dinner and lunch late to not stand out – and made no fuss as to what we want or do, which is mainly me and Gordon sitting in deckchairs, holding hands and reading this and that online. Lord knows where Sadeeq spends his time – reciting Byron to the diesel pistons for all I care. In any event, he did get us out of San Diego and away from the clutches of my crazy ex.

I heard two people talking, and they were coming my way. One voice was deep and rounded by calculating tones, and might be called self-possessed. The guy he was chatting with sounded just about the opposite: flip, glib, high tones pinged with a…a Vietnamese accent.

My heart sank. That particular combo of resonances – unmistakable.

I curled up a bit, drawing my knees to the side so I could get the blanket over my head.

Every now and then along the boat deck, the handrail jutted out to form a little niche where crewmembers would stand in the event of needing to lower the lifeboats, which were locked into place on davits overhead.

Lloyd and Sang Trọng stepped into the nook nearest my deckchair, presumably to drink in the view I myself had been enjoying.

"I'm anxious to get this settled once for all," Lloyd said.

"I know, sweetie, but the gods would not steer us wrong."

'Gods…?' I wondered.

The sea captain was angry. "It's been too much! The humiliation those two piled up—"

"Don't aggravate yourself, Lloyd, darling."

"Trọng, it helps to vent these things. Not only have I lost my wife and could lose a big fat cash settlement if my lawyers can't find a loophole in my prenuptial agreement. But what's worse is how I've lost face in the eyes of my competitors. Business is suffering, and my enemies are going around cutting off my supply, calling me *Capitán El Puto*. And it's all the fault of that Kraut! I want revenge, and the god wants the return of his sacred cult object to my possession. He won't be appeased until things are righted. Then maybe my business dealings will get back on course too."

"There, there, I know, darling. I too feel betrayed and humiliated in the basest of ways. That sexy-ass Gordon suddenly spurned me and ran. No one ever dumps Trọng! And it's that Kohl's fault too. I just need to get my precious Gordon away from his evil clutches. A day or two behind closed doors will teach that twink a lesson, and 'educate' him not to mess with Sang Trọng – I have claws and will use them."

"He visited me again last night."

"Neptune?" Trọng asked.

"Aye – the Great God of the Sea, the one to whom I owe everything."

"What did he show you this time, dearest?"

"Same as the last three nights – that Kohl and Gordon are on this ship, and that we will bump into them sooner rather than later."

"Yes. The Great One – Lord of the forest and field – has come to me every night as well with a similar vision. That our enemies, the ones we most seek bloody vengeance upon, are on board. Priapus will deliver them into our hands. I have no lack of faith."

Lloyd said, "It's just a matter of laying low and cornering them. I have men aboard who are standing by with concrete loafers for those queer boys to try on."

I heard a shiver emerge as a sputtering of Trọng's lips.

"Shall we, Lloyd? I'm getting chilly."

"Yes, dear."

As they continued walking, a shiver of my own ran down my spine. It was not necessarily caused by the threat of death – that I guess I'm used to by now – but by the freaky insight that I was not the only one visited in my dreams by the Phallic One.

There may not have been much room to pace in our little seamen's cabin, but that's exactly what I'd been doing for the last hour, trying not to panic.

I was half-glad I didn't go with Gordon and Sadeeq to the lame-ass lounge show – all sequins, tits and showgirls – for then we wouldn't have gotten the jump on the drug lord and his Vietnamese moll.

More panic! What if those two nut-jobs, or their hired goons, had bumped into Gordon?! My boy could already be fish sticks....

I froze, hearing laughter from the corridor. Sadeeq and the teenager entered, and I immediately launched a hug on my boyfriend.

Gordon chuckled, hugging me back. "Possessive much?"

That pissed me off slightly, but more so the mad poet's just standing there with open mouth like a guppy. I released my boy, moved Sadeeq aside and gingerly closed the door. In another second, it was locked and I could take a breath.

"You okay, buddy?" Sadeeq asked.

"No!" I nearly shouted, then slapped shut my own mouth with a hand.

I started pacing again, which was even harder with the two more men in the cabin. "I can't believe it. I can't believe it...."

"What?" my boy asked.

"They are here! They're on board."

Gordon's face puzzled, half-amused. "Um – who?"

My ire flashed on the poet. "And what *about* you! Did you know they'd be on? Is this a setup—"

"Woah. Calm down, dude."

"Kohl!"

Gordon's tone of concern brought me around. "Yes, hon?"

"Who are you talking about?"

I grabbed him by the upper arms and sat him down for safety. "I was covered up on the boat deck, alone, when a big guy comes strolling by. He stops and I overhear his conversation: how he was stolen from; how he was outed on live TV; how he wants revenge on the German guy who did it all to him! Know who I'm talking about?!"

Gordon, being the boy he was, howled with laughter, slapping his knee and rolling on the bed trying to regulate his breathing.

"Oh, yeah," I told my boyfriend. "Well, in case you think he was rambling to himself, he wasn't. Trọng is on board too, and the little hussy wants to divide us so he can corner you, alone, and quote-un-quote, teach you a lesson."

Now Gordon slowly panicked, rising to his feet and pacing along with me. In his stead, Sadeeq sat on the bed and watched rather removed from the drama. He idly petted his ponytail.

"You mean," he asked, "Lloyd – the *Lloyd* – owner of this ship, and the entire Neptune Line?"

"Yeah, yeah," I clipped briskly. "You know him?"

"I do indeed. And I can confirm he's a dangerous man. His cruise line, and this ship primarily, is his main means of smuggling drugs from Mexico. He does it by the tons."

Me and Gordon stopped and held onto one another. I asked, "You know him personally?"

"Yes, I do. And"—he added wryly—"congratulations. It's no mean feat for a pair of nobodies, like you fine gentlemen so obviously are, to become the enemy of such a powerful man."

Gordon inquired with strained restraint, "Did you know he'd be on board?"

"Nope." He crossed himself. "Swear to God. Hope to die."

That answer was too pert for my personal taste. "It's your fault! You jumped us from the flame into the broiler, and now we're trapped in a floating sardine can. What are we going to do!"

The poet leaned back on the bed, using his elbows as props. "Well, first, I suggest you guys calm the fuck down. Secondly, sit the fuck down and let's think this thing out; explore our options; brainstorm."

Based on his intellect, I doubted Sadeeq could muster much of a brain drizzle, let alone a storm, lol. Nevertheless, I took my boy's hand and we sat on the cabin floor in front of the social media celeb.

"Before we do anything else, we need assumed names," said Gordon. "We're not on the passenger list, so Lloyd can't be a hundred percent certain we're on board."

"Yes. Good idea," I said. "Who are you going to be?"

"Um – how about something trendy…. Grayson…Hewitt."

"Grayson Hewitt…." I repeated it a few times to set it in my memory.

Sadeeq grinned. "That's lovely, Gordon. Matches you to a tee—"

"Yeah, yeah," I interrupted. "Now me. Trendy, huh? How about… Mason…Polyaenus?"

The two rolled around in breath-snatching fits of laughter.

I copped the expression of that flat-lined, slant-eyes emoji. "What? You guys are ignorant. Don't you know your Homer, poet? That's one of the epigrams – epitaphs, whatever – for Ulysses."

They only laughed the harder.

"Means 'the man of many legends,' and/or 'the man who has many tales to tell.'"

I elbowed my boy.

"Okay, okay," he finally said. "That's a good one, Mason, but maybe you should keep in the back of your head that you're Mr. Smith from now on. Got it?"

I nodded, skulking. 'What's wrong with my choice,' I wondered. 'The state of learning is something appalling these days.'

"Well, faux Ulysses"—Sadeeq meant me—"let's pretend we've just wandered into the cave of the Cyclopes, where Jove's very thunder claps are made, and need to think our way out again."

"But we're on a boat," Gordon said flatly. "We can't escape, can we?"

"We can sink it," I offered. "Leave our fate to Fortune."

My boy frowned. "Are you serious? That's a terrible idea."

I was about to argue the point when Sadeeq held out his hands. "Maybe there's a smarter way."

"Like what?" I demanded to know.

"We could get chummy with the night crew on the bridge. Maybe bribe the pilot with goods and favors." His lecherous brow flared at Gordon, and his hand stroked his ponytail like a fetish. "And he'll get us off somehow – after Gordon gets him off, that is." He laughed, and laughed alone.

"Or," I suggested, "simply tell him my boyfriend is too seasick to go on and he must put us ashore."

"In the middle of the night…?" Gordon sounded dubious.

"Why not?" I said. "You're a good actor. Ham up the green eggs, et-cetera, and make him believe it."

"Green gills," my boy corrected me. "That means seasick."

"But…who would have green grills in their mouth…?"

"I'm not so sure, Kohl, about your idea," offered a pensive poet.

Some silence followed, in which the three of us each followed the course of our own earnest meditations.

"What about…" I started, but then faltered. "No. Never mind."

More deliberation-time ensued.

Gordon said, "We could always just steal a lifeboat—"

"Containers!" the poet exclaimed.

"What?" I asked.

"We'll pack you and Gordon in some shipping containers in the hold."

My boy scowled. "Are you delirious?"

"No, young man – I'm *serious*. We'll pack you up, put in some food, water, a pottie, and when you're offloaded in Puerto Vallarta, I'll come to collect you. Easy peasy."

"No, no." I kye-bashed the whole thing. "Too many variables – what-*IFs*. What if they cover the breathing holes; what if we run out of water; what if they open the crate up in Customs? Too many possibilities to go way wrong."

"Yeah, and"—Gordon pointed out—"we don't know where Lloyd's drugs are in the ship. We could get hauled off and opened up the middle of a grow operation. Too risky."

We nodded in agreement.

Several minutes of concentration followed.

Sadeeq suddenly cried out, "Black face!"

Me and my boy were astounded. We asked in unison, "What…?"

The poet copped a Cheshire-cat grin. "Why not? It works in the movies!"

"This is not the movies," said Gordon heatedly. "It's real life. We can't become Black guys just because we mask our skin with makeup. Why not circumcise each other so we can pass ourselves off as Jews?"

"I'm already—" Sadeeq started.

My boy snipped him off. "My point is, has any person just one mark of distinction? You want to wrap our heads in table napkins so we appear like Palestinians? Want to chalk our faces and pencil in eyebrows so that with barrettes on our heads we look 'French'? How about piercing and tattooing our skin all over so we look like Hipsters. Would that work? Would that fool anyone…. I. Think. Not."

I guess my boy had a lot of POV on this subject, one quite frankly I'd never even considered.

"No," Gordon went on. "That's the problem with our world nowadays. We form opinions on how certain people are supposed to be – the Jews, the Arabs, the Irish, the Queens, the Queers, the basic bitches, the farmers, the urbanites, the rednecks, the progressive, the backward, the bible-humpers, the God-haters – and assume in total arrogance that *our* opinion of them is all there is to those people. When the hell will we stop assuming and start listening again? This can't go on much longer, for it's impossible for a functioning society to be so mired in belief-based dismissals, or act on what's just really another form of head-in-the-sand escapism. We need Truth, for God's sake!"

When Gordon had finished and realized we were staring at him lacking comprehension, he threw up his arms, rolled his eyes and exclaimed, "Fuck! Why don't we just jump overboard and end this entire farce."

Into the quiet that followed, Sadeeq mumbled, "Farce...? Did you say...? Farce!"

He stood up and made for the door.

"What?!" I asked.

"Wait here. I'm going to borrow some clothes from my crew buddies."

"Uniforms?" I wondered out loud in Gordon's direction.

"Better!" said the poet. "I've come up with a surefire method."

My boyfriend grumbled, "We should just take a lifeboat...."

"Trust me." Sadeeq painted on a greasy leer.

After he'd slipped out the door, I thought, 'Trust him.... That's the last thing I want to do.'

Gordon popped up and latched the door, but when he came back, he slid despondently into my arms. My better half lay his head on my chest, and I stroked his lovely, curly hair.

"Gordon, honey, will you listen to me for a second?"

"Yes, Kohl." He didn't move, other than to hug himself tighter to my midsection.

"Trọng and Lloyd were talking about...well, it seems weird."

"You can tell me. Talking about what?"

"Dreams. How both of them got 'messages' we'd be aboard this ship, for this specific cruise. Do you believe in that stuff?" I hoped I could delicately investigate if Gordon was dreaming about Priapus too.

"No," he said. "I mean, I've never had that kind of experience, so, I don't know." He looked up at me. "How about you?"

"Me, believe in that stuff?" I faked it. "No! It's all BS. It has to be... right?"

"Yeah." He settled his head back against my heart.

I sighed. "I'm sorry, Gordon. It seems we're no closer to our goal. I've led you right back into the heart of my cursed existence."

My boy hushed me. "That's bull shit, and you know it. I'm right where

I want to be, with the only one I ever want to 'experience' things with, Kohl."

"But still…" I hesitated. "I, um, long for a time when we're settled. A future when things are better, or maybe just easier for us."

Gordon chuckled. "You saying you want to go back to Aptos? My dad will give you a job."

Laughing, I said, "Yeah, mucking out the compost heap for twelve hours a day for the rest of my life. No thank you."

As my boy sighed and snuggled in deep for a few minutes of quiet and soul-to-soul contact, my mind skimmed over a few new lines of verse.

> 'What are we but the playthings of the gods? –
>
> Their whims, our fates become;
> Their threats crack troublesome,
> Like thunder worrisome
> To make us chill and numb.
> Their cruel delirium
> To man is burdensome,
> When their laughing loathsome
> Makes us only feel glum.
> Then to flight we succumb,
> Escaping meddlesome
> Retribution awesome
> And enforced martyrdom.
>
> So, are we not the playthings of the gods? –
> Tossed aside to uncertainties,
> Like dice rolled with little care of the odds,
> And only to up *their* antes.'

Chapter 26: "I Got You, Babe"

I had to stop and adjust my pantyhose.

Sadeeq, walking two paces behind me, said, "That's not very ladylike."

"Fuck you" was my reply. "Why do we have to go so public anyway?"

"Simple. Hiding in plain sight makes you invisible. Now, shall we?" He extended the crook of his arm. I took it, and we strode into the ship's main lounge for breakfast.

As the pair of us stepped leisurely to the buffet, Sadeeq's hand slipped down my waist to settle objectifyingly on my upper ass.

I removed it.

"What...?" the poet asked mildly. "Just trying to blend in. Plus, you better get used to this kind of treatment, now that you're a...." He let the final word trail off.

"A lady!" I said, and grabbed a plate to start looking over the scrambled eggs, sausage and bacon. My mind was awash with uncertainty concerning this new and unwanted situation. Last night, it turned out the mad poet's idea was – just as he'd reminded me – to conceal ourselves out in the open, as women. I'd never done drag before, and as I scooped some eggs, I mused how most straight women assume Gay men have closets of finery we flit about in when no one's looking. I selected some pork links. Last night had been something of a flap. First Sadeeq needing to convince us of the sound-ness of his idea, and then a squadron of his fey Filipino friends transforming me and my boy. I resisted tooth and nail their wanting to shave my eyebrows, but in the end, they won, and now I have to admit the rakish, pencil-thin, black-liner brows really change the shape of my face. I selected a slice of toast, glancing around the room. I'd never been so nervous about acting 'nor-mal' before.

Just as I dabbed a spoonful of jam on my plate, I tensed up, feeling my nuts get squashed again. I wanted to slam my food down, pull and yank the bindings free right then and there...but I didn't. Instead, the fake smile I had plastered on for Sadeeq became a real one when I considered how Gordon was still back in the cabin, getting the finishing touches of his 'look' done by the poet's flamboyant friends.

Sadeeq led us to a table – his hand on my ass, again – and we sat down.

I snapped my napkin and used it to cover my crotch while I tugged on the polyester torture device to finally get some relief. As I picked up my fork, I told the poet honestly, "We should've run the boat aground."

"Don't be silly."

I rocked back on my chair. "Don't *be* silly?! Look at me."

Sadeeq speared one of my sausage links. "What? You look hot, babe. Good tits, nice ass; you're as qualified as any woman in Trump's America could be."

Suddenly Lloyd and Trọng were there. Waiters stood behind them holding food plates.

Lloyd greeted Sadeeq with a chin bob. "Hello, old friend. I'm pleased you could join us on our little excursion south after all."

The poet grinned, cool as a watermelon. "Wouldn't miss a trip like this for the world, Lloyd, ole buddy."

I started to fumble with my purse, and was relieved to find a rhinestone-encrusted compact there. I pulled it out to appear self-absorbed and busy, but accidentally caught a glimpse of my worried expression. I was glad one of the crew lent me some violet-colored contacts.

Still looking in the mirror, I heard Trọng ask, "Mind if we join you?"

I panicked. Surely Sadeeq would send them away.

"No, please do!" said the poet happily.

Lloyd and Trọng sat down. The food was set before them, and now to my continuing horror, I recognized one of the waiters as that redheaded psycho Popeye from the ferry and flea market!

I glanced around, and sure enough, this boy's insane junior officer boyfriend was similarly dressed and bussing tables. His jerky movements and ugly scowl told me he was just as surly as ever.

'No doubt,' I considered, 'they want their revenge for the Rose Bowl fiasco. What are the odds they'd be on this boat too...?'

Lloyd's typically resonant tones sounded while he inquired of Sadeeq, "Aren't you going to introduce us to your lovely companion?"

I thrust a ladylike hand for the sexy sea captain to take. "Why, it's an outright pleasure to be making y'all's acquaintances, I do declare – y'all." On the spot I had decided to put on an outrageous mush-mouth Southern accent to hide my naturally beautiful one, however, I sounded more like Foghorn Leghorn channeling Carol Channing, lol.

Lloyd, the real corny type, kissed the back of my hand. As I withdrew it, I could tell the Vietnamese guy had been goaded into some mild jealousy.

After a moment of silence, with the newcomers looking expectantly at me and Sadeeq, Trọng finally asked, "And your name? Didn't catch it."

I opened my mouth to rattle off something sweet and forgettable – something ending in 'Smith' – when Sadeeq interrupted.

"Polly. Her name is Polly Aenus."

All at the table were astounded, including me....

Sadeeq casually took a bite of scrambled eggs. "Stage name," he explained. "Her and her wife are female female-impersonators."

I drained my mimosa.

"A *female* female-impersonator?" Lloyd asked.

"A woman playing.... A woman?" Trọng seconded the query.

I smiled, sat back and let Sadeeq go over the details.

"Sure! Her and the missus have studied the art of being a woman from all the best drag queens in the world, and they carry it onto the stage."

'That's not what I was thinking at all.'

Lloyd and Trọng glanced at one another. "Really?" they asked simultaneously.

Sadeeq crunched on the end of a bacon stick. "Absooolutly. I hear it's exactly what Lady Gaga and Maggie Thatcher did. Learn from the masters, right, Polly?"

I tried to chuckle. "Saq – sweet pea – you know it's not quite true. I—"

"Oh, yes. I see what you mean. Obviously, Martha Stewart studied drag too – what else could explain her."

"Hmmmm," I cleared my throat. Although the notion that someone like Angela Merkel could use lessons on the finer points of femininity stuck me as highly plausible, I wasn't sure where the mad poet was leading all this.

"Oh, yeah! Oh, yeah," Sadeeq added excitedly. "Actually, Polly's ball-n-chain is what they call a Drag King – a girl who's studied the macho arts. You know, from the likes of Steven Seagal, Mitch McConnell, Mr. T; them types."

"Fascinating," said a stunned Lloyd.

I smiled and nodded at our table-guests, stealing Sadeeq's mimosa and draining it too. The sight of the lipstick on the glass startled me. 'Maybe time to dig in my purse again,' I wondered.

"So…?" Trọng said inquisitively. "You were hired as lounge acts. How interesting."

"Yes," added Lloyd. "We look forward to seeing you perform tonight."

Sadeeq piped up, "Me too!"

Gott im Himmel, I could have killed him.

Lloyd picked up his napkin and gestured towards my plate. "Let's eat, shall we?"

The four of us settled down to our food, and I wished to melt away like butter in a muffin. The redhead sailor was standing by Lloyd when the sea captain said to him, "Get more mimosas for Sadeeq, and Ms. Aenus." He then chatted with us. "How are you liking the cruise so far? We've had fair weather and calm seas."

"Indeed," replied the poet.

"Yes. Sturdy as a rock," said the captain with pride, "She's a fine old dame, and they don't build 'em like this anymore. The *Ekdíkisi* had her keel laid in 1977, only she was christened as the *S.S. Gerald Ford* back then."

"Really?!" asked Sadeeq with false enthusiasm.

…I had a vague recollection about it being bad luck to rename a vessel….

"It's true. I rescued her after the President Line sold her to a San Diego scrapping outfit."

"Yes, sweetheart. And then poured ten million dollars into interior renovations to make the old gal look wrinkle free. If only every 'fine old lady' could be gussied up with a mil or two." He chuckled vainly. "But we're not talking about Doris anymore, are we?"

After a tepid grin, Lloyd leaned forward a bit towards us. Lowering his tone, he asked, "Just wondering, but have either of you seen suspicious characters on board?"

"Oh, yes!" confirmed Trọng. "Two in particular. A lovely, sexy teen boy with wavy hair, and a sauerbraten Kraut with surly lip, mousy brown hair and bile-colored eyes."

'Hey!' I thought. 'That doesn't sound like yours truly at all....'

Just then, I turned and made accidental eye contact with Tanguay as he was setting my glass down. After that, he stood behind Lloyd and glared at me suspiciously.

"We'll keep our peepers peeled," Sadeeq assured them. "But tell me – what'd they do? Must have been something awful." He stroked his ponytail and pivoted his glance on me.

Lloyd appeared pained by the subject, but willing to explain how I'd accidentally outed him on television, however, Trọng laid a hand on his arm and snapped Lloyd out of it.

The drug lord frowned and divided attention between me and Sadeeq. "Let's just say, we need to have a serious talk with those two scoundrels." He cracked his knuckles.

"Don't excite yourself, dear. We know they're on board – they will be delivered unto us."

"How do – y'all – know?" I asked.

The sea captain bobbed his manly chin at Sadeeq. "Tell me, poet, do you believe in dreams?"

"What do you mean by *believe?*"

The couple glanced at one another for a second, as if seeking and granting permission for the other to speak freely.

"I have dreamed this four times, poet. Most recently just last night," said Lloyd. "Tell me what you think.

> "It always starts with fog. I'm cold, wet and afraid, trying to get away from something off the stern of my rowboat on the sea. Just then, the mist fades away and I can see the Statue of Liberty rising about a quarter mile behind me. It's her I was running from. As I watch – right before my eyes, as they say – the copper-clad goddess with all her folds of drapery transforms into the awesomely lean and naked form of Poseidon; he's still the same ravishing verdigris color though.

> "The god comes to life, lowering his head to look straight at me. He opens his mouth, and the air around me vibrates with his mighty, electric tones. 'Woe betide the man who let My image be defiled by unclean hands – allowed my holy shrine be defiled and robbed.'

> "Just then, as if in slow motion, the god crouches down on the massive stone pedestal, and uses his trident to touch

the sea. Three times, he rakes the tines through the waves, and three times, the ocean becomes more violent and infuriated.

"Again his eyes fall upon me. 'The villain you seek has been led aboard your flagship vessel. Go and consign his earthly form to my depths, or—'

"Then my dream ends. I wake in a cold sweat."

"Oh, my darling," cooed Trọng, "our visions are so similar, you'd have thought we slept the same sleep together, not merely in the same bed.

"My dream starts with me roving barefoot in the woods, the sunlight strobing on my face cubed by the leaves overhead.

"Suddenly, I hear a scream and go towards it. Under the shadows of a grove of poplars, I find a white bunny in a cruel snare. I release the poor, frightened thing and hold it tight, stroking it and saying all will be made right.

"Just then, I hear a twig snap. Behind me stands The Blue-Green One, his disheveled hair and slightly soiled cheeks leave me in no doubt as to who he is – that and his enormous penis, obviously.

"Anywho – I say, 'Oh, Great God, why show thy presence to humble little me?'

"'Look again,' he says and gestures.

"The place he bids me look is down, and the rabbit in my arms is the lovely Gordon – my Gordon.

"As I stroke his curly hair, Priapus tells me, 'Know this, in your search for the boy you love, I have entrapped him on Lloyd's main ship.'

"I awake with a smile and sweet, sweet desire – the God's ultimate gift."

'Brazen hussy,' I think, 'lusting after another's pet....' But I had to admit I was freakishly enthralled to hear another describe the dark, dirty face that visits me. Only when he comes to me, it's with the intent to torment.

Sadeeq finished the last of his eggs and placed the cutlery noisily on his china.

"Well," asked Lloyd. "What do you think?"

"About dreams?" said Sadeeq dismissively. "I think they are merely vague remembrances. Yes, the residual electrical activity of a tired brain.

That's all."

Trọng asked, "Don't you trust in signs, or portents of the future?"

"From *above*?" The poet sputtered with a frown. "No. The gods are so distant, they are hardly a concern. Now, man's avaricious nature – that, as they say, is an ever clear and present danger. As for somnambulatory visions, I say:

"No message from the gods are our dreams –
Often it's digestion woes disturb
Our erstwhile indifferent night slumbers.

When sleep comes to lift our burdens,
It's neither Heaven nor Hell that 'sees,'
But every chest reliving what it needs.

Whatever 'tis in which we take delight,
And think of most by day, we dream at night.

Soldiers and boys with video games
Slaughter at night as much as at day –
Dreading a bullet will bite their frame.

Panhandlers and lawyers alike plead
Their case in public opinion's court,
Knowing everyone judges them wrong.

Conscience's plain, half-drowned in blood afar,
Comes to those who by day noised it at the bar.

Bankers and elected men count coins
And ferret out where to hide it best –
Offshore accounts or money schemes.

Stockbrokers dream of crashes and falls
Whereby the richer only get more
To stamp the little man in the ground.

These soulless types are the worst among men,
Thinking God it's blesses them and their ken.

And so thus dogs will run in their sleep,
And the hunter too, if I'm honest –
Pursuing the hare through the dark woods.

While other sports fill the lonely head;
The hard-up only find what's not there,
Looking for sex in all the wrong spots.

Thus the good wife dreaming of her stallion's charms,
Oft seeks pleasure in her cuckold husband's arms." [27]

I stood up, having taken all I could stand.

Lloyd rose to his feet as well, like a true gentleman, while Sadeeq simply continued munching his toast.

Singsong, I sang, "It was certifiable pleasure, I'm sure, to make y'all's acquaintances, but I must be off, to...um—"

"Rehearsal for tonight, Polly," the poet added most unhelpfully.

"Yes. Rehearsal. It was a pleasure to meet you, all – y'all."

I saw Trọng react to my voice like he was trying to place something familiar.

Distracted, I felt someone assist with my chair by pulling it out of my way. I smiled and turned straight into the face of the fanatical Caribbean sailor. The man also seemed to spark with a dim recognition.

I quickly made my way to the door, as ladylike as my pinched testicles would allow.

"Oh, thank God." I hooked onto Gordon's arm just as he was about to enter the lounge.

"But, I'm hungry," he cried as I dragged him in the other direction.

"We'll go someplace else. Lloyd and Trọng are in there."

As we walked down the corridor, away from a roomful of danger, I started to chuckle.

"What?"

"Your getty-up. It's...adorable."

And indeed it was. My handsome boyfriend had been transformed into a butch *boi* – a drag king of the sweetest description.

Clothes of vaguely 1970s vintage flare made him seem like a Filipino fembot. But his cutest aspects were how his naturally wavy hair had been teased and sprayed into near-Afro proportions. A little eyeliner and blush softened his facial features, while a mascara 'stache rounded out the Shakespearean liminality – that is, the out and out gender-fuck – of a man playing a woman playing a man.

I kissed my 'wife,' feeling blessed.

After we got Gordon some food, we spent hours hiding out in the loneliest place on any cruise ship: the library. Not a soul bothered us, and we began to feel a little more optimistic.

At about four o'clock we decided it was as good a time as any to sneak below decks again. We made our way casually along one of the cabin levels. With no one watching, we ducked through a service door used by the maids for bedlinens.

As we walked into the abandoned staging area where the commercial laundry baskets on wheels lined up, I tugged on Gordon's sleeve to halt him.

"I need to talk to you about something. It can't—"

Gordon stopped up my mouth, whispering, "Listen."

Our luck sprung again, and sure enough, it was the voice of Hesus, the mad sailor, talking to his redheaded partner.

We quickly assessed they were coming out way. I removed Gordon's hand from my face. "What do we do?"

"Hide!" He picked up sheets and buried himself in a basket.

I hiked up my pantyhose – which had become surprisingly supportive and 'refreshing' – and climbed into the neighboring cart.

In a second, I was totally covered and regulated my breath as our enemies' voices drew nearer.

They stopped by our baskets, with Tanguay saying, "Hold on, Hesus, ve need to talk about those losers on this here woyage before ve get on deck again."

"Oh," said Hesus, "I'm a-keepin' my eyes on the alleged woman-impersonator. Something fishy – or, more than supposed to be fishy – if ya catch me drift."

"I do. But Captain Lloyd's telling all this wessel's crew to be on the lookout made him up his bounty to five grand, a head!"

"Oh, my boy, I'm spittin' mad all right. Them two water varmints got us sacked from the *Mrs. Jared Kushner* for a-brawlin' with passengers. And look at us now! Sunk to the lowest rank of sea-work – waiters on a cruise ship. Humiliatin'!"

"There, there, love," the hothead redhead cooed. "Ve'll get back on our feet soon as ve put a vrong right. Ve're avaiting Poseidon's werdict to see vhich vay his wendetta goes. But one thing's certain – as long as those two are on board, ve're all in danger."

Back in the cabin, I ripped off my wig. Pacing, I told Gordon, "I think you were right, honey. Why don't I ever listen to you...? We should just steal a boat and be done with it. Plus, if we pull it off, it's a good opportunity to dump Sadeeq."

My boyfriend, the voice of reason, halted my step. "It will never work. Even if we get one of the lifeboats to lower and shove off, this ship will stop until the 'rescue party' hauls us back. I think we should stay in the cabin until the *Ekdíkisi* docks. Sadeeq can bring us food."

I took his hands and led us to sit on the bed. "Look, there's something I've been meaning to tell you. This, god, Priapus – well, not only did he hex my prick, but he visits me in my sleep."

He opened his mouth to speak, but I intercepted and pressed on. "I know, I know – just dreams. But last night, this is what happened.

"I dreamt I was in this secluded desert, looking for you, desperate and lonely. The sun struck my dry eyes, but then from one corner appeared this mini cyclone – a sand devil, I think they call it.

"It moved towards me, but I had nowhere to hide, so ran. It gained on me and sucked me up. Spinning around and around, I heard 'His' voice – gruff and rustic. He said awful things, about you, sweetheart, the gist of which is that you only loved me for my, um, potency, and now that it's gone, so is your affection.

"Anyway, this is where it gets weird, because the dust devil thing ends and puts me down on top of a craggy mountain overlooking the desert. I can see for miles and miles.

"Hearing a noise, I turn, and there is the Dirty One himself with a hand on your shoulder, and a giant bag of money in his other hand. Oddly enough, I realize we are standing by the corner of a church, and look up to see its bells ringing.

"His voice makes me look down again. 'Choose,' he tells me.

"And then I wake up in a cold sweat."

Gordon hugged me. "You don't have to – it is just a dream, Kohl. Just a silly...silly, dream." He tenderly kissed the side of my neck.

"We have to find a cure for me, Gordon."

There was an abrupt noise at the door. We jumped up, and I armed myself with the nearest 'weapon' – a giant hand mirror.

The door burst open, knocking the mirror out of my hand anyway. Behind it was Sadeeq, and he'd brought a small army of Filipinos. Draped over the arms of one was a long white dress, beautifully fringed and beaded.

Sadeeq said, "Come on, time to change. Chop, chop! No time to lose."

"Poet—" I started.

"That crafty Trọng is already suspicious. There's no other way"—the social media celebrity smeared on a sly grin—"you'll just have to trust me."

❑ ❑ ❑ ❑ ❑

Be-feathered showgirls high-kicked it while a lounge-lizard type of guy in white tails sang on stage.

In the wings, I could peek out through the heavy side drapes and see the auditorium had been transformed. Now small tables with lamps were peppered with small parties of people, including Sadeeq, Lloyd and Trọng at one front and center. The "maximum occupancy" count for the lounge was about 300, and a good 250 – or most of the passengers – were out there having fun.

Another scan of the room showed me those two sailor-waiters moving about serving drinks, and eying passengers suspiciously.

Gordon touched my arm, for he had wise words to offer. "We've done this a million times at karaoke. Just relax, enjoy the moment, and it will all be over soon."

"I'm worried it's us who'll be 'all over soon' – all over the deck boards after the crazy drug lord puts a bullet through our heads."

Gordon smirked. "Always seeing the bright side, huh?"

The showgirls were gathering for their finale, and a kick-line is guaranteed to generate applause, lol. The backstage area was crowded with as many of Sadeeq's maid and steward friends as could get off duty. They were here to see their handiwork – me and Gordon – perform.

The music crescendoed; people clapped; the feathered headdresses curtsied; and my nerves ratcheted up a notch. They trooped offstage on the other side.

Gordon took my hand just as the MC announced, "And now, ladies and gentlemen, please welcome to the Omonoia Room of *Neptune's Ekdíkisi*, Polly Aenus and Spike Hardfist doing a dear old standby."

Applause rang out and I was suddenly seized with the realization that they were for me and my boy. Effortlessly, I snapped into character. I was gorgeous in my white gown, so I tossed back my long black hair, and whipped my microphone cord like a pro. I gave Gordon a wink and croaked, "Shall we," applying tongue firmly to upper lip.

We strode onto stage like we owned it. And why not? We were all that, and a natural smile came to me regarding my cute boyfriend in his Beatles wig and monkey's foot mustache. He wore a vintage wine-colored tux with huge lapels, and a big floppy bowtie.

While the ovation was still going on, the music started, and me and my boy assumed the positions – moving our feet and bodies rhythmically to the sway of the music, and glancing at one another adoringly.

Gordon was right. We had sung Sonny and Cher's "Heaven Sent" a million and a half times together, because it was our song.

> "*They may try to keep us apart,*
> *Criticize the length of our hair,*
> *Think our journey's doomed from the start,*
> *But them putting us down's not fair.*"

We sang the first chorus and got lost in the realness of the emotions. This set us rocketing into the verses.

> "*This month we may not make the rent,*

But what's cash when you're heaven-sent;
When your hand in mine feels so right,
And our future looks only bright.

Who's to tell us what is golden
That to the past we're beholden;
We'll make our own way, you and me,
And prove them wrong so they will see."

Before we knew it, our hands were joined, and we pulled each other close. These words were so personal for us, we down-geared into the concluding chorus with true feeling.

"They may try to keep us away,
Make fun of us in what they do,
But we know we're blessed day by day
Cuz our dream's already come true."

We ended on a high note, staring straight into one another's eyes.

The music ended in raucous applause – some of it coming from the assembled showgirls and Filipinos in the wings.

We kissed, and Gordon said in his natural voice, "I got you, Kohl."

"And I got you, babe."

At first I was too distracted to notice a vengeful Trọng rise and point with his full arm.

"It's them!"

The clapping ground to a halt.

Glancing at Gordon, I hiked my skirt and mic cord, and we hoofed it.

The Filipino crewmembers and dancing girls shrieked together and piled onto the stage.

Bedlam followed as me and my boy ran for the nearest door. However, the sailor couple headed us off, and hauled us back in arm-locks to the dance floor in front of the stage.

Lloyd, Trọng and Sadeeq stood there waiting. The poet tried to ham up the shocked and dismayed routine at our deception. The drug lord turned to him. "Don't pretend you're not a part of this."

Trọng shoved the poet to the 'wrong' side – to stand next to me and Gordon.

A soon as he got there, Sadeeq pointed at me, shouting, "It was his idea!"

No one paid him any attention, but all eyes wandered to Lloyd to see what he'd do. Hesus restrained me tighter. The drug lord walked up to me, eyed me coldly for a moment, and then gripped my package through my Bob-Mackie beading.

"Hello, Kohl. I'd recognize your dick anywhere."

And true, when it still worked, I'd discovered Lloyd was hardly the 'total top' I'd imagined. Instead, he'd worshiped my *Schwanz* many a Catalina night on his knees. I glanced at Gordon for a moment because that was something I didn't want him to necessarily know.

I broke out of the Caribbean sailor's grip. "Evening, Lloyd; Trọng. Nice to see you again."

The Vietnamese guy advanced with ire. "Is that all you have to say?! After you humiliated us. After you.... Did what you did to Lloyd! OMG."

"Let's play nice," I said, "like old times. What do you say? We were good friends once, and can be again."

Lloyd asked with icy reserve, "Is that what you want, Kohl?"

"Yes." I chuckled, glancing at my fearful mate.

Lloyd slapped me. "Ask what I want."

I swallowed. "What do you want, Lloyd, besides your statue back?"

"I want to know why when we're harmed by a stranger we call him a thug, but when hurt by a friend we have to 'make nice'?"

"Um..." I stammered – he had a good point.

"I also want to *disappear* you, Kohl. After you tell me who has my stolen idol, I'm confident no one will come looking for you."

Trọng screeched petulantly, "But what about me! I want to know if criminals are still flogged at sea. And what's more than that, I want to get my sweet Gordon away from such an awful Kraut, and in a room, alone."

Hesus cleared his throat, as he'd decided to speak up too. "Beggin' pardon, sir, but dees two done wrong by us as well. Worse! Day've angered the mighty god o'da sea."

"That's right," piped Tanguay in agreement, finally releasing Gordon. "I've seen it with my wery own eyes, sir. This one"—meaning my boy —"clipped his nails on board a wessel, vhistled a tune in the vind, told my partner to go drown himself, said the vord 'goodbye'! And worst of all, ate a wivid yellow banana—"

The surly redhead was cut off by the uproarious laughter coming from the stage. Chorus girls and cabin crew alike regarded those as silly things to be angered over.

Hesus demanded of Lloyd, "As a man of da sea, Captain, you know how serious these affronts be to Poseidon. For ever and a day, them der cracked actions have been forbidden, and for good reason too. We can't change the rules of shippin' just for two fly-by-night hipsters."

"Yeah!" chirped his boyfriend. "So let us take care of this punk in our own vay. Ve'll appease the god, for sure, and do it wisibly."

Trọng was indignant. "No one's gonna harm my precious Gordon...."

"Look, look, friends!" At this point, Sadeeq, 'trying to help,' told the entire room, "This poor bastard, Kohl, has suffered enough – his limp noodle was behexed by some crazy sex cult. He can't get it up, and for a Gay guy, that's a fate worse than death!"

I thought, '*Gott im Himmel*, I could kill him all over again.' Meek as a sheep, I glanced around the room, which was now in full-snicker mode over my condition. I saw it was especially evident in the sailors-cum-waiters.

Sadeeq pleaded, "Lloyd, take pity. The gods have done worse than you ever could." He went up and laid a commiserating hand on Gordon's chest. "And as for the boy, you can see, he's already been punished enough."

"No so fast!" shouted Trọng, who went over and roughly snatched the Beatles bob off my Gordon's head.

Pissed, I told him, "Don't you dare lay a finger on him, you demented China Doll!"

That angered Lloyd, who said, "Watch your language."

Sadeeq said, "More political correctness run amok."

Me, Gordon, Lloyd and Trọng shouted in unison, "Shut up!"

That offended the poet's Filipino friends who came streaming off stage, the befeathered showgirls caught with them in mid-stream.

The sailor-waiters tried to fend them off, but one cabin steward smacked a shoe upside the redhead, freeing Gordon fully, who came and clung to my beaded dress.

Hesus took affront to his boyfriend being abused, and within a matter of seconds, sides had formed, with all of the lounge wait staff battling the cabin crew. The showgirls with their gorgeous, sparkling costumes, bopped whomever they could over the head.

Trọng flew towards Gordon to try and grab him. I got angry, and with the brawl all around me, I shielded my boy behind me. I started to move us slowly back, waving my microphone cord at Trọng like a whip. "You stay away from him, you crazy bitch. You're the only one who deserves a flogging on his sip."

I ripped off my wig and threw it in his face.

The fighting halted our step, but now Lloyd was pissed off again at the way I'd spoken to his partner.

The sea captain directed more waiters to "Get them!"

Me and Gordon picked up chairs and fought them back lion tamers, the cord of my mic stinging the white-jackets with stinging stripes.

The brawl raged on.

Suddenly through the din, a loud *Tap, Tap, Tap* was heard. The spotlight came on and swung around to stage center.

Alone up on the platform, hugging the microphone stand passionately, Sadeeq Amergin delivered these words:

"A Poem on Peace.

"There's a futility
   To constantly being on edge;
There's real danger as well
   That the razor-blade of anger
Cuts the wielder as deep
   As the intended victims do.

But by seeing ourselves
　In the faces of others, we heal;
By wielding forgiveness
　Can we the gods themselves absolve."

Somehow, by some alchemy of magic unknown, the poet's words struck home. All seemed stunned into misty-eyes compliancy. Gordon and I set down our chairs and hugged. Lloyd and Trọng – and Hesus and his redhead too – moved to stand calmly next to their partners.

"Let's end this," said Trọng.

"All right," I said, stepping forward, "but let's formalize it in a kind of peace treaty. For which, I agree to tell Lloyd who has his idol, and work with the current owner to restore it."

That seemed to calm the sea captain, somewhat.

"And I," said Gordon to Hesus and Tanguay, "promise to do the proper rituals to undo my 'sea sins.'"

That appeased the Caribbean.

"But," I cautioned Trọng, "you must make concessions too."

"Like what?"

"Like, you agree to stop trying to force me and my boy apart."

The Vietnamese throt looked not too sure.

I sweetened the pot. "And as a penalty clause, if any of the parties to this agreement fail to live up to the promises, $100 for each violation will be proffered in cash. Agreed...?"

"And," added Gordon to Trọng, glancing at the younger sailor, "I think I know where your precious Gucci gym bag can be located."

Trọng and Hesus looked amenable, but Lloyd and Tanguay less so.

"Lloyd, darling, it's the best way forward."

The sea captain stepped up to me. "I can forgive and forget, but I have fear in my heart."

Despite his concluding sentiment, he shook my hand to seal the deal.

"Oh, dear," laughed Trọng. "There's no need to be nervous. Sadeeq was right about dreams. They are no more omens of the future than exit polls; only after they 'come true' do they seem to be halfway believable." He kissed Lloyd's cheek.

All the warring factions, from showgirl to black-eyed waiter, hugged it out at Trọng's insistence.

Just as I finished one of these enforced signs of peace, I turned around to face Hesus. Tanguay was at his side.

I stuck my hand out, and much to my relief, the Caribbean took it. However, the red-haired boy remained dismayed. He muttered, "This wictory ain't right."

Hesus replied, good naturedly, "All be forgiven, nug."

"Maybe so vith us, but that don't mean it's over in their wiew."

"What do you mean?" I asked, chuckling.

Tanguay looked me square in the eye. "Since vhen is concord among men in the best interests of the gods?"

Sadeeq tapped on the microphone again. He cried out, "I could use a drink. Who's with me?!"

A tremendous cheer went up.

"Okay then, the night is fair, the seas are calm, so let's go celebrate in style!"

Chapter 27: Pool Party [of the Gods (???)]

Someone did an ugly-ass belly flop into the pool. The feelgood music was temporarily drowned out by screams and the sounds of chlorinated water slocking those sitting poolside.

A moment later, laughter bubbled as freely as the flowing booze, and the party tunes came back into focus in my ears. Everybody was suitably loose as midnight rolled by unnoticed.

We were gathered by the stern of the vessel, and I personally had a perfect view of everything from my seat at a table. Off the portside, obscure masses floated by a few miles away. I took them to be the craggy hills and shoreline of a sparsely populated Baja California. Behind us, two ever-expanding wakes churned up white foam from the *Ekdíkisi's* props, but other than that, the sea was dark and still as a black mirror.

No moon was out, so atop the surface of the ocean a milky abundance of stars stretched from one horizon to another in their slow-motion of dance. However, not singly or *en masse* could any of those fiery bodies compete with the sheer beauty of my boy emerging from the pool in his yellow striped trunks. He had a radiant smile for me.

After the lounge brawl and truce accord, a contingent of Filipinos went with me and Gordon to our cabin to change. They used some sort of white cream to clean off our make-up, and then one of them kindly instructed me on how to paint on fairly believable eyebrows. I was glad my boy was spared this indignity. After they left – and after a quick-but-loving hand job for my better half – I slipped into cargo shorts and a tank top to enjoy the flowing libations and perfectly warm night up on deck.

Gordon toweled off poolside, and then joined our table. He sat with the terrycloth draped around his neck, but soon the lank stares by Lloyd and Trọng made my boy shift the towel to cover his exposed nipples, especially from the Vietnamese guy's lascivious lip-licking.

Our table had a pitcher of margaritas, so I poured my boy a salty glass and topped up everybody else's too. We were having a good time, and our formerly hard feelings seemed to be fading. For that matter, Lloyd was growing downright friendly again.

We heard loud laughter and shouts of "Don't do it!" Turning, we saw Sadeeq shaking a champagne bottle and spraying a small constellation of twink boys, one of whom appeared to capture the middle-aged poet's fancy with his brooding good looks and short dark hair.

The four of us settled back to our drinks.

"May I propose a toast?" Lloyd held up his glass, and we at the table followed suit. "To – renewal in all its varied forms. Cheers!"

Yum. The Tequila was nice and strong. The taste of agave made me think of the Mexican interior just a few miles to the east.

"So, Gordon," said Trọng, reaching his hand across the table. "It's so nice we can be friendly again."

My boyfriend briefly shook the offered hand, as if that was what Trọng had in mind.

I chuckled. "Maybe we should have gotten our peace treaty in writing."

"Why not?" Lloyd shrugged. "Plenty of paper here." His left hand fell on a stack of dry cocktail napkins.

"Have a pen?" I asked.

Trọng pulled one from his bag and handed it to his partner.

"Okay," said Lloyd, "what's first." The pen clicked, ready for action. "But," the sea captain warned, "both sides must have and offer up something the other – aggrieved – party wants."

We all withdrew into ourselves a moment and became pensive.

Lloyd, inspired, scribbled and told us, "All right, let's start with the absolutes, the back and whites if you will. Article 1: In exchange for info on the whereabouts of my golden statuette, Trọng and I promise to stop hunting you." He looked up at me and Gordon. "Fair?"

"Yes." We nodded.

"Now for the penalty clause," said the sea captain.

I joked, tapping on a fresh piece of paper for Lloyd to write on. "Article 2: I agree to pay a cash penalty if I ever, accidentally, defile one of your shrines again."

We laughed, but the man in charge wrote it all down anyway. "How much?"

"Um," I said, "$500 for each occurrence."

The captain objected. "A thousand for the first occurrence. Five hundred for each subsequent defilement."

"Agreed," said yours truly.

Trọng twittered, "Oh, that's just silly. Can we put a clause in there that Gordon Sanchez promises not to be so goddamn cute?"

I shook my head. "I don't think that's possible."

We all laughed again. Trọng poured the next round of drinks.

Lloyd passed the pen and the stack of cocktail napkins to me. "Now, it's your turn to state what you want."

"You do the honors, babe." I slid the 'contract' towards my boy.

Gordon leaned elbows on the table and got into writing position. "Okay, where do we start?"

I jumped right in. "Do you, Sang Trọng, being of sound mind, promise from the bottom of your heart to never gripe, bitch or complain about past grievances – real or imagined – received from Gordon in the past?"

"Geeze, Kohl…!" my boyfriend said as he scribbled to catch up. "What are you, a fricken shyster-jackleg?"

We laughed, but when my boy was caught up, I asked Trọng, "Well, do you?"

"Yes – if he pledges not to withhold his *friendship* from me – I agree."

"And furthermore," I stated litigiously, "Sang Trọng hereby affirms he will never force kiss, coll, or closer hug on my boy without forfeiture of one hundred dollars for each and every occurrence."

I was going to ask for agreement, but Gordon interjected first with mercenary exactitude.

"That is," he said, "as long as we tally you up, and you pay cash-money first. No lay-away plans."

That made everybody bust up, but Gordon recorded it in the notes as soon as Trọng licked his lips and nodded enthusiastically.

"Agreed," he said.

"Now, the articles between me and you, Lloyd," I said. "Do you, being of sound mind, promise from the bottom of your heart to forgive and forget all that's occurred before this date in time?"

"I do."

"And do you furthermore promise to refrain from threatening my life directly, or contracted through others to achieve the same, with the payment of $2 million forfeited to Gordon Sanchez if I be so killed?"

There was a tense moment of deadly serious quiet. All eyes trained on the sea captain to see what he'd say.

"Agreed."

I smiled, watching my boy put the finishing touches on our demands.

"However," said Lloyd, "you must agree to our part of this bargain as well."

"What do you want?" Gordon asked.

"We want," Lloyd announced sternly, "for you to keep secrets better. The fine for each loose lip of indiscretion is will not be paid in dollars, but – affection. Trọng and I are to collect kisses and BJs for minor slips, and a thoroughgoing fucking for major infractions."

I glanced at Gordon. We agreed, but I first joked, "My ass has never been 'fracked' before, but so help me *Gott,* if I ever accidentally out you again, my cherry is yours for the plucking, Lloyd." I gave him a shit-eating grin, lol.

"So write it," instructed the grave sea captain – quite frankly, turning me on....

The sounds of the raucous party going on all around us re-interceded. We cheered one more time, and affixed our signatures on the motley, cocktail-napkin concord.

After that, we settled down for a while, and I noticed a sort of sentimental mist settle over my boy's eyes. He was feeling all romantic and took my hand.

To our shipboard hosts, he asked, "How did you two first get together? Was it a 'story'?"

Trọng chuckled. "I know what you mean. I get bored with people telling me they met at a bar or on a dating app." He took Lloyd's hand too. Trọng's tone became soft and choked with real emotion. "We have a story. I was this big stud's personal mani-pedicurist. And one day, after about six months, he gave me an extra big tip – right down my throat!" He flushed with joy. "I'll never forget it."

Me and Gordon exchanged glances. We were going to be 'good' and not laugh our asses off, but it was hard.

"And what about you?" Trọng asked. "How did you and Kohl meet?"

"Um, um..." Gordon stuttered. "I was just out of high school—"

I cut him off, knowing he was going to deliver a story fairly close to what actually happened, but I knew the mood called for some wild tale: one fitted to modern ideas of violence and love equaling 'romance,' à la *Pulp Fiction* or *The Living End.*

"Let me tell it, hon. This goes back a couple years. Gordon had started community college in Portland, Oregon, and gotten into the wrong circle – tweaking all the time and selling meth."

Lotto!

Trọng gasped. Lloyd's interest perked up too as the couple closely inspected my boy's now-blushing face.

"Yeah, so," I continued, "the good news is he got into this high-end rehab facility where I was a day nurse. Anyway, the court acted the fool and wouldn't let Gordon go free"—I noticed my boy rapt to my tale just as intently as our hosts; he was hinge-ing on every word—"so I busted Gordon out with a pistol, and a shotgun. That's how we met."

Lloyd and Trọng were suitably amazed, and so was Gordon for that matter. I kissed the back of his hand and added, "And now I feed him the only 'junk' he needs – my love." I cocked my head and looked at him all lovey-dove.

That was almost too much. My boy's eyes glowed like coal, primed and ready to explode in laughter.

Suddenly Gordon squeezed my hand, and his expression went cold and sad. He asked Trọng, "Is it too late to go back to these article thingies?"

"Why?"

"I was wondering if you'd help us with one more, very important item?"

Trọng glanced at Lloyd. "Me?"

"Yes." Gordon explained. "You're connected with the cult that cursed Kohl's.... That cursed Kohl. Can you put us in touch with some 'good' Priapeans to take it off again?"

Trọng looked uneasy, and that was hard to do with him.

"Well..." he started slowly, "no guarantees, but after we get to Puerto Vallarta, perhaps we can take a road trip. There's one particular holy site, and maybe—"

Gordon didn't let him finish. He burst out with a "Thank you," and nearly tipped the table over reaching to hug Trọng.

While they were still thus engaged – the Vietnamese guy using his shirt to dab at Gordon's happy tears – Lloyd leaned towards me and spoke low and dark.

"We'll see how long it lasts."

Just as I was trying to digest these ominous words, someone slapped my back with loud laughter.

"Hiya!" Sadeeq called out, slamming down a bottle of tequila on the table. He then put his arm around the dark-haired pool beauty, who had accompanied the poet over to us. "This is Michael-Francis." He then sat down without further ado and poured a slug of liquor.

After the boy took a seat, we all did our own intros, and I realized this smiling cutie was a grifter too – takes one to know one, they say. Michael-Francis must be scamming the old fart under the misconception that the social media 'poetry biz' is a lucrative one.

Sadeeq poured us all a drink, announcing generally, "I'm glad your fences are mended, or as Robert Frost would versify – your New England stone walls are re-stacked."

Michael-Francis chuckled with an eye-roll and reached for the bottle. "I'll drink to that, babe!"

I shivered internally, but then caught Gordon's smile at the newcomer's antics.

"Michael-Francis and I have just been discussing matters of truth versus perception," said Sadeeq. "Take for example Twitter. Did you know they've been working behind the scenes?"

"Doing what?" Gordon inquired.

"Working quietly, undercover to identify and block Kremlin-sponsored cyber espionage in the US. They rolled out the new bot-detecting software all at once one fine morning. And poof!!! Just like that, Donald the Dumpster lost over 360,000 so-called supporters. Their fake-ass, Russian-accent accounts blocked and erased in an instant. Just gone, like the So-Called himself needs to be, if people woke up and realized they have the power to bring real democracy into action."

Gordon chuckled. "Yeah, right. How likely is that to happen."

Michael-Francis cleared his throat and addressed the table generally, "So, what have you guys been talking about?"

Trọng got weepy again. "We were just talking about 'grand connections' – tales about how we met the love of our life"

Sadeeq squealed, "Ours is simple! Twas twenty minutes ago, over by the pool."

We all laughed at that.

My muse took over, almost beyond my willpower to wrestle her down. The fact was, my boy's eyes goaded the loveliness of my thoughts.

"You know," I said, "the beauty of this calm, clear night, the reunion of friendship and love reminds me of a passage from Golding's translation of *Metamorphoses*. It goes:

"The King of Gods did burn everywhere in love for Ganymede,
The Phrygian lad who was found where Jupiter kept steed,
And rather be than what he was, could the god not beseem
The shape of any other bird but the eagle we most esteem?
And so, he soaring in the air with borrowed wings, trussed up
The Trojan boy who still in heaven even yet you shall see,
Bringing Him sweet nectar, though against Dame Juno's will it be."

Into the comparative quiet of contemplation, Sadeeq stroked his ponytail and said, "True, true, but if it's love and devotion you want, I've got a story for you. This happened to a friend of mine, so you know it's real.

"My tale begins in that bastion of projected male power and authority – Fort Leavenworth, Kansas.

"The Federal Prison there is famous for housing the best and the baddest thugs in the land.

"So it happened that a certain infamous North Jersey mobster was caught up in a well-planned and tried RICO case, and sentenced to thirty years on a tax-payer funded retirement plan.

"Now, his wife was beautiful – long, Sicilian dark hair, a killer body, self-control – and it was obvious to the casual observer how she was about three decades younger than her made-man husband.

"Whether Gianni knew the type of woman he'd married before his sentencing, he sure knew afterwards. Livia, who had been living like a princess, sold all her Prada and Gucci to buy a trailer next to the penitentiary. She dumped all her plans for life, her friends; her cell phone! She was hell-bent on being the ideal Mob Madonna and spend all of her time worrying and doing what she could to make Gianni's prison life more bearable.

"Her daily routine was this: up at the crack of dawn, she'd dress all in black; make her *padrone* the finest espresso she could from Italian beans she'd grind by hand; once breakfast was made, she'd pour the coffee into a thermos, pack his morning vittles, and troop sadly over to the side entry, where the visitor sally port lived.

"Through a series of bells and whistles, and sounds of metal gates sliding open, she'd find herself in the sparse check-in room.

"'Back again, eh, Mrs. Vitantonio?'

"The young buck of a prison guard was someone the Leavenworth Matron had a hard time keeping her horned-up eyes off of. Tall, fair, studly – and able to fill out his tight polyester uniform slacks like few others she'd seen – she tried to keep her Madonna gazes averted from his soul-searing blue peepers. His warm smiles also helped her not a bit.

"'Yes, officer Aramis,' she replied meekly.

"'No, please call me Bruno. We see each other every day, and have for a year now – when it's just you and me, call me Bruno.'

"She glanced around. No insider – rat-fink informant – eyes were around that might pass word on to her husband. 'Well. In that case, I suppose you may call me Livia, if you like.'

"She could not avoid that radiant, manly smile now. It stirred her parched and lonely lady-parts down below.

"'Then, Livia it is.'

"Flushing, she waited to be led to a visiting room.

"Once there and alone, she sighed deeply, wondering what had become of her full and active life. Although it's true she has been a 'good girl' to please her father and never had sex before her wedding night, the allure of the non-Italian, non-'lifestyle' men she knew always turned her on. In high school, it had been a positive torment to attend the football games with her girlfriends and see the tightly-clothed male buttocks on bent-over display. It made her tingle to think about the slight protrusions of the jockstrap through the silken material. I mean, come on! No one can resist a man in uniform.

"She was startled with surprise. Her husband was shown in through the other door, and she realized with horror she'd forgotten to lay out his breakfast. She quickly unpacked and poured him an espresso while the man sat down in lordly ease across from her.

"'You're a saint, you know that?' Gianni told her.

"'Um...I just do—'

"'You do a lot for me. You make my life bearable.'

"She glanced at his wrinkled and gray face. The man was tough, and she had always told herself she loved him...in her heart....

"'Where's my breakfast, baby?'

"'Here. I made an asparagus frittata—'

"'What! Again?! *Marron.*'

"Later that night, as she did every night after a long day of feeding her man trailer-made manicotti, baked ziti, penne alla vodka, amaretti di Saronno and mascarpone-stuffed cannoli, she fell to her knees and prayed to the Virgin Mary to remove the lust in her heart for the sexy-ass guard.

"What she could not have known, being young and innocent, was how Bruno Aramis wanted to drill her both for snitch-level intelligence on how Vitantonio continued to be the boss of his operation from behind bars, and literally.

"One fine day in spring she had a break in her cooking-visiting-prayer routine. Giada came to visit from the East Coast. Gianni's youngest sister was vivacious, brash, beautiful – in a totally fake way – and about the same age as her brother's spouse.

"'Oh. My. GAh-awwwd,' she screeched after ducking her power-hair below Livia's trailer doorway. She looked around and saw the cramped quarters of penance the Leavenworth Matron was forcing herself to inhabit. 'You "lives" here, Livvy?'

"'Yes.' Livia added, lying, 'It's not so bad. I like it anyway.'

"The other Jersey girl let her Versace handbag slip dramatically into the crook of her arm. She popped a bubble inside her mouth. 'Me and yous needs to have a talk, sis-in-law girlfriend.'

"Sitting down to coffee and uneaten cannoli from the day before, Giada laid it on the line for her sister-in-law. 'Sweetheart, you know I loves yous, so I say this with mad respects, but shakes out of it, girl! I look at yous and think: "Weak!" See, honey, sweet-tits, now that Johnny is in the pen, it's your times to party a little, and have lots a fun. If he ever get outs again, then you can revert to being the saint-wife these men make up and tell themselves in their heads. But you don't gots to be a fricken livin' Saint Chasity-Belt here while he's out of the ways. *Marron*, grows up a little, girl. Live, Livvy!'

"The young matron was not too sure, and dared to confide in her in-law that there was a blond man who'd caught her fancy.

"'Then fucks him!' Giada cried. 'Screw his brains out. Go for it – gets your rocks off where and when you can. Lord knows I do's.'

"About a week after Giada returned to the coast to screw her brains out, Livia was alone in the supermarket. Her daily routine left little 'free' time – what with the morning feedings and evening suppers – so she needed to spend the noon-hour shopping for more mobster fuel: pasta, tomatoes, cheese, red wine.

"'Livia...?'

The distracted woman turned nearly into the arms of Bruno Aramis.

"'Oh, my God, it is you. How are you doing?' he asked.

"In Livia's mind the 'doing' word stuck and threatened to become her total *undoing*.

"'I'm fine, Bruno. Just taking care of a few things.'

"She omitted to ask what he was doing in the store that time of day, distracted by the ripples and teasing rolls of his off-duty jeans, faded and worn-in with sexy aplomb.

"The guard helped her, and finagled his way into her trailer, ostensibly to assist with all the ricotta-filled shopping bags.

"'Well, sit down, if you like.'

"His shy smile said he liked indeed.

"'Can I make you a cappuccino?'

"'No, no – you wait on your man hand and foot. I don't need anything from you, except maybe for you to sit and talk with me.'

"Slowly, she pulled out a chair. 'Talk about what?'

"'Just things. I'd like to know....well, if you are happy, I guess.'

"Dirty pool, Livia thought to herself with a frown. He knew very well....Her thoughts had to pause. For in them, he'd taken her on the trailer tabletop, and she liked it.

"They talked for hours, both opening up to one another, and both becoming more and more enamored with the other.

"That night, Livia called the prison to let them know she would not be coming, and missed her first regular appointment with her husband. Instead, she spent the evening and sleepless night on her knees, begging for the Madonna to show her some mercy. If her lot in life was to suffer, she could take it, but why then tempt her with matters of the flesh – big, strong, blond-haired flesh that made her go weepy in all the wrong places. A Verdi-like figure she struck, a second Desdemona with clenched fingers, on her knees, solemnly saying her Ave Maria with pained passion for clarity.

"The next morning, she awoke late and realized with horror she hadn't made a thing for Gianni to eat. She scrambled to get her act together. She'd have to change her routine and arrive with a mid-day repast.

"She'd never been to the visiting rooms this time of day, so was not too surprised to find some other guard on duty, however, she let her heart acknowledge how disappointed she was not to see Bruno's smiling come-ons greet her as she signed in.

"'Umm...' the middle-aged guard stammered.

"'Is there a problem?' she asked, snapping back to reality.

"'Mr. Vitantonio, he is, um—'

"Following a premonition, she walked boldly to the room she and her husband usually occupied and peeked through the square window. Another woman was there, handfeeding a smiling Gianni spoonfuls of tiramisu.

She went back to the guard. 'And who is that?'

"'His wife Linda. She comes every day at this time.'

"Livia calmly picked up her food basket and dumped the whole thing in the trash.

"She then found Bruno and shagged his brains out in the pat-down room. She'd never been so satisfied, or felt more alive.

"After that, she sold the trailer, ratted on her husband's 'business dealings' to keep him in jail the rest of his life, and ran away with Aramis to Florida – where else?"

Sadeeq laughed to finish and deliver the moral of his story. "So you see, dear friends, *The Leavenworth Matron* is a memento mori: let this corpse of a tale be a lesson to us all. Make the most of life while you still can. Live each day as if it's your last."

While the mad poet had been delivering his mad morality play, I had been noticing punk-boy Michael-Francis drinking more and slowly souring on his mark, no matter how much money he thought Amergin had. To entertain himself, the dark-haired guy started to smile suggestively at my Gordon. That was something I did not appreciate one bit – but I had vowed to be better, and I was trying hard, so I simply took Gordon's hand in my lap and held onto him lovingly.

Yet, as Sadeeq continued to drone, I also began to perceive things around us change. The weather turned moist; the sea, a bit choppier. And then the breeze began to pick up from the west. However, I have to say it was all a tad blurry to me as I focused most of my attention on the boys and only looked at the rest of the world through the green-eyed lenses of my jealousy.

The tale completed, I realized the party was over. The music was

dead, and the few people still left on the stern deck by the pool were bund-
ling up and heading indoors.

The wind had picked up precipitously.

Chapter 28: Gordon's Ultimate Love-Act

We stood at the stern handrailing. The pool party was long dead, and Gordon had slipped on his sweatpants and a tee-shirt. We were the last on deck and would soon head off to our little, cramped crew cabin to crash, but for now, we simply enjoyed the quiet and each other's company.

"Look." I pointed up to the sky. "The stars have gone to bed too."

"Yeah," Gordon mused without energy, "it's a lot more cloudy than it was."

We both gazed west. An inky-black formlessness in that direction seemed to further blur the definition of horizon, sky, and water into primal chaos.

"Hey," Gordon said.

I smiled, the kind a person does when they are caught rouge-handed. "Yes?"

The boat heaved like it was riding a giant swell; the sound of the engine became louder for a moment as the props had less to push against.

"You okay? You seem distracted, Kohl."

I was, but I lied. "I'm fine, just thinking about the fake-ass nature of everything."

Gordon laughed. "Oh, thinkin' about everything is your definition of 'fine,' huh?"

I draped my arm around his shoulders. "You probably didn't hear it, but after you got up from our table to put your clothes on, Sadeeq told Lloyd his Leavenworth Matron wasn't a true story at all."

"No?"

"Nope. The mad poet revealed it was actually his screenplay, and wondered if Lloyd knew any showbiz types Sadeeq could pitch it to."

"Yep." My boy nodded gently with the sways of the sea. "That's pretty fake-ass all right. And I halfway bought that story as real too. Just goes to show, you can never be too careful with what people say and the way they act."

I let go of my boyfriend and stepped a pace away. Lightning streaked off the starboard side.

'Oogh,' I thought. 'That comment comes really close to the heart of what's on my mind.'

"Kohl, for God's sake, what's eating you?"

"You going to force me to say it, even if I vowed not to?"

'Well, you better say something."

The boat pitched heavily again, this time in the other direction.

"Okay, here it is then."

Thunder crackled like spitting bacon.

"I saw the way you were flirting with him."

"What! Flirting with who?!"

"Sadeeq's hustler boy, that Frances-Michelle."

"You mean Michael-Francis, but Kohl—"

"For all I know"—I was stupid with anger—"you were playing secret foot-rub-footsies with him under the table. Believe me, I wanted to pop down there and see for myself."

"Oh. My. God."

The dark sky split open and lit half his face again. Thunder cackled immediately while the wind picked up and pelted us with the first drops of icy rain.

"I saw you – you can't deny it."

"And you call Amergin mad. You and your fucked-up jealousy, Kohl, I swear."

I brooded in silence a moment, wiping the rain or tears away with my hand, not knowing or caring which they were.

Gordon touched both of my lower arms. "Are you even serious right now?"

The ship's engine slowed; the rumbling coming through the soles of our feet lessened; more lightning and thunder intruded publicly on our private scene. In the meantime, the rain picked up and began slamming into our bodies at a forty-five-degree angle.

All of a sudden, I regretted my upset: maybe I was building a mouse-hill from a mountain again.

"Kohl?"

"Well...." The boat lurched back to the left and nearly toppled my boy into my arms.

'Fuck it.'

I reached out and embraced him firmly. Instant fulmination, like an old-fashioned photographer's light bulb, lit up every nook and recess of the stern deck brighter than midday for a moment.

"Kohl," he said very calmly and close to my rain-soaked lips. "Sadeeq and that guy went off together to fuck, didn't they? And I'm here with you, aren't I?" Gordon – my sweet boy – was halfway between pissed and tender. Grumbling thunder from the horizon sounded like the Cyclops in his cave while Jason and company were escaping.

"Yes," I admitted lamb-like, all my fury gone.

"Good. Just remember the big things." He suddenly smiled, just as a rolling wave made the ship lurch to portside.

"It's always the same old same old with you." He laughed. "I should have gotten a peace treaty with you too. Even if you only handed over a dollar for each flare up of your jealousy, I'd still be a millionaire in no time!"

More lightning broke, and as I kissed him. Thunder instantly crackled right over our heads.

A couple of sleepless hours later, Gordon lay in my arms. We were fully dressed, in the bunk of our crew cabin with the light on, and counting the perilous swells like sheep jumping off a cliff.

The engine slowed even more, and now and then the lights flickered in a moment of menace, which it did again right now, but came back to 90% almost instantly. At such times of looming darkness, I was forced to think of something I'd suppressed. However...time seemed....

Hugging my boy tighter, I said, "I have something to tell you."

"Oh?"

"Yeah. While you were saying your good-nights to Trọng, Sadeeq and Michael-Francis, Lloyd came up to me at the handrail. We looked out, across the waves together, and he said something to me."

"Oh. Was it serious?"

"Yes. That's why I thought it best to play mum and not let you know. But he told me:

> "'Remember how I said earlier, in the lounge when we agreed to our ceasefire, that I can forgive and forget?'
>
> "'Yes....'
>
> "'Well, it's true, but I still have fear in my heart.'
>
> "'Fear of what?' I asked.
>
> "He sighed. 'Poseidon and Priapus each alerted us of where we'd find you.' The drug lord turned his unflinching gaze on me. 'I may be a professional killer, but I'm not a cruel man. I can't say the gods are the same. However, I accept knowing I might suffer the penalty I've spared the two of you.'"

"What do you think that means, Kohl?"

I swallowed down my distress and shrugged, knowing even my boy's willingness to believe me was not enough to hide my anxiety concerning his wellbeing.

Our cabin went dark all of a sudden. The rumble through the rivets and steel plates of the *Ekdíkisi* sputtered to a grinding halt. All was quiet as the ship rocked helplessly on the stormy seas.

"Oh, my God," Gordon said.

An emergency light went on over the door moments before an intercom crackled to life. We tried not to panic.

The announcement had been for all passengers and crew to put on life vests and proceed to our emergency escape positions. That was all well and good, except that me and my boy had been stowaways until a few hours ago, and had no idea where to go or what to do.

Now, holding onto the slippery handrail and trying to climb our way up to the boat deck, we kept pausing because the vessel was dead in the water and buffeted this way and that in the howling throes of the storm.

We'd managed to find one life vest under the bunk in our crew cabin, so I personally strapped it on Gordon and told him not to take it off under any circumstances.

The boat deck, which is called that because it's where passengers board the rescue craft if need be, was total bedlam when we finally got up there.

Crewmembers tried to keep passengers from being terrified, but found it was a hard task. That was mainly the boat's fault, for foundering as she was, one moment the ship was blown in the eddying direction – pounding everyone on the starboard side of the boat deck with punishing rain and hurricane winds – and then after a few minutes, she'd list hard to port as the *Ekdíkisi's* prow pointed vaguely to the dark and menacing Mexican shoreline.

One bridge officer appeared unexpectedly. He had with him a megaphone and announced to the sailors, "Hurry! We've lost all power and are being driven into the underwater reefs offshore. Don't panic the passengers!"

All the passengers within earshot screamed and began to fight one another for a spot in a lifeboat. Me and my boy, who'd been standing back, feeling confident we'd get a spot once the crew started to load themselves, began to wonder if we should join the melee.

The battery-powered davit motors started to lower the first full lifeboats nearest us. The ship then steadily began listing to starboard, obviously taking on water. We held onto each other and the handrail attached to the wall.

As the boat commenced to right herself, me and Gordon thought about making a move.

Suddenly – with winds screeching and lightning and thunder stronger than ever – Lloyd and Trọng were in front of us. The Vietnamese guy was with his small luggage, including the repatriated and precious Gucci bag.

Even through the din of the storm, the sea captain's angry words were crystal clear. "It's all your fault!"

Without warning, the strong man bent his knees and reached out for Gordon's arms and legs.

A second later, he'd picked him up, saying, "A sacrifice must be made."

Trọng screamed, and both me and him launched ourselves at the crazed man heading towards the boat-deck railing. He was going to toss the teen boy into the drink.

The ship had no intentions of staying level, and quickly listed in the opposite tack from before – to port – or away from the direction Lloyd wanted to go.

The drug lord slipped on the soaked deck boards, and wound up losing his balance, unintentionally throwing the boy into my arms. Trọng came up to our sides.

We moved back towards the wall as the ship slowly returned to horizontal again.

Lloyd, looking like a man possessed, got to his feet and exposed a lot of the lower whites of his eyes as he tilted his head down and stared boreholes through us.

"Atonement must be made, or we all die! Hand him over."

The stalemate set fast, as Trọng tried to shield Gordon from Lloyd's view.

The sea captain faked us out, reaching right but ducking left, where he had a clear shot to grab my boy.

Just then, the *Ekdíkisi* violently rocked starboard again, right as the winds moved the prow south, and brought our side of the ship into the full wrath of the tempest.

For a moment, a strange, time-frozen moment, Lloyd stood perfectly erect. An oddly resigned placidness came over his face. An instant later, fulminating lightning lit up the scene like midday again, and I swear to you, something like dark, invisible fingers reached up from the top of a crashing swell to latch onto Lloyd.

Another impossibly long second passed, and the drug lord was pulled backwards off his feet and into the waves a few stories below.

The three of us ran to the railing, Trọng naturally distraught and crying out simultaneously for help for his partner.

More anger from the sky lit up the scene, and we saw the drug lord tossed like a ragdoll in the churning foam. His light-colored clothes remained visible to us when the darkness returned, and we helplessly watched him be swirled round and round, and eventually swallowed whole by a whirlpool.

Trọng screamed, but just then, a sailor grabbed him, throwing his Gucci into the waves, and tossing the man into a full lifeboat. The crewmember jumped in himself, and the vessel started to lower.

Me and Gordon watched it, only becoming aware that it was the final lifeboat once it got halfway down.

The rain pelted us again, and just then, mid-side along the port hull, the ship struck a reef, hard.

We grabbed onto the railing and each other. The lifeboat crashed into the side of the ship, and terrible screams erupted.

Gordon and me looked over the side, and the boat was still lowering, only now rolling its gunwales over the surface of the *Ekdíkisi*, and threatening to spill out all the passengers and crew into the water.

Just then, the ship careened off the reef again, hurling the lifeboat horizontal and upright onto the swelling seas. A second later, the lines were detached, and me and my boy were left alone on this doomed vessel.

With every swell now, the boat listed less and less. It was clear her hull was rapidly filling with water.

Walking at near forty-degree angles into the brunt of the rain, me and Gordon clung onto one another and began climbing up to the top deck.

Hanging on for dear life, we got as far forward as we could go, for now the swimming pool at the stern of the boat began to slip into the sea.

"Oh, my love, I'm so sorry," I told Gordon. "If not for me, you'd be safe and sound in Aptos, probably with a decent boyfriend and happy."

"Kohl—"

"It's too soon, my boy. Did some great plan unite us only to see us ripped from life before we really had a chance to live it on our own terms – to build our happily ever after?"

The boat turned back away from the storm, as if the keel was affixed to something underwater, creating a pivot point. But, the ocean continued to rise up to our level.

I told him, "The sea is swamping our boat, baby. It won't be long now, so, please – please – come here and give your man one final kiss, before the angry fury of Nature severs our embrace of life."

Gordon didn't come to me. In fact, he disobeyed me completely and undid the clasps of his life vest.

"No!" I shouted, but my boy instantly hugged me, and with a deft hand, lashed the ties around my waist and midsection. We were two within one life preserver.

"Oh, Gordon," I mumbled, feeling tears sting my eyes.

And then, just as I had asked, he kissed me. "Kohl, listen to me now. No matter what takes place, we'll be carried to our fate, together. If we're to die today, then we'll be married in death. If the sea turns compassionate and washes our bodies to land, then I hope some kind stranger will see us, and pile rocks over us through pity, but will keep us together. If the sea has no such heart, still we'll be sunk to the bottom in our embrace, and let the uncaring sediment cover us over, together. Either way, Kohl, our love won't die with us."

He could say no more, for my tearful kisses stopped up his mouth.

Just then, the boat neared a critical angle as it rotated Gordon and me back to the tempest's dreadful anger, and we slipped.

While we were sliding and grasping out to hold onto something, anything, I must have hit the back of my head...and...remembered no more, other than suddenly feeling very wet and sinkingly afraid.

"...deorsum fluens..."

— Part Nine —
Temptation in the Desert

#Château-Wogga-Wogga,

#blue-ships-line, #just-be,

#coerced, #foul-smell,

#beautifully-morose,

#in-a-biblical-way,

#shore-was-clear,

#self-torment,

#Squiffy,

#donkey

Chapter 29: "Fish, Flame or Worm"

If gravity had a color, it would have been black. For dense blackness was what I felt compelled to move through. Sensations of gradually twirling pulled me in all directions at once, as if caught in the invisible tentacles of a formless eddy.

I suddenly panicked. 'Where is Gordon' became an all-consuming refrain in my mind. 'My boy; my boy; my boy; where are you?'

As I continued to be drawn down, down and around into an uncertain event horizon, sadness seemed to sink in the center of my being as well. I felt I had lost my Gordon forever and wished for nothing but insensibility.

Without warning, I perceived a flash of white foam forced to move in the whirlpool of energy with me. Using all my might, I began to 'swim' to it, with each breaststroke feeling hope revive, for the shape was human. Could it be my Gordon? Perhaps I had not lost him after all.

Through herculean efforts to live, to *be* despite darkness insisting that I give up, I reached out to the form. Just barely making contact with the shoulder, it rotated.

Lloyd's frightened eyes made contact with mine. He was the figure, and he was the one sinking to nihility with me.

The dying man reached out arms to grab me. I moved back, out of his grasp, and anger arose within him. Though I could not hear a sound above the static tingle of the vortex, I clearly saw the man's lips move. He said, "It's all your fault!"

He lunged for my throat, and I voicelessly screamed, shielding my eyes.

After a moment or so of abject fear, I gradually perceived the sensation of falling had ceased. It felt as if I were on *terra firma,* and in another moment, birdsong greeted my ear, and then the soft lick of sunshine and a summer breeze touched my skin.

I slowly removed my hands one at a time.

Greenery was all around me. I stood in a slight depression cupped out of the living earth – a hoe was cradled in the crook of my arm.

A foul smell seeped into my nose and I looked down to see I stood at the base of a compost heap, mucking it out as it were. A wide-brimmed Mexican straw hat shielded my eyes from the bright California sun.

I suddenly knew where I was. Aptos.

But before I could even think another thought, a glorious sight appeared. My boy wearing overalls and pushing a wheelbarrow of flowering potted plants.

As he passed on a trail about fifteen feet away, Gordon's sly face turned to me. He smiled, in his sexy way, and jostled his head towards a particular greenhouse.

I waited a couple of minutes, watching Gordon round the side and disappear from view by the building he'd indicated. I felt relief, that, and happiness. I had my boy; all was well.

After a while, I looked around. The shore was clear, so I climbed out of my hole and wiped hands on a bandana from a back pocket. I inched my way around the corner of the greenhouse, full of the pleasure of anticipation – I was hard as a rock.

Before I could see anything, I heard odd sounds. I freed my view beyond the final turn, and there was Gordon bent over a potting table, pants and drawers down by his ankles, Priapus' huge member fucking my boyfriend from behind.

The dirty god's face turned to me, and he shoved with more force, making my lusty partner moan in increased rapture.

With every indication of submission and pleasure, the ugly god-face smirked at me in greater triumph.

My grating breath caught, and I jerked bolt-upright.

Confused, while the sights and emotions of the horrible vision faded, I glanced around. I was in a living room of sorts: wood paneling; bunk seats with cushions; a television mounted near the relatively low ceiling. Small windows and lit wall fixtures told me it was night outside.

My skin was clammy and wet, but I wore a dry robe. It took the rolling of the sea beneath the boat to make me realize this 'living room' was the main cabin of some oceangoing vessel. I looked to my side – Gordon was there.

I scooped up the robe-wearing and sleeping boy tenderly. My happy tears woke him up. He opened his brown eyes and slowly used a thumb to brush my cheek. I vowed internally, most solemnly, that I wanted never to argue or accuse Gordon through jealousy again. There is a quote in German. *Eifersucht ist eine Leidenschaft, die mit Eifer sucht, was Leiden schafft*, which means, Jealousy is a passionate pain, passionately seeking self-inflicted suffering. But I felt done with self-torment through my innocent boy. He deserved none of it.

He indicated a wish to do so, so I helped him sit up. We assessed one another by touch, feeling limbs and legs. Nothing was broken.

He asked, "Do you know where we are?"

"No, baby, but I guess a boat dragged us out of the sea and saved us."

"Oh."

Gordon seemed a little shell-shocked, so I joked, "Think of it this way: it may have required extreme methods, but at least we are free of that mad poet."

All of a sudden, the boat reverberated with the deep and hearty laughter of about a dozen men. In the center of which rose a familiar shrill voice speaking Spanish.

We rose to our feet and followed the sound down a narrow corridor. It opened up at the end into the captain's cabin. There Sadeeq sat, as if a jester in a royal court, entertaining with bawdy stories and jokes.

"Ah!" he cried out, getting up and coming over to us. "You're awake. Good! There will be some grub soon, but in the meantime, I've been telling my new amigos about a true story, *La Matrona de Altiplano*—"

"Where are we?" I wanted to know.

"On a boat, dummy."

"I think that much we got, Sadeeq," said Gordon.

"Oh, yes," the poet muttered. "Seems once the first lifeboats hit the shore, a bunch of fishing vessels, like this one, went out to pick through the shipwreck loot. But when they got there, it turned into a rescue mission."

Gordon asked, "Where is Michael-Francis?"

"Safe. He sent me a text from shore before the boat went down."

By this time, many of the Mexican fishermen had risen. A couple of them squeezed past us, and now the sounds of pots and pans in the galley clanged.

The captain spoke to Sadeeq.

In another minute, the poet turned to us and said, "Now that you're awake, we'll eat, chat and open the tequila!"

As the wet sand and minute particles of debris squished through my toes, my mind drifted onto a promise made and broken long ago, if 'history' is to be believed anyway. I remembered Noah in similar circumstances interpreting the appearance of a rainbow as God's vow to never again hurt mankind in a biblical way, but maybe the gods today heed no such honorable pronouncement. Man certainly doesn't.

It was the morning after the storm, and me and my boy walked along a stretch of shoreline. The incredible blue-azure of the Pacific, along with its plate-glass composure, made it almost impossible to believe a horrendous outburst of bad weather had passed over its surface only twelve hours previous. There were however some wispy dark streaks of cloud in the sky to remind humankind that tempests will be our lot until the end of time.

The little village our rescue vessel pulled into just as dawn was breaking could be considered anything but romantic. A collection of modest houses, and lots of blue tarps here and there to augment roofing shortcomings efficiently.

We had learned many of the *Ekdíkisi's* lifeboats had landed to the north, and the Red Cross was assisting with necessities. We also learned that teams of volunteers had been dispatched to comb the beaches from our village to the main point of contact. So far, about a hundred passengers and crew were unaccounted for, and the official search and rescue mission had progressed to a search and recovery phase.

For the three of us picked up by the fishing trawler, the crew itself had invited us into their homes, but Gordon and I needed to get away for just a bit. The trauma of events weighed heavily on us, so we just held hands and walked; no words were needed for the pair of us to acknowledge just how close to death we'd come, and how precious the new day dawned in our eyes.

My love for my boy knew no bounds, and with this renewal of our lives, I wondered how and when I'd find my cure. When and where we'd be able to lift this curse. A faint hope existed though when I recalled Trọng saying he'd take us to some place sacred to Priapus once we landed in Puerto Vallarta. Sadly, we were many miles north of there, marooned on not just an island of sand, but one in the form of a mighty peninsula, stretching nearly a thousand miles long, while the width of land separating the Sea of Cortez from the placid, blue Pacific was a hundred miles for most of its length.

Baja California had a foreboding kind of beauty. It's craggy bluffs, wind-shorn by eons of precipitation offered little by way of human sympathy, while its interior mountains, hills and parched hallows seemed only fit for rough and tumble plants and armored creatures like armadillos and horned toads.

Gordon tugged on my fingers and led us to a place where the exposed cliff face formed a stony niche.

We sat there for quite a while, just watching the surf roll in.

I eventually put my arm around his shoulder; he rested his head against my chest.

"Are you all right? It's been – well, something awful."

"I'm okay, Kohl. You?"

Did I dare answer the truth? There was always the risk that a 'no' would be misconstrued.

"Getting there," I said. "But I'm glad to be here, with you."

He hugged my waist, pressing his cheek deeper into my shirt. "It makes you think, doesn't it? I mean, is life so tenuous that one moment you can be...and then the next—"

"It's all right, honey. What matters is that we made it somehow. We are now two of the 'lucky ones,' the ones who get a second chance to do more, be more – strive to forge the connections that will matter the most. Do you...feel the same, baby?"

"Yes, Kohl. I feel like – what the hell – how did I make it out okay when others didn't? Is there something I, we, were meant to do."

"All I know is that I'm a hundred percent determined to get rid of this curse. I'll go where I need to, do what I have to to be free of this – for both of us, and for our future, baby."

He stretched and kissed me, and how sweet it was too. My heart beat faster, flushed with the incredible renewal of my life's blood.

I rose to my feet, pulling my boy up and brushing sand off of his backside.

Hand in hand, we continued to walk...until....

It was about a hundred yards farther along, in a very similar niche to the one where we had sat. At first, a dash of out-of-place color drew our attention. We walked up and found Hesus and Tanguay. They were dead, but lashed together with blue ship line – the ship's ropes – expertly knotted in front. So we knew they had done the same as Gordon did with us, tied themselves to one another for better or worse.

Through our tears, we went to work. While I prepared a shallow depression on top of the cliff, Gordon collected rocks. Eventually, we undid the ropes, picking up Hesus and placing him first in their joint grave. We positioned his left arm to lay flat. Then we moved Tanguay, the fire gone out of this feisty redhead, and positioned him in his partner's embrace.

We carefully wound the cordage and placed it at their feet. Then we moved the sandy soil over them, before covering over the grave with enough stones to keep carrion birds and coyote at bay.

Again, no words passed between Gordon and me; none were needed. We were performing the sad obsequies Gordon had prayed on the *Ekdíkisi* would be done to our remains. Here, unexpectedly, we were doing it for others, not so secretly glad we were the ones allowed to find them and honor their love by carrying it forward into the grave.

Once we'd finished, the afternoon was getting long in the tooth, but we stood by Hesus and Tanguay's burial place, arm in arm.

These words came to me, and I said them for our mirrored selves in the tomb.

> "Hand and foot are we thus tied to the wheel,
> Fortune raising one, and the other drown,
> While all the while just daring us to feel
> Her decisions are mean, cruel or unsound.
> Too often the injustices are great
> That life forces upon our attention;
> Too much havoc in our souls they create,
> When what we want is rest and redemption.
> Hand in hand, let us stand as life's witness
> To celebrate what little time we share,
> And thereby acknowledge our love's greatness
> To shoulder with us the burdens we bear.
>> Chaos and cruelty, come do your worst,
>> For the human spirit won't be coerced."

We slowly made our way back, feeling like we'd completed a day of penance. Hunger returned as we neared the village in the long light of early evening, but things were not right.

Going up to a tightly clustered crowd on the beach, we found Sadeeq there too.

"What is it?" I asked, pulling his shoulder back slightly.

"See for yourself."

Gordon and I excused our way to the front of the assembled people, all of whom had removed their hats and clenched them tightly at their waists. We arrived just in time to see two men remove a braided noose of kelp from a drowned man's neck.

Lloyd's body was still soaked, as if a vengeful sea had only now disgorged the drug lord's lifeless remains back to the land for burial within it. Humanity was called upon to deal with one of its own.

Chapter 30: Marigolds

An alabaster pediment glowed sadly near the ceiling. It was held in place by two Corinthian pillars, which also shimmered softly from the funeral parlor lighting within. This was the setting afforded the final rites of a feared and honored drug lord.

From back to front, the wall enshrined by the columns and pediment supported a large framed picture of Lloyd in black and white. Around it were foliage and blossoms of yellow mums and marigolds, while on a table below the portrait rested a bust of Jesús Malverde, the Mexican narco-saint. His pediment too was bathed in soft light and sat atop palm fronds speckled with more golden-orange flowers.

The stoic plaster eyes of this venerated icon stared straight over Lloyd's open casket; Malverde presided in judgeless gravity while the rest of us got on with life and the burying of our dead.

Flanking it, two tall pillar candles demarcated the head and foot of Lloyd's coffin, and off to their sides stood six-foot-high easels, festooned with wreaths of green and yellow foliage.

To the left and right, tables were piling up with gifts: bottles of Scotch and tequila; cartons of cigarettes; bright red pastries; green and yellow citrus plucked with healthy stems and leaves still attached; mounds of banana and plantains. And all was illuminated by tiers and tiers of flickering tea lights.

As people made a slow progress past the dead man lying in state, no one seemed to begrudge Lloyd's orientation in life, at least not under El Bandido Generoso's carful inspection.

Uniquely, Lloyd was dressed in a suit with a turtleneck sweater. When I saw him, I gasped at knowing why; the bruises under it were brutal, and their existence meant he was still alive when the kelp cordage asphyxiated him.

"Beautifully morose ceremony, isn't it?" Sadeeq asked in a low voice from my side.

As honored guests, and near-family to the deceased, we'd been given positions to stand beside one of the gift tables. Our duties were light though, and mainly consisted in nodding as passersby made deposits of presents for the afterlife.

"It's very solemn and beautiful," I told him.

"Octavio Paz said: 'For the inhabitant of New York, Paris or London, *death* is not spoken, lest it burn the lips in passing. The Mexican, by way of contrast, belittles it, cherishes it, calls it sweetheart.'"

I stared the poet in the eye. "Pablo Neruda: 'If nothing saves us from death, may love at least save us from life.'"

He nodded his head. "Well played, my fellow poet."

"I want to take a couple of these flowers for later."

"Ah, yes." A smile arose on the mad poet's visage. "Gordon will like that, and since he couldn't attend this—"

"Well, he had to make arrangements, and he speaks Spanish, so...."

"Yes. Taking a few flowers is a perfect idea." His hand reached out to stroke a vibrant saffron-colored blossom. "Do you know the significance of marigolds to Mexican culture? It dates back to long before the Spanish arrived."

"Flower of death?"

"Yes and no. To them it's both a remembrance of death and sacrifice – Aztec rituals to the sun god – but so too it has meanings of reunion and connectedness in love and relationships."

He had said this in a warm way, and naturally. I smiled. "So, it's perfect then."

Sadeeq nodded. "We'll get a pair for your lapels."

It excited me to know the lives of me and my boy – no, correction: of Gordon and me – would be changed by the early hours of the evening. However, that notion put me in mind of Lloyd's partner. "It's a shame Trọng couldn't be here, where he belongs."

"Well, as I said, it seems most of the *Ekdíkisi's* survivors have already been put on busses for San Diego."

"Yes, but still—"

"I know. But he's here in spirit."

Just as he said that, a large group of young men filed in. They all wore suits similar to the photos I'd seen on the wall of Lloyd's shrine. Bearing no gifts, other than the intense gravity set upon their shoulders, the others in line to view the body stepped aside. The young men came up to the casket like a sad troupe of pilgrims, individually trekking to an icon of sacrifice each and every one of them was prepared to make because of their chosen profession.

Christ's words about living and dying by the sword have never been better actuated or exampled than by this line of young men paying tribute to a fallen comrade.

As I watched, I thought that if this life is rightly considered, shipwrecks are lurking at every turn, looming partially seen over every horizon. If so, then which is better? To die in the cold depths of the sea; to go out in a blaze of glory for what you consider a worthy cause; or to molder and die in bed as a faint whisper of your old self – you tell me which is better. Which inequity can be said to be any nobler than the others when fish, flame or worm, all of us are supposed to be consigned to what we consider a painless hereafter. So, rather than live in fear of it, we should acknowledge Death is all around us. Moreover, it has the power to be a great unifier – the ultimate equalizer – for gluttons die in feast; misers in soul-starved suffocation; health fanatics and joggers of heart attacks; slackers of thrombosis. Simply put, there is nothing about life that is not fatal.

What matters is to choose it actively every day.

A few months ago, I wondered where 'our future' lie, and back then the obvious answer seemed a joke. Today, no. Life is no joke, nor is it something to run from. It's been twenty-four hours since my boy said yes, proving he loves even the broken version of me, but my better half and I will re-commit to finding a cure and putting things right. Or, I have no doubt, we will die trying.

□ □ □ □ □

"So what," Sadeeq said flatly. He'd propped elbows on the small table and was twisting his sparse ponytail in mock nonchalance. "So what? We couldn't stay with the fishermen in their homes any longer. They collected coins and convinced the hotelier to put us up, didn't they?"

Gordon stated the obvious. "Yeah. For one night; after that, who knows."

"Well, sometimes one night is all it takes." The mad poet laughed at his own insider-joke. My boy and me just stared him down.

"And," I added on a serious note to Gordon, "this one night *is* special —"

"I know; I know!" Sadeeq barked like a bounding puppy.

I turned to him. "So, stay out of our room for the night, please. Just one night, Sadeeq – please."

He smiled and nodded, leaving me to believe he'd gotten the point. We'd see.

"Where will we stay tomorrow?" Gordon asked sadly.

"We'll be together, honey. That's what matters." I raised his hand and kissed it.

"Yeees," cheeped Sadeeq. "As the old saying goes, one day at a time, but at least we'll be together."

My boy and me glanced at each other, just daring the other to laugh. Instead, I told the poet, "Or, maybe it's better to quote your President Lincoln, who said 'It better to take things one war at a time.'"

There was only one hotel in town, and it was orientated as a series of walled haciendas with terraces and sea views. The bar, where we were relaxing now after a long day, was likewise comprised of an indoor area and a long, ocean-facing patio.

The cooling breeze on my arm around Gordon's back felt great, and the rhythmic crashing of the surf always soothed.

Not too many people were out here on the terrace with us, but at the bar sat a pair of handsome local boys killing time and looking for girls or guys to hang out with. Right now, they were laughing at some antics occurring at the other end of the bar.

I followed their eyes to a seated woman – perhaps a 'professional' –

and a standing man leaning heavily on the bar to talk to her. He stuck out like a sore toe, for not only his wrinkled linen sack of a suit and shapeless Panama hat, but for his off-kilter speech. I didn't have to know the language to realize he was speaking Spanish with a thick, mush-mouth British brogue – or speech impediment, as that word means – for it was pompous almost to the point of incredulity. The half-drunk man tried to ooze charm on the young lady, no doubt fishing for a pity-drink from her.

I broke off watching, not wanting to draw his attention to us, lest he sniff his way over here like a hound scenting a bone.

Turning my attention to Gordon, it was easy to get lost in the rich brown pools of his gaze. Over the yokes of our chairs hung our borrowed suit jackets. Seeing them, and his eyes, put me in mind of standing in the courtroom this afternoon and noting the likewise-borrowed marigolds in our lapels from Lloyd's wake. I took my vow to Gordon with 'death till we part' sincerity. The ceremony was simple and honest, and would have been perfect if not for the necessity of needing the mad poet there as witness.

A smiling waiter arrived. In his arm he cradled a napkin-encased bottle; gold foil protruded from the end.

He set down a folded card, and Gordon picked it up first.

While the server began to uncover the cork, and uncage the libation, my boy read and translated the accompanying message.

"It's from – well, here. Listen:

> "Congratulations to the
> young *señores* on their nuptials.
>
> A long, happy life to you both!
>
> Captain López,
> *El pez espada*."

POP!

The champagne cork unleashed a tremendous sound.

Gordon and I kissed, and the whole bar erupted into applause and raised glasses. With my eyes closed, and the celebratory clatter in my ears, I was happy but troubled too. Our wedding night would not be as it should because of the curse, but I'd please my boy – my husband – of that I was sure.

When I opened my eyes, I noticed Sadeeq looking at something to my left.

The disheveled *gringo* from the bar was making his way over. He sat down, effortlessly crossing his legs and latching onto a glass. "Don't mind if I do." A sticky grin parted his thin lips as he held the drinking vessel up for the server to fill.

Sadeeq nodded at the waiter, who obviously knew the panama-hat-wearing intruder was a parasite, but poured anyway.

The lanky Brit impatiently waited as the rest of us were attended to.

"What's the joyous occasion, if you don't *mind* me asking?"

He removed his hat, using a knee as a hall tree. The man then brushed back his thinning and greasy badger hair – black with a central white streak. His face was gaunt, although engaging eyes tried to flicker out from his semi-permanent drunkenness to take in his surroundings. The man and his clothes had the smell of fuel about them.

Sadeeq explained, "The occasion is the wedding of my friends here, Kohl and Gordon."

The Brit stranger raised an eyebrow, but he also lifted his glass. "Cheers. Many happy returns and *many* blissful years together."

He downed his champagne before any of us could get a glass to our lips. Then, as the waiter was leaving and setting the bottle down, the man grasped at it and poured himself another.

Just then, one of the ubiquitous stray dogs about town came up, sniffing at the shabby drinker's pant cuffs. The man grunted and swept it aside with his wing-tipped foot.

"Damn mongrels, they have a *penchant* for not leaving me alone. Squiffy Wellington, *at* your service."

"Sadeeq Amergin." The poet forced a handshake on the man. "Social media poet and internet sensation. Follow me at *American-4-all.biz*."

"Ahh," Squiffy eked out audible disdain, "an American. *How* charming. And you two...?" He vaguely motioned our way before draining and refilling his glass again.

"I'm German. Gordon is from Northern California."

"Well, as I said – Squiffy Wellington. Yes, *that* one."

The three of us exchanged glances.

Gordon asked, "That one, what?"

"My dear boy," he said, highly exasperated. "There's only one *me*. Squiffy Wellington!" He squeegeed his greasy hair with a free palm.

We gave him no reaction, nor indeed, had any to offer.

"Come now; come now. You must *know* me; celebrity tell-eey chef. *Squiffy Sautés Africa*; *Squiffy Stews South America*; *Squiffy Stir-Fries the Orient;* I had my own bloody BBC cookery show *for* decades."

I resisted the strong urge to ask: 'So, how'd that work out for you?'

"Yes, yes," Wellington mused, grabbing a passing waiter by the arm and popping the now-empty champagne bottle in his hands. "Shall we"— he asked us—"order another bottle? They make *them* so small these days. Hardly enough for one...or something different—"

Before we could answer, he'd already told the server, "*Una botella de vino tinto*, por *favor*."

"So what do you do now?" Sadeeq seemed to be drawn in by the man's insufferable affability.

"Now, my dear North-of-the-Border friend, I do *as* I please: I go where I like; I eat...what I can....I sleep beneath *the* stars some evenings on the warm *Playa público*, while other nights I slumber in an abandoned tequila vat."

"In a what?" Gordon asked.

"It seems a former mayor used to indulge himself and *his* local political party in quite a *penchant* for the fiery stuff. He had it shipped in by the barrelful. One of the old wooden containers rolled down hill to the city dump, and forms my own little corner *of* heaven. It retains the sweet smell of mother's milk in it, and I find I need it to get to sleep these days."

"And is Squiffy your real name?" the poet asked out of curiosity.

"Good gracious, no. It's one *of* those old-boy names one acquires in public schools – which naturally enough means exclusive, *private* schools in Britain – and it stuck. I'm not even sure I could conjure my *real* name anymore. 'Squiff's' even on the passport."

A bottle of red wine arrived, and Squiffy topped up his champagne glass to the brim. To be frank, he looked a bit nervous. "I don't usually come out this *time* of night, however, this evening is the exception. You see"—he glanced around the room with hunched shoulders—"the wife of the current mayoral *alcalde* fancies me, and has arranged a tryst for later on. I'm here to fortify myself for *a* performance of a different kind than cooking in front of a camera."

He laughed at his own joke.

I asked, "Did the mayor's wife give you any cash for the arrangements?"

"No. Why...?"

"Because we're broke too. We're survivors of the *Ekdíkisi* disaster." I paused for acknowledgement of our dire straits; none came.

After sitting back again and languorously draining half his glass, he said blasély, "Oh. Do tell."

Gordon, incensed, quipped, "We're marooned here. No money. No homes."

"Yes, rather like me then." He 'shooed' away another dog with a meaningful swoosh of his heel. "You're not *an* American, are you?"

"I'm German."

"Ah, yes, indeed. Dreadful cuisine – all crimson cabbage and *red* vinegar. No wonder you're in Mexico; you wanted to get something decent to eat."

I gave up. I didn't see the point in arguing of our poverty with someone who didn't care.

"So, you sleep in a tequila vat. That sounds interesting," Sadeeq said with genuine interest.

I just realized something. "Didn't some old Greek do that?"

Blank-eyed, Squiffy inquired, "I beg *your* pardon?"

"A philosopher. I remember something about one living in a wine barrel in Athens."

The washed-up TV chef took a sturdy drink. "Never heard of him. And I hardly do anything 'Old Greek' anymore. At least not since my fagging days at school. Not that I mind *your* love-style, young man. Get your wild oats sown while *you* can, and luckily you won't get snared by *a* shrill harpy who'll divorce you *a* mere four decades later...." [28]

His tone drifted off into a general grumble concerning the female of our fickle species.

"You, young men," he finally said with conviction and a pointing finger, "*are* lucky."

And to that I wholeheartedly agreed by smiling and taking Gordon's hand above-table.

"But regarding knowledge of this Greek *philo* chap, I suppose I do not feel comfortable *with* anyone openly willing to display more knowledge *than* me. It's the sort of intellectualism run rampant these days."

I scoffed silently to myself. What a typical Drump-head contempt for 'intellectuals' this man just coughed up like phlegm. I laughed. "Only in this brave-less new world could a lazy, shiftless German substitute teacher like me be ridiculed as an intellectual. Well, so be it."

The man popped on his formless hat – backwards – and stood up. He slurred something about "needing the loo," but grabbed the bottle firmly by the neck before skulking off.

"That's it," I said. "We're rid of him. See? He's already slipping out the door, thinking he's stiffed us with the tab."

The three of us laughed, but I was gladdened by the thought that I'd never see Squiffy Wellington again.

At least the archaic PC in our hacienda could access the internet, and Gordon called me over to watch something, once he'd found an old cooking program. "This one is the opening episode to the *Squiffy Simmers Down Under* series."

I pulled up a chair, not knowing what to expect.

The opening sequence was a gorgeous shot of blue ocean: a large sailing yacht slicing through the waves with sails vivacious and full of air.

The scene cut to a well-appointed galley where Squiffy – looking at least ten years younger than the desiccated specimen we knew – stood there miserably as he swayed back and forth with the moving vessel.

He held a bottle of champagne tightly on the countertop for support.

"Welcome to our new series. Currently I'm – *God* knows why – somewhere on the Indian Ocean, off the shore of sun-parched Perth"—he made mocking-fun of the Aussie vowels—"Auuuh-STaaa-leeah."

He unwrapped the foil-clad bottle as he continued.

"My producer, that is my darling wife, thought it would be *fun* to film a sequence on a moving yacht, but where is *she* when I need her *producing?!* Projectile-tossing vegemite Lamington cakes over the side of the boat. So it's just me and my intrepid cameraman, Harry."

The cork popped and a spew of bubbly erupted, which the middle-aged man slurped up with mouth to bottle.

"So, as you *can* see"—he moved to the stove, not daring to let the bottle out of his grasp—"I have water, a mess *of* garlic for our Australian friends, and now we add the clams with a healthy dose of Aboriginal wine. You may choose your favorite *varietal,* such as a fine Sydney Syrup, or if unavailable, a pinch of Cuvier Reserve Château Wogga Wogga will do." He looked sly all of a sudden. "You Monty Python fans out there will know *what* I mean. Oh, dear. Now Harvey, I mean Hubert, is scowling at me." [29]

He held up the bottle.

"*This,* my friends, I have been assured is some *of* Auustraalia's finest, and I take their word *for* it, but when in Rome, drink like a slave, I suppose."

Squiffy dumped in some onion and chopped parsley. They smoked violently while he set the empty dishes on the counter.

The boat suddenly ratcheted up its rocking.

"Steady on, and aim the camera properly, Harold, darling. Get my best side, there's a good chappie."

By now Gordon and I were helplessly laughing our asses off. It was like watching a circus where the animals were holding the whips over the humans; you didn't want to watch, but you couldn't turn away!

In another second, the unfilled ingredient plates went crashing to the floor, making a nerve-shattering racket.

"Oh, well," announced Squiffy. "It was cheap, *local* crockery anyway. At least I saved *the* so-called sparkling wine."

He held the bottle to his lips, and the rest of the sequence was devoted to making the audience at home watch him drain the bubbly while his clams burned in sooty billows behind his back. Once empty, he frowned at the camera and said, "Welcome to bloody Down Under."

We couldn't stop howling with laughter, gripping onto one another for support.

Now we knew how and why he had had a show for decades; it was produced like a reality TV sitcom. Oh, man. We book-marked more links to watch later. The series called *Squiffy Smokes Through Canada* looked highly promising for its comedic content; or, maybe the *Squiffy Shishkebabs the Middle East,* lol.

We had left the poet about an hour ago in the bar, with me giving him one final warning to leave us alone tonight, of all nights, and he agreed, although with puppy-dog eyes and a pouting lower lip.

Now, after we'd showered and changed into shorts and tees, the cool ocean breeze coming from our fully open terrace felt great on our skin, prickled with laughter as we were.

Suddenly, Gordon placed tender palms on both my cheeks and drew me in for a kiss. My heart thumping with mirth, easily transitioned to beating hard with love for my spouse. We may not have known what tomorrow would bring, but the here and now was what mattered.

"Honey," I said, pulling away after a few minutes. "The funeral this morning made me re-vow to do what I need to to end this hex on my *Schwanz*."

"I know, Kohl. We'll track down Trọng's Priapus lead, and actually, one old woman today told me the place we may want is not near Puerto Vallarta at all."

"No?"

"No. She told me it's closer to us right now, and on Baja California. It's an ancient place, she said."

"Did...she...say...how long—"

I was stopped mid-thought, for behind Gordon, I saw a white, formless thing be thrown over one of our hacienda walls.

We stood up and walked to the open patio doors. Our 'visitor' was a crumpled panama hat.

A moment later, sounds of excursion and pants preceded Squiffy Wellington clambering up to the crest of wall.

Once he was fully straddled across the top, roast-pig fashion, he paused, noticing our astounded stares at him. "Evening, gents. Lend *a* hand...?"

I honestly felt like getting a broomstick and poking him back where he came from, lol. But my better half pulled me with him to the wall, and we helped the drunkard down onto our terrace.

Once on his feet, he sprightly scooped up his hat, and ushered us into the room. He then closed the doors and drew the blinds.

Stopping him as he was turning out the lights, I asked none-too politely, "What is going on?!"

"My escapade with the mayoral missus went horribly *a*-wry, and now I need *to* get away."

"What happened?" Gordon asked.

Squiffy turned to me. "It's something you know about, dear boy – I can't *get* it up."

"And how, pray tell," I inquired with false patience, "would you know such an intimate detail about me?"

"Your social media *friend*. After you two left, I went back and drank with him. He went on and *on* about your condition – your peckless pecker, shall *we* say."

Just then, Sadeeq strolled in the front door, toting a six-pack of beer, "Hi, guys, It's me. What'er we up to?"

'*Gott im Himmel*,' I thought as I walked past him and locked the door. 'Just one night! That's all I asked.'

Sadeeq spotted the down-n-out TV chef. "Ah, Squiffy, *Old Boy*, how was the rendezvous?"

"Dreadful, dear soul. Simply *dreadful*. I'm afraid it's the usual problem again. But now I must flee, because there's nothing worse than an unsatisfied woman. I fear she'll turn the town loose on me."

"Oh," Sadeeq said.

"Um—" Gordon tried to say, but was cut off.

"What *I* need – what this young man here needs"—Wellington put a hand on my shoulder—"is the Spanish fly. The real stuff made from the aquamarine shell of the blister beetle. I've heard tell of a town in the desert where one can get it, and the Aztecs used *to* go there to 'take the cure,' or pluck the feather of Quetzalcoatl, as they used to *call* it."

I glanced at Gordon, feeling, I for one was not too sure about joining forces with the TV hasbin, but my boy seemed more optimistic.

"I don't know if we should leave this place," Sadeeq said. "The people here have been generous supporting us."

"OH, dear sport. I've had further intelligence that this town *in* the wilderness is an eccentric place where poetry and poets *are* highly valued."

A slow smile crept across Amergin's face. "Welcome to the gang, Squiffums, old chapareeno. It's settled, and we'll be off to this town then!"

"Wait a minute; just wait a minute," I said. "How are we going to get to this weird shang-gra-la-la land where poets are valued?"

Squiffy popped the hat on his head, holding himself a little more erect with the pride of purpose. "Allow me. I have a friend who *can* arrange means of transport." He moved to the front door to make an exit. "We will leave at first light, so be ready. And," he added gratuitously, "don't *do* anything strenuous tonight. You'll need your strength."

His leaving the hacienda left me with a feeling I was still not too sure about. We needed to find Priapeans to un-*Behexen* me, and it seemed unlikely the donkey dick folks would have a desert outpost. But then again, with them you never know, and I have come to realize...they are rather like fly poop – everywhere you look.

Chapter 31: A Journey Inland

The way the exposed strata of cliff faces angled sharply in the afternoon sunlight reminded me of bolts of fabric seen from the folded end.

Darker layers of stone were probably the bottoms of ancient seabeds, but now ribboned themselves through berms of softer sandstone to form vistas and valleys. On the floor of these hollows, scrubland plants fought tenaciously for life, refusing to give up hope on the monsoons yet to arrive.

The sky behind this scenery of green and rock was plate-glass blue, and clung on jealously to little wisps of clouds. These formations were not enough to provide shade down on the ground, so despite knowing how silly we looked, I was glad Sadeeq had picked up some broad, workman sombreros at the public market for our journey.

And what a journey it'd been. My aching backside could tell you stories of sore. It turned out the mode of transportation Squiffy Wellington had in mind were donkeys. His friend had lent us the pack animals, which although slower, allowed us to avoid the main road and its patrolmen. We cut straight across the desert, and keeping my eye on the subtle changes in landscape took my mind off my discomfort for the most part. Especially the differing forms of the towering saguaro cactus. These with arms of two, three, and sometimes four, housed intrepid birds who'd peck out cozy nesting cavities amid the barbed-wire line of vertical needles.

Clumps of paler-green paddle cacti littered the canyon floor here and there, and although the wrong season, I knew the tops of each healthy 'pad' would produce a shower of red flowers in celebration of the life-renewing rain.

Some other, even lighter-colored plants popped up singly from the sandy soil. They grew taller than the paddle cactus, which they seemed to congregate around, but looked for all the world like spiky sea coral, sprouting serpentine branches from a crinkle-crankle stalk.

Despite my best efforts to keep my poetic mind occupied with the slowly passing environment, I couldn't quite shut out the endless inane patter the former celebrity chef and current-day mad poet kept up from the backs of their burros. No amount of ambling or dry heat seemed to rob them of speech, unfortunately. I'd come to regard Squiffy's manner of expression as unpleasant – a mouth parched for loquacious moisture seemed apt analogy – for with this British man, his word choice aimed to sting. However, worse yet was the way a certain acid tinge inflected emphasis on syllables which tended to be languid in the mouths of others. But not in his, either passing under or over his sharp, ever-honing tongue.

I glanced to my side, to my boy. We had nothing, but it felt good to travel light, and he looked cute on the back of his mouse-colored donkey.

"Are you all right, honey?" He looked tired.

"Wish we were there, that's all."

Squiffy shouted back, "It's not far now. As the nooseman said to the condemned, 'Just *hang* tight. It'll be over before you know it!'" He laughed and laughed; did so to the point of needing to pull out his canteen, which we knew was full of firewater. The man took a swig, raising squinting eyes to the sun slowly but surely retreating in the west. It was back along the way we'd come.

Just then my burro stiffened his muscles below me, and a great horned lizard scurried lightning-fast off the narrow trail in front of us.

Following the way it ran, I was surprised to see large-eared coyotes peppered along a nearby ridge. Brazenly, they just hung out like medium-sized dogs commanded to 'sit' and watch our little party pass. They were well within sight, but clearly out of reach if one or all of us decided to go after them.

If the sun hadn't broiled my brain yet, I might have persuaded myself that their canine eyes stayed locked on the currish TV chef. It crossed my mind how every stray seemed interested in the food sophist-savant.

"And this mysterious place we're going to, where poetry and poets are admired, does that extend to some of the more 'eager' young men?"

Squiffy bounced a hard laugh off the canyon walls. It was delivered at Sadeeq's expense. "You mean, randy *old* sod, to stir the creative juices?"

"Precisely," replied the poet in all due seriousness.

Wellington bounded back on his donkey for a moment in silence, then used his panama hat as a fan, saying, "I'm sure you won't have trouble finding *eagers* of both genders."

"I was just thinking," enthused Sadeeq, "what with 'the cure' in the waters and the availability of the genuine Spanish fly, I should be more than ready to accommodate any willing young acolyte looking for a mentor."

"Oh, I know, dear chap. I know. There was a time young women threw themselves at my feet, or kitchen clogs, to *be* more accurate. Why, I remember a time in Rio, this fine young *senhora* had bundled herself on the bottom shelf of a room catering *trolley*. Let me tell you, *the* service at the Ao Al-mofadinha Hotel was exquisite."

'Yeah,' I thought, 'and I'm sure the girl's services were duly included on the hotel tab.' It was the kind of story that sounded made up anyway. As such, Sadeeq felt honor-bound to try and top it.

"That's nothing!" exclaimed the mad muse-abuser.

"Nothing...?" The chef was astounded.

"Indeed. Here's a hotter incident that happened to me. When I first started my social media blitz, this boy – underage boy – contacted me from Israel. He was a real kosher firecracker, this kid, and started flirting shamelessly with me. Anyway, comes his summer break, and his family in Israel are shipping him off to relatives in Seattle. The crafty bugger booked a *lay-over* – if you know what I mean – for six hours in L.A. I won't go into details, but let's just say the boy's flight to the Pacific Northwest was a hard one to sit through, but I'm sure he was grinning the whole way."

'More made-up rubbish,' I thought. 'Total BS.' I bet these guys had never been even halfway close to an honest brush with the law.

Sadeeq cried all of a sudden, "Who wants to hear another one of my masterpieces?"

Since he was looking at me, I shrugged, with both Gordon and his donkey turning accusatory eyes on me. I guess I should not encourage him; our mad poet had been droning out his own lamentations and elegies for most of the afternoon.

"This one," he announced with pride, "I call the *Reykjavik Rainbow*:

"From besieged Moscow and Washington they came,
To a barren strip of volcanic sand,
Close by Reykjavik, before it had fame
As the place two troubled leaders would stand
Halfway between their capitals in Iceland;
 Great opportunities came so seldom,
 Especially those of equilibrium.

Old men in overcoats, there the two stood,
Amidst October winds and a bleak sky,
A shot at peace seemed a real unlikelihood,
For forty years of stalemate could belie
Neither side was willing to give peace a try
 Because the military industry
 Said concord was nothing but a travesty.

The Hofdi House, a charming gingerbread treat,
Hosted this unusual world event
In a home so charming it seemed obsolete
For a world of nuclear weapons bent
To propose no less than Man's extinguishment;
 To say we teetered on the brink is true,
 As minutes on the Doomsday Clock did accrue.

Handshakes for cameras, Gorbachev already
In the house, anxious to begin the talks,
And soon the scope would prove Reagan unready –
At total peace on the table he balks –
Threatens that the Americans and he walks
 If such high-faluting stakes are at play
 As changing the course of the world in a day.

Inside then, and settled in the dining room,
The Soviet laid it all on the line:
His people suffered the Cold War's deepest gloom,
Plowshares beat to swords seemed no longer fine

If privation and hunger were to consign
    The future they had to a distant past;
    And leave the skies permanently overcast.

Unready was Reagan, on that gray-cloud eve,
To trust his so-called enemy at all,
So nothing was accomplished one could believe
Proved a new world was born this day in fall,
Yet something like Fate's writing was on the wall:
    'Encourage the bold and let it be your guide;
    Never seek war as a cozy place to hide.'

Unable to sleep, the tired man sought counsel.
George Shultz was cagy, uncompromising,
But even he thought this accord could chronicle
A change others might be recognizing
As a great diplomatic thaw before spring.
    Armed, the next day's meetings would rearrange
    The distrust among men and bring about change.

Agreements flew fast and steady all that day
As Gorbachev saw four decades of neglect
Be patched up one by one without delay –
And all the misconceptions made correct
Where man to man two opinions could connect.
    Great the will of man when it's put to use,
    Free of bias, prejudice and all abuse.

And to seal the peace, then the gray skies parted,
Showing over Reykjavik a rainbow,
Reminding us how God's vow started
Post-flood, when new life had a chance to grow,
That never again on Man would He bestow
    The threat of our destruction if not our own;
    If not ready for our own sins to atone." [30]

Sadeeq was far from done, but as he drew in a breath and contemplated what came next, Squiffy interjected.

Swaying lightly on the back of his burro, the ex-celeb said nonchalantly, "I met Reagan, *once*."

Gordon perked. "Oh, really?! We learned all about him in History class. About how he bankrupt the country by giving arms dealers free rein, trickled up all the tax benefits to the rich, and made ketchup a 'vegetable' on school menus. So what did you say to him?"

"I said, 'Get out *of* my light.'"

Sadeeq was stunned. "Really? Get out of my light?"

"Yes, old chap. We were about *to* start filming a segment for my

Squiffy Skewers America series. It was on *how* to debone a pardoned Thanksgiving turkey on the White House lawn. And then, *he* interrupted so I told him to move."

We weary pack of travelers were a bit speechless, and if I'm honest, the burros even seemed to shrug at that one.

Exasperated, Squiffy Wellington exclaimed, "The show must go on, dearies. I suppose you'd have to be *a* celebrity like Ronald Reagan or myself to understand." Being misunderstood as he was, the man resorted to the 'comfort' of his 100-proof canteen. "Yes, I've known PMs, presidents, princes and the lot, but not a one of them would bow to me today, so far *have* I fallen."

"Cheer up, Squiffy, old boy," Sadeeq told him.

"No, no, it's true. As a bum and a beggar, I make *a* tragic-but-profitless figure."

"How so?" Gordon asked.

"Simple. Put a lame man out there, *on* the sidewalk with a tin cup, or put a woman with a white cane *in* a train station with a plate for coins, and they'll be able to profit a bit by their misfortune. It's true. They'll be able to eke out a living from the *able*-bodied masses. But, put me *in* the same locations...?"

"Yes? And what would happen?" I asked.

"Why, nothing would happen. I'd starve. *Do* pay more attention, dear boy. The moral of *the* story is this: People will mindlessly toss coins at *the* lowly in an attempt to assuage an angry Fate from making themselves go limp, or as tribute to a capricious godhead who might smite them blind at any moment, but none of those selfsame *kindhearts* ever imagine they could be *a* down and out television celebrity, so I'd go hungry. Just me and Matt Lauer, I suppose...."

Gordon and I exchanged eye-rolls. We wanted to laugh in relief of the tension, but it would have been wrong to chortle at another man's genuine misery, no matter how flamboyant a form that suffering took.

"And worst yet," added Squiffy, "never mind hunger – I *thirst!*"

"Not with us you won't, my friend." Sadeeq was quick to reassure by patting the extra canteen of jet juice he'd packed on his donkey. The sagacious poet knew the man leading us through this wasteland as guide had to be placated and properly lubricated, lest he turn as capricious as the godhead so recently cited.

The landscape opened up again and the trail began to rise. It appeared as if we were heading to a pass through two sloping mesas, but it would still be quite a long time until we surmounted the highest point.

Our donkeys started to labor a bit with the incline, and I looked to my boy. He'd been a bit quiet on this trip.

"What about you, young man," the washed-up TV personality said to me. "Any war stories about conquests?"

Gordon laughed. "Don't ask him. We'll be here for days."

"Yeah," Sadeeq chimed in. "I imagine as a teacher, some temptation or other has presented itself to you."

Not immediately acknowledging Gordon's blush – because the poet's description fit Gordon's taking me in the supply closet to a tee – I said, "No, not really."

The lecherous poet smiled in a way I knew would get me in trouble with my boy.

"Well, there's one personal experience I could be convinced to share..." Sadeeq got into storytelling mode. "This happened pretty soon after I graduated from college. I needed some money, so I accepted a job as a live-in tutor to shape up this boy's ability to take university entrance exams.

"I knew I'd just be living there for a few months, but this kid – let's call him 'Ralph' – proved a huge temptation, not the least of which was because of his innocent face belying an already-raunchy heart. He was truly beautiful and I wanted him, only learning later that he'd already seduced every boy in his class.

"One fine evening, we were studying in my room well past midnight and he fell asleep on my floor, only I knew it was all an act. So I knelt by his side and pretended to pray. 'Dear god of Love, who art in heaven, or wherever, if only I might kiss this boy without his awakening, I'll give him a pair of video games as reward.'

"Once he heard the value of the requested favor, he started to snore.

"So I 'stole' a few passionate kisses with the hot boy lying there like a faker, and good to my word, the next morning I trotted off to the store and got his games.

"As soon as we found ourselves in the same situation, a couple of days later, my prayer became '...Let me kiss and caress his body all over – and I'll give him a puppy.'

"Well, never a stone slept more soundly than that boy. Again I started with kisses, but soon made off with his clothes. The result was me giving him a half and half, where his little moans of pleasure and the fact that his 'rover' was stiff long before I got down to it told me I was not trespassing in the least.

"So the next day I go down to the shelter and picked out a nice poodle puppy for my boy.

"Ralph was so happy and appreciative, the same night while we were studying, I decided to let the kid take charge. Pretending to fall asleep on the bed, I heard the young man say, 'Oh, god of Love, if I go all the way with Sadeeq, I pray he'll give me a car!'

"Well, no shrinking violet was Ralph, and I had a devil of a time remaining 'asleep.' But the boy on top knew what he was doing, and eventually I moaned and made his dream come true.

"Now, cars are not as easy to come by as games or puppies, but I walked around town until inspiration struck.

"That evening, when he entered my room to study, he dropped all pretenses, along with his books. He came up to me, wrapped hands around my neck, and gave me a cock-rousingly hot kiss.

"'Please, Sadeeq,' he said. 'Where's my car?'

"'Here,' I said, and presented him with a radio-controlled toy *Porsche*.

"He looked at it disappointed, and then laughed, saying the god of love can be such a tricky little trickster.

"I agreed, but soon his laughter turned to more kisses, and we made love for the first time with our eyes open.

"Now, after Ralph had properly initiated me, I had no qualms about seeking his favors. Whenever he was too tired or not in the mood, he'd tell me pettishly, 'You better watch it, or I'll tell my father.'

"One night, the teen was particularly randy, and even though we'd had our fun three times in one evening, his little probing hands woke me up for a fourth shag. I hugged him tight and said, "You better watch it, randy little boy, or *I'll* tell your father." The poet ended with a rhetorical flourish. "Now that's a true story! You can put it in the bank."

The chef rattled off some horrible mangling of vowels. "*Nihil est tam arduum, quod non improbitas extorqueat.* Or, 'There is no task is too arduous for a dearth of ethics to surmount.'" [31]

The allusion to scruples – or lack thereof, lol – raised my hackles. I turned to see the cause, and realized too late that Sadeeq's big mouth had given away lots of sordid details previously withheld from my dear spouse. Ooops....

"That's a piece of schoolboy Latin I remember," explained Squiffy. "Not that I remember much of last week, but fifty years ago – now that is clear as a bell."

"That *is* a true story, isn't it, Sadeeq," stated Gordon, "but not yours."

The poet grinned and split guilty glances between me and my newly-wed husband.

I told Sadeeq, "Remind me to never tell you anything in 'strictest confidence' again. If I want a thing advertised, I'll do it myself."

"So that was *your* adventure, young man," said Squiffy, totally bored. "How interesting."

"I agree." Gordon had an arch tone to his voice. "Details not even *I've* heard before."

"Why don't you finish the story for us then," asked the tipsy 'travelling gourmet.'

I smiled at my boy. "Not much to tell really, just that Rolf got me in trouble. In Germany, he was old enough to choose on a lover, but not old enough to know any better concerning money."

Gordon said, "What do you mean?"

"I mean, I didn't ask him to do this, but he started giving me coins from his father's bullion collection. One gold coin per fuck, he said, to keep as souvenirs of our times together."

"So, that's why you had to leave Germany," my husband observed.

"Yeah!' exclaimed Sadeeq. "Cuz they fucked a *LOT!*"

'Oh, *Scheisse*,' I thought. 'I'll have a great deal to make up to Gordon this evening.' But, on the other hand, at least now the full story was out to my boy.

Our donkeys were plodding along switchback trails, leading us gradually up and up to the side of this scrubland cliff.

I changed the subject. "And what about this place we're going to… what's it called again?"

"Crotones, old chap. *There's* a sad story of how adherence to rote convention obscured the average person's ability to accurately evaluate human avarice, evil, *etcetera*."

"What do you mean, exactly?" Gordon asked.

"Once rich, they rolled headlong into decline as people allowed the profiteers to squander public wealth on an *army* too large and *grand* to ever use. To appease the masses, these Crotonian political carpet-baggers imported tons of trinkets from overseas, and all the *rest* of the peoples' hard-earned pesos poured into foreign banks."

Sadeeq laughed. "Bullets, not bread – what a way to go."

"Yes, old soul. Subsequently, nowadays the only *way* for Crotonian fat-cats to hold onto power through *the* people's misery is by misinformation and fear. Lie to them, tell them it's all the fault *of* outsiders, not the consti-pated men who have had *their* hands on the levers of power for decades and sold them out. It's a sad situation not to trust what you are told. It reduces once-honest men into two camps, and two camps *only:* the cheat or the cheated."

"Yes," I said, "but what about the *reason* we are going there?"

"Oh, that. Well, my fine Germanic Schatzi, Crotones is a very ancient settlement, and existed long *before* the Spanish set foot on Baja. In the center of town is a spring, which all the people used to visit to take the cure *for* their sexual problems. At *one* time, Crotones had a massive festival to the Aztec god of fertility, with many days' *worth* of feasting, drinking and orgy. They believed the pool was where the feathered serpent god bathed before *taking* his eternal journey to the west."

"They don't have this festival anymore?"

"Well, perhaps they do, but it's different, dear boy. Everything's different. The Spanish rolled *in,* walled off the sacred precinct and built a church atop the springs."

Sadeeq chuckled. "Horny priests. They keep all the sacred love juice for themselves."

"Funny thing is," explained Squiffy, "the church uses the spring as the source for its *holy* water. People come, fill up bottles from the stone founts to take home and souse their privates in private."

The poet joked, "Would Jesus approve…? Probably."

"And I hear the hospitality of the people is generous, as long as they think there's something in it for them. Keep *that* in mind…."

While Squiffy prattled on, and as our burros neared the summit, my mind was stuck on the image of Quetzalcoatl bathing in the waters. Maybe it was simply my imagination, but there seemed something positively Priapic about it.

I glanced up in time to see Gordon's ass keeping an eye on me with a spark like a knowing smirk. Perhaps we were being led here the whole time.

Just then, we finally cleared the crest of the hill. Down below us was a desolate valley with a glittering walled town in the center of it.

'Almost there...' I thought.

"...fascina fugiens..."

— Part Ten —
Spanish Fly

#¡Bienvenido-amigo! #harridan,

#wicked-lives, #yes-so-tired,

#just-happy-to-be-useful,

#elote, #uniform-sexy,

#firecracking-petardo,

#man-whore, #rest,

#what-a-woman,

#almond-bloom,

#the-stuff

Chapter 32: High-Life on the Public Peso

BANG!

A little black powder singed the air, for it was fiesta time in Crotones.

The sounds of the fireworks punctuated the dance music and stomping feet coming from the main stage. The crackle of light in the sky blended with the colorful flashes from the costumes in motion.

Sadeeq, Squiffy and I stood watching from one end of the public plaza in the center of town. It was a good place to observe sights, sounds and smells, for indeed, luscious scents drifted our way from the adjacent food concessions.

"*¡Bienvenido, amigo!*" The nine-hundredth person of the day hailed Sadeeq as both a friend and someone wonderful. The poet had been continually glad-handed by hungry-eyed men drifting past us as they got closer to the dancing and festivities.

Sadeeq turned a sly leer on us. "This place is amazing! All the locals are throwing their daughters – and *sons* – my way with prospects of marriage. Although being married to my Art as I am, I know what a tricky spouse I'm already committed to. Poetasters, who would rather flirt than bed down with versifying for the long haul, scribble a few lines and smugly think they've changed the world. Sadly, the urge to *poeticize* has led many a young man astray."

I thought to myself, 'Yeah, you would know all about being a stray, lol.'

I changed the subject. "So, Squiffy, how goes the search for the Spanish fly?"

"It's proving very elusive, old chap. Everyone keeps *harping* upon the fact that it can kill, as if that has any bearing on my obtaining *it*."

"People are like that," Sadeeq added, apropos of not very much. He probably wasn't listening anyway. I hate it when people do that.

The dancing crescendoed. Applause followed, and then the master of ceremonies went to the microphone and raised his hand in our direction. Sadeeq was being called forward to the stage. Several hundred faces from the crowd turned to us, and Amergin copped a 'humble poet' attitude, complete with a double-handed clutching at his heart. He savored the moment as he made his way through the adulations being piled on thick. Once on stage, he said "Gracias," and started to recite in Spanish. It was a companion piece to his *Reykjavik Rainbow* called the *Berlin Wall Across the Mexican Border*. I was glad I did not have to hear it again in English.

"Oh, there's nothing I abide with *less* leniency," muttered the has-been TV chef.

"Bad poetry?"

"No, no, dear boy – false modesty."

He had a point there.

Squiffy continued, "Do pay attention. You see, I've gave it some thought *and* found the perfect analogy."

I waited for him to address his own rhetorical point. "Dogs."

"Dogs?" I asked shrewdly. "Like the kind that seem to 'hound' you everywhere you go?"

"Precisely. Witness how I lived in a tequila vat because it was cozy *to* me. As long *as* I have a wee dram to tipple now and again, and a dry place *to* bed down eventually, I can eschew the trappings of success – house, car, clothes, family, wealth, fame, fine food – women – you *name* it."

Out of the corner of my eye, I observed one of the Crotones strays drifting through skirt hems and ankles, slowly making his way to my philosopher-savant companion. "And the dog part of it?" I inquired mildly.

The hat came off for the briefest of seconds, just long enough for him to slick back his badger hair. "Do try *to* keep up, young man. The canine contingent of the *aphorism* is this: Humans overthink all the best gifts of Fortune, Nature, God – you name it. But in contrast, dogs live at ease in the present, without anxiety. Thus, they have no use for money, medicine *or* 'psychopathic help,' bless 'em. Dogs are a shameless race, not because they know they are superior to all modesty, but because it's no show with them." The wandering homeless mongrel arrived as if on cue to sniff at Squiffy's heels

As I knew he would, this cynic shooed the mutt away with a tidy little kick, muttering, "Be gone, *you* worthless blighter."

He rambled on with more of his sophisms, but I tuned him out, just as I had done with Sadeeq's poetry over the loudspeaker. Instead I surveyed the lay of the land. The spring church was on a hill to the right; steps looking suspiciously like the recycled stairway of an Aztec temple led up to a stuccoed edifice surrounded by a wall. All painted in white, with coral accents along the cornices and central dome, it shone in the desert sun.

The plaza where we stood was tidy and roomy enough for the whole community to gather, like now, for the *Fiesta del El Azul-Verde*.

I considered how well we've been treated the week we've been here. Gordon and I used Gay soap-opera worthy aliases – my boy becoming the adorable Grayson Hewitt, and me, his husband, Mason Hewitt. Why Sadeeq and Squiffy didn't cough up fake names the minute we got here, I shall never know, especially seeing how the poet devised a grift. Our town's hospitality is based on Amergin conning them into thinking he's waiting on a huge insurance payoff because of the shipwreck.

If caught, I'm sure the poet will point fingers at us faster than a crow can fly south out of town. And now I thought about it nervously as I spotted Gordon helping out at the grilled corn-on-the-cob stand. 'When you live outside the law, you're just waiting for the other flip flop to drop.' Finally one of Sadeeq's endless quotables came in handy. Again, this one was from his beloved Burnaby:

'Heavens! How ill it fares with wicked lives;
They ever expect a fate they'll despise.' [32]

Squiffy interrupted my musings. He jostled my elbow and gestured out over the sea of people. "They're all biting their tongues at Sadeeq's horrible Spanish." He laughed.

That was the teapot calling the toaster black. However, I was glad I didn't speak Spanish so I could avoid the mad poet's ramblings for at least half the time. Among us, Gordon's language skills are the most natural, because he grew up with it as a necessity for the nursery. Sadeeq's ability was good enough to make people groan and roll their eyes behind his back, which, let's admit it, is exactly what people did with his English. To his face, these Crotonesians praised him effusively, or at least enough to make him exclaim, "¡Respetan a los poetas aquí!" Gordon translated it as 'They really do respect poets here.' The irony was that Sadeeq – a grifter himself – was oblivious to all of these pretend artsy-fartsy types just grinning and bearing with his babbling because they were counting on a payday.

I glanced back to the failed TV celeb. As for Squiffy Wellington, his was the worst among us, speaking a ghastly Queen's English type of Spanish that made even me cringe.

I told Squiff, "The con is one thing, but I wish Sadeeq hadn't told the town to put us up on the public *peso*, and in exchange, he'd make Crotones famous with his verses on the internet. The people are seeing tourist dollar signs anytime they spot one of us."

"And, dear boy...?"

"*And,* attention is not always a good thing."

He gaped wide-eyed at me like I'd just blasphemed. The truth was, this curse was like an excess of divine attention, and I longed for the day when 'the gods' went back to not giving a flying fuck about yours truly. I much prefer the bog-standard godly apathy that we're so accustomed to.

Such hopeful thinking again brought me back to Gordon. His job was simple. Once the corn was grilled, he brushed on white, American mayonnaise from a jar, liberally sprinkled with crumbled dry cheese – rather like a mild Mexican version of Feta – and served the *elote* to a smiling customer.

It makes my boy happy to be useful, and thereby fills my heart with joy.

For a lark, I quizzed Squiffy. "What do you think of *elotes?*"

His face contorted into a sour pucker.

That's what I thought he'd think, but nonetheless, it's real and honest Mexican food, which contrasted sharply to the *haute* monstrosities served at Tre-Princely Knight's dinner.

Sadeeq on stage came to a particularly dramatic lull in his epic recitation, and paused for the captive audience to gasp/applause/whatever. A few did, and he was satisfied. Squiffy and I scanned the faces of the crowd for sport. Most attendees appeared bored and had plastered-on smiles as they faced the bard on the boards. One exception was a very old woman who leaned on a broom of acacia switches and openly derided Sadeeq's perform-ance with raspberries and expressive hand gestures.

"Look at her," Squiffy said close to my ear. "Bless her, the hoary old harridan. I bet she's seen the likes of us come and go *by* the score – i.e., as the Yanks might say – she *knows* the score."

While we were thus watching, a pretty girl approached us through the assembly. She came to a rest by my right side, hands immediately going to her hips as she candidly appraised me up and down.

"Why, ¡*hola!*" Squiffy said, oil dripping from his tone as he reached across my chest to shake her hand.

She did not take the philosopher-savant's mongrel paw. Instead, she told me flatly, "You look like a cheap man-whore."

"What?!"

"Yes, yes..." Her accent wasn't Mexican, it was more elaborate and spicy in the vowels. "Look at you: no hair out of e place; eyebrows e painted on; a cruising looks; e studly gait like you got huge *cojones*. You're a hustler walk-ing, and I a can e spot your kind a mile away."

Getting hot under the collar, I retorted, "You're mistaken, sweet-heart."

My non-chivalrous companion simply said, "Squiffy Wellington, at your service, *señorita*. And what might your name *be*, most bewitching crea-ture?"

"Cáliza. From Puerto Rico. Don't a confuse me for one of these Mexi-canas." She resumed taking my measure with disapproving eyes. "I work for a rich family here, and my *ama de casa* – my how you e say, mistress-lady-boss – she has a taste for gutter trash."

"And what's that got to do with me?" I wanted to know.

Her eyes grew round with mirth. "Oh! *El señor e-fiesty. Bueno.* She'll like you. E see, e some women have the wild *extravagancia* to be in love with filth. They a can't help it. For them, when the bullring is full of men on e sat-urday, they a choose the rough lover of the nose-bleed e seats, with his dirty face and oaken e staff, over all the gentlemen in the boxes with their metro-e sexual"—she wiggled the tip of her finger—"tooth-e pickers." [33]

I shrugged. "I don't think I'm what your lady-boss is looking for. Just tell her I said I'm unworthy."

"No, no. I am her maid, and know what she likes. You're e perfect. A cheap and a cheerful. You e see, when you will be e saying 'I am unworthy,' you turn my lady on even more. The more the e street-walking boy, the better. Then, e speak up – on the market? Okay; she will a pay. If you are a slut"—she made air quotes—"*donating it* to females, then she's waiting in line already."

"Um—" I started

"As for me, I e personally only e sleep with wealthy men, e soldiers above the rank of a corporal, and...." She drew out the end seductively, laying big brown eye-flutters on Squiffy for the first time. "Los acelebrities."

The TV host immediately straightened the lank frame in the slack confines of his linen suit, and twisted his dusty tie a tad.

Warming to the comedy afoot, I grinned and asked Cáliza, "Now tell me the truth, are *you* the one really so in love with me?"

She doubled over with laughter, leaning across me to get support from Squiffy's arm.

Our personal noise and commotion were enough to draw the attention of Gordon. Seeing his questioning glance raised a spark of a notion in me.

I gently latched onto Cáliza's shoulder. "And is she ready, this lady of yours?"

"*Sí.*"

"Where?"

"Not too far. We acan walk."

"I'll want $500, up front."

The shred maid pulled up a fat roll and peeled off five hundred-dollar bills from the top.

"Dear boy," Squiffy said, sounding genuinely alarmed. "What about your hus—"

I hushed him silently. When we turned back to Cáliza, she'd taken out her phone and sent a text. "*Bueno.* You acan follow me."

"Me as well?" inquired Squiffy with hangdog sincerity.

The woman's brows flared. "*Sí.*"

She led us out of the busy plaza, with me giving one final, compassionate look to my boy.

As soon as we left the center of town, the streets were completely abandoned. Everyone was at the *fiesta*, and the sounds of the renewed dancing hovered in the still air like an ambient haze.

She took us to a bolted door set within a high adobe wall. Knocking three times in a certain way, the iron-strapped portal opened from within, and a security guard let us in.

To my amazement, the wall I'd just passed through surrounded an immense orchard of mature almond trees. Right now, delicate white blossoms filled the blue sky to the horizon, and along with high desert clouds, bees buzzed in the air as if already drunk on pollen.

The maid took us to a patch of grass not too far from the entrance. The older man at the gate had returned to his rickety chair, pulled his hat over his eyes and snoozed again.

Cáliza stopped. "Señor Wellington and me will wait here. You go on."

"Go on, where?"

She gestured vaguely, towards the deep run of trees. "Just estart out. Estallida, my mistress, will find you."

I reluctantly left, wondering if this was a set-up of some kind, mystical or otherwise.

Starting to venture beneath the canopy of blossoms, I shed one final look and saw the firecracker maid settling down on the grass with the washed-up TV presenter.

I moved slowly amidst the tree bark, straining my ears for any sound not coming from the sky-echoing festival.

Around the bend of one tree, I spotted a cloud of white fluttering close to the ground, and went towards it.

A woman – and what a woman – was dressed in lace and reclining with legs tucked on a large blanket. Enchanted by her beauty, for such I felt, each step bringing me closer to her filled my head with notions of how the Arts would fail. Painting: would fail to capture her animate spirit in oils. Sculpture: would come short in portraying her noble bearing. Poetry: could only mangle her beauty on an unworthy rack of gilded words – all this, and I'm fucking Gay!

Almost as if in a dream, I glided down and sat on the picnic blanket across from her.

"Estallida, what are you?" I asked.

"Just a woman; a woman who fancies a strong young man." She smiled, and it was like the moon breaking free of clouds in all her beauty.

If I had looked around the groves for statues of men frozen in action, I would now have been surprised. However, my eyes never left Estallida.

A shadow of doubt obscured her face. "But the young man I desire is, alas, already married to another. I would not be homewrecker to the lovely Gordon for all the world, Kohl."

My mind reeled a second; she'd caught me off-guard. "But," I said at last, "I imagine you are married as well, and – well, and, what the gander does not know won't cook the goose."

"How exceedingly clever you are." She moved closer to me, stalking my wilds like a jaguar on her knees.

"I have grapes, and walnuts, and wine too."

She plucked a sweet yellow grape, the dewy blush still upon it.

Reclining, she drew my head into her lap. The lapis sky above her dark hair was no match for the openness of her downward gazes.

She fed me – motherly, I suppose – and made me imbibe a sweet red wine too, allowing all my mellowness to come to the fore.

Poetry dribbled from her lips like drops of pancake syrup:

> "Jove, just a ray of golden light,
> Fell upon Danaë's tender skin;
> He, the mightiest bull in sight,
> Europa's resistance wore thin;
> While to Leda, a feathered kite,
> He sailed a swan to her chagrin.
>
> Thus each fell prey to mortal sin,

But sank through heavenly delight."

"Brava, Estallida. I ask again – which goddess are you…?"

"No god am I." She chuckled, slyly hiding her face a moment. "Perhaps you are my"—her fingers walked down my chest, to my waist, and then, to my crotch—"my god of love. My tempting fate…." Her tone tailed off.

Then her palm roughly palpated my soft-as-a-sock trash.

"What is this?!" Her voice was completely different. "I don't turn you on?"

I sat up. "Um…" I fell back on the hustler's best friend. "This has never happened to me before. I swear."

Suddenly she got mad and super Latina in one swift kick. Her accent started to come through to my otherwise honey-drenched ears.

She stood. "Is this the way you treat an a high-class woman like me?!"

"I—" I got to my feet as well, defensively.

"No, no." She wagged a scolding finger at me. "No esscuses."

Estallida pulled out her cellphone, fumbling over a harried-typed text.

I asked sheepishly, "What is it you are doing?"

"E-see for yourself. Sending instructions to my maid. Here, read."

She held up the screen.

All it said was: "Bring the e-stuff."

Chapter 33: An Abject Low

"You. Did. What...?"

I held up the five one-hundred-dollar bills. They'd become moist lying on the blanket under the almond trees. "Half-a-grand, honey...."

"Geeze. Un-fucking believable."

Despite my husband's shock and anger, I couldn't help but notice how cute he looked in his *elotes* uniform. The desert twilight, enveloping Crotones as the fiesta mellowed into an outdoor drinking symposium, bathed my boy and me in the room of our third-story *posada*. The town leaders had put us all up in a three-hundred-year-old hostel in the center of the city.

"Look"—I tried a reasoning snicker on for size—"no point in getting yourself railed up. It was a flop encounter anyway. And. I'm sorry...."

He paced the room, nearly glowing ghostlike as Gordon silhouetted his profile against the light of the open window. "It's don't get *riled* up. Riled."

"So it's 'run out of town on a rile'...?"

"No. Run out of town on a rail."

I blinkered. "Same thing, right? Or close enough."

"It's not." He sighed. "Even what we perceive of as small differences matter."

"Um—"

"It's like this. So a cop pulls over a driver. 'Sir, you failed to come to a complete stop at that stop-sign back there.' Driver laughs. 'Big deal, officer. I slowed down, didn't I? A slow-down is as good as a stop.' The cop starts punching the man's shoulder as hard and as fast as he can. Man says 'Owww! Quit it!' Cop says 'Now, you want me to stop, or just slow down?'"

I chuckled. "Cute story, babe."

"Oh, my God." The frustration got the better of him. He placed hands on his chino-clad waist and strode up to me. His beautiful brown eyes were so full of hurt, I had to look down.

He lifted up my hand with the cash. "Kohl, what the fuck. We don't need money in this place, and we shouldn't be hustling out in the open in such a small town. You're exposing us to danger."

A part of me knew he was right. My boy – my wonderful man, my spouse – had always been much smarter than me. "Um—"

"Don't give me any more bullshit. I need to know what you are thinking."

I blurted in a well-rehearsed stream, "You're right. It was for more than cash. I needed to see if the god cursed my dick for women too. I want to 'prove' myself, and maybe Priapus will allow it to work when—" My tirade had slowed with every single word until it came to an abrupt stop. The withering look of 'cut the crap' in Gordon's eyes made me hesitate.

"Kohl—"

"It worked on Doris! I was just wanting to see if Estallida could give… yours truly a"—I had the distinct displeasure of realizing I was saying way too much—"blowjob, like on Catalina…behind Lloyd's house."

He let go of my hand. Back to pacing, he exclaimed to the exposed rafters, "Unbelievable."

"But, I did. She was able to—"

"Kohl." There were nearly tears in his voice. "Let's be truthful with one another. For God's sake – the real, absolute truth."

"I don't know what you mean, honey."

"I mean, for example, there is no way in hell Alcibiades rose a virgin from the philosopher's bed, despite all the fake-ass whitewashing, and moralizing, and using it as an example of a bull-shit purity that does not exist."

"I get it. But, I told you my—"

"Spare me the diatribe of 'your truth,' the one you've made up in your mind to make you comfortable – like Socrates' supposed lack of a sex-drive. So, I'm asking you one more time to not give me the sanitized 'truth,' but to give me the real stuff and tell me what's going on."

I sighed, hearing him completely and giving up my embarrassment. "Gordon, I wonder what part of me is still a man. Without *that* part of me, how much of me is real…? I'm desperate."

He lifted my chin to face him. The light framed the back of his head like a halo. "Being a man, Kohl, doesn't mean, isn't defined by sleeping with a woman. It's shown by being a faithful person to the one you love. To the one who loves you – who has given up everything to be with you." He started to cry, but his tears of rebuke were angry ones. "How right is it that you walk around, accusing me all the time of being a slut, when you're the only one with real faithlessness in your heart?"

"Gordon—"

"No. No!" He regulated his thoughts and took a step back. Wiping his tears, he said plainly, "You wanna be a man, then let your husband fuck you. I need that connection too, Kohl, or maybe there is no you and me anymore. You won't let me love you all the way, and yet you pimp your ass to some random woman! That's disgusting. It makes you gross."

Internally, I agreed. I felt utterly disgraceful.

Our door suddenly burst open. Behind it was female laughter; Cáliza and Squiffy sauntered in, the perfect picture of relaxed familiarity.

"This is not a good time," I told them.

Ignoring me, and only smiling more broadly, both approached us. Squiffy held up the maid's hand. In it, a plastic baggie held half a dozen little blue-green pills. It was the first time I'd seen a genuine expression on the TV cook's face; a happy one.

"What's that?" Gordon asked tersely.

"*La mosca española.*"

I asked Cáliza, "What?"

"The Spanish fly, my boy!" Wellington was so excited, he was ready to burst. "Here it is *at* long last."

"*El Señor Esquiffy* is right. This is the real estuff." She opened the bag and displayed two of the encapsulated aphrodisiacs in the palm of her hand, telling me, "You must take it and wait twelve hours. Get a good esleep for it to take effect."

My husband asked, "What is she talking about, Kohl?"

The maid copped a businesslike scowl for Gordon. "My mistress has already epaid and esspects eperformance in es-change."

Gordon turned to me, more anger flaring. "You agreed to see her again?!"

"Oh…" I stammered, and then smiled. "Didn't I mention that…?"

Cáliza said, "Have esex with her or epay back double the money. That's what you esaid."

"Steady on," Squiffy said in my defense.

"No!" exclaimed Estallida's servant. "It's eput up, or eshut up time."

Gordon talked reason to Cáliza. "We'll get you the money. Kohl, give back the five hundred now."

I hesitated, fingering the dirty wad of lucre still in my south paw. Glancing at my man, tragically, for just the briefest of moments, I lunged for the pills in Cáliza's palm with my right hand. A split second later, they were traveling down my throat with an unpleasant burning sensation.… Because…I had swallowed them.…

I couldn't look my Gordon in the eyes.

The next morning found me determined to make my re-scheduled attempt with Estallida a success. In my hand was a piece of paper Cáliza had given me. I checked the address again for the hundredth time looking for the place of my rendezvous. The house numbers were actually house names in Spanish: *Casa cuerno de rinoceronte; Casa bulbo de orquídea; Casa filtro muscari.*

The sounds of the third day of the fiesta drifted to my ears. It seemed uncomfortable reminder of how mad my husband had been last night, but he was made even more so when I kicked him out of bed, explaining that I was worried the *fly* would kick in all of a sudden. I didn't want his errant tickling of my side undercover to sap my strength, if indeed any had returned. I felt I had to prove myself, thready pulse and pounding headache be damned.

At last, I turned the corner and found the *Casa de las ostras.* Cáliza met me there with a wicked grin.

"How is *El Señor Peña* today? The *mosca* help?" She glanced down suspiciously at my fly.

I shrugged. "It feels...tingly," I said, but then so did the rest of me, lol.

The maid took us to a darkened room with no windows and only one door. All the walls were draped in pleated black fabric. A single bare bulb hung from the ceiling.

She sat me at a little table. On it were strange things to eat: a jar of honey still oozing from the comb; a plate of oysters; sliced avocado; figs stuffed with hunks of chocolate; watermelon; and most strangely of all, a bowl of red-hot chili peppers.

Cáliza poured me a shot of tequila. I downed the glass, becoming aware of the maid putting something on my wrist. It was a broad leather cuff with sturdy stainless-steel rings.

She poured me another, and I drank it while she did up my other wrist.

Cáliza pointed to a stack of clothes. "Eput those on." She left.

I stood and discovered the term 'clothes' had been generous. All that was included were a pair of ankle cuffs, a leather harness and a pair of codless short-shorts.

Dressing in the ensemble, I tried to stay focused on my agenda, but afterwards, felt funny about my dangly bits dangling out in the fresh air. I pulled my boxers on top of the fetish-dudgeon *lederhosen*.

There was a sound behind me; Estallida. "Well – my deedless dandy, my featherless cock, my smothered flame – have you brought all of yourself to play with me today?"

The woman was in a black spandex one-piece with long sleeves, but cut low in front. The floor clicked beneath her knee-high stiletto boots, strapped with a half-dozen buckles, each. For accessories, a silver and turquoise belt hung loosely about her slender waist and broad hips. Around her neck was a string of black pearls.

I chuckled. "Do the best of your work, *señora*. Don't ask me to tell; rather give me a try for yourself."

In truth, the charm of this seductress I'd met rhapsodically under the almond blossoms was greatly diminished in this dingy sex vault.

'Stay focused,' I reminded myself.

She picked up something from a bench. "Be careful what you wish for. Present your neck."

Gulp.

I did, and the matron placed a studded leather collar on me; a chain was attached doggie-style, and she maintained a firm grip on my leash.

She tugged it and drew me backwards to the wall.

"Um—"

She lifted one of my hands, and clipped the cuff to an iron ring revealed beneath the wall-fabric.

"Um.... Maybe—"

"Do you believe in fate, Kohl?"

I couldn't answer; couldn't think. I simply watched her as she attached my other wrist to the wall.

"Um—"

Estallida laughed sharply and clapped her hands.

Cáliza entered pushing a rattling medical cart. On it were 'toys' of the most non-innocent type: clothespins; a leather flogger; dick cages; a dildo chastity belt; an e-stim apparatus with dangly wires and sticky pads for the skin. However, most sobering of all was down below, for taking up the entire bottom shelf, was a bullwhip coiled like the devil around the tree of knowledge on the day of Temptation. It lay in wait for its mistress to unwind and use its multi-forked tongue on Man – on me!

"Um. This is not what I had in mind. You can let me go now—"

"*¡Silencio!*" Estallida screeched in full dominatrix mode.

The women bent down and attached a wooden bar between my ankles, clipping it in place and making my stance uncomfortably wide and helpless.

Estallida then picked up a huge pair of scissors, like the kind used to shear bolts of tailoring fabric.

I didn't want to look as she strode up to me, but Estallida tugged my chain hard and forced my head down to her task. "Don't...."

I felt the frigid bite of metal against my inner thigh. She cut away my drawers.

She stepped away, leaving me relieved but also as cold as Patagonia in spring through my nether regions.

"Let me go. This is not the way to rouse yours truly."

"No? This is the way *normal* men get turned on, when an estrong woman takes control."

Gulp.

'If so, then shame on those poor straight buggers,' I thought.

Funny thing was, this woman – who in dappled sunlight raised 'magic' enchantment in me – now became a *bruja* of horrifying ordinariness. She was older and more wrinkled than I let myself see in the beginning. This was no Doris II. Estallida was the kind of girl a guy marries in the blindness of lust, and then gets home only to discover the woman's mother has moved into his bed.

She came up to me, applied her lips to mine and aggressively pushed her tongue in my mouth. I again had flashes of Prussia projected on the back of my closed eyelids, but they didn't help!

Estallida's hands were like potato mashers against my chest, tummy and thighs. The fury of her sloppy smooches became vacuum-like and robbed me of air. I grew light-headed.

At long last, foreplay at an end and me gasping, her palm laid on my noodle, which was as flaccid as any Republican's moral stance.

The woman was furious. She stood back, akimbo, and berated me. "*¡Puto!* You esissy man – or half an esissy man! You disgust me, faggot."

Cáliza took her mistress' hate-speech hard.

Through welling feelings of anger and self-loathing, I held Estallida's stare. "You're right. When I agreed to try and have sex with a woman, it's about the gayest thing I ever did in my life! So excuse me, Hautia. If I can't get it up for a harpy slut, it's because I've hurt the one I love to even try to fuck a publicly traded commodity like you!"

The woman was stunned, grumbling, "¡...el puto malo...!"

Estallida picked up the cat-o-nine-tails with slow deliberation, stroking the long tendrils of punishment. Each leather strip was tipped with a cruel-looking metal stud – a pointy cone facing up, and flat metal rivet on the back.

She struck me. The stainless steel dug into the flesh of my lower back on the left side, and then raked forward to the searing stripes she had just raised on my tummy.

She went at me again, this time doing the same motion, but breaking skin open over my right kidney.

I wanted to flinch, become angry at the injustice, but I couldn't.

Instead, as Estallida grew more reproving with each flog and hit me harder and harder, I glanced up and held my tongue and tears. In my mind's eye, I saw my Gordon doing this to me, and accepted every bitter lash as a mild form of retribution, considering all the pain I'd put him through.

The woman's breathing resounded with exertion as she cracked me the hardest yet. She'd moved lower and hit my upper thighs and backside.

Cáliza looked distressed now and cleared her throat. Her glance to Estallida caused me to hold my tormentor's eyes as well.

The boss-lady appeared furious. "Why don't you cry, puto! Why don't you act faggotty, whine and whimper like all the rest of your kind and beg for me to stop? You think you some kind of man and can take it!!"

I swallowed the lump in my throat, knowing I was not going to snivel for the likes of her: a stranger, a meaningless nobody to me or my story. Nevertheless, I did tell her the truth. "Do your worst. My penance is not you, but to my beloved husband. Whatever misery you cause me, I know I hurt him worse."

"All right," Estallida said like cracking ice. "You want to hurt worse, I can help you with that." She frowned towards the bullwhip, letting the bloodied flogger drop to the floor by her stiletto boots.

Cáliza arrested her employer's motion to the cart. "Enough, señora. You knew he was a-gay right from the beginning, so just let him go."

Estallida, more incensed that ever, made a clicking sound with her mouth and bent to pick up the whip anyway.

Cáliza immediately snatched it out of the other woman's grip. "I said no! This low-aclass man whore is epunished enough. Now, let him go." She curled up the leather snake and hid it behind her back.

The dominatrix retorted sarcastically, "Want me to let him go.... How about this, eh, Cáliza...? I let you both go. Get out. You're fired!"

Estallida plodded out of the room, her heels sounding loudly on the hard floor. At the door, she paused and shouted at the top of her lungs for more servants.

Cáliza quickly undid me, but not before four burley men of the *casa* pounced and dragged us to the front door.

A horrible thump later, we were lying in the middle of the street, and one of the men dumped my clothes into the muddy gutter.

Still in the fetish gear, bruised, bloody and nearly naked, the passersby howled with laughter while I crawled over the unforgiving cobbles to find my trousers.

An hour later, the sounds of the town's fiesta still drifting in through the window, I was back in our room alone to lick my wounds, both physical and those to my stupid ego. I tried to drive the repulsive notion out of my head that this is how poor straight bastards feel every time they have to debase their pure manly energy just to copulate with a female. It was enough to make me shudder, so I did.

Once thrown out of the *Casa de las ostras*, a tearful Cáliza moved off mumbling something about the washed-up TV host. I didn't pay too much attention, for she was gone quickly. And hurriedly was the way I had to dress in the middle of the street too – just slamming my clothes over Estallida's bondage outfit. Then I ran as best I could to our inn barefoot.

At the front desk, the woman seemed concerned, pointing to her cheek, so I guessed there was a cut on mine. I told her I was sick and asked everyone to stay away.

"*¿El Señor Grayson también?*"

"*¡Sí!* Especially him...." I ran away before I started bawling from shame.

An hour ago, I had wiped the blood off the nick on my cheek, and stripped to finally be rid of the woman's restraints. I saw plenty of bruises starting on my body, and was relieved to think they, like my internal anguish, would be easy enough to cover.

Now I sat on the floor, wearing a set of sweatpants and a tee-shirt, and gaping mindlessly out the window to the desert-blue sky.

The weirdest notion yet entered by beleaguered brain; I scrambled to my knees, folding hands together, and casting meek eyes to the all-seeing ether, prayed:

> "Oh, you – powerful god – if it was faith
> You sought to drive home in my heartbeat,
> I humbly beseech you to hear my plea.
> Priapus – delight of Bacchus and Nymphs,
> Still secretly adored in wooded places

Where your power has never been questioned
By the mistrusting minds of modern man –
Great Blue One, lend attentive ears to me,
For though nothing about me is sinless,
You have feebled me, drove me as exile,
For an affront I did not mean to give,
And are not the ignorant meant to be shown
A loving leniency once the lesson
Is taught, and the supplicant shows remorse?
Such a one am I. Debasement now beats
Throughout the shambles left of my being,
And yet, I cling to hope for one reason;
That the joy so long delayed between me,
And the boy who so patiently endures,
Will be rewarded in ultimate bliss.
For that reason, not for my own selfish
Outcome in this miserable twilight
Of being only half a shell of a man,
I say: 'Do your worst, but after, forgive.
The only hope of Man is that our gods
Are more absolving and perfect than we.'"

Settling back on my haunches, I began to feel angry. What injustice never leads to frustration and spite? Where's reason now if by complaining we ease our discomfort – but do the blind curse their feet; do the lame, their eyes? Do actors on stage cover their ears when they see a horrible sight? Do dentists speak of moral decay into their patient's mouth; the shamster preacher of the importance of flossing to his flock? No. So why blame god when my prick is at fault; why pretend I have anything to blame other than the offending member?

I pulled down my waistband, exposing the object of my disgrace. After smacking it a few good times, I addressed it thus:

"And you, coward, who at one time
I could depend upon to stand
Suited up and armed to the teeth,
Ready to charge into battle;
You who cried courageous mottos:
'Hold back and fire only when
The whites of the eyes you can see';
'Damn torpedoes, full steam ahead';
And no divebombing Zero could
Rend the air with a more frightening
Shout of 'Tora! Tora! Tora!'"

I beat my Benedict Arnold some more.

> "But now see your disgraceful state!
> How like a Sherman tank are you:
> One with its gun turret pulled in;
> Or like a cowardly army,
> Sent into total disarray,
> Retreating into the safety
> Of your all-protecting 'helmet.'
> Your stiffened spine has now become
> Limp macaroni, so I should
> Stick a white feather in your cap,
> Set you on a pony, and give a slap."

A key sounded in the door.

I quickly crawled into bed and pulled the covers up to my chin.

Gordon entered with a tray. He was in his roast-corn uniform.

He set it down, and said while closing the door, "They told me you are sick. I brought soup and some bread."

He sat on the bed. Never was my husband's caring nature on more annoying display.

He touched the top of my hand. "You want to eat?"

I shook my head, drawing my hand out of his grasp and placing it below cover.

Now he looked concerned and a bit of a shield appeared. "How did it go with that woman?"

Gordon must have already heard about my public humiliation. Was he just rubbing salt into the wounds?

Angry, I said, "Fine. You'll be happy to know I could not perform—"

"Kohl. Please."

"No. You asked. You should get the details."

"I don't want details."

"Then what do you want?!" I demanded to know. "I was wanting to be left alone."

He was silent for a while. A tear formed, which oddly only hardened my heart.

"I'll go then—"

"Tell me one thing though."

"Anything, Kohl. I have no secrets from you."

"That night – *the* night – you ran away from yours truly to fuck around with Assauer, was he content to leave you alone, or did he take his pleasure away from you by force?"

He stood up, shocked and unhappy. As he paced, one hand was on his beltline while the other shielded his eyes in a gesture of disbelief. My inquiry had sapped all the good humor out of the boy who'd arrived so jovially.

"What exactly is it you think you are doing, Kohl? I know this can't be easy on you, but how much do you think I can take? Look around. I'm the only one who cares enough to be in your life anymore."

I sat up in bed, pissed off and picking road-dirt out of my nails. "Maybe it's your devotion to me that beggars the imagination."

"First of all, it's 'buggers the imagination,' and secondly, is that your honest opinion? Really. You can't understand why I'm here?"

I shrugged. "Does opinion really matter?"

He walked up and looked over me in bed. "Well, what I think is you're playing a game, trying to mislay blame by acting the fool. And trust me, there's nothing more deceitful than a ridiculous opinion." [34]

My silence made him stomp off. But as he was leaving, he paused in the doorway to tell me, "And by the way, to answer your question – no force was needed."

SLAM!

Tears came. I wondered what in the hell I was doing.... Just heaping more hurt onto my boy....

I'd come to an abject low, not knowing how things could be worse, or which way to turn.

Then, in a sudden, inexplicable flash of clarity, I realized why Crotones' spring church had always been vaguely familiar to me.

I rose out of bed, drawn by the drifting smell of good food and the sounds of fiesta music to stand by the window. Through my blinding tears, I could look across town and see sunlight glinting off the structure's dome. From this distance, the building atop its manmade hill, I was able to recognize the place from my Priapus dream.

'Maybe,' I thought, as I wiped my eyes with a forearm, 'he *has* been leading me to this spot the whole time.'

Chapter 34: *da pedicure*

Kneeling in church, I prayed not to the man on the cross, but recited slowly the plea I'd rehearsed in the inn to Christ's more ancient, purer incarnation.

At my back I could feel the breeze coming from the west through the huge open doors. On this movement of air rode the continuing sounds and smells of the Crotones fiesta.

I felt a sudden pressure on my right side. I opened my eyes and saw an old woman sitting at the end of my pew. As I got up and settled into the seat next to her. I recognized her as the same ancient grandma Squiffy had pointed out the first day of the festival. Here was the same 'harridan' laughing freely at Sadeeq's poetry while leaning on the handle of a rustic broom.

She flashed a rumpled grin and a gold priapic pendant on her chest. "Are you a friend of the God?"

I slowly shook my head, deathly afraid, but more scared of inaction. "I believe he hates me. What is your name, old one?"

"You may call me Fala Diosa."

"My name is Kohl."

"Yes. The God told me what you are called, and that you would be seeking something very vital."

"Yes. Vitality itself."

"But you look tired, *niño*."

"I am."

"Fatigued of more than just body; of spirit too."

"Yes, so tired of it all."

The Wrinkled One gestured to a small door. "My *casita* lies just beyond. Come." She stood cheerily. "I will refresh you there."

A few minutes later, I was seated in a crude little lean-to built against the side wall of the church. The corrugated tin roof seemed to transfer the desert sun in oven-like effect. My brow began to sweat from both warmth and nervousness. What did this old witch have in store for me?

Fala Diosa was busy near a central arch built into the exterior wall of the church. She grunted, and I heard water slosh from some depth. "Can I help...?"

"No, child."

In another minute, she had a dripping bucket setting on her table. A knowing grin lifted her kind lines of care. "The blessed waters of the sacred spring. This, my boy, is the reason why you are here."

Gulp.

She grabbed a shiny, freshly polished brass bowl and ladle from a peg on the wall and returned to the table. Fala Diosa filled the vessel with spring water and set the bucket on the floor. "Come. Get closer so you can see what

I can see, *niño.*"

The priestess sat and pulled a chair over for me. I drew close to her side and joined her. The bowl she placed near the corner of the table where we could both look into its crystal-clear depths.

"Through *adivinación,* the great Blue-Green One will show me what I need to know.... How to help you."

She stared into the pan, and although I personally witnessed no change in the *agua,* the woman's eyes became round with wonder.

"Your *novio* is very special."

"My boyfriend – I mean, my husband?"

"*Sí.*"

"Yes, he's very special."

"I mean, blessed, my boy. The God has kept his eye on Señor Gordon for a very long time."

"Really?" I looked harder into the seemingly bottomless pot. If info on my boy was in there, *Himmel,* I might swim in it.

"Gordon has a green thumb, which is a gift and blessing of the God. *¡Dios!*" she exclaimed without warning.

"What...what?"

"I see an accident at sea: a wreck and great loss of life."

"Oh. Yes. I'd rather not think about—"

"It occurred because an argument arose between *Neptuno* and the God. As I say, Priapus is fond of your Gordon. He has had his protection on the nature-boy for a very long time. But Neptuno was insulted by Gordon's attitude and sea-mistakes. The Wet One vowed to punish the *niño* by inflicting a fate worse than death – Tr̥ong!"

She rocked back on her seat, as if the sight was too horrible to bear. She held my eyes and said soberly, "Neptuno wanted your boy humiliated sexually to effect his revenge."

"But.... That didn't happen."

"*No?*"

"No."

She leaned back in to get an update.

"Ah, I see; I see. Because Neptune's plans were thwarted, in his rage he raised a storm at sea to kill all who signed the truce."

She looked up to me again, saying, "*La concordia* among men is not in the best interests of the gods."

I puzzled a moment, knowing I'd heard that somewhere before. "But, Fala Diosa, I'm more concerned with Priapus' hex on my dick. I never plan to be on the ocean again."

Once more, her stooped frame bent to the story in the sacred waters. Once more, her wicked smile rose up to me. "He has shown me what to do." She stood, taking the bowl from the table. "But, *niño,* are you ready to endure the retribution He demands of you?"

Gulp.

I had a moment of my typical instinct to run from tough circumstances, but then I thought of Gordon, of how happy he looked at the corn stand, and I wanted that contentment in him forever. "Yes."

"All right." She pulled out a smaller bowl and dipped some of the sacred water into it. Then she retrieved a saucer with which olive oil seemed to half fill it. These items were set on the corner of the table before the Old One went to a cabinet. In another moment, she returned to me and held out a large object wrapped in cloth. As she lifted the fabric corners, I stumbled backwards to my feet. "But that's.... That's...."

"A dildo, *sí*."

No ordinary sex toy, it was attached to a wearable set of leather straps – not to mention the *Schwanz* part of it was of herculean size!

"Where did you get that?!" I asked, moving towards the door out of the *casita*. I was freaked, but the old woman laid a dry hand on my forearm. After a moment, she shrugged. "*El eBay.*"

The ordinariness of the reply had a bit of a calming effect. It was enough at least to remind me of my resolve, for Gordon's sake.

She gently led me back to the table, where she drew off my tee-shirt. Her hands tugged at my sweatpants, and I dutifully got naked for her, feeling no embarrassment.

"Lie on the table, facing up."

I did, but it was only large enough to accommodate my back and head. The rest of me dangled off one end. I propped myself up a little on elbows to watch her actions.

She took the saucer of oil and mixed in some powdered items of black and green. The old one cracked a wrinkled grin and bent down to show me the sloshing contents. "Here...see: *granos de pimienta negra molida, con semillas de ruda, y aceite de oliva.*"

'Cracked pepper...rue seeds...olive oil,' I went over the ingredients in my mind like a demented grocery list.

Fala Diosa tapped the rim knowingly, setting the saucer down. But what I saw next was disgusting. She spat in the smaller bowl of holy water and stirred it all around with a finger.

Starting at my lower extremities, she anointed certain parts of my body, reciting an incantation and blessing.

First, the soles of my feet became wet.

> "Covertly, he asks of you:
> 'Give me all that you may,
> And offer it every day.'"

My thighs were moistened one by one.

> "'Give to me my rightful due
> As Jove the boy carries
> To heaven and there tarries.'"

Her wet fingers – now mingling the water with oil – caressed the length of my soft shaft.

> "'Like the shy bride, afraid to screw,
> Suggests *instead* on her wedding night,
> So her 'virgin part' stays all right.'"

Fala Diosa drew a line of liquid along my abdomen, up to my heart.

> "In plain English, he'll say anew:
> 'Offer up to me your ass,
> And your bliss will never pass.'" [35]

She was nearing my face now, and I halted her hand.

Gently, she said, "Lie back, *niño*. The sacred water will cure your current blindness."

I nodded, released her wrist and lay back. Small pinholes in the tin roof let shafts of sunlight animate the milieu of dust particles in the air. Some of them fell on the priestess like laser spotlights.

Fala Diosa dipped her right index and middle finger in the water, and then brought it to her mouth where she liberally placed a wad of spittle.

I closed my eyes, and she anointed them, making more soothing sounds as she rubbed the moisture in.

When she'd finished, and I opened them again, my environment seemed changed. A warmth and tingling in my sight rounded edges, hazed the light, and brought a beautiful mystery to everything. Part of me felt drunk and unresponsive. Another part of me had never felt more connected and alive.

Time became lost and irrelevant. Vaguely, I was aware of her preparation, and a slight sensation of oily coolness on the entryway of my passage. The spices then began to sting, but along with that feeling spread a delectable warmth as she worked them in and out.

It seemed more time passed, and then I felt her climbing on the table – my back sliding up so my head lolled off the end drunkenly. She pressed against my hole, but I gaped at the fuzzy shafts of light, feeling relaxed and prepared.

She entered me and paused. I reeled with pain at first, but I had a vision of Gordon from my dream. He pushed a wheelbarrow along the paths of his family nursery, and passed me a look of pure love and unwavering devotion.

The tension left me, and Fala Diosa fucked me with a strength not her own. The initial stinging sensation quickly gave way to unbelievable pleasure, and I remembered what it felt like with Gordon when he sometimes wanted to use 'warming gel' as the lube. It was incredible.

At the height of passion, I forced my head up. The laser jets of light remained softened and struck the crone's face with caresses. As she pummeled me, and as I watched mesmerized, her face melded with that of the god's. Now he did not look angry as he locked his steady eye-contact with mine. He looked on approvingly at my pleasure, for pleasure it undeniably was.

My lubricated cock was rock hard and throbbing with each downward stroke of the god's member. It became sandwiched between us as he reached back to support my neck. I watched the curly-haired, unruly appearance of the god sharpen into focus above me while he thrust harder and deeper. His animalistic pants and grunts grew faster and more insistent. His eyelids faltered a moment – and for him, because of the pleasure I was clearly giving him – I orgasmed hands-free. He must have felt the intensity of my long-pent-up release, for he slackened his grip on my head, letting it fall back. The god/the priestess let out one final, primal yell, and collapsed on top of me in the exhaustion of a godly climax.

I blacked out in ecstasy. I'd finally let go and had a meeting of spirit and flesh in its purest, most exquisite form.

I had found where I belonged.

Chapter 35: "What *about* Sadeeq?"

Just beyond the civilizing confines of Crotones, the sun beginning to set over the desert produced the most beautiful sherbet colors in the sky. Fingers of them reached overhead, almost like a sign that everything was put back into proper order; as if God – or at least one of them – was content and had had his ire satiated.

A snippet of schoolboy Latin resurfaced in my mind as I glanced upwards.

> *Sicut erat in principio,*
> *et nunc, et semper,*
> *et in saecula saeculorum.* [36]

Buoyant and curse-free, I ran back to our inn, avoiding the main plaza as much as I could and the delays I'd encounter there caused by the ongoing fiesta.

"*¡Hola!*" I sang out to the front-desk woman before mounting the steps two at a time.

I rushed into our room. "Honey!" He was not there…. "Gordon?" What if it was too late….

I heard some muffled sounds back from the way I'd come. After a minute or two of investigating, I figured out where they were coming from and burst into Sadeeq's room.

Still holding onto the doorknob, I stood frozen, forced to witness an unaccountable scene.

The poet was astride his bed, lying face up, hands supporting the lower back of the young woman he was buggering, reverse cowgirl! Neither one was plussed by my presence, and I glanced down and saw a boy in his late teens sitting in a chair and also watching intently, as if taking mental notes. He occasionally tugged at the erection in his cargo shorts, and I judged the girl and boy to be siblings, for they both looked exactly alike.

"What ya up to, Kohl?"

"Have you seen Gordon?" I asked the poet.

"Nope."

I was halfway out the door, when I turned back out of sheer curiosity. "But Sadeeq – you're fucking a girl." Confusion sounded in my tone.

"I know. The sacrifices I make for my Art."

'Huh?' I wondered.

Continuing to rodger her, the mad poet explained, "You see what I must endure? The mother dropped them off before heading to the fair, so I'm tutoring them per the mother's express wishes."

He winked at me lewdly. To the boy he said, "Don't worry, your *lesson's* coming up next." Then the social media maven caught the youth eying my crotch. Sadeeq gallantly asked me, "Unless you'd like to do the honors, Kohl. You can be *my* substitute teacher to the chico if you want."

"*Gracias*, no. I have to find Gordon—"

Just then the boy in question appeared at the door. He was smiling, peering over my shoulder at the scene in Sadeeq's room, and still wearing his *elotes* uniform.

I grabbed him, closed the poet's portal behind us, and ushered my husband into our room.

After I closed our door, I joined him in the center of the space to hug and kiss my boy.

Fairly astounded, Gordon held my shoulders and pushed back a little, "What has happened?"

Giddy as a schoolgirl, I bit my lower lip, enjoying the sweet savor of anticipation.

"I'm on club nine, or in seventieth heaven – however you say it."

Gordon scowled.

I winked and smiled, ending his suspense. "I got it back, baby."

"Got.... Got *it* back...?"

I nodded. "Yep. My ju-ju. Want to see?"

"I can see already, husband." He grinned, reaching down to caress me through my sweatpants.

I pulled off Gordon's shirt, and then my own.

The ruby twilight burnished his body to perfection.

Barely able to suppress my giddiness anymore, I stepped back, tugging open the bow closure of my running pants, and lowered both them and my drawers to my ankles. I stood fully upright again, hands on my hips to give my man an unencumbered view.

Gordon's eyes popped. His jaw went slack as his noggin did a boyish doubletake.

"I'm cured, honey. Come check it out for yourself."

He approached slowly, and I used Gordon's hands – both of them – to cradle my gradually tubbing member.

"Kohl...?!"

"I know, right."

"How did it happen?"

"Remember my dream on board the *Ekdíkisi?* The one where Priapus took me to the top of a hill and had me choose the world versus you? He wanted me to choose."

"Yes, I remember," he said distractedly, already beginning to play with me.

"It's here! The hill is the top of the spring church. I went there, and this priestess used the holy water, oil and then...."

"And then what?" He held my eyes.

"She smeared it all over an eBay strapon and fucked me like she meant it. I know, you're thinking 'he's never let me—' But this *was* my first. I swear it, honey."

"And this fucking cured you?"

"Yeah. Well, while she was 'doing it,' I had a vision that Priapus was finally pleased with me, and you know what? I shot a huge load – just buckets – I never came like that before."

My boy smiled in a sultry way. I was fully hard now.

"Oh, oh," I added, "and I have this for you." I took off one of two identical priapic pendants from around my neck. I placed it over Gordon's head, telling him, "Fala Diosa, the priestess, gave us these to wear. She said it's a sign to other initiates that the God has blessed us. She said, 'Go and spread his seed, my sons.'"

Gordon blinked with doe-y eyes and caressed the golden cock upon my chest.

Only when it was against my man's alabaster skin did I realize it meant all those others we'd seen wearing this ensign – during our seemingly endless quest for a cure – had been fucked by the nature spirit too.

'Gott im Himmel,' I thought. 'That's some way to develop a loyal cult following – screw 'em one at a time, lol!'

Wondering, and following a hopeful notion, I touched Gordon's basket. I undid his chinos and lowered them. Using my fingertips, I traced the outline of his cock over the fabric of his boxer briefs, and kept going, and kept going...halfway down his inner thigh.

My man was amazed, but I wasn't. "You've been blessed too, baby."

I pulled his shorts off, salivating as I dropped to my knees.

Raising it up – with both hands – I lifted my grateful eyes and said sincerely, "I've been a lousy lover to you, Gordon. I promise to do better, to be the full man you deserve. And I vow to make up for lost time...starting right now...."

He smiled, but wordlessly laced fingers through my hair, guiding me assuredly to my work.

I licked along the shaft, making him moan in pleasure, and causing the mighty member under my control to have its first jolt of life.

Holding it up along the sides, so the head passed his navel, I caressed it with my tongue from base to flaring tip. It became increasingly difficult to restrain it, so I let it fall into my open mouth. Again, finding and maintaining contact with his eyes, I slowly let it slide along my tongue with no pressure. Halfway in my mouth, I allowed my lips to encircle his shaft and suck.

The fingers on my scalp convulsed in pleasure, and the rod in my throat pulsated once or twice.

Letting it come back out, I repeated the procedure, and this time savored the honey-sweet taste of my beautiful man's precum.

I settled back on my haunches, where I could be comfortable for a good long time, and let Gordon take control. In another thrust or two, he was face-fucking me, getting acquainted with the new length and girth of his dick, and boldly training my throat in the same dimensional equations.

I loved to apply suction as he withdrew, knowing how incredible the pressure feels when the hood draws back to the lips like this.

My hand found my own stiff 'blessing' and slowly worked it up and down. I did not want to go too fast, knowing the second orgasm after a long period of abstinence feels even more incredible than the initial breaking of the fast. And I wanted Gordon and me to come at the same time. It was going to be incredible.

His hands stroked the back of my neck, shoulders and caressed manfully along either side of my spine. My ass tingled with longing, knowing it had been missing so much for so long....

I stood into Gordon's kiss. We hugged and helped each other kick and step out of our clothes. Then I led him to the bed, asking – pleading really, "Please. Will you please, Gordon, fuck me?"

Happy and amazed, a joyful sort of moisture gathered in his eyes.

I lay down, head pointed towards the window while my boy retrieved the lube from the top dresser drawer.

Climbing on, the gilding light from outside animated his sleek form. His feline movements made me think of the spotted leopard so beloved of the boy-god of wine. He could devour me now if he wanted; I'd die happy.

Instead, he knelt by my lower extremities, cradled my legs over the top of his thighs and spread some lube on two fingers.

"Ready?" he asked.

A nod and eyebrow flare later, he was pressing the cool wetness around the perimeter of my portal. Actually, it felt soothing compared to the olive oil and pepper mix Fala Diosa had used.

I arched my lower back slightly to signal, and he slipped a finger in.

My dick reacted with an awesome bounce on my belly, and deposited a pearl of precum there.

He worked his digit in, going deeper at my insistence. Soon, the second finger was in there too, exploring and lubing the walls of my passage from every angle. He twisted his hand, and made me moan.

My neck arched too, allowing me to see out the window, but the only visions I'd see from now were of my husband's incorruptible loveliness.

He withdrew, and I settled back on my pillow to watch him. More lube came out of the bottle and anointed his holy member, with him paying special attention to leaving the bulk of the slippery stuff on the head.

Gordon dumped the container and scooted up on the mattress, lifting my feet in the air as he did.

Romantically, just as I often did when first entering him, Gordon used the weight of his upper body to pin my legs down. His hands rested on the bed to the right and left of my ears, and he brought his face close to mine.

We were only inches apart, ready to gauge and savor the other's pleasure, so I reached underneath with one hand and guided his cock in.

Breaching the opening initially made me wince – which caused my man to hesitate for fear of causing pain – but I latched onto both of his thighs, held his eyes steady, and pulled him deeper into me.

The sensation was amazing: life-altering, really. And Gordon felt the same, if I judged his tender blinking and searching of my features with his eyes, and the mouth standing open and exhaling a sweet breath of astonishment were any clue.

He continued halfway in, and I tugged on the back of his knees to give him more space. He took advantage of it and sank his dick into me to the balls. I thought I might lose consciousness for a second, but the insistence that my cock was having an incredibly good time kept me alert.

My man's gaze on me was so beautiful. As he pulled out and began to develop a rhythm of fucking me, my fingers played with the curls near his ears.

He glanced away, concentrating on his work, and I told him, "Feels so amazing, baby."

"Uh-huh," he grunted.

"Baby...."

"Whaaat...."

"I love you."

"Uhhh...I...."

"Honey...?"

"Kohl, less...talk. More...fucking."

I pulled him down for a kiss. My husband was always right, and I settled back while he worked up an amazing head of steam.

Eventually, Gordon raised himself kneeling position, holding my legs in both hands, and thrusting me good and deep, over and over.

I could tell by the quickness of his breath that he was nearing a magic moment, and I allowed myself to touch my dick – which was aching from neglect.

I paced my movements to Gordon's incredible march to climax, matching him stroke for stroke, never feeling more alive or connected to the world, and all though the ministrations of a particular 'one': the man I loved more than life itself.

His eyes suddenly fell on mine with a mixture of pain, ecstasy and determination.

I stroked harder.

"Kohl; Kohl?" he said.

"Yes, baby."

"I"—he slammed me balls-deep again, making my prostate teeter on the verge—"love the hell out of you. You're my man. My only one."

I started to cum, and I mean really cum. Jets of it sailed past my ears, towards the twilight locked in the frame of the window.

He fell on me, and I felt his mighty member unload in me. It didn't stop, and matched the rhythm of my sexy stud's breathing close to my ear.

I caressed the back of his head, felt the slight slick of perspiration on the back of his neck with loving gratitude. At last I knew what it meant to be a true man.

"Thank you, Gordon. I love you so much, and always will."

He moved his head and kissed me.

Without another word, both of us drifted off to sweet, dreamless sleep – his dick still firmly rooted where it always should have been.

Late at night, the moonlight poured into our room.

Gordon and I lay arm in arm, exhausted but able to slip some clothes on at last. Our sunset *siesta* hadn't lasted very long, and now, after several verse flip-flop sessions where the life-affirming juices flowed in both directions, we just enjoyed the peace.

Sounds of the fiesta coming to an end drifted through the window. "It's a shame," said my husband. "But the party will be over and done within an hour or so."

"You enjoyed working there, didn't you?"

"You know, I did. I like rolling up my sleeves, getting my hands dirty, and making things happen. It's all the better when it brings joys to others too."

A sight of the Sanchez family nursery flashed across my mind. "I know you do, hon. You're so good at so many things. You're much brighter than I am, that much I know for sure."

"Finally admit it, huh?" He poked my side with a laugh.

"Yes. I'm finally admitting a lot."

There was a gentle rapping on the door.

"Who is it?" I called out.

"It's me, Squiffy Wellington, dear boy. Do *open* up."

We stood, smiling. I flipped on the light and unlatched the door.

The former TV star allowed Cáliza to enter first, then trundled in behind her with a pair of bags. He hurriedly closed the door.

"What's going on?" my husband asked.

"*¡Ay, señor!*" the unemployed Puerto Rican maid said, running up to and grasping at Gordon. "You are in danger."

"It's true, old boy – both of you. Cáliza and I are getting out on a northbound truck right now. But there's a bus leaving in half an hour, carrying the fiesta musicians back home to a neighboring state."

"*Sí.* You better to be on it!"

"But why?" I asked. "What's changed?"

Squiffy explained, "The town's wise to the poet's scam and are planning a suitable revenge."

"Oh, geeze," Gordon muttered.

"Revenge for his awful poetry...?" I remained a bit cloudy, gleefully fucked stupid as I was.

"No, old sport. Revenge for promising to pay out *large* when this non-existent shipwreck money rolled in. They know none will be coming."

"Ohhh."

Cáliza and Squiffy rushed to one another and stood in the center of the room like a spotlight was pointed there. They embraced dramatically. "You see," said Wellington, "my dear girl, angered by the rough and rude conduct of *that woman*, sneaked into Estallida's supply of Spanish fly and took it all."

They giggled, and Squiffy pressed a finger to her lips. The washed-up TV presenter continued seriously. "This dear *girl* and her lovely blue-green pills have cured me, my boys. Cured! And better yet, I don't want to drink – much – when I'm with my little fire-cracking *petardo*."

More tittering laughter followed a pair of tweaked noses. Then they indulged in a long-lasting tongue kiss. Gross! I wish they wouldn't force their 'lifestyle choice' down our throats....

Cáliza broke off first, glancing at her watch. "You're on your own, and they will be acoming for you too. So, epack – now!"

I scrambled for our bags; the het couple skittered for the door; but my husband stood still and asked very insistently, "Um, guys – what about Sadeeq?"

Cáliza stamped her little foot. "There's no time to warn him. He's being feasted now by the *Concejo Municipal*."

"By the town council, chappies – being fatted by the powers-that-*be* before slaughter."

Gordon pleaded straight to me as the others picked up their bags, "We have to warn him."

I said, "But baby, now with my cure, it's time to start our HEA. No more getting dragged into crazy adventures."

Cáliza puzzled. "Hay-chee-eh?"

I stared right into Gordon's eyes. "Our *Happily Ever After*."

Gordon slowly reached out and took my hand. Then he said hastily, "We'll text him from the bus."

Well, that's our story, and now it's done.

As for what happened to the hasbin TV chef and the laid-off lady's maid, El Señor Esquiffy and Cáliza post things periodically on social media. They've relocated to Monterrey, Mexico, so the firecracker can pursue her career in Country Music singing. You might be happy to know Squif is back on the boob tube! But he appears now as the laughable, bungling weatherman for a local station. People are once again checking out the movable trainwreck that is Wellington on their televisions, and the man's ego is suitably oblivious as to why. Bless his heart that he could live all these many years never knowing people are laughing *at* him, and not with him. In any event, Cáliza and he seem happy, and they've even opened a dog rescue center. Aww. I can see Squiffy now, the cynic-savant, taking care of the poor mangy mongrels – or, not. lol.

That's about it.

Oh. I guess I can hear you asking 'So, what *about* Sadeeq?'

We texted him from the bus. Whether or not he read it in time, we can't say for certain. However, after Gordon and I got to safety, we checked all of Amergin's social media sites. On his Facebook page, we found this one final, sad posting from the mad poet.

Mondo, addio!

How like Prometheus is an artist,
Punished for bringing enlightenment's spark;
The brighter the flame, the more the catalyst,
The more target he becomes with a mark.
Critics rip the creative man's liver
Like the Titan's immortal vultures do,
But envy drives the literary skiver
To tan the writer's hide each word anew.
And so, fair world, farewell – I've tried my best –
If my life is judged to have fallen short,
Chain my soul on the mountaintop with the rest:
Better to try than ever Art abort.
    Gladly I'd die than bow to attackers,
    For my work shall live, despite detractors.

Ultimately, he sacrificed himself willingly as a creative soul, because the next day, the town pushed him off a cliff.

I can hear his final words echoing off the canyon walls as he went.

"Nobody respects poets

anymore –

more –

ore...."

Gott im Himmel, he died for Art's sake, for Fuck's sake. Poor bastard absolved the sins of the rest of us. Well, good on 'im, I suppose. In other words, better him than me.

Speaking of yours truly, part of me is aware just how melodramatic an ending this has turned out to be. But, if it was good enough for great Gay artists like Petronius, Oscar Wilde and Tennessee Williams, I guess it will have to be good enough for the truth.

Sometimes, as even the critics will admit, the truth is a hell of a lot stranger than any fiction, and so it turned out for us.

Oh. And then I suppose you'll want to know a bit about what happened to my husband and me. Right...?

Let's just say, Gordon and I are out there, doing what's needed to get by. But we're happy. Just look around carefully and you may spot us. There's a lot of us out there, and don't you ever doubt it.

So if some day, while out walking, you spot two suspicious yet loving-looking lads up to no good; or if on a Sunday you're kneeling in church, or having a picnic in the park, or grocery shopping and happen to see a blissfully happy same-sex couple; or perhaps you find yourself in a restaurant and see young love on display as a quiet exposing of tender hearts to the trust of one another – say one milkshake with two boys attached via straws – know we will be there too.

It matters not if our story were two thousand years old, fresh as a daisy and set right now, or revised and re-packaged two millennia in the future – *we* will always be out there, loving each other, living our lives, doing what we need to get by, and making ourselves happy.

So, that's our tale of getting my mojo back, and as they used to say in print books of old, this is the end {for Fuck's sake}.

"...*omnes sapientes semper feliciter*..."

Cicero

~

Post Scriptum: A Curtain Call

P.S. Oops. After finishing the summary that ends chapter thirty-five, Gordon – my eternally smarter better-half – reminded me I should fill you in on some of the other 'characters' we've met along the way. After a little digging, I found out that adding a *post scriptum* to an account has a long and colorful history. For example, Jonathan Swift's *Tale of a Tub* is blessed with a damn funny one.[37]

Although "Mojo" is no *Tale of Tub*...or tub of a tale, for that matter...this is what Gordan and I have found out about some of the other people mentioned in our adventure. Please stand back and let them take a curtain call.

Let's see, we learned....

» Sang Trọng understandably took the death of his partner hard. After six months of isolation {Saint-Tropez, naturally}, he sold all his designer earthly goods and joined a monastery. He occasionally posts status updates under the name of Brother Moon and Stars. Gordon and me suspect the Brethren secretly worship the cock as well as the cross, just like that old-timey pope mandated.

» The news for the so-called religion about an alien, a volcano and a beauty college is mixed. Seems the Internal Revenue Service was sniffing around, and the FBI opened a RICO case – or a Racketeering Influenced Corrupt Organizations criminal investigation. The last we heard, Sprag, McFearsome and the rest of them had already moved to a glorious tax haven – the Caribbean Island of Turks and Caicos – where they've cornered the market on the local supply of asses' milk. We'll see if they are ever brought to 'justice.' And if so, maybe they'll get a pardon from the Great Pharmapseudocologist in the sky.

» On a much happier note, 'Bergeofftram' continue to be adorable together. They decided to stop collecting frequent flyer miles and outright move to Washington. The Gay Grapevine has it that the Racial Kink Cult leader was given space right in RNC headquarters. He turned it into an atonement chapel, and evidentially it's fast becoming the most frequented house of worship in the D.C. area. At least Bertram tells me that with a smile. Geoff, bless his heart, stated his strong desire to "make a difference" in these uncertain times of transition and disappointment, so he started a Names-Project-type charity for disillusioned Dump voters to send in quilted squares. From the pix, Geoff's "National Duvet of Regrets" is already big enough to cover half the Washington Monument – condom like. "Ah, healing," he tells us. Let's hope so.

» Speaking of *Hope and Glory*, you may not believe it, but last we heard, my ex and Hojax have been permanently reunited. Assauer made up for our pilfering, but in the process, convinced the captain to take up a different hobby. Now they can be found any Sunday of the year at the Rose Bowl Flea, liquidating Hojax's war knick-knacks and nazi what-nots to focus on a joint collecting endeavor: Hollywood treasures from the age of drunks. Kitsch items dating between the death of James Dean and the demise of Jim Morrison is what they buy.... It's still morbid if you ask me. We're glad they're happy, but I imagine my *Exfreund* often has an angry bottom, thanks to the captain's form of corporal love, hehe.

» Red and puffy also reminds me of beef-cheek, nitrate-laced hotdogs! The Sparks are still roving the California countryside in the warm-weather months, feeding contented people contented corndogs and ye olde jalapeño poppers. Seems they found a new employee who likes Alisoun's bedroom proclivities, and probably gives Karl's backside a well-earned rest now and again.

» And then we come to Angekwekwa. The power-saluting days of Ms. Umfume-Kintay are officially over. As Maggie once more, and by a process of guilty workings unknown, she woke up one day and decided to embrace her inner honky. I suppose she regretted turning her back on her own inborn nature as a through and through dull person, for with no qualms at all, she became a meditative candle and soap maker in the Green Mountains of Vermont. She and her partner – Candice Hargrove-Whipplemeyer-Stapleton-Johnson-Smythe III {Man! How white can you get} – opened a Lesbian bookstore-coffee-clutch center in Burlington, and spend weekends canvassing for voters to *Feel the Bern* in upcoming elections. {Oh, yeah. That white!}

» As for the rest of the cock god people, who knows. They are perhaps still meeting in hotel ballrooms to indulge in wand envy and dummy fisting. All the best to 'em.

» But what of Maggie's former employer, the disgraced ex toady tool of the Grand Old Partisans you ask...? Unlike Smythe III, he did not mend his ways, perhaps preferring The Hammer's correcting blows, but instead went farther to the dark side – um, I mean, to the ultra-pasty side – and hooked up with David Duke to be technical advisor on the Wizz's scheme called "Let's get 'em all out to the middle of the ocean." So far, according to the project's webpage, a swamped pontoon boat and a pair of dinghies have been donated to this "voluntary" effort.

» Despite the way they were raised to always stay out late, and never think of the consequences, Claude and Domingo Germaine-Klaassen are early to bed, early to rise type folks. They have their own tube channel now on heritage farming to give other fast-lane city boys an aspiration to hold on to. In their videos, they show how to farm with oxen, and rig horses to go logging in winter with sledges. Claude tells me they sleep with a new Amish girl every other night, and reminds me wickedly that lights go out at 6:00 PM most evenings. They are living the Ohio dream.

» In terms of dreams – or maybe sleepwalking fits better – Napoleon Trueblood and Neil Campbell moved from L.A. to the 'next *it* spot,' Topeka, Kansas. They discovered unmotivated people with cash can be found outside of Hollywood too, and also learned their self-actuated dollars go further in the Sunflower State. Plus, Napoleon informs me the clogged drains are just as shitty. *Ca-CHING!*

» And then, I think, that only leaves us with Tre-Princely Knight and Prospera Texas-Ivy. Tre's missus keeps busy promoting her own line of celebrity gin, called The Husband Pacifier™. She hawks it online and on home-shopping cable channels. Apparently, Melania Trump was an early advocate, endorsing the elixir on-air, but of course that was before the So-Called got dragged away. Other than that, Prospera still enjoys cooking Mexican food with all the best chefs born above the 40th Parallel. And as far as her husband goes, from what we read in the news, the former biggest male bottom in porn accepted a job from the new Democratic Administration to head up programming over at PBS – the Public Broadcasting Service. Perhaps he got the job by pitching a new puppet show, à la Mr. Rogers-cum-Wes-Craven, or said "There just aren't enough wolfman acrobats on TV...." Who knows. The only thing that's for sure is he'll have to change that part of his epitaph assuring mourners he took no job in The Capital, unless it's too late and Gavin Coruptti has already carved it in stone. If so, then once again, the truth be damned.

finis

— Appendix —
All the Priapean Extras!

#for-further-reading, #and...

#text-notes, #umm-quotes,

#poems, #ahm-resources,

#yes-that-is-all-folks,

#Bye! #but-still-here,

#oh-still-reading?

#no-one-respects,

#poets-anymore!

#more, #are...

Mojo Appendix: For Further Reading

One can easily encounter English-language versions of the ancient Roman fragment of novel known to us as the *Satyricon*. This should not be surprising, for since its rediscovery in the Renaissance, it's never been out of print. What should qualify as hard to believe is that all of the plotting and wild adventures surviving to us represent excerpts from perhaps two or three chapters of the original novel, or from two or three "Books," to use the correct phrase. There were perhaps thirty-seven Books to the full *Satyricon,* with new installments issued quarterly, which is when people received their salaries, and when bookbinders advertised their new editions. This quarterly release of new titles is still the common practice today.

From the choices of these many English translations, I will recommend two must-have volumes for those who are curious about my sources for *Mojo.* Both are rather inexpensive and available from online book dealers in either new or used form. I will also list one or two other noteworthy tomes to acquire if you find your Benusian interest growing. For both the essential and the optional choices, I will lay out what I feel are their strong suits and blind spots, if they have any.

Following the *Satyricon* material, I'll give a few online sources for further reading concerning the various ancient religions encountered in *Mojo.* Hopefully the links will provide fun areas to investigate on your own.

Books given (Parenthetical) designations before the title will be referred later in these notes by those monikers. Page number references are for the editions highlighted.

For Further Reading: *Satyricon*

» (Burnaby) *The Satyr of Titus Petronius Arbiter*, The Modern Library, New York 1953. This reprinting of William Burnaby and associate's 1694 translation {under the slightly altered title of *The Satyricon of Petronius Arbiter*} is accurate to the original and easy to acquire.

This is the first must-have. Many scholars have wondered out loud what inspired the birth of the modern novel, in its perfect form with no experimentation, to emerge from London in the years leading up to 1700. It seemed to pop up fully developed from the hands of several authors at once. The long-neglected answer is Burnaby's {and his unnamed-but-credited co-author's*} delightful version of Petronius. Their 1694 edition of the first English translation sparked an understanding in writers like Jonathan Swift of how a story should flow and develop in ways to criticize current times as instructional entertainment. For all the many translations that have followed Burnaby, none have matched the purely open and Gay-positive tone this edition brings unaltered from the original Latin – and indeed, the majority of later English versions tried to 'hide' the fact of *Satyricon* as a brilliant satire on the lives of Gay men. {And the book's doing so via our classic obsession with big *eggplant*.} Many of these 19th and 20th publications try to force a hypocritical, anti-gay, sexual-relationship-only "shame" onto the characters that has nothing to do with Petronius. We will be avoiding these, for if such repressed Freudian commentators cannot admit our author wrote one of the most loving and tender portraits of boyfriends that still survives, then they have been blinded by their own bigotry. Or, as Petronius put it: "Nihil est hominum inepta persuasione falsius." (*Satyricon*, CXXXII)

Two drawbacks face a modern reader diving into Burnaby. First, the "juicy bits" are printed untranslated in the book. The authors never excluded scenes of tenderness and love between Encolpius and Giton {our Kohl and Gordon}, but they did obscure most of the out-and-out sexual encounters by keeping them in Latin. The second drawback is one not often encountered in the work, but to avoid a censorious removal of the book for sale by the government, some of Burnaby's English phrasing is pointedly quaint, to say the least. A perfect example is when the old harridan produces her honking great dildo to work The God's cure/revenge on Encolpius, and Burnaby says she drew out "... a leathern ensign of Priapus..." (Burnaby, page 229). For those familiar with the wording in the Latin, Burnaby delights them here; but for newcomers, "ensign" fails to conjure the requisite fake-penis image.

Currently, The Modern Library Edition is posted online here:

https://archive.org/details/
in.ernet.dli.2015.113231

Also currently available is a scan of Burnaby's original 1694 edition, which can be found here:

https://play.google.com/books/reader?
id=sURoAAAAcAAJ&hl=en&pg=GBS.PA1

or

https://books.google.com/books?
id=sURoAAAAcAAJ&pg=RA1-PA47&lpg=RA1-
PA47&dq=%22when+in+a+dream+presented+to
+our+view
%22+burnaby&source=bl&ots=35AUYFQdPc&sig=
0oyPyOsPfh0AtQp7sbg0nvB8I20&hl=en&sa=
X&ved=0ahUKEwi4ncLxjNfVAhUK22MKHSYCD4
QQ6AEIKDAA#v=onepage&q&f=false

* It's possible Burnaby's "another Hand" and co-author was
poet-playwright William Byrd II (1674-1744). See here:

https://books.google.com/books?
id=GzLqCQAAQBAJ&pg=PA37&lpg=PA37&dq=willi
am+burnaby
+poetry&source=bl&ots=LICUWxY2qZ&sig=
ACfU3U3eYokT1J9RsoOOWR4ZBjs9OtXsCA&hl=
en&sa=X&ved=2ahUKEwja3uORm5n-
pAhUI5awKHSbnAkcQ6AEwAnoECAcQAQ#v=

onepage&q=william%20burnaby
%20poetry&f=false

» (Dent) *Petronius Satyrica,* J. M. Dent Publishers, London 1996, ISBN 0 460 87766 6. Translated with commentary by Bracht Branham, Daniel Kinney {and their university students, who are thanked for working on some of the poetry}.

This is the second must-have. The publication of this book was met with reviews and printed comments on how "gay" the whole thing was, these well-seasoned reviewers having no idea *Satyricon* was not a Roman exposé about orgies of men with women, as it had been presented for decades. This was the book that came out at the other end of the tunnel from Burnaby's 1694 version, and it has many notable features. No other commentators I am aware of delve into understanding the satire inherent in Petronius' poetry like this volume's authors do. It is also admirable for some very snappy, and downright Petronian dialogue. They capture not only the words' meaning, but recreate the punch a contemporary reader of the novel would have gotten from the writer's firecracker Latin.

The downsides are that the translation, despite the hype at the time of release, is not as accepting of same-sex love as current standards require. This 1996 version still uses derogatory slurs to talk about Gay characters, in opposition to the original Latin terms being neutral or positive. The authors' disinterest in or knowledge of LGBT people in Roman society is all too apparent. I may just point out how neither Branham nor Kinney understand that *frater* {brother} in Latin – as indeed in many ancient and current languages – is the term of endearment men in partnerships use for one another.* See footnote 9.1, page 8, for Dent's confusion, and Joseph Jay Deiss' *Herculaneum,* New York 1985, p. 147, for several direct, firsthand attestations of frater's romantic meaning in Roman times. Shakespeare for one well understood it, and a glance through his *Julius Caesar* will reward with all the best-known Gay couples in the play using the term. "Romans, Countrymen and Lovers!" {III, ii}.

Petronius also provides a burlesque chuckle in the text when Circe {our Estallida} tells the narrator she knows he already has a boyfriend {*frater* – 'brother'}, but he might as well have a girl-friend {*soror* – 'sister'} too (Dent, page 131).

A partial impress of the University of California's edition of Dent is available here:

https://books.google.com/books?
id=XrNEns3_yd0C&pg=PA157&lpg=PA157&dq=
%22AL+651,+Bu
+30%22&source=bl&ots=HN3G0mOQtg&sig=ACf
U3U1T7p88sytLOFVqXc0UDOdV__WWtA&hl=en-
&sa=X&ved=2ahUKEwjHoNba2NHoAhVQKa0KHU
x-AJEQ6AEwAHoECAIQKQ#v=onepage&q&f=false

*As an example of Dent's unfriendliness to – and unwilling-
ness to show respect for – same-sex love, more often than
not, the book refers to Encolpius and Giton as quote-un-
quote "sexual partners." {for example, see Dent page 76.}

A limitation on both the Burnaby and Dent volumes is a lack of
the running original text in Latin next to the translations. For
such scholarly editions, the following two are the among the
best.

» *Petronius Satyricon,* Volume 15 of the Loeb Classical Library, Har-
vard University Press, Cambridge 1913. Translated by Michael
Heseltine and W. H. D. Rouse. Revised by E. H. Warmington.

» *The Satyricon, by Petronius,* The Panurge Press, New York 1930.
Translated by Alfred Allinson. This version was originally privately printed, and later, some "genius" re-printed it as the
work of Oscar Wilde.

Currently, an online version can be found here:

https://www.sacred-texts.com/cla/petro/satyrlat/
index.htm

□ □ □ □ □

For Further Reading: on Priapus

» *Carmina Priapea: Testo latino con traduzione in lingua italiana,* Bolzano 2009. Translation by Edoardo Mori.

This text is something like the Rodney Dangerfield of Classical studies; it can't get no respect! Comprised of many Priapus-related poems, epigrams, and no-trespassing-type curses, it has long been assumed by scholars to be a hasty anthology of some "naughty" pieces and no more. Now that a few scholars are looking at the collection with fresh eyes, some have published opinions that the *Carmina Priapea* appears to be an esoteric liturgy, or several, and indeed, the ancient Greeks were known to celebrate Priapus at harvest time with country picnics and ceremonies. Some experts even think they recognize the hand of no less a poet than Ovid in preparing the Greek originals for Latin use. These points are conjecture for now, but the work is fun to go through.

Currently, there is a Latin printing with an Italian translation off to the side. It's available online, and DeepL.com will help turn the Italian versions into more-than decent English renderings:

https://www.mori.bz.it/humorpage/carmina.pdf

» *The Poetics of the "Carmina Priapea"* Philadelphia 2015. Peer-reviewed paper by Heather Elaine Elomaa:

http://repository.upenn.edu/cgi/viewcontent.cgi?
article=3484&context=edissertations

The Northern Europe folk-culture and/or worship of the great

Blue-Gray One did not pass into obscurity with the demise of Roman governance. Quite the opposite. It stayed underground, under threat from a hostile Church, but signs and symbols of Priapus remained common personal amulets until well into the Renaissance. See the following paper for a brief survey.

» *Pious Phalluses and Holy Vulvas: Some Sexual Body-Part Badges in Late-Medieval Europe (1200-1550)*, Gambier, Ohio, 2017. Peer-reviewed paper by Ben Reiss:

https://digital.kenyon.edu/cgi/viewcontent.cgi?
article=1291&context=perejournal

Additional evidence for the widespread veneration of Priapus in medieval times survives in a large anthology of songs and poems collected together about the year 1200. Several songs to The God are included.

» *The Carmina Burana: Songs from Benediktbeuern,* Third Edition, Los Angeles 2014. Translation and commentary by Tariq Marshall.

Currently, the entire Latin text is posted on the website Marshall maintains for his book:

https://the-carmina-burana.webs.com/

For Further Reading: on Abraca

» *Carl Jung's Seven Sermons of the Dead,* Wheaton, Illinois, 1982. Translation by Stephen A. Hoeller.

Despite how unlikely it seems, the Cock God of the Las Vegas chapters is based on an important ancient deity. Carl Jung featured this chimera entity in one of the most unusual written works imaginable. Although *Septem Sermones ad Mortuos* was penned and published privately, for the doctor and his close family members, it was nevertheless printed widely and became something of a bestseller. How such a book – reputedly composed over the course of several drug-induced 'research' highs – did not wreck the psychiatrist's reputation, I do not know. Different times, I suppose, where the occult was not viewed as dangerous, but more of a parlor entertainment. A snippet from Sermons No. 3 is provided below in the "Notes on the Text," under the listing for Chapter 19.

Currently, Hoeller's text is hosted online by The Gnostic Society Library:

http://gnosis.org/
library/7Sermons_hoeller_trans.htm

Mojo Appendix: Notes on the Text

These endnotes are mostly brief and meant to be digested after having read the entire book. However, if you are like me, you will keep a bookmark in this section and follow the notes as you go along. I hope they are not too intrusive if read in this manner.

[1] Epigraph Page:
"Talent borrows; Genius steals" is oft attributed to Oscar Wilde. It is also commonly stated how the Wilde quote is a Petronian-esque distillation of the following:

"Immature poets imitate;

mature poets steal;
bad poets deface what they take,
and good poets make it into something better,
or at least something different."
— T.S. Eliot

That Wilde could condense Eliot's meaning down to a mere four words makes for an ingenious display of the type of stealing indicated. It also makes a good story, which it is, as Wilde had been dead at least twenty years when Eliot published this bit of wisdom. Never mind; the charlatan who stole to give the famous playwright-poet-novelist more luster was displaying their own sort of ingenuity.

[2] Chapter 1:
"Just fearmongering topics and saber-rattling prattle," I said. "I think I've heard someone say that before."

The place Kohl heard this is Petronius:

> ...nunc et rerum tumore et sententiarum vanissimo strepitu...
> (*Satyricon*, II)

> [Literally: "...now only cancerous issues, and cyclonically polished sentences..."]

The *Satyr* translates it as "the inordinate swelling of matter, and the empty rattling of words," (Burnaby, page 2). Other renderings for our times of this pithy adage might be:

> – Merely inflated bellowing, sounded amid burped assumptions
> – Just puffed-up spin, and swanky prattle
> – Overinflated subject matter, and factious *beaux mots*
> – Just hot-air talking points, and whirlwind blarney
> – Political hype in hateful huffs

[3] Chapter 1:
Here are two videos providing some of the history, gory as it is, concerning Napoleon Trueblood's self-help rap:

Gag reel with some of Junior Bushy's 'presidential' lowlights:

https://www.youtube.com/watch?v=8Ux3DKxxFoM

The Cheney-shot-a-guy-in-the-face-gate scandal {Ah, the days when life was simpler...}:

http://www.cc.com/video-clips/ed8966/the-daily-
show-with-jon-stewart-headlines---dick-cheney-
shot-a-guy-in-the-face-gate

[4] Chapter 3:

Setting amusement aside for a moment, I will tell you in all seriousness, this chapter is dedicated to the memory of the Ghost Ship Tragedy in Oakland, California. It is for this Queer community of artists and thinkers I have attempted to capture 'their world' in an impossibly small cage of words. I also wrote it in tribute to their families, partners and loved ones; as well as to the survivors.

[5] Chapter 8:

"Pasadena got its launch more than a century ago by its very own cult leader!" Kohl has confused towns. Actually, it's Atascadero, California, established by Edward Gardner Lewis, a leading light of the City Beautiful Movement, and indicted miscreant of his followers' funds. Before this legal hiccup, his original base of operations was the leafy and elegant University City, Missouri, which he founded in 1902.

Here is a general article on the man:

https://stlgs.org/research-2/community/st-louis-
biographies/edward-gardner-lewis

The original tower built by Lewis for his day-to-day operations
is cult-worthy for sure. Now University City's City Hall, its interior is one of the finest *belle époque* spaces in North America. See
here:

https://i.pinimg.com/
originals/70/4b/49/704b49a00103433
bab8ba2f812c90369.jpg

Lewis also provided the tower's exterior with flash; literal flash
in the form of a perpetual-motion searchlight, no doubt to guide
the willing to his destiny's calling. See here:

https://nebula.wsimg.com/
dbd67a9292a895c75cbbe94e1ba19081?
AccessKeyId=53D64AF43A7E16F831E8&dispos-
ition=0&alloworigin=1

{You simply can't make this stuff up....}

[6] Chapter 9:
"Queer Art generated for viewing by Queer smarty-pants." Here

are pictures of Brunswick's neo-postmodern statue of Hercules and Antaeus grappling.

https://upload.wikimedia.org/wikipedia/
commons/8/85/Ringerbrunnen_Braunschweig.jpg

https://
live.staticflickr.com/6067/6208269899_dd8ef-
11bfe_c.jpg

[7] Chapter 9:

"The wind's blast may rage," etc. is translated after *Carmina Burana* No. 83:

> Sevit aure spiritus, et arborum
> come fluunt penitus vi frigorum;
> silent cantus nemorum.
> nunc torpescit vere solo
> fervens amor pecorum;
> semper amans sequi nolo
> novas vices temporum
> bestiali more.
>
> [The wind's blast may rage,
> And the leaves stream away from the trees
> Before the first of the violent frosts.
> It's then that birdsong falls silent;
> Then the randy pulse of the beasts,
> So lusty in spring, goes dormant.
> 'But I,' sayeth The God, 'But I,
> The lover of all things holy,
> Refuse to bow to the temporal,

The changeable whim of the seasons,
And the mere drive to brute dumbness.']

[8] Chapter 10:

"Unter allem Diebesgesindel," etc. is Kohl's panhandled quote while in the sauna. It's from Goethe:

Unter allem Diebesgesindel
sind die Narren die schlimmsten.
Sie rauben euch beides,
Zeit und Stimmung.

[From amongst thieving riffraff,
the foolish ones be counted the worst.
They steal not only your time,
but your finer sentiments as well.]

[9] Chapter 11:

Floorplan of the Getty Villa. The arrow on the plan is pointing to the room where Tre's dinner occurs.

https://pictures.abebooks.com/
DIATROPE/15700073337_2.jpg

[10] Chapter 11:

"Unhappy mortals we," etc. is modeled after Burnaby, page 51.

[11] Chapter 11:

"For as long as you thrive," etc. is after *Carmina Priapeia* No. 80:

Dum vivis, sperare decet:
tu, rustice custos,
huc ades et nervis, tente Priape, fave!

[For as long as you thrive, live in hope:
I, the Rustic God, will stand by your side
To gird your loins with priapic favor.]

[12] Chapter 12:

"Afterall, what's a day? You get swept up into one, and it's night again." The original is a great example of why Petronius' Latin is so much admired. It is crisp, biting and clear as ice water.

> Dies, inquit, nihil est. Dum versas te, nox fit. (*Satyricon*, XLI)

> [Literally: They may say, what's a day? It's nothing. You turn around, and it's night.]

[13] Chapter 12:
"Hard as a horn" is borrowed from Burnaby, page 63.

[14] Chapter 12:
The phrasing of "Moot points" is delightfully lifted from Burnaby, page 72.

[15] Chapter 12:
Developed after an analogy mentioned in Dent footnote, page 48. Tre-Princely's Spanish is decidedly off. The crowning chorus to Gershwin's opera *Porgy and Bess* is the moving and glorious "Oh, Lord, I'm on my way, On my way to the Promised Land." Tre's version actually says: "Oh, my God, let's get out of here."

For those unfamiliar with the caliber of humor Benny Hill purveyed on television, here is a highlight video:

https://www.youtube.com/watch?
v=epKqu_VHbQU

[16] Chapter 13:
"Forgive these guys because in a situation like this, it's the defeated who win the day". The original is another wonderful example of Petronius' laser-focused style:

> Semper in hac re qui vincitur, vincit. (*Satyricon*, LIX)

> [Literally: Always in such matters, the vanquished come out victorious.]

[17] Chapter 14:
"I know that old Roman Senokot said don't think you're better than them." Here is a part of the "Senokot" quote; the full quote follows in the Poetry section of this appendix.

Vis tu cogitare istum, quem servum tuum vocas, ex isdem seminibus ortum eodem frui caelo, aeque spirare, aeque vivere, aeque mori! tam tu illum videre ingenuum potes quam ille te servum. Mariana clade multos splendidissime natos, senatorium per militiam auspicantes gradum, fortuna depressit, alium ex illis pastorem, alium custodem casae fecit; contemne nunc eius fortunae hominem, in quam transire, dum contemnis, potes. (*Ad Lucilium Epistulae Morales*, 47-10)

— Seneca

[Kindly remember that he whom you call your slave sprang from the same stock, is smiled upon by the same skies, and on equal terms with yourself breathes, lives, and dies. It's just as possible for you to see him a free-born man as for him to see you a slave. As a result of the massacres in Marius' day, many a man of distinguished birth, who were taking the first step toward senatorial rank by service in the army, were humbled by Fortune, one becoming a shepherd, another a caretaker of a country house. Despise then – if you dare insult Fate – those to whose social station you may sink to at any time, even going down as you are despising them.]

Translation by Richard Gummere *Seneca Ad Lucilium Epistulae Morales*, Volume 1, London 1917, page 305.

[18] Chapter 14:
Tre's epitaph is inspired and developed along the lines suggested by Dent, page 66. Compare with Burnaby, page 108.

[19] Chapter 15:
"*Bucco, bucco* – cheek by jowl – how many fingers can I get up your ass before you howl?!" and "*Bucco, bucco* – dunderhead, chin by cheek – how many fingers do you need to count all the fools both dumb and weak?!" are modeled on part of *Satyricon's* dinner sequence. The reference to "fingers" in my version is inspired by Dent, page 59.

Non moratus ille usus est equo, manuque plena scapulas eius subinde verberavit, interque risum proclamavit: "Bucco, bucco, quot sunt hic?" (*Satyricon,* LXIV)

[Going for it, he made use of his 'horse,' and laying his hand full on the shoulder blades, beat the man's ass from time to time, amid the laughter, proclaiming: "Blockhead, blockhead, how many of your kind are there here?"]

[20] Chapter 17:

"Hans *und* Franz" is a reference to a series of comedic skits, airing now long, long ago…

https://www.youtube.com/watch?v=PTxA35jKufc

[21] Chapter 18:

Cher in her 'half-breed' phase:

https://www.youtube.com/watch?
v=TOSZwEwl_1Q

[22] Chapter 19:

"Abraca, speak unto this boy / That which is sacred and profane," etc. is modeled after Sermo I and III in Carl Jung's *Septem Sermones ad Mortuos* ["Seven Sermons for the Dead"] (Stuttgart 1916). For the flavor of this highly unusual publication, here is an excerpt from Sermo III:

> Was Gott Sonne spricht, ist Leben,
> was der Teufel spricht, ist Tod.
>
> Der Abraxas aber spricht das verehrungswürdige und verfluchte
> Wort, das Leben und Tod zugleich ist.
>
> Der Abraxas zeugt Wahrheit und Lüge, Gutes und Böses,
> Licht und Finsterniß im selben Wort,
> und in derselben Tat. Darum ist der Abraxas furchtbar.
>
> [What God speaks through the sun is life;

what the devil speaks through anything is death.

But Abraca speaks the venerable and cursed;
The word that is life and death simultaneously.

Abraca begets truth and lies, good and evil,
light and darkness, in the same word,
and in the same act. Thus is Lord Abraca terrifying.]

[23] Chapter 22:
"The rich feast off the misery of the poor," etc. is a paraphrase of:

Itaque populus minutus laborat
nam isti maiores maxillae
semper Saturnalia agunt. (*Satyricon*, XLIV)

[The little man toils and starves
Just to make the jaws of the rich
Think every day is Christmas!]

[24] Chapter 23:
Reiterating that some things are just too fantastical to be made up, behold the 2,000-year-old cannikin of asses milk face cream:

https://www.theguardian.com/uk/2003/jul/28/
artsnews.london

[25] Chapter 24:
"For nature had so qualified him for a lover," etc. is after Burnaby, page 139.

[26] Chapter 24:
"Once enjoyed, we straight to a new desire," etc. is after Burnaby, page 140.

[27] Chapter 26:
"No message from the gods are our dreams," etc. contains couplets for Sadeeq's dream poem that are modeled after Burnaby (page 159). Additional inspiration for the verse sections comes from the poetic fragment attributed to Petronius known as *Burman 30*, or *AL 651:*

Somnia, quae mentes ludunt volitantibus umbris,
non delubra deum nec ab aethere numina mittunt,
sed sibi quisque facit. nam cum prostrata sopore
urguet membra quies et mens Sine pondere ludit,
quicquid luce fuit, tenebris agit. oppida bello
qui quatit et flammis miserandas eruit urbes,
tela videt versasque acies et funera regum
atque exundantes profuso sanguine Campos.
qui causas orare solent, legesque forumque
et pavidi cernunt inclusum chorte tribunal.
condit avarus opes defossumque invemt aurum.
venator saltus canibus quatit. eripit undis
aut premit eversam periturus navita puppem.
scribit amatori meretrix, dat adultera munus ...
et canis in somnis leporis vestigia latrat
in noctis spatium miserorum vulnera Durant.

[When, in our Dreams, the Forms of Things arise,
In mimic Order placed before our Eyes,
Nor Heav'n, nor Hell, the airy Visions sends
But ev'ry Breast its own Delusion lends.
For when soft Sleep the Body lays at Ease,
And from the heavy Mass our Fancy frees,
Whate'er it is in which we take Delight,
And think of most by Day, we dream at Night.
Thus, he who shakes proud States, and Cities burns,
Sees Showers of Darts, forced Lines, disordered Wings.
Fields drowned in Blood, and Obsequies of Kings:
The Lawyer dreams of Terms, and double Fees,
And trembles when he long Vacations sees:
The Miser hides his Wealth, new Treasure finds:
In echoing Woods his Horn the Huntsman winds:
The Sailor's Dream a shipwrecked Chance describes:
The op'ning Dog the tim'rous Hare pursues:
And Misery in Sleep its Pain renews.]
           — John Dryden

[28] Chapter 30:
Squiffy's "fagging days" is a reference to a longstanding custom at English boarding schools where boys starting as young as eight become 'fag' to an older one. They are treated like low-level servants, and required to do menial tasks, like serve the older boy meals, do his laundry, polish his shoes, go on errands, etc. It's possible this term {deriving from a meaning of 'close to exhaustion'} is the origin of the hate-speech term we know all-too well

in North America. Wellington's comment here makes it clear his menial tasks included sexual favors for his elders, an almost goes-without-saying expectation of the 'fagging' institution.

For more on this topic, see Julian Mitchell's play *Another Country*, Oxford 1982.

[29] Chapter 30:
Australian Table Wines, a Monty Python sketch:

http://www.montypython.net/scripts/
austwine.php

[30] Chapter 31:
The Reykjavik rainbow, October 1986:

http://cdn.mbl.is/frimg/9/15/915395.jpg

[31] Chapter 31:
"There is no task is too arduous for a dearth of ethics to surmount" is modeled after Petronius' firecracker original:

> Nihil est tam arduum, quod non improbitas extorqueat. (*Satyricon*, LXXXVII)

> [Literally: No task is so arduous that wickedness cannot tear it to shreds.]

Some alternative translations might include these words and phrases:

> – Shamelessness; a want of principle; a lack of conscience; a shameful dearth of ethics; a shocking lack of integrity; a total lack of self-respect; a mortgaged ethos {sound like any elephantine political cabal you may know...?}

[32] Chapter 32:
"Heavens! How ill it fares with wicked lives / They ever expect a fate they'll despise," etc. is modeled after Burnaby, page 204

[33] Chapter 32:
Cáliza's "oaken estaff" vs. "the metro-esexual tooth-epickers" is modeled after Burnaby, pages 204-205.

[34] Chapter 33:
"There's nothing more deceitful than a ridiculous opinion" is gleefully hoisted from Burnaby, page 219. His translation for this line is unsurpassable.

[35] Chapter 34:
"Covertly, he asks of you / 'Give me all that you may,'" etc. is a translation/adaptation of the *Carmina Priapea* No. 2:

> Ludens haec ego teste te, Priape,
> horto carmina digna, non libello,
> scripsi non nimium laboriose.
> nec musas tamen, ut solent poetae,
> ad non virgineum locum vocavi.
> nam sensus mihi corque defuisset,
> castas, Pierium chorum, sorores
> auso ducere mentulam ad Priapi.
> ergo quidquid id est, quod otiosus
> templi parietibus tui notavi,
> in partem accipias bonam, rogamus.

> ["Covertly, he asks of you:
>   'Give me all that you may,
>   And offer it every day.'"

> "'Give to me my rightful due
>   As Jove the boy carries
>   To heaven and there tarries.'"

> "'Like the shy bride, afraid to screw,
>   Suggests *instead* on her wedding night,
>   So her 'virgin parts' stay all right.'"

> "In plain English, he'll say anew:
>   'Offer up to me your ass,
>   And your bliss will never pass.']

[36] Chapter 35:
"Sicut erat in principio," etc. is part of the Latin mass, borrowed

from the Book of Psalms, and means:

> As it was in the beginning,
> it is now, and shall ever be,
> world without end. {Amen.}

[37] Post Scriptum:
For Postscripts used as concluding chapters, please see here:

https://www.thoughtco.com/postscript-ps-
meaning-1691520

❑ ❑ ❑ ❑ ❑

Mojo Appendix: Some More (Awful) Poetry:

Just for the record, I do not consider what follows to be awful. Think of the word here as a hashtag or enticement. You've come this far, right?

First, A Word or two from a Roman or two:

» Seneca's epistle advocating the treatment of Roman household slaves/staff as part of the family was not a new concept. Romans of the Republican era were repulsed by Greek notions of race-based slavery, and said so. As the wars of conquest progressed, the novelty of 'owning' a man or woman to assist a person was converted to a family model. The *pater familias* {head of the household} was just as responsible for seeing to the welfare of these unfortunates as his own blood. And unfortunates is the right word, for the Romans prided themselves in living in a system where personal slavery could be ameliorated by brains, wits and odd jobs for others. With these savings, including gifts from their *pater*, they could save and buy themselves freedom, and with enough cash, even buy themselves a Roman citizenship. To the Greeks, this was abhorrent; they thought there were inferior "races" who should be enslaved, worked to death, and bred to produce more starving hands to toil.

Tre-Princely loads up the table late in the night with the servers, performers and manicurists from his Happening. The following excerpt from Seneca's letter on slavery paints a very vivid picture of such a setting, so I will quote it at some length.

> "Kindly remember that he whom you call your slave sprang from the same stock, is smiled upon by the same skies – and on equal terms with yourself – breathes, lives, and dies. It's just as possible for you to see him a free-born man as for him to see you a slave.

> As a result of the massacres in Marius' day, many a man of distinguished birth, who were taking the first step toward senatorial rank by service in the army, were humbled by Fortune, one becoming a shepherd, another a caretaker of a country house. Despise then – if you dare insult Fate – those to whose social station you may sink to at any time, even going down as you are despising them. (Epistle 47, Verses 10-11)

> I shall pass over other cruel and inhuman conduct towards them; for we maltreat them, not as if they were men, but as if they were beasts of burden.

> When we recline at a dinner, one slave mops up the disgorged food, another crouches beneath the table and gathers up the leftovers of the tipsy guests. Another carves the priceless game birds; with unerring strokes and skilled hand he cuts choice morsels along the breast or the rump. [...]

> Another, who serves the wine, must dress like an adolescent and try to repress his ripening years; he cannot get away from his boyhood; he is dragged back to it; and though he has already acquired a soldier's physique, he is kept beardless by having his hair shaved away or plucked out by the roots, and he must remain awake throughout the night, dividing his attention between his master's drunkenness and his master's sexual thirst – in the bedroom he's got to be a man, but at the dinner table, a boy {i.e., a top in bed, but a bottom in front of company}.

> Another, whose sole duty it is to put a valuation on the guests, must stick to his task, poor fellow, and listen and watch whose sycophancy and whose braggadocio, whether of appetite or of bluster, is to get them an invitation back for tomorrow.

Think also of the poor purveyors of food, who note their masters' tastes with delicate skill, who know what special flavors will sharpen their appetite, what will please their eyes, what new combinations will rouse their fatted stomachs, what food will elicit their loathing through sheer satiety, and what might stir them to hunger on any given day of the year.

With Slaves like these, who serve him so well, the master cannot bear the thought of actually eating with them; he would think it beneath his dignity to associate with his slave as equals at their table! Heaven forfend!" (Epistle 47, Verses 5-9)

Translation after Richard Gummere *Seneca Ad Lucilium Epistulae Morales*, Volume 1, London 1917, pages 303-307.

* *Glabri, delicati,* or *exeoteti* were favorite slaves, kept artificially youthful by Romans of the more dissolute class. Cf. Catullus, lxi. 142, and Seneca, *De Brevitat Vitae,* 12. 5 (a passage closely resembling the description given above by Seneca), where the master prides himself upon the elegant appearance and graceful gestures of these favorites. (Gummere's original note from 1917.)

» Another Roman voice we should lend our ear to is far less dependable that Seneca, and in fact, comparing the two would be like pitting the journalism of the *New York Times* against the "paid inside sources" of the *National Enquirer* {whose informants will make up anything the paper wants to buy}. I am speaking, of course, of that muck-peddler and darling of the Classicists, Juvenal. He wrote exposé pieces with about as much wit and sophistication at today's rag-mag hacks, but he can give us a window into what Romans at least thought was possible. To that end, I note the following chatterbox quote is purely anti-woman, but in one detail, it makes my interpretation of the ceremony Kohl and Assauer intruded upon plausible. For in the Roman mind, which is what matters, this sort of sensationalistic thing could have been going on around them. It's the classic suspicion of human nature to think "Neighbors. You never can tell...."

Nota bonae secreta deae, cum tibia lumbos
incitat et cornu pariter uinoque feruntur
attonitae crinemque rotant ululantque Priapi
maenades. o quantus tunc illis mentibus ardor

concubitus, quae uox saltante libidine, quantus
ille meri ueteris per crura madentia torrens! [...]
tunc prurigo morae inpatiens, tum femina simplex,
ac pariter toto repetitus clamor ab antro
'iam fas est, admitte uiros.' dormitat adulter,
illa iubet sumpto iuuenem properare cucullo;
si nihil est, seruis incurritur; abstuleris spem
seruorum, uenit et conductus aquarius; hic si
quaeritur et desunt homines, mora nulla per ipsam
quo minus inposito clunem summittat asello.

[Everybody knows the *mysteries* of the Bona Dea,
when pipes whip up the privates of those ravers for Priapus,
excited to a high by both the horny sounds and the alcohol,
they toss their hair around, hootin' and hollerin'.
Oh, what sick impulses tweak their breasts!
What moans of illicit passion start vibrating down below!
How slick their inside thighs get with 'dribbled chardonnay'! [...]
And then, when lustful depravities will brook no more waiting,
these wantons unleash their true colors
and echo one voice from all sides of the playroom:
"We're ready for men! Show in the studs!"
If one popular young man soon passes out,
another is called to put up his hoodie and get in there;
when this *classier* sort can't be sourced anymore,
a cycle is made through all the servers;
if they too peter out, the dishwashers will be bribed next.
If there *still* aren't enough men, these women
waste no time, and hoist their butt cheeks up
for a puissant donkey to be lowered on top of them.]

And Now, Some Poetry

» Sticking with The Great Blue-Green one for a moment, there is
a charmingly licentious quatrain from Geoffrey Chaucer. In the
Merchant's Tale, a wealthy man is giving a tour of his new pleasure garden, hinting sexual romps are part of the landscape too.

Ne Priapus ne myghte nat suffise,
Though he be God of gardyns, for to telle
The beautee of the gardyn and the welle,
That stood under a laurer alwey grene.

[No, Priapus. No might not suffice,

Though he be God of gardens, for to tell
The beauty of the garden and the well,
That stood under a laurel allée green.]

» Next up is a "teachable moment" concerning {the end of a} marriage, and the heroine of the poem happens to be a certain Doris....

Cupid, Hymen, and Plutus

As Cupid in Cythera's grove
Employed the lesser powers of love;
Some shape the bow, or fit the string;
Some give the taper shaft its wing,
Or turn the polished quiver's mould,
Or head the dart with tempered gold.
    Amidst their toil and various care,
Thus Hymen, with assuming air,
Addressed the god: 'Thou purblind chit,
Of awkward and ill-judging wit,

If matches are not better made,
At once I must forswear my trade.
You send me such ill-coupled folks,
That 'tis a shame to sell them yokes.
They squabble for a pin, a feather,
    And wonder how they came together.
The husband's sullen, dogged, shy;
The wife grows flippant in reply:
He loves command and due restriction,
And she as well likes contradiction:

She never slavishly submits;
She'll have her will, or have her fits.
He this way tugs, she t'other draws:
The man grows jealous, and with cause.
Nothing can save him but divorce;
And here the wife complies of course.'
    'When,' says the boy, 'had I to do
With either your affairs or you?
I never idly spent my darts;
You trade in mercenary hearts.

For settlements the lawyer's fee'd;
Is my hand witness to the deed?
If they like cat and dog agree,
Go, rail at Plutus, not at me.'

> Plutus appeared, and said, 'Tis true,
> In marriage gold is all their view:
> They seek not beauty, wit, or sense;
> And love is seldom the pretense.
> All offer incense at my shrine,
> And I alone the bargain sign.
>
> How can Belinda blame her fate?
> She only asked a great estate.
> Doris was rich enough, 'tis true;
> Her lord must give her title too:
> And every man, or rich or poor,
> A fortune asks, and asks no more.'
>   Avarice, whatever shape it bears,
> Must still be coupled with its cares.
>   — John Gay

» A French essayist had this to say {tongue in cheek} about Petronius' versification:

> "An excellent poet may be a very ill man."
>   — Charles de Saint-Évremond

» A well-noted philosopher admired Petronius' Latin, as have generations before and after him.

> "Who could finally even dare to make a German transla-
> tion of Petronius, who, more than any great musician be-
> fore him, has been the master of the presto, in inventions,
> ideas, words – what is the ultimate cause of all the quag-
> mires of the sick, bad world, even the "old world", if, like
> him, one has the feet of the winds, the lift and the drag,
> the freeing cynicism of a compass that drives all things to
> be healthier by making all things fly!"
> (*Jenseits von Gut und Böse,* 28)
>   — Friedrich Nietzsche

» This poem about never appreciating what comes easily should
sound a bit familiar, at least thematically to current times and
mores.

Epigram, from Petronius Arbiter

Things got with pain, and difficulties rare,
Indulge our fancies, and oblige the fair:
We scorn the wealth our happy isle brings forth,
But love whatever is of foreign growth;
Not that the fish which the poor Tiber breeds

Do those excel which chaste Sabrina feeds.
Not Tyrian Gods in nobler purple shine,
Or shew a dye rich as, Augustus, thine;
Nor can the flecks which breathe th' Iberian air
With Evesham's Vale for fleecy sheep compare.
But these are cheaply got –
Whilst moving plains, and rough tempestuous seas,
Make the dear-bought and far-fetched follies please.
— William Burnaby

» Back to the philosophical side for a second, here's another snappy
epigram.

"A wise person's most valuable trait
is a justified instinct for what not to believe."
— Euripides

» One of the early English novelists took on the *Satyricon* fragment
about dreams too.

On Dreams, an Imitation of Petronius

Those dreams, that on the silent night intrude,
And with false flitting shades our minds delude
Jove never sends us downward from the skies;
Nor can they from infernal mansions rise;
But are all mere productions of the brain,
And fools consult interpreters in vain.

For when in bed we rest our weary limbs,
The mind unburdened sports in various whims;
The busy head with mimic art runs o'er
The scenes and actions of the day before.

The drowsy tyrant, by his minions led,
To regal rage devotes some patriot's head.
With equal terrors, not with equal guilt,
The murderer dreams of all the blood he spilt.

The soldier smiling hears the widow's cries,
And stabs the son before the mother's eyes.
With like remorse his brother of the trade,
The butcher, fells the lamb beneath his blade.

The statesman rakes the town to find a plot,
And dreams of forfeitures by treason got.
Nor less Tom-t--d-man, of true statesman mould,
Collects the city filth in search of gold.

Orphans around his bed the lawyer sees,
And takes the plaintiff's and defendant's fees.
His fellow pick-purse, watching for a job,
Fancies his fingers in the cully's fob.

The kind physician grants the husband's prayers,
Or gives relief to long-expecting heirs.
The sleeping hangman ties the fatal noose,
Nor unsuccessful waits for dead men's shoes.

The grave divine, with knotty points perplext,
As if he were awake, nods o'er his text:
While the sly mountebank attends his trade,
Harangues the rabble, and is better paid.

The hireling senator of modern days
Bedaubs the guilty great with nauseous praise:
And Dick, the scavenger, with equal grace
Flirts from his cart the mud in Walpole's face.
                              — Jonathan Swift

» And here are some of the Petronius poems appearing in translation by Burnaby. We'll start with a poem Encolpius composes
after making love to his boy. As you can tell by the words, it's getting harder and harder these days to pretend the couple is only
in the FWB zone. No, they are in love, and have been for near two
millennia now. That won't change, despite the denialists who
can't let anything from history be "gay," especially *not* the Gay
stuff!

I.
Who can the charms of that blest night declare;
How soft ye gods! our warm embraces were?
We hugg'd, we cling'd, and thro' each other's lips
Our souls, like meeting streams, together mixt;
Farewell the world, and all its pageantry!
When I, a mortal! so begin to dye.

II.
Laws bear the name, but money has the power;
The cause is bad when e'er the client's poor:
Those strickt lived men that seem above our world
Are oft too modest to resist our gold
So judgment, like our other wares, is sold;
And the grave knight that nods upon the laws
Waked by a fee, hems, and approves the cause.

III.

How e're the case appears, the cause is won
Every rich lawyer is a Littleton
In short of all you wish you are possest
All things prevent the wealthy man's request
For Jove himself's the treasure of his chest.

IV.

The merchant's profit well rewards his toil:
The soldier crowns his labours with the spoil:
To servile flattery we altars raise:
And the kind wife her stallion ever pays:
But starving wit in rags takes barren pain:
And, dying, seeks the muses aid in vain.

V.

What's soon obtain'd, we nauseously receive
All hate the victory that's got with leave:
We scorn the good our happy isle brings forth
But love whatever is of foreign growth:
Not that the fish that distant waters feed
Do those excel that in our climate breed;
But these are cheaply taken, those came far
With difficulty got, and cost us dear:
Thus the kind she, abroad, we admire above
Th' insipid lump, at home of lawful love:
Yet once enjoy'd, we strait a new desire
And absent pleasures only do admire.

VI.

Who e're has money may securely sail
On all things with all-mighty gold prevail
May Danae wed, or rival amo'rous Jove
And make her father pander to his love
May be a poet, preacher, lawyer too:
And bawling win the cause he does not know:
And up to Cato's fame for wisdom grow
Wealth without law will gain at bar renown
How e're the case appears, the cause is won
Every rich lawyer is a Littleton
In short of all you wish you are possest
All things prevent the wealthy man's request
For Jove himself's the treasure of his chest.

VII.

Sure amorous Jove's a holy tale above;

With fancy'd arts that wait upon his love
When we are blest with such a charm as this
And he no rival of our happiness:
How well the bull wou'd now the god become:
Or his grey-hairs to be transform'd to down?
Here's Danae's self, a touch from her wou'd fire
And make the god in liquid joys expire.

VIII.
Where lofty plane-trees spread a summer shade,
And well-trimm'd pines their shaking tops display'd
Where Daphne 'midst the cypress crown'd her head;
Near these, a circling river gently flows
And rolls the pebbles as it murmuring goes;
A place design'd for love, the nightingale
And other wing'd inhabitants can tell
That on each bush salute the coming day
And in their orgies sing its hours away.

"Fancy and Art in Gay Petronius, please;
The Scholar's curate wit, meets Everyman's ease."
— *after* Alexander Pope

www.ingramcontent.com/pod-product-compliance
Lightning Source LLC
Chambersburg PA
CBHW051536250626
47157CB00001B/65